PRAISE FOR KELLEY ARMSTRONG

"Armstrong is a talented and evocative writer who knows well how to balance the elements of good, suspenseful fiction, and her stories evoke poignancy, action, humor and suspense."
The Globe and Mail

"[A] master of crime thrillers."
Kirkus

"Kelley Armstrong is one of the purest storytellers Canada has produced in a long while."
National Post

"Kelley Armstrong is one of my favorite writers."
Karin Slaughter

"Armstrong is a talented and original writer whose inventiveness and sense of the bizarre is arresting."
London Free Press

"Kelley Armstrong has long been a favorite of mine."
Charlaine Harris

"Armstrong's name is synonymous with great storytelling."
Suspense Magazine

"Like Stephen King, who manages an under-the-covers, flashlight-in-face kind of storytelling without sounding ridiculous, Armstrong not only writes interesting page-turners, she has also achieved that unlikely goal, what all writers strive for: a genre of her own."
The Walrus

HIGH JINX

KELLEY ARMSTRONG

Cover Design by Cover Couture www.bookcovercouture.com

ISBN-13 (paperback): 978-1-989046-45-6
ISBN-13 (hardcover): 978-1-989046-44-9
ISBN-13 (ebook): 978-1-989046-43-2

ALSO BY KELLEY ARMSTRONG

Rockton thriller series
City of the Lost
A Darkness Absolute
This Fallen Prey
Watcher in the Woods
Alone in the Wild
A Stranger in Town
The Deepest of Secrets

A Stitch in Time time-travel gothic series
A Stitch in Time
A Twist of Fate

Cursed Luck contemporary fantasy duology
Cursed Luck

Standalone Thrillers
Wherever She Goes
Every Step She Takes

Past Series
Cainsville paranormal mystery
Otherworld urban fantasy
Nadia Stafford thriller

Young Adult
Aftermath / *Missing* / *The Masked Truth*
Otherworld: Kate & Logan paranormal duology
Darkest Powers paranormal trilogy
Darkness Rising paranormal trilogy
Age of Legends fantasy trilogy

Middle-Grade Fantasy
A Royal Guide to Monster Slaying series
The Blackwell Pages trilogy (with Melissa Marr)

CHAPTER ONE

"Ooh, this doll definitely looks cursed," Hope says from across the shop where she's glued to my laptop, surfing eBay.

When I don't respond, she turns the laptop around. "Don't you think it looks cursed, Kennedy?"

"Bookmark it," I say. "Right now, I'm a little busy with this mirror, which is *definitely* cursed."

We're in my antiques shop, which has been open for a month. It's mid-June, and I'm madly preparing for full-blown tourist season in Unstable, the little town where Hope and I live with our older sister, Ani.

Turani, Kennedy and Hope Bennett. Yep, our parents named us after famous curses, fitting for a family of curse weavers. At least half the items in my shop are formerly hexed objects. That's my specialty. In Boston, I'd hidden the "formerly cursed" part. In Unstable, it's a selling point.

Right now, I'm trying to get this tabletop mirror uncursed before the shop opens. I've already had three people knock on the window. I'm considering investing in drapes. Luckily, in a town like Unstable, nothing intrigues people more than a shrouded store window.

Hope walks up behind me and reaches for the sheet covering the mirror. I catch her hand. "Uh-uh."

"But I want to see."

"No."

"You looked. What did you see?"

I don't answer. I try to focus on the mirror again, listening for the music of the curse.

"Kennedy?" she says. "What did you see?"

I glower at her.

She sets her hands on her hips. "I don't see why you're removing the curse. It's a great tourist draw. A mirror that emphasizes your greatest flaw."

"Yeah, and only someone who looks like you wants to see that, Hopeless."

She rolls her eyes. "I already know what I'd see. My skin. I thought I'd stop getting zits when I turned twenty. No longer a teen, right?"

"It doesn't work that way."

"Did for you. Oh, wait. You *never* got zits. Anyway, if I already know my biggest flaw, what's the big deal?"

"The big deal is that there's a difference between knowing it and seeing it magnified a hundred times. Your skin is fine. The problem is in your head. So now you want to see what's in your head actually showing on your face? No one needs that. It's a nasty little hex, and I'm getting rid of it."

She's quiet for a moment as she leans against a butler's desk.

"What did you see?" she asks, her voice softer now, concerned.

Nothing. That's what I saw.

I imagine telling Hope that. She'd tease me about thinking I'm perfect if I didn't see any exaggerated flaws. It's not that. I literally saw nothing. I looked into this cursed mirror, and there was no me, and I'm not sure how to interpret that. I'd panicked, as if I were looking into a scrying ball for my future and seeing none. That isn't it. That can't be it. It's just a hex.

It's the sort of curse I specialize in—a joker's jinx—though personally, I'd say this one edges closer to a misanthrope's malice. I like my jinxes fun. Light-hearted pranks. This one bears the sharp teeth of cruelty, and I have no time for that bullshit.

I keep telling myself that's why I don't see my reflection—as a weaver who specializes in the jinx, I see through it. Like on April Fools' Day, I saw through other kids' pranks and exposed the cruel ones, and the bullies who liked their jokes nasty stopped trying to play them on me. Pouted and said I was no fun, no fun at all. Which always made my friends laugh. Kennedy Bennett, no fun? There's a reason I specialize in jinxes. I was the class clown, the carefree girl who adored a good prank, even if it was played on her. I just don't like cruel jokes, and so maybe this mirror is like those bullies, pouting and refusing to show me anything in its reflective surface.

A good theory. And I don't believe it for a second.

"I saw *your* chin on *my* face." I shudder as I rise from crouching before the mirror. "The stuff of nightmares."

"We have the same chin, K."

"Huh. Really?" I tap mine. "Looks better on me, though."

She raises a middle finger.

I lift the shrouded mirror. "Open the storage room. This hex is going to take a while to uncurse, and you are not going to let me concentrate."

She opens the door. "Because I want to see myself in it first."

I set the mirror inside and shut the door. Then I take the key ring from my pocket and wave it before locking the door. "Good luck with that, kiddo."

"Spoilsport."

"I know. I am no fun. No fun at all." I head for the sales counter. "Now, show me this doll."

Hope specializes in cursed dolls the way I specialize in cursed antiques. Her actual weaver specialty is the lover's lament, colloquially known as the ex-hex. As for the dolls, that would be my fault.

Hope is five years younger than me, and as a proper big sister—and a proper middle child—I'd done my best to terrify her. I'd tell her stories about cursed objects, especially dolls. Contrary child that she was, she loved it and now has a room filled with formerly cursed dolls. And I have four of them in my shop.

I'm still not quite sure how that happened. When I'd been low on stock, Hope insisted I take a few of her least favorite dolls on consignment. They'd sold within two days. I'm still half-convinced she hired the buyers. I mean, who the hell walks into an antique shop, sees a creepy old doll with glass eyes that follow you across the room, and says, "I want that in *my* house!" Apparently, a lot of people, at least the sort who visit Unstable.

So I now have four truly creepy dolls whose eyes follow *me* everywhere. And I have a summer employee, in my sister, who somehow went from "Can you sell these old dolls of mine on consignment?" to spending her days here, which wouldn't be so bad if she didn't also expect a paycheck.

When I move to the laptop, I resist the urge to pick up my phone and casually glance at my messages.

Expecting a text, Kennedy?

No, not at all.

Wait, you weren't checking to see whether Aiden read your last message, were you?

Ha-ha, no. That's not me. I pop off dozens of texts a day, whether to my sisters or friends or clients, and I never check to see whether they've been read unless it's life-or-death urgent. Yet my fingers itch to pick up my phone, and my pride slinks down into my sneakers.

I don't want to be this person. Definitely don't want to be this woman. Connolly and I aren't dating. We're friends. Have been for nearly a month. Would I like more? Yep, I won't deny it. But I'm currently under an unbreakable curse, one that will visit doom and despair on any guy who falsely claims to love me.

That should be a good thing, right? Who doesn't want a romance lie detector? The problem is that I'm not sure that's how the curse works. It might also hurt a guy who *thinks* he's interested and later realizes otherwise. Or who says he loves me and later realizes he doesn't. That's not curseworthy. It's just part of picking your way through the minefield of romantic love, making mistakes and figuring it out as you go.

The truth is that, while the curse scares me, it's also made me slow down, and that's a good thing. If I have a life motto, it's carpe diem. Looking before I leap is foreign to my DNA. When it comes to Connolly, though, I want to get this right.

Therefore, I should be fine with him not rushing to answer—or even read—my texts, right? Take it slow. Don't go wild. Ease in. But he *didn't* ease in at first.

Connolly is naturally reserved, with the kind of standoffishness that can be mistaken for arrogance and ego, and in Connolly's case, that wouldn't be entirely a mistake. Yet he was different with me. He'd send the first text of the day. He'd read my response right away. No games, and I appreciated that, but now something has changed and I'm racking my brain to figure out what.

I only know that he's no longer jumping at every excuse to hang out. I invited him antiquing in New Hampshire this past weekend, and he *had* jumped. Yes, that sounded like fun. He'd clear his schedule. He knew a great spot there for dinner. Then, three hours before he was supposed to pick me up, he texted to say he couldn't make it. He didn't call. He sent a vague "something came up." Since then, he hasn't initiated a single conversation or answered a text within thirty minutes.

I should take the hint, right? Say screw him. If he's backing off, that's his loss, and it's not as if I'm sitting at home, waiting for his call.

That's what I want to say. Instead, it's like that empty mirror. I look into it, and I feel as if there's a message I should understand, and I don't. I know I didn't do anything wrong, but a little voice keeps whispering that I must have. That I did something to deserve this.

I shove my phone into my back pocket and look at the laptop screen.

My cat, Ellie, hops onto the stool. She takes one look at the doll and hops down again.

"Yep, Ellie, that is one ugly doll."

"So, cursed?" Hope says.

"Not every ugly doll is cursed."

She rolls her eyes. "It doesn't matter whether it's cursed or not. It *looks* cursed. That's what counts."

"It looks dead."

She squints at the screen. "Kind of?"

"It looks like a dead *baby*."

"And that's a bad thing?"

"Yes, kiddo. It's a bad thing." I wave at the shop. "Our clientele is people like our parents. Middle aged. Middle class. Looking for a conversation piece."

"A doll that looks like a dead baby is a conversation piece."

"Would Mom have wanted that in our living room?"

She sighs and slumps. As I pretend to tidy, I study her for a reaction to the mention of our parents. It's been five years since a careless driver stole our father. Two years since cancer stole our mother. We are easing into a place where we can talk about them without diving into the tar pit of grief, and I am glad of that. I don't want to talk around our parents. I want to talk *about* them. Bring them to life the only way we can.

"Fine." Hope flips to another browser tab. "This one?"

"It looks possessed," I say.

"So, yes?"

"Yes, but if we don't sell it within a week, I'm turning it to face the wall for a time-out."

"Ooh, no. We should do that right away. Hang a sign warning that shoppers turn it around at their own risk."

When I don't immediately say no, she brightens.

I smile over at her. "Yes, that'd be fun."

"This is why I'm going into marketing. Ani's the oldest twenty-seven-year-old on the planet. Like a stodgy grandma. *No, Hope, you can't run a sideline hexing exes. No, Hope, you can't vlog a client's cursed objects on your TikTok. No, Hope, you can't tell people they'll be eaten by a rabid dog if they don't get Aunt Maude's tea set uncursed.*"

"Mmm, gotta agree with her on the last one."

"But you'd be fine with the first two, which is why you, dear sister, will be the benefactor of my upcoming college education. I'm going to run all my test cases using your shop. Right after I convert that corner"— she points—"into a cursed-doll gallery."

"Four dolls, kiddo. We agreed on four. No more."

I'm about to turn away when my gaze snags on the bottom of the webpage. It disappears as Hope closes the tab. I take the laptop from her and reopen it, zooming to the suggested listings. The one I thought I'd seen doesn't appear.

I type two words in the search box, and the entire page fills with results.

"Cursed paintings?" Hope says. "New sideline, K?"

I flip through the list, most of which is paintings of cats, which could mean the search engine thought that's what I mistyped . . . or it could think it means the same thing. It wouldn't be wrong. I glance at Ellie, who's contemplating sharpening her claws on a three-hundred-year-old chair.

I scroll down and click a listing. A painting of a crying girl fills the screen.

"Holy shit," I whisper.

"That isn't creepy," Hope says. "It's just depressing. You don't want that one. Here, let me—"

I smack her arm as she reaches across the keyboard. "You don't recognize it?"

"Uh, should I?"

"Salvo Costa. *Crying Girl.* The *most* famous cursed painting. Well, one of them. It was part of a quartet. All cursed."

She frowns.

"You never read Mom's curse scrapbook, did you," I say.

"Just the pages on dolls."

I sigh. "Fine. Curse history lesson, just for you, baby sister. It's the seventies. Guy paints a series of sad kids. Why? Because it's the seventies, and people ate that shit up. Or that's how it began. He only meant to paint one and have copies made. He holed up in his studio to do this painting—*Crying Girl.* When night comes, his wife brings him dinner, and he says to leave it outside the door. Doesn't touch it. Doesn't touch breakfast, either. For three days, he drinks nothing but coffee. Lots of coffee. When he emerges, he's completed a series of four paintings, all of sad kids."

"Did anyone suggest therapy?"

"No, but when his priest saw them, he suggested an exorcism."

She peers at the screen. "It's just a crying kid."

"While they're called the sad children, this is the only one who's crying. There's a boy about thirteen who looks eerily determined. Determined to do what? That is the question. Then an older girl who looks as if she's lost her last friend in the world, and an older boy who looks as if he murdered that friend. A wee bit too demonic for the priest's taste. As for Salvo Costa, all he wanted was to get the damned things out of his house."

"But he'd just finished painting them."

I shrug. "That's the legend. He painted them and immediately wanted them gone. His art dealer took them and sold them. That's when the crying started for real."

"Let me guess. They make people cry?"

"No, they kill. Violent death and madness follow the paintings wherever they go."

"Ooh, now it gets good. It's story time, yes? Please tell me it's story time."

I lower my voice. "They say that Costa was possessed by the spirits of the four children. He and his wife had just moved into a new home. Little did they know that it harbored a dark secret."

My sister fairly vibrates with glee, and I have to bite my cheek to keep my expression suitably somber.

"An entire family died in that house," I say. "Parents and their four children. They perished in a fire. Except . . . that's not the whole story."

Hope bounces, glowing as if she's seven again, the two of us under her covers while I unspool a new ghost story.

I continue, "They say the parents died first. And it wasn't a fire. It was . . . the children."

I let that one hang for the required three seconds. "They say the oldest girl and oldest boy murdered their parents. Killed them in their sleep. For the next month, no one knew. The kids said their parents were busy, their parents were sick, their parents had just stepped out. All the while they were rotting in their beds. The youngest girl wouldn't stop crying. She missed their parents and didn't understand why she wasn't allowed in their bedroom. Then came the fire."

"Did the little girl set it?"

"That, my dear sister, is the question. Some say it was indeed the little girl. Some say it was the younger boy, the one who looks so determined in the painting, perhaps determined to punish his murderous siblings. Some say it was the older girl, and that explains her expression—she's broken by guilt and remorse. Or it's the older boy, who'd had enough of the crying and decided to stop it for good. There is another story, though. One where the youngest—the girl in this painting—escaped and ran to tell the neighbors. The neighbors came back . . . and set the house on fire. At the last minute, they pushed the little girl into the flames to perish.

After all, she shared the same blood as the two who'd killed their own parents. A bad seed."

Hope gives a delicious shiver. "That's a good one."

I lean back. "I think so. Anyway, that's the origin story for the paintings, which this seller doesn't even seem to know."

"Lousy marketing."

"Right?" I scroll through the listing. "They don't seem to know there are other paintings, either."

"What about the deaths? Do the children come out of the paintings at night and kill the owners?"

"Kill them or drive them mad. Everyone who has survived insists they saw the child in their painting come to life. My guess is that the curse is actually a hallucination, causing the owner to believe they see—"

Hope sticks her fingers in her ears. "What's that? You're trying to explain away a cool story? La-la-la, I can't hear you."

I smile and shake my head. "Fine. I'll keep my theory to myself. The point is that, yes, it's widely believed that the paintings *are* actually cursed and that the curse *has* killed people. Better?"

"Much."

"And, since it's a deadly curse on an item that is for sale, I am honor-bound to buy it and uncurse it."

"Then resell it, with the full story, for double what you paid."

"That's the idea." I sign into my account. "Looks like the bidding is at a hundred bucks. Let's make it two."

CHAPTER TWO

I'VE LOST HOPE. Three of them, in fact. One, I keep getting outbid on that damned painting. Two, I conceded defeat in the phone-checking battle, only to discover Connolly *hasn't* read my message. Three, I've lost the actual Hope, who got a call from Ani needing her at home. Ani runs the family business: Unhex Me Here. As the name suggests, they uncurse whatever people need uncursed. Or, more often, whatever people believe they need uncursed. Ani needed Hope to handle a client trying Ani's patience, which is honestly not hard to do.

Business is brisk for a Tuesday. I've already sold three items, and I'm closing in on the sale of a doll. I may have told Hope that our clientele was mostly middle-aged antiquers, but her dolls—and my jewelry finds —pull in a different crowd: fifty percent Gen X former goths, twenty-five percent my fellow millennials and twenty-five percent Hope's fellow Gen Zs. These two fall into the last category. Trust-fund babies who think that a cursed doll is exactly what their tony Boston apartment needs. So ironic! Can you believe people actually thought it was cursed?

"So the curse has been removed," the blond one says. "You can guarantee that?"

"I can guarantee that the doll is not cursed." *Because it never was.*

"Is there a certificate or something?" Blond smirks at Brunette. "A certificate of de-cursing authentication?"

A click behind me, as Hope must come in the back door. Both young women look over.

"Well, hello," Brunette murmurs. "Please tell me *you're* for sale."

I presume she's talking about my sister. Then Blond says, "Wait, wasn't that Aiden Connolly?"

I turn so fast my sneakers squeak. I don't see Connolly. I do, however, see the storage room door swinging shut.

"That was Aiden Connolly," Blond says, her voice as breathy as if she just spotted a movie star. Which tells me two things. One, Connolly just walked in the back way and immediately turned tail and fled. Two, I was right about the background of these young women. When I called them trust-fund babies, I was kinda snarking. Seems I hit the bull's-eye because Connolly isn't a movie star . . . unless you're a society girl who's memorized Boston's most eligible bachelor lists. Connolly is on those lists. Hell, he's in the top three.

Hope has shown me the lists. At first, I thought she was creating fake ones to tease me. Oh, I know Aiden Connolly is hot. I have eyes. Also, I know he's rich. Son of a very wealthy, old-money family, and he has his own successful insurance company. But, well, he's Connolly. A little straitlaced, a little standoffish, not exactly a charming playboy. I mean, the guy runs an insurance company. He geeks out over actuarial tables. Except that kind of ambitious stability is catnip to many of the women who pore over those lists. And if they prefer the "charming playboy," well, there's always his younger brother, Rian . . . who has been secretly dating Hope for the past month.

"That was Aiden Connolly," Blond says again. "I know it was."

Her friend curls her lip as she looks around. "Here? No way."

"Yes way. I heard he's been slumming it with some . . ." Blond's gaze turns to me. "Oh my God."

I fix on my most neutral expression and pause before speaking, as if they are engaged in a personal conversation, which I hate to interrupt.

"We don't have certificates of de-cursing authenticity," I say. "How-ever, I do offer a store guarantee. You may return the doll within three days, no questions asked."

"That *was* Aiden Connolly, wasn't it?" Blond asks.

I pause, again so politely that Ani would be proud. Then I fix on my blank shop-clerk look, the one that says I know my clients aren't addressing me.

"Hello?" Brunette says, waving her hand in front of my eyes. "We asked if that was Aiden Connolly who just came in your back door."

I glance toward the back door and frown. "Someone just dropped off a delivery. Is your friend a courier?"

I check my watch. "Oh, would you look at the time. I'm sorry, ladies. I have a video sales appointment in a few minutes. Perhaps you'd like to think on the doll a little longer?"

I raise my voice loud enough to be heard in the storage room. "Or perhaps, if that delivery guy really was your friend, you can slip out the back door and catch him."

The young women must not know Connolly personally because they don't take me up on my offer. Nor do they leave nearly fast enough, instead flouncing and whinging because I have the nerve to turn down a sale.

The pair finally leave after shooting back that if I were really selling uncursed objects, I'd offer a certificate of authenticity.

I return to my desk. Less than ten seconds later, the storage room door creaks open before swinging wide as Connolly strides in.

"That *was* you," I say, gaze on my phone as I check the cursed-painting bid.

"Yes," he says. "I left my phone in the car."

A perfectly valid excuse if you're me. If you're Connolly, it's like saying you left your right arm behind.

There's no reason for him to lie. He could admit he heard the young women recognize him and retreated because it made him uncomfortable, which is true. Plenty of guys campaign to get on those lists. To Connolly, it's like topping the list of prize breeding bulls. Or, more accurately, top investment opportunities.

He sets something in front of me. The smell of fresh bread wafts out, and I glance up to see a picnic basket, complete with a bottle of wine.

"My apology for this weekend," he says. "I'm hoping you'll have time for a picnic, but if you don't, consider this a delivery service."

I slowly lift my gaze over the basket, which is a mistake. I said Connolly was hot. I suspect he'd find that adjective as uncomfortable as being on those lists. That doesn't mean he hides his light under a barrel. I've been told that Connolly dresses extremely well. Maybe I should have realized that myself, but male fashion isn't my thing. Hell, *female* fashion isn't really my thing, as evidenced by the fact that I'm working in a T-shirt and sneakers.

Connolly dresses as if he's heading to a GQ magazine shoot. Today, that's an ivory shirt tailored for his lean body, paired with a tie that I'm sure cost more than I'll make this week. He's on the other side of the counter, so I can't see the rest, but I'm sure it's not jeans and cowboy boots. He looks freshly shaven. Gorgeous green eyes. The exact right number of freckles scattered over his nose, as if his creator counted them out one by one.

When anyone finds fault with Connolly, it's always his hair. Not the style, which is impeccable, between fashionable and corporate, with just enough wave for flair. It's the color that puts some people off. I happen to have a thing for redheads, so yep, even this is a point in his favor.

He reaches into the basket and pulls out a tin. "I brought brownies."

When I still don't answer, he shifts, almost imperceptibly. I'm usually the one who'll swing in, basket in hand, to tease him with sweets, a temptation he avoids.

"I am sorry about the weekend," he says.

"Ah." I count two beats. "I didn't get that impression." I take out my phone, flip to the texts and read his. "'I need to cancel this weekend. Something came up.' Nope, nothing apologetic there."

His brows knit. "Are you sure? I could have sworn I said more." He shakes his head. "My phone has been misbehaving all week. I knew I should have held off on the software upgrade."

"Ah."

Here is the quagmire of a new friendship, especially one with the potential to become romantic. If I demand an explanation, am I being needy? Scaring him off?

I hate the "scaring him off" part. It makes me sound desperate. I like Connolly because there's an amazing natural level of comfort between us. This is the opposite of that.

Screw it. If Connolly is having second thoughts—if he's feeling pressure for "slumming it" as those girls said—that isn't my problem. I don't want a friend who can be scared away by the expectation of common courtesy.

"I understand things come up," I say evenly. "But we did have a weekend planned, and I had to scramble to make alternate arrangements. That deserved more than a five-word text."

He flushes, and I struggle not to be charmed by that. Fair skin means the guy blushes easily, and it *is* charming. It's also proof that he saw my point even before I brought it up.

"I am sorry," he says. "If I didn't text more, it's because I got caught up in the situation I was resolving. That's no excuse. I should have called."

"Would you like me to stop texting you, Aiden?" I ask. "If so, just say that, please."

He frowns.

"You aren't reading my texts," I say.

"But I am. They come to my watch." He holds up his wrist. It's a gold watch with an analog face. When I arch a brow, one corner of his mouth lifts, and he taps the face to reveal a digital version.

"Fancy," I say.

"Yes, well." He clears his throat and then injects a too-bright note with, "You have told me I fuss with my phone in the car too much."

"You do."

"So I was receiving your texts, but as I planned this surprise visit, I decided not to respond until I saw you."

Maybe this should make me squirm. But it wasn't as if I was sending a dozen texts a day and freaking out when he didn't answer. It was our usual daily check-in, which he had started last month, texting me over his morning coffee each day and turning that "Good morning" into a twenty-message thread, casual back and forth as we got ready for our days, which turned into another dozen over the course of the day, more of them instigated by him than me.

I'm not being needy. I'm not being demanding. He's changing the rules to a game he started, and I don't know why.

He taps the basket. "Do you have time for a picnic lunch?"

"I have an appointment in thirty minutes. Also, I lost Hope, so I need to eat inside."

He waves at the showroom. "Let's pull up a seat then."

My phone dings. I glance down at it and sigh. Then I swipe it open, explaining with, "Bidding war."

He takes the basket to a dining table, and before I can say we can't risk scratching that, he whips a tablecloth from the basket. A white linen tablecloth. With matching napkins.

I'm still entering my bid as he sets out lunch.

"May I ask what you're buying?" he says. "If it's for the business, that is, and not personal."

"Cursed painting," I say.

"A painting you believe is cursed? Or one advertised as such?"

"Both. Salvo Costa's *Crying Girl*."

He pauses while dishing out salad. His head tilts as if accessing an inner data bank. "I don't believe I've heard of that one."

"Because it's kitschy."

I show him the photo, and he struggles against a moue of distaste that makes my lips twitch in a smile. Another ongoing mock battle of ours. His impeccable taste versus my predilection for, well, kitsch.

"Even I wouldn't hang this in my house," I say. "Sad-eyed waifs are not my thing. Now, if it was a sad-eyed puppy . . ." I catch his look. "Kidding. No sad-eyed anything. But this is part of a quartet of infamous cursed paintings." My smile fades. "Dangerously cursed."

"Fatalities?"

"Yep, which is why I'm trying to buy it. Uncurse it if I can, and if I can't, then I'll get rid of it. Safely."

I'm putting my phone down when it dings again.

"Seriously?" I mutter. "Sorry about this."

"Cancelling a weekend at the last minute is a cause for apology," he says. "Trying to remove a cursed object from the world is not."

I shift on the chair, hoping I don't look too uncomfortable. I want to be angry with him. Annoyed, at least. He's not making that easy.

I open the bidding app and let out a profanity that has his brows shooting up. He sets down his sandwich as I show him the screen.

"Some guy just *doubled* my bid."

It was already double what I wanted to pay. I don't say that. Even the current bid would be pocket change for Connolly.

I turn over my phone and set it down. "I'll figure that out later. The auction doesn't close for another couple of days."

"Tell me about the painting."

I shrug. "Definitely cursed. Definitely lethal. Not much to say beyond that."

"Really?" he murmurs. "There's no story?"

His gaze meets mine, green eyes glittering. He knows there's a story, and he knows I love to tell them. Still, I hesitate.

Was this week a temporary withdrawal? He wasn't sure that he wanted to continue the friendship, and now he is? He has the right to reconsider, especially given my curse. If that's what he's done—and he's now showing me that he's past that—then okay. Let's do this.

I sip my wine. I take a bite of my salad. And then I start the story.

CHAPTER THREE

BY THE TIME I finish the story, we're done with the meal and ready for the brownies. I slip into the back to make coffee. There's a machine up front —a one-cup brewer with inexpensive knockoff pods. That's fine for customers, and it's fine for me, yet I've invested in a pour-over system in the back, along with single-origin coffee, for the guy sitting out front. Not that he wouldn't drink the pods. I've seen him drink worse when his caffeine level runs low. But learning a new brewing technique and buying better beans is my way of showing that I "get" him.

Am I overdoing it? Trying too hard?

Gah! I'm overthinking this, and I don't like it. Don't like it at all.

As I take him his coffee, he has my brownie set out, with his own cut into tiny cubes, and I have to laugh at that. It's an in-joke—I'd once cut his up when he was in the balancing phase of a luck-roll. Connolly is a luck worker. He can manipulate luck, but when he does, he suffers a bout of bad in return for the good, when even a bite of brownie could send him into a choking fit.

Ellie sits on a dresser, watching him, narrow-eyed, as she always does. I could take that as a bad sign, but she doesn't dislike Connolly. She's just suspicious of this new person in my life. Maybe suspicious of the role he's filling and how fast he's filling it.

I pass over the coffee, and I'm about to sit when my phone buzzes.

"Oh, look," I mutter. "The bid has gone up again."

I flip over my phone and unlock it. The bid pops up. I read it and swear under my breath.

"Something wrong?" Connolly asks as he eats a tidbit of brownie.

"Someone paid the full asking price. Two grand."

"That's inconvenient." He washes the brownie down with a sip of coffee. "Is there any way of tracking the buyer? You could contact them and try to uncurse it."

"How? *Oh, excuse me, that painting you bought really is cursed. But I can fix it. For free.*"

"I wouldn't say *free*. Ask for a few hundred and then negotiate. People are overly suspicious of *free*."

I shake my head. "While I highly doubt the buyer will let a stranger see their new painting, I can reach out. It's a username with an account. Damn. It's a brand-new account, created a few minutes ago. Username . . ." I glance up at him. "PotOfGold7. You bought it."

"Me?" His brows arch as he pops another brownie bit into his mouth. "That sounds like a leprechaun reference. It certainly wouldn't be me."

"Did you just pay two *thousand* dollars for a cursed painting, Aiden?"

"Certainly not," he says. "I invested two thousand dollars in a painting that can be uncursed and resold."

"Not for two grand."

He lifts one shoulder in a shrug. "One must make a few poor investments to properly appreciate the good ones."

"Somehow, I don't think that's your family motto."

He takes another bit of brownie. "No, our motto is *Oderint dum metuant*." He pops the bit into his mouth. "Let them hate, so long as they fear."

"Well, I *hate* to break it to you, but I *fear* you've wasted at least fifteen-hundred bucks."

"It's not wasted if it removes a cursed painting from the world." He lifts his coffee. "Do they offer charitable donation receipts for that?"

I sigh. Then I meet his eyes. "Thank you, Aiden, but—"

"You did not ask me to buy it, or even hint that you wanted me to. Allow me the occasional good deed, Kennedy, even if it doesn't earn a tax write-off." He checks his phone. "It says the seller is in New York state. May I suggest we pick it up in person? Perhaps tonight?"

I peer at him.

What's going on, Connolly? You just did a one-eighty, from canceling our plans and ignoring my calls to buying me a two-thousand-dollar painting and wanting to drive two hours to pick it up.

"Is everything okay, Aiden?"

He meets my gaze again, locking it in. "Everything is fine with us."

I hesitate. I can't miss his wording. He's saying that whatever is going on has nothing to do with me. Which suggests something *is* going on.

"And you?" I say carefully. "Is everything okay with you?"

His cheek twitches, even as his gaze stays steady. "Everything will be fine."

I don't miss the nuances in that answer, either, but it's all he's giving me, and I do not have the right to press for more.

"Sure," I say. "I close at five, and I'm free after that."

"Excellent. I will make the arrangements and pick you up at six. We'll have dinner in the city."

———

I'M WAITING outside the house at six. I have a backpack over my shoulder, one containing a lead-lined blanket that we call a curse shield. I'll need it to bring the painting back.

Hope is with me, while Ani is in the house making dinner. When a car rolls up in front of the house, Hope bends and squints at the driver. The car stops, passenger window rolling down.

"Traded your wheels, huh?" Hope says. "Gotta say, I liked the other one better."

"As do I," Connolly says. "However, it's in the shop."

"This is the courtesy car? Last time I took ours in, we got a ten-year-old Kia that leaked when it rained." Hope pats my shoulder. "You kids have fun now."

"Have you heard from Rian lately?" Connolly asks.

Hope fixes on her blankest look. "Me?"

"If you do, please tell him I need to speak to him. It's urgent, and he isn't answering my texts."

I bite back the urge to snark that I know what that feels like.

"I'll tell him," Hope says. "But if you want him to answer, you have to stop marking them all as urgent."

"I mark them all urgent because they always are."

"Then maybe, just maybe, you could occasionally text him to say hello, and not only when there's a family emergency you think he's caused."

"I don't think—" Connolly cuts himself off. "Point taken. However, you might also remind Rian that when I *do* message to say hello, he accuses me of checking up on him."

She sighs. "Noted. I'll talk to him. Also, I'm going to start billing you two for sibling mediation services."

I slide into the car and wave goodbye to Hope. I wait until we've reached the edge of Unstable before saying, "Everything okay with Rian?"

He makes a noise in his throat. In the Connolly family, Aiden is the good son. The golden boy. Rian is the disappointment. The black sheep. All siblings are cast into stereotypical roles. In our family, Ani is "the smart one," and I often feel overshadowed by that. Hope is "the pretty one," and I feel overshadowed there, too. I'm "the fun one," and they feel that shadow cast by that, as weird as it seems to me.

But *our* roles were assigned by outsiders. To Mom and Dad, we were all smart, all pretty, all fun to be around. With Connolly and Rian, it was their parents who assigned their roles, and their parents who keep them in them, and their parents who use those roles to pit them against each other. Connolly must look after his wild younger brother and rescue Rian from whatever scrapes he gets into, even if they're half a lifetime past being children, and even if Rian resents the interference, understandably so.

It's messed up. That's all I can say. Hope wasn't joking about sibling mediation. It's almost like being an interpreter between people who don't speak a common language. "When you say this, your brother hears that." "When you do this, your brother feels that." I'm just glad that they're both willing to listen.

I'm also willing to listen, yet Connolly only makes that noise in his throat that says yes, there's an issue, but he doesn't want to discuss it.

I'll deduce, then, that whatever's been wrong in the last few days does indeed have nothing to do with me. Another family emergency that Connolly got sucked into. He had to cancel our weekend, and he didn't mean to be so abrupt with it. He was just distracted.

I can grumble that if it's not about me, then I shouldn't be affected. But while Connolly can be the model of considerate behavior, you don't grow up in a family like his without developing a strong kernel of self-absorption.

"Hope's good for Rian," he says as we reach the highway.

"Um-hmm."

He glances over. "The question is whether Rian is good for Hope, with the answer being 'probably not.'"

"I've come to accept that if she gets hurt, she's old enough to deal with it. He's good for her, too, in his way. My concern is mostly that he'll be careless with her. He hasn't been so far."

"Agreed." He exhales the word, as if in relief.

"You aren't your brother's keeper, Aiden. If Hope *does* get hurt, I'm not going to blame you. I'm just going to kick Rian's ass."

His lips twitch. "I'll hold him down."

"Thank you."

His phone rings. With this not being his car, the caller doesn't show up on the dashboard. He doesn't check his watch, just taps the Decline button. He knows who's calling, and I'd bet my life savings it's his mother.

"You need to set ringtones," I say. "So you know who's calling."

"I always know who's calling."

"There's also a handy call-block feature. Or one that sends certain callers straight to voicemail."

He only gives a humorless quirk of his lips.

His phone rings again. Again, he taps Decline.

"Aiden?" I say. "Not getting up in your business, but I'm guessing whatever's going on explains your sudden urge to fetch a cursed painting tonight."

A strained chuckle. "I had hoped my motivation wasn't quite so transparent, but yes." He hesitates. "Is that all right? I *do* think it's safer to get it ourselves. I wasn't trying to rope you into an unnecessary trip."

"You didn't."

He relaxes into his seat. "Then, yes, if you can temporarily block calls from my mother, I would appreciate that. I would have done it myself, but I told her I was working at home tonight, and she usually respects that."

I pick up his phone and then hesitate. Is his car really in the shop? His mother has been known to track him, going so far as to send security personnel to "check up" on him if he isn't where she expects him to be. She treats him like a teenager with a behavioral issue who's lost the right to privacy. He doesn't live under her roof. He doesn't work for her business. He doesn't give a damn about his inheritance, so she can't even hold that over him. Yet she holds something, and we haven't reached the stage where I can ask. I only know that it's not a matter of telling him to cut the apron strings. These aren't apron strings—they're cast-iron ankle monitors.

I won't ask about the car. Better he thinks I buy the excuse than force him to admit he had to rent a car to play hooky with me.

I open the phone. "Uh, it's not your mom. It's someone named Taylor Silver."

His brows knit. "That's the seller. Can you check for a message?"

I hold the phone out for him to unlock it with his face. Then I tap voicemail and hesitate.

"Ignore all the ones from my mother."

"And your father?"

"My father's calling, too? Now I'm really in trouble."

He rubs a hand over his face and murmurs an apology, as if that flicker of annoyance had been a raging tantrum. Sometimes I think a raging tantrum might do Connolly a world of good. Whatever lessons his parents have injected, they include keeping his cool at all times, and if that hardened into an icy wall that might be mistaken for arrogance and indifference? Well, it's better than the "weakness" of an emotional reaction, right?

I'm about to listen to the seller's voicemail when I notice another message.

"Oh, you also got a voicemail from a Theodora an hour ago. I'll let you listen to that, presuming it's business."

He stiffens, hands clenching the wheel before relaxing. "Yes, I'll take it later. Thank you."

Not business then. Theodora O'Toole. The surname screams Irish, and the given name screams money.

"Pretty name," I hear myself saying before I realize it.

He makes a strangled noise, and my heart thuds down into my feet. I take a deep breath, as quietly as I can.

If he's seeing someone, that's none of my business.

Easy to say. Logical and rational. And inside me, something wilts. No, it is pulverized, like a flower crushed under a heel.

It takes me a moment to remember why I'm holding his phone. Then I force myself and hit the Play button on the seller's message.

"Hello?" A woman's voice wavers with uncertainty. "Mr. Connolly? I tried to message you on the platform, but I haven't received a response. I wanted . . ." She pauses, and when she comes back, her voice is firmer. "I needed to notify you that the painting has been sold to another buyer. No charge was made to your account, and I apologize for any inconvenience this may have caused."

"What?" I say, my voice rising. "She can't do that. Can I call her back, or do you want to?"

He doesn't answer, and when I look over, his gaze is distant. I remember the other message. I remember Theodora. He's still thinking about that. Still trying to figure out how to tell me.

Stop it.

"Aiden? Did you want me to call back?"

"I'm considering our options."

I relax a little. He switches lanes and then says, "I propose we don't return the call. That we pretend I didn't receive the message. I am driving, after all."

"Show up on her doorstep expecting the painting? Making her face us when she says she sold it out from under you?"

"Precisely."

CHAPTER FOUR

AFTER WORK, I'd changed my clothing in case Connolly's idea of dinner out was a place with a dress code. It's happened before, to our mutual embarrassment. I mean, if you're the kind of guy who dresses like him even on Saturdays, you don't realize when places have dress codes because no one ever stops you. Even if he's not wearing a tie and jacket, they'll make an exception because he's still better dressed than three-quarters of their patrons. On the other hand, if you're me, you can't remember the last time you went to a restaurant with a dress code.

So, while I'm not exactly in black-tie garb, I am wearing a dress and low heels, and I'm glad of that as we walk to Ms. Silver's front door. I look as if I'm with him, and not an employee he brought along to carry the painting.

He rings the bell. When no one answers, he pushes again, harder. The door cracks open, and the sliver of a woman's face appears.

"Hello?"

"Aiden Connolly," he says. "I've come for my painting."

"Didn't you get my message?"

He frowns. "Message?"

"I called."

He takes out his phone. "Ah, I have it on Do Not Disturb when I drive. Did you need me to meet you someplace else to pick it up?"

"I, uh, I can't sell you the painting."

He stares at her for five excruciating seconds before speaking, annoyance sharpening his tone. "I said it was a two-hour drive, and you called when I was already on the road. Is there an issue with me taking possession tonight?"

"I . . ." She takes a deep breath. "I sold the painting to someone else."

Silence. Connolly lets it stretch a beat too long before he says, "I believe I misheard. You seem to have said you sold it to someone else, which cannot possibly be the case because I bought it." He looks her square in the eye. "In good faith."

This is where he wields his privilege. His bearing. His expression. Even his accent, more Boston than my own, more clipped and cultured. The guy bought a cursed painting off eBay, but he acts as if he purchased an old master from Sotheby's, and the seller quails under that look.

"Did I not agree to pay the asking price?"

"Yes, but—"

"Did you not accept that offer?"

"Yes, but—"

"Do I not have"—he raises his phone—"proof that you accepted my offer, on a legitimate sales website." His chin jerks up, as if a thought has just occurred to him. "Did you perpetuate a scam, Ms. Silver?"

"W-what?"

"A scam. I purchased goods intended to be sent through the mail, across state lines, which makes this a federal offense. You intended to take my money and withhold the goods. Only I arranged to pick them up—at an additional fee, despite saving you the mailing charge—and you didn't know how to say no without it seeming suspicious. So you agreed and then messaged me that it was already sold, meaning I cannot prove you never had the goods in the first place. Or so you think. Fraud can certainly be proven. My lawyers will make sure of it."

She tries to withdraw.

"Yes, it is your right to close the door, Ms. Silver. I will take that as a sign that you wish me to leave your property, which I will do. At that point, the matter is in the hands of our respective attorneys. I will leave my lawyer's card in your mailbox. It's a small firm and perhaps not terribly impressive, but that is the price one pays when one's family employs their own team of lawyers."

She stops closing the door. "It wasn't my fault."

"Does that mean you wish to discuss compensation?"

"C-compensation?"

"Not money, though if the lawyers are involved, obviously money will be required. They may be employed by my family, but that does not mean their work comes free. I believe their current rate is five hundred an hour. However, it is my hope that we can resolve this without involving lawyers or any form of cash compensation."

The door cracks open a little more. She says nothing, just waits.

"Let us start with you explaining how you came to sell my painting to another buyer."

"I didn't want to. He threatened me. With legal action. Just like you're doing."

"I'm threatening you because you committed fraud against me. What was *his* excuse?"

"He painted it."

I rock forward before stopping myself. Connolly nods toward me.

"This is my partner, Ms. Bennett."

Her gaze travels over me, and I feel the weight of the assessment. She's trying to figure out whether he means business partner or personal, and I'll admit to being gratified that the answer doesn't seem immediately obvious.

"Ms. Bennett is an expert in the field of anthropologically significant art," Connolly says.

"Anthro . . . ?" she repeats.

"This painting is the subject of a well-known urban legend, as you alluded to in your listing. Ms. Bennett believes it is the original, and she came to confirm that before I bought it."

"You said the *artist* bought it?" I say. "The original artist? I'm presuming he showed identification."

"I-I . . ." she begins. Then she opens the door a little wider as she nods decisively. "Salvo Costa was the name of the painter, and it was also the name on his credit card."

"So Mr. Costa contacted you and offered to buy it for more?"

"No, he contacted me and insisted on buying it for the asking price, or he'd call the police and say I was selling stolen artwork." She straightens. "If it *was* stolen, I knew nothing about that. I bought it in good faith, from a reputable dealer. I tried to say that, but Mr. Costa started rattling off legal gibberish. I'm not an art dealer. I'm just a regular person trying to make a little extra to get by. I decided that if he was willing to pay the same as the buyer, then there was no reason I couldn't sell it to him."

"Except that it's a clear violation of eBay's policy. And also a really shady business practice."

"I didn't have a choice. He's the *artist*."

"Right. And if I sew a dress and sell it to you, is it still mine? Can I ask for it back? Demand to buy it back? Mr. Costa gave his art dealer that painting right after he finished it in 1977. It sold within a week. It has not belonged to him since."

"B-but he said—"

"Do you even know how old he'd be now?" I say. "Over eighty. Did you see him?"

"He sent someone to pick it up an hour ago."

"That was quick," I murmur, just low enough for Connolly to hear.

He tilts me a nod and says to Ms. Silver. "Then there is no point in pursuing this matter with you. We will take it up with Mr. Costa directly. I presume he provided contact information? We'll need that, everything you have, including a description of whoever picked it up."

She pulls back. "I'm . . . not sure I should give you that."

"All right, then. We are back to lawyers again." He takes a card from his pocket. "I will notify them to expect your lawyer's call. Is one hour sufficient?"

She hesitates.

"It's your choice," I say. "We're eventually going to need to pursue it with Mr. Costa in small claims court. We can speak to him directly with the information you provide, or we can get the lawyers involved. Mr. Costa lied to you. You legitimately owned that painting, and he bullied you into breaking faith with a customer."

"He did," she murmurs. "He was very abrasive."

"Which you did not deserve, and now he's endangered your reputation by forcing you to violate eBay's policies. If Aiden reports it, you'll lose your account and everything you've built on that platform. That's not fair. You're a small business owner, and Mr. Costa screwed you over."

"He did."

"Then do you allow him to keep screwing you over? Or do you let Aiden—with his very expensive lawyers—show up on Mr. Costa's doorstep instead?"

Her lips curve as she envisions that.

"Come in, please," she says. "I'll give you what I have."

———

I AM SORELY TEMPTED to have a little chat with Ms. Silver about the dangers of inviting online buyers into your home. Of course, one could argue then that we're equally gullible for walking into her house. Still, we're careful, only stepping into her front room and keeping the path to the door open, with my weapon and Connolly's luck at the ready.

I have a gun in my purse. That's not the real weapon, though. It's not a weapon at all, considering it's a modified paint gun. The real weapon is my Magic 8 Ball I always bring on curse-related jobs. Just as Connolly needs to balance his good luck with bad, I need to balance my uncursing with cursing. I cast them all into a Magic 8 Ball. Curse bomb at the ready.

I don't need my gun here, or my curse bomb, or Connolly's luck. Ms. Silver is exactly what she seems to be—a seller who was taken advantage of by a bully and is eager for retribution.

Ms. Silver hasn't been in the online business long. She stumbled into it after reading an article about someone paying a few hundred for a fountain pen once owned by Al Capone. Ms. Silver hatched a scheme—sorry, business plan—to buy objects with a colorful history and leverage the story during resale.

I could roll my eyes, but that would be wildly hypocritical, given what I do for a living. I'm only amused that she still seems surprised anyone was willing to shell out two grand for a cursed painting. Obviously, she's never set foot in Unstable.

She'd bought the painting in an estate sale. The previous owner had died, which may seem suspicious, but he'd been seventy and in hospice care, never having had any trouble with the painting.

She got it cheap and put it up for sale this morning. It might seem like incredible luck that we found it on the first day of sale, but credit goes to the platform's algorithm. Hope was searching for cursed dolls, so eBay also suggested its newest cursed object.

Ms. Silver provides us with the details she was able to get from "Mr. Costa." I'm damned sure the buyer wasn't actually the artist. While she gives us an address, I'm sure it's fake. I'm also not sure what we'd do even if it isn't.

"Follow up, of course," Connolly says as I ask this once we're back in the car. "It's less than an hour away. While I agree it's likely a fake address, we should check it. Either way, we'll find that painting."

I bite my lip against the obvious question of *why*. Yes, when I saw the painting for sale, I wanted it. An infamous cursed painting for a couple hundred bucks? Hell, yeah. Buy it, uncurse it and resell it. Altruism plus profit. It doesn't get better than that.

Then Connolly bought it at a price I almost certainly can't recoup. I'd felt a nudge of guilt, scrubbed away by the reminder that he didn't expect full repayment, and uncursing it was a good deed. If he wanted to drive and pick it up, I could justify that, too. A cursed object isn't something you should toss into a FedEx box.

But now the painting is gone, and our only leads are almost certainly fake. This is where we need to stop. To say that we've done our best. It's not as if the painting hasn't been in the world for decades, along with three others, and I've hardly felt compelled to track down any of them.

My mother's scrapbook of famous cursed objects is thicker than any published book on the subject, and half of *those* would be fakes. Her book contains only the real thing. I have only ever seen three of those objects. One that my grandmother uncursed, one that my mother did and then the Necklace of Harmonia, which I uncursed . . . and, in doing so, took on the curse myself.

In an ideal world, I'd devote my life to tracking down those infamous objects and removing the terrible curses. In that ideal world, I'd also have a multimillion-dollar trust fund plus the skillset of a trained private investigator and undercover operative.

In other words, the best I can do—like my mother and grandmother did—is keep my eye out for those objects crossing my path. Now one has, and as much as I long to pursue it, I know that makes no practical sense. I have spotted one deadly fish in the sea, and I cannot dive in after it. But I want to. Damn it, I want to.

Connolly is offering to help me to dive in after that fish. The guy who does have that multimillion-dollar trust fund plus the skillset of an insurance investigator. So why argue?

Because I'm me, and I can't let him dive into dangerous waters without warning.

"Should we bother?" I say. "Even if it's the real address, this guy's not going to sell us the painting."

"We don't know that until we try." He glances at his watch. "Oh, I did promise you dinner, didn't I?"

"That is the least of my concerns, Aiden."

"If you're worried about the time . . ." He taps the address into his phone GPS. "We're long past rush hour, so we should be able to eat, check the address and return you to Unstable by midnight. Is that all right?"

"That means you'd be home after one. On a weeknight."

"There are benefits to being the boss."

His voice is a little too chipper, as if he's forcing himself to remember that he *is* the boss.

"Aiden." I take a deep breath. "I get that you want a distraction, and I'm more than happy to provide one, if that's why we're doing this."

He straightens. "No, no, of course not. While I welcome the distraction, I wouldn't drag you all over New England for that. This painting bears a terrible curse, and if you can remove it—regardless of whether we can purchase it—that is for the best."

I wait as he drives to the highway. Then I twist to face him. "I can't sneak into the room and uncurse it while you distract the owner. It'll take time."

"Then I'll buy the painting."

"I'm saying that if you need tonight as a distraction, I'm here for it. I'm here for *you*, Aiden. We can track down this painting, or we can grab a burger and drive all night. I don't care. I just don't want you running around chasing a cursed painting because you think I need it." I meet his gaze. "Or because you think I'm upset over last weekend. Yes, I was annoyed. I worried that I'd done something wrong."

"You didn't," he says emphatically. "It was absolutely not you."

"Or that it was us. Our friendship. You were pulling back, which is your prerogative."

"It wasn't you, and it wasn't us. If I thought you might think that, I would have clarified. This is my problem. It does not . . ."

He trails off and snaps out his sunglasses before realizing the sun has sunk too low to need them. He hesitates, glasses in hand, as if robbed of the chance to hide behind them.

"It does not directly have anything to do with you," he says.

I remember that name flashing on his screen. Theodora O'Toole.

It does not have anything directly *to do with you, Kennedy.*

"I would like to check out that address," I say, "whether it's to distract you from an external issue or just for the sake of crossing that off the list, since we're in the area."

He exhales and signals to change lanes for the highway. "Excellent."

"I'd like something else," I say. "In the interests of being honest. Something is going on with your family. I know it's none of my business. But if you'd like to talk about it, I'm here, as I said. I just need a yes or a no, so I stop hovering, wondering whether I should push. Do you want to talk? Or should I drop it?"

He turns onto the highway. Drives another mile before saying, "I believe we should discuss it as it does . . ." He clears his throat. "It tangentially involves you, though I am trying very hard to keep you out of it." Another throat clearing. "We should talk. Perhaps over dinner?"

"Let me find something along the way."

CHAPTER FIVE

WE'RE AT A CAFE. I get a salad with enough feta and pecans and candied fruit to ensure it's no healthier than a fast-food burger. Connolly is far more virtuous, as always, selecting a baby greens salad and wrap. It's a warm night, and we take our food outside to eat. We're the only customers on the patio. The only customers at all, with the shop due to close in five minutes.

I eat my salad and sip my seltzer as Connolly picks at his food. Then he says, "My parents have decided it's time for me to get married."

My head jerks up so fast that, for a second, I'm sitting with lettuce hanging from my mouth, like a cow disturbed at the trough. I quickly shovel it in and swallow before I laugh, tension leaching from my shoulders.

"Ah," I say. "You *are* closing in on thirty, after all."

"I'm twenty-eight."

"Like I said, closing in on thirty." I grin at him. "Time to start pumping out little Connollys."

I expect him to at least roll his eyes. He only stabs his salad.

"I'm kidding, Connolly. Your parents might want grandbabies, but you are under no obligation to provide them."

He keeps eating.

"Aiden? Is this an inheritance thing? Or a trust fund thing?"

His gaze cools. "I do not care about my inheritance. Or about my trust fund."

"I'm sorry. That wasn't an insult. I got an inheritance, and technically, it's in a trust fund. I've drawn from it before, and I will again. No judgment here."

"Your situation is different," he says, his voice softening. "And I didn't mean to get defensive."

"Point is, you don't need money. Your parents can want grandbabies all they like, but they're stuck hinting and grumbling, like every other parent with adult kids."

"It's . . ." He stabs a tomato. "Different for us."

"Different how?"

"New England luck workers practice arranged marriage."

I blink. Then I blink some more before I manage to give a strangled, "What?"

"Arranged marriage. It's common in many cultures." His voice takes on a clipped tone. "In our case, it isn't religion—it's custom. To keep the magical bloodline strong, we marry within it."

I remember hearing that his parents were both luck workers. I'd gotten the impression that was by design rather than choice, but I hadn't made the jump to arranged marriage.

"All right," I say slowly. "So your parents are arranging your marriage, and you're dealing with the stress of that. I'm sorry if it seemed as if I was mocking your traditions."

He stares at me for a moment and then makes a strangled sound, halfway to a laugh. "I don't *want* my marriage arranged, Kennedy. I want to marry whomever I choose, whenever I choose."

I keep my face impassive and pray I don't look as relieved as I feel. "So tell them no. You're financially independent. The only thing they hold over you is their love." Now I really have to keep my face straight in hopes I don't give away my thoughts on *that*. "They'll be disappointed, maybe even angry, but ultimately, you're their son. They won't stay mad for long." I quirk a smile. "Hey, you might even get a few interference-free months out of it."

He doesn't return the smile. Doesn't meet my eyes. Just pushes around the salad on his plate. "I am not entirely financially independent. I owe a debt I cannot yet repay."

"Okay . . ."

"When I received my admission letter for Harvard, I made an agreement, and when I turned eighteen, I signed the contract for that agreement. My parents paid for my tuition. In return, I agreed to allow them to arrange my marriage. If I default on that, I owe the tuition. Immediately."

My mouth opens and closes at least three times before I say the only thing that comes to mind. "That can't be legally binding."

"Forcing me into an arranged marriage wouldn't be, but by tying the contract to my tuition, they circumvent that. The marriage is a private matter, which the court would remove from its consideration, leaving only the debt, due to be repaid by my thirtieth year. I thought that meant when I turned thirty."

I wince. "It means when you turn twenty-nine."

His lips twist. "If only I'd had you to consult with before signing. My parents verbally led me to believe the money was due when I turned thirty. That was the age that stuck in my mind, and if I ever revisited the contract, I skimmed that part for other details."

"They misled you. Used archaic wording and let you misunderstand it. Then, when the time drew near, if you wanted to repay it, you'd think you had another year to get the money together."

"Yes," he says finally. "Exactly that."

"You did plan to repay it, right?" I ask.

This is the longest pause yet, and he visibly shifts in discomfort. "I . . ." Deep breath. "When I agreed to the contract, I was not vehemently opposed to an arranged marriage. I grew up expecting it, and at the time, my parents seemed to have a strong relationship, as did other members of our circle. It's not as if my parents would choose a woman and force me to marry her. I would have multiple potential partners, whom I would get to know."

"I'm sorry," I say. "My question was presumptuous. I know people who come from cultures that arrange marriages, and sometimes, it works out a lot better than the alternative. I apologize for sounding judgmental."

"You didn't expect it from my particular cultural background. It was a shock." He sips his coffee. "I would like to say that I have been saving to repay the debt since I graduated. But my early profit went into repaying the start-up loan to my parents and then expanding the business. The contract had no effect on my relationships. I dated whomever I wanted, with no interference from my parents. Had I been serious about anyone, I suspect that would have changed, but it was never an issue."

I remember the first time we met. He'd checked that I was actually a curse weaver using an ex-hex. A mirror supposedly given to him by a former lover after he'd broken it off when she became serious. The lie had come easily to him, so much so that I never questioned it, which makes me suspect it was a variation on a situation he'd encountered before. Young, wealthy, handsome and single, he'd have had no problem finding women. But his job and his ambition meant that none of those relationships approached a level of commitment his parents deemed dangerous.

He continues, "If anything, knowing my parents would help me find a life partner freed me from looking for that. I could enjoy company without commitment. The fact I was never tempted to commit also seemed to support their philosophy. Then, two years ago, Rian asked how much I'd saved to get out of my contract."

My sister's face flashes. "Rian is under the same contract, isn't he?"

Connolly shakes his head. "Rian refused to sign, so my parents refused to pay for his education, and he had to drop out after his first year."

I say nothing, but my expression must speak for me because Connolly nods. "Yes, that was a horrible thing for my parents to do, and I regret that I didn't realize it at the time. To me, it was just Rian being his usual contrary self. It wasn't as if he cared about school. Wasn't as if he'd gotten into Harvard."

He makes a face. "Yes, I was an ass. Nothing new there. But then he mentioned it, presuming I planned to save up the money. That made me think. I spent a year mulling it over before deciding yes, I should repay it. I still intended to let my parents suggest possible partners, but I wanted the freedom to buy my way out if I didn't like their choices."

"Good plan."

"I thought so. Then . . ." He trails off and sips at his coffee before folding his hands around it and saying, "I recently . . . I began to doubt . . ."

He clears his throat, and I wait for him to go on. Was he going to say . . .? Say what? I'm not sure I dare guess.

He continues, "I decided I did not want to go through with the matchmaking."

I sit there, poised for more, only to realize that's all I'm getting. Maybe that's all there is to get. Still, whatever his reason, he doesn't want the arranged marriage.

"Good," I say, maybe a little too emphatically.

"Yes. I wished to repay the money. I turn thirty a year from this September, and I was on schedule to pay the debt."

"Then you found out it's actually due this September."

"Yes."

"How close are you?"

He shifts in his seat. "Not nearly as close as I thought. When I began accumulating the funds, I asked our accountant how much my tuition had cost. I knew I was expected to pay interest, so I factored that in based on the historical prime rate, plus five percent. Last week, my mother told me it was time for me to meet their choices, and I asked for the bill. That's when I found out about the date difference. It's also when I discovered that the contract specifies the interest rate is tied to a specific index, which has done very well in the last decade. My bill has doubled."

"They want you to repay *double* your tuition?"

"It's more than tuition. I am repaying the cost of my *education*, which apparently includes the apartment they rented for me—premium Boston real estate—plus all expenses. They'd given me an unlimited credit card and encouraged me to use it. I worked very hard at my studies, and so I deserved to indulge myself. That's what they told me, and so, being young, I did."

"They encouraged you to rack up your bill, and *that* was the reward for your hard work?"

He shifts. "They played me for a fool, and I am dealing with that humiliation. I'd rather not discuss it further, if that's all right."

"Of course. So the point is that you're not going to be able to repay them by September. What about taking out loans?"

"I am still investigating that, but all my past loans have been through them, which means I have little in the way of a credit rating."

He straightens. "Here is where this discussion becomes truly awkward. First, let me assure you that I have no intention of going through with any arranged marriage. I *will* find a solution. Therefore, I should have left you out of it."

"No, if you're dealing with something, it helps me to know that. We are, uh, friends, right? I'm not just here to ply you with forbidden sweets, as much fun as that is. Chasing cursed paintings is fun, too. But I'm also here for the less fun parts. Like supporting you in a difficult situation, whether it's brainstorming solutions or just cheering you on and cheering you up."

He's quiet for a moment, and I think I've gone too far, presumed too much of a new friendship. But when he speaks, his voice cracks a little as he says, "Thank you. I . . . haven't been that kind of friend to anyone, I'm afraid. Not even my brother. Not being it means I can't expect it from others, but . . ." Deep breath. "You can expect it from me, and so I appreciate it from you. I'm trying to change, for Rian, too, and this helps."

"I'm happy to be your supportive-relationship training wheels."

His lips quirk. "Thank you. However, I still wouldn't have presumed to burden you with this issue if it didn't involve you. Tangentially, as I said. The problem . . ."

He pulls at his collar and then stops fussing. "I'll be blunt, as embarrassing as it is. There is a reason why my parents decided it was time to suddenly start foisting"—he pauses, pulls a face—"*introducing* potential partners to me."

His gaze lifts to mine. "It's you."

CHAPTER SIX

Connolly clears his throat. "No, that's not quite the wording. That sounds as if you've done something to cause this, which you have not, unless you can take the blame for existing."

"Ah, let me guess. You've been hanging out with an unattached young woman, and that has them worried."

"Yes."

No surprise here. I'd once accidentally—okay, not so accidentally—overheard a video chat between Connolly and his mother. What did she call me? Right. A manic pixie girl. Which insulted her son as much as it did me, with Marion Connolly making it obvious that she thought Connolly also fit the usual romantic foil for such girls. A respectable and responsible guy wrapped up in his work, thrown for a loop by a reckless and flighty young woman. Okay, that's fifty percent Connolly. Also fifty percent me. But it reduces us to stereotypes we *don't* fit. Connolly is hardly the boring guy who doesn't lift his head from his studies, and I am—I hope—a little more grounded and responsible.

Still, this is what his mother sees. Poor Connolly, the hardworking, uber-successful guy, fallen prey to the flibbertigibbet who wants to take him on a wild ride . . . and win herself a passport to their high-society world.

"Have you told them I'm not your girlfriend?" I ask.

He gives me such a look that I sputter a laugh.

"Fair enough," I say. "Maybe you should have gone on that weekend trip with me, left them an itinerary of our plans and let them send one of their people to follow us, see nothing was going on."

"They'd know it was a setup."

"Right. Or they'd think I'm just holding out for a fifty-carat engagement ring."

His lips twitch. "You wouldn't be able to lift a fifty-carat ring."

I bat my eyelashes at him. "Give me one, and let me try."

He laughs under his breath, and then sobers and shakes his head. "I am sorry, Kennedy. This is very embarrassing."

"Stop saying that. Practicing arranged marriage is not embarrassing. Signing that contract is not embarrassing. You were a kid, and *someone* took advantage. Your parents worrying about me isn't embarrassing, either. I'm flattered that they see me as a legitimate threat to their family dynasty. So much better than having them write me off."

"Well, thank you for being kind about it, and I'll stop moaning about the humiliation."

"Good. So, now that you're done that . . ."

I pull a chocolate macaroon from my takeout bag and divide it with my plastic knife. He puts out his napkin, ready for the treat. Instead, I take a bite and say, "You were an ass, Connolly."

I take another nibble, savoring it as he watches. "You stood me up with no notice and no explanation. Left me to spend the weekend wondering what the hell I'd done wrong."

"I—"

"You said it wasn't about me. I get that. You were wrapped up in this marriage problem, and the last thing you wanted was a weekend of antiquing."

"I *did* want that."

"Fair enough. You could have used the distraction. The real reason you canceled was so your parents wouldn't find out and make things worse."

He exhales. "Yes."

"That's a shittier excuse than just being busy. I understand you wanting to dispel their concerns. But the fact that it involves me means, well, it involves me. You should have said something. Instead, you blew me off and dodged my messages, then snuck over—"

"I didn't sneak."

"When you were recognized in my showroom, you retreated and lied about forgetting your phone. Then you show up tonight in a different car and lie about yours being in for service. You're trying to convince your parents that you aren't having a secret fling with me . . . by sneaking around to see me. If you aren't supposed to be with me, tell me that, and if you aren't supposed to be with me . . ." I look him in the eye. "Maybe don't be with me."

His lips tighten. "I am not allowing my parents to interfere in my relationships."

"Then tell them that. About me and about this arranged-marriage business. Unless you think that by playing their game, you can buy some wiggle room—an extension or a reduction."

"I will not get any concessions. Either I marry, or I owe them the money. I will repay the money. As for telling them to leave me alone about you, I can't. Not without putting you in danger."

"Danger?"

"Not physical danger. My parents don't do that. But there are other ways to hurt people. Financial ways. You are vulnerable to that."

"How? I rent my shop. My car is paid for. I live in my family home, which is also paid for. If there's one good thing about not having a lot, it's that someone can wipe out my savings, and it's hardly a catastrophe. I'll just keep going."

"Unless your professional reputation is damaged beyond repair. Unless your family home is suddenly discovered to have a mysterious lien against it. Unless your trust fund suffers catastrophic investment losses. My parents can ruin you, Kennedy. If the situation reaches that stage, they will."

"And you know this?"

"I've seen them do it before."

"No, I mean you know that they could and *would* do this to me, and yet . . ." I wave at him. "Here we are, sneaking around together, with me having no idea that we're sneaking or why. With me not having the option to say whether I accept the risk."

I push up from the table and stride away, phone in hand as I tap the screen.

Connolly comes after me. "I'm sorry, Kennedy. I didn't think it through."

"No, you didn't. Like you didn't think it through before ghosting me this week."

"I didn't ghost—" He stops. "All right. Yes, I did, but I didn't mean it that way."

"You meant it to get your parents off your back, and then you decided you weren't letting them run your life, so you snuck off to see me and put me in danger without asking whether that was okay. Without allowing me to make that choice for myself."

I peer back at the shop we just left, and then I stab the name into the phone app. Connolly edges close enough to see the screen.

"Yes, I'm calling for a ride share," I say.

"You don't need to do that."

I hit the button to match me with a ride. The wheel spins as it looks for a driver.

"What about the painting?" he says.

I fix him with a glare, and he has the grace to color under it.

"You never gave a damn about the painting, Connolly. This was about giving you a night off. You're tired of sitting in the parlor while your parents parade in marital prospects."

"That's not actually how—" He clears his throat. "Yes, I understand what you mean, but no, I didn't need a break. I wanted to see you."

"To tell me what's going on? Warn me that I'm on your parents' hit list for having the audacity to hang out with you?"

"I did not think it through," he says, gaze on mine, each word enunciated. "I said that I am not accustomed to thinking of others, and I meant it. I—"

He runs his hand over his mouth. "Excuses. I'm making excuses and shifting the blame. I can do better."

He straightens. "I made a mistake. Multiple mistakes that disrespected you and our friendship and possibly put you in danger."

He pauses and gives a sidelong look, waiting for me to recognize the bravery in acknowledging his mistakes.

I look down at the phone. Still spinning.

"I had no intention of allowing you to be endangered," he says. "That's why I stopped returning your texts. That's why I showed up in person, instead. That's why I rented a car. However, that was patronizing of me."

Another of those looks that begs for a little credit. I tap the phone as if that can make it find me a ride faster.

He continues, "If you feel in danger now—which is your right to feel —then please allow me to accompany you on the ride share, for your safety."

"How the hell does that help? I'd still be with you."

Silence. More silence. The wheel on the app slows, only to pick up speed again.

"You'd prefer not to be with me," he says, "under the circumstances."

"No, Aiden. I would prefer to have that choice and to know the circumstances." My phone blips, and I look down to see a "match not found" alert. I let out an oath.

"Allow me to drive you home, Kennedy," he says. "If you would prefer not to, then allow me to summon a hired car for you. That will be both safer and more efficient."

I hit Search again, but when the message pops up immediately, I shut the app.

"I'm furious, Connolly."

"As you have every right to be."

"And I would feel very stupid—and gullible—getting into a car with you after what you've done."

"I understand, but I'm also the one who put you into this situation." He holds out the keys. "Take the car. Please. I can rent another."

"You're not giving me your car, Aiden."

"It's a rental. I'll have it retrieved from Unstable tomorrow."

"I'm not stranding you here."

"You are unable to book a ride share because no driver wants to take you all the way to Unstable. I can easily get a lift to a rental company."

He takes out his phone and punches in the address. A moment later, "There. My driver will arrive in five minutes."

I shove my hands in my pockets. "It probably seems as if I'm over-reacting—"

"It doesn't."

"But it feels like it." I exhale. "It also feels, though, like if I let you drive me home, I'm sending the wrong message. Saying what you did is no big deal."

"It is a big deal. I understand that now, and allowing me to take you home in no way implies a lessening or undervaluing of your anger."

I hunch my shoulders and peer down the darkening street. "What if I accept the ride and say I want to check out that address for the painting, since we're almost there?"

"In that case, I would conclude that you are accepting the ride because you are understandably concerned about the painting. Concerned enough to permit that to override your anger."

I scuff one heel against the sidewalk. Then I mutter, "Cancel the ride. I really don't want to be in a car with you right now, but it'll keep me awake at night if I don't check it out."

"Understood."

CHAPTER SEVEN

"I'm GOING to need something from you," I say as we hit the road again.

"A promise that I will not permit my parents to interfere in your business?" he says. "You have it." He glances over. "I will handle this, and you will not suffer in any way for our friendship. I swear that."

His expression is so earnest that I can't bring myself to point out the impossibility of such a guarantee. Connolly's biggest problem with his parents is a lack of control. He's spent his life moving this particular goalpost. As a child, he'd have set it at his first year of college. Just get out of the house, and he'd be free of their influence. Okay, so he won't be truly free until he's eighteen and legally an adult. Move the goal post there. Okay, he's an adult now, but he's still a dependent in college. Move it to graduation. Hmm, now his parents want to invest in his business, and he doesn't have a credit rating so, fine. Start the business. Skimp and save to pay them back. There, free at last. Oh, wait. There's Rian, who still works for the family business, and so Connolly has to run interference. Fine, but now Rian is finally making moves to become independent and . . .

And then there's the marriage contract.

Connolly is like a fairy-tale prince locked in a tower. He gets out of the tower, only to find a shark-infested moat. Clears that to discover he's in an endless forest. Oh, and then there's the desert beyond . . . With each obstacle, I'm sure he blames himself for miscalculating. Yet everyone else can see the truth—that the wicked king and queen are erecting new obstacles as fast as he clears the old ones, and unless he does something drastic, he's never escaping their hold. They won't let him.

At some point, Connolly is going to need to make hard choices. I can't make them for him. I can't even suggest them. He needs to see the weapons laid out before him and select one, rather than keep dodging the fight. He's looking for compromise, and his parents see only a refusal to take up arms, which suits them just fine.

"I don't need a promise, Aiden. If I am part of this, then I need to take control of my corner. I want to speak to your parents."

In his silence, I make the mistake of sensing Salvoy. He sees my point and—

"Absolutely not."

My hackles rise. "Is that an order?"

"If I could give that order, I would. As I cannot, it is only the most extreme advice. You do not want to do that, Kennedy, and if you insist, I will do everything in my power to keep you from making that mistake."

"Mistake . . ." I say, my voice low.

He hears the warning in my voice and looks me square in the eye. "Yes, mistake." He turns back to the road. "There is no possible way you can confront my parents and win, and if you see that as an insult, it is not. I presume you don't mean to confront them in any aggressive sense. You intend to reason with them, yes?"

"Yes. You think I'm incapable of that."

"No, I think *they* are incapable of that. They will turn this into a confrontation, and they will use it against you. You cannot reason with anyone who does not respect you."

"They don't respect me because they don't know me."

His hands adjust on the steering wheel. "I have spent my life trying to win my parents' respect, Kennedy. If I say you will not do it in an hour, that is no reflection on you. They have cast you into a role, and they will not allow any deviation from it, as they will allow me no deviation from mine."

"My role is 'gold digger.' I get that. There must be a way to prove I'm not. Maybe I can . . . I don't know, sign a contract or whatever. Forfeiting any right to your money under any circumstances."

"Signing a contract is what got me into this mess in the first place."

"Right. Okay. But I think you're too close to this, Aiden. How about we ask Rian? See what he says."

Connolly snorts. "He will say that having you confront our parents is an excellent idea, and also that he insists on being there and hopes you serve popcorn."

"You think he'll want to see your parents eviscerate me?"

"No, the opposite. He'll want to see you go after them, because it would be entertaining. He'll consider the bomb, not the fallout."

"I think you're wrong," I say softly. "I think you don't give him enough credit. I'd like to ask him."

"Go ahead."

"I don't have his number."

There's a pause that stretches for at least a half mile.

"Connolly? Please tell me you have your brother's number."

"He has several, and I am never quite certain which he is currently answering."

I sigh and text Hope, who passes over Rian's number. He answers on the fourth ring, just when I've decided he won't pick up.

"Hey, Rian. It's Kennedy."

"Hey, yourself. What's up?"

"It's about your brother. Do you have a moment to talk?"

"What's Aiden done now? No, wait. Let me guess. He's being an asshole. A prissy, inconsiderate, arrogant asshole."

When I don't answer, he says, "He's right there, isn't he?"

"Kind of. Sorry. I forgot the warning label."

Rian only laughs. "It's not anything I haven't said to his face. So what's up?"

"It's about his marriage contract."

A creak, as if Rian is getting comfortable. "You found out about that, huh? Don't worry. Aiden's not marrying anyone he doesn't want to marry. I reminded him of it a few years back, and he was already putting aside money. He'll have enough before the chit comes due."

I glance at Connolly. "You haven't told him?"

"Aiden tells me nothing personal, Kennedy, and with him, *everything* is personal."

Connolly says, "I've been trying to contact him, so he knows the situation and hears it from me."

Rian says. "Okay, I heard that, and I concede his point. I've been ducking calls. So what's up?"

I look at Connolly, who nods, telling me to go on.

"Well," I say. "He may not have begun saving as soon as you think."

"Really? Okay, that *is* a surprise. Still, he'll have it by next year."

"It's due *this* year. On his birthday. He misunderstood the terms."

"Misunderstood?" Another creak, as if he's sitting up quickly. "That's not possible. This is Aiden we're talking about."

"The contract says the money is due at the beginning of his thirtieth year. He didn't realize that you're in your thirtieth year of life right after you turn twenty-nine."

"Shit. I wouldn't have gotten that, either. Wow, screwing over your *kids* in a contract. Our parents are winners, huh?"

"Mmm. The point is that Aiden is stuck. He doesn't have enough yet to pay it back, and your parents are trotting out the marital prospects early because they're concerned about me."

"They don't believe he just wants to be friends? I'm shocked. *Shocked,* I tell you." His laugh sounds uncomfortably close to a cackle, and I shift the phone to my other ear, away from Connolly.

"Aiden is concerned that they'll make a move against me."

Rian stops laughing. He's stone-sober when he says, "Yeah, Kennedy, they will. They know where to apply pressure. For Aiden, that's you, which will seem to prove that you two are more than friends and dig that hole deeper."

"I want to talk to them. Meet face to face. Work this out."

Silence.

"Rian?"

"Aiden isn't going to let you do that, right?" He raises his voice. "Tell me you are not letting her do that, bro."

"He is advising against it. Strongly. I thought you might have a different take."

"Sorry, but I'm with Aiden. Anything you say to them will only make things worse. They'll use it against you and against him. The best thing you can do is let Aiden handle it."

———

WE'VE ARRIVED at the address "Salvo Costa" gave Ms. Silver for the painting purchase.

"You know what would have helped here?" I say as Connolly pulls into the drive. "Satellite view."

Connolly makes a noise between annoyance and agreement. We'd plugged the address into the car's GPS, but an online search would have brought up a photograph of the house and saved us the trip.

"Maybe we're being too hasty," I say. "He *is* an artist. This place certainly has character."

Connolly rolls his head to the side, giving me such an un-Connolly look that I sputter a laugh.

"Fine," I say. "It's a pigsty."

"I believe that would be an insult to pigs."

We're at the end of a long road leading to what can best be described as a stunning example of rural decay. It's the kind of derelict homestead that photographers love to capture, complete with dead trees and one lonely tire on a rope, swinging ominously in the breeze.

"Do we check it out?" I say.

He glances at me and then squints at the house and turns on the high beams, as if one of us clearly suffers from poor night vision.

"No one lives there, Kennedy."

I shrug. "Sure, but we're here now. We should check it out."

"Whoever bought the painting found an abandoned house and gave Ms. Silver the address. There's no actual connection between this farm and the painting."

"I'm going to check it out. You can wait here. Keep your shoes clean."

"Kenn—"

I'm already out of the car, the slap of the door cutting off the rest as I stride toward the abandoned house.

CHAPTER EIGHT

I GET ABOUT TEN STEPS—JUST far enough for him to be sure I'm serious—and then his door slams shut with more force than necessary. When I turn, he's striding toward me, ignoring the puddled ruts in the dirt driveway. Once I'm no longer looking, though, I catch sight of his reflection in a half-broken window as he picks his way through, nose scrunching in distaste.

I clamp my mouth shut. If I tease him, he'll take that as a sign that we're fine, and we're not.

I tramp through the overgrown front garden. I might be wearing low heels, but they're washable. There's nothing in my closet that isn't.

"Watch out!" he says as I lean toward the broken glass.

I can see the jagged edges, and I'm not getting that close. I edge as near as I can and shine my phone's flashlight inside.

"There is no one here, Kennedy," he says as he stops outside the garden.

"I can see that."

I peer in and lean close enough to the glass to make him rock forward, his reflection catching my eye.

"I think the painting's here," I say.

Silence behind me. I swear I can hear the internal debate raging. He suspects I'm just looking for an adventure. That *is* what brought me out of the car. Now he's trying to decide whether I'd stretch the truth to continue that adventure.

"I sense a curse," I say.

Reluctance shadows his voice as he says, "Is that normal?" In other words, he's skeptical but hates to doubt.

"It depends," I say as I survey the house. "I can usually sense them when I'm close, occasionally when I'm farther away. I'm not saying it's definitely the painting, but there's a cursed object in there. Which is a problem."

"Because you don't know what it is, and we could trigger it."

"No, because . . ." I wave at the derelict building. "The chance of there being a cursed object at a random empty house is next to nil. If there's a curse in there—painting or otherwise . . . ?"

"It's a trap." He pauses, and there's double the reluctance in his tone as he says, "Is that plausible?"

I exhale. "That's the bigger question, right? I found it while Hope was online looking at cursed dolls. It's not as if someone emailed me the listing. I'm not even the one who bought it. So how *can* it be a trap?"

I throw up my hands. "Maybe I'm wrong. I'm on edge, and I'm imagining that I feel something inside because I want a distraction."

I turn to the car. "Let's just go."

"No," he says. "Even if there isn't a cursed object inside, you sense something."

"Possibly just frayed nerves."

"All the more reason to be sure. We don't see how this can be a trap, so there's no danger. No reason to walk away without satisfying your curiosity. Otherwise, you'll wonder whether the painting might have been here after all, whether someone could have arranged that listing to lure you in, and if so, then it's better that we know before they try again."

"But we agree it's not possible."

"I didn't say that. Showing you that listing involves technology, which means we cannot say it's impossible, neither of us being experts in the field. Is it possible to hack a company that size? Probably not, if the sole purpose is to entice one visitor with one item. At the other end of the spectrum, is it possible to hack *your* computer and nudge you with that listing until it catches your eye? That seems more likely."

"But again, I didn't buy it."

"No, I did. Using my credit card. Under my real name." He looks up at the house. "I am concerned someone could be targeting you because of me."

"Your parents." I rub my arms. "You think this could be them?"

He doesn't answer for a moment. Then he says, slowly, "I'm torn between saying they wouldn't do this and knowing I have said that far too often in my life, only to be proven wrong. However, usually when I say that, I mean they would not go so far. This is different. If I say I can't see them doing *this*, it's because it's overly complicated. Also, it leans too far into the magical side of our world, and they prefer the business side."

"Destroying my credit rating rather than zapping me with a curse."

"Yes. They see our luck working as a tool that gives us a business advantage if we wield it with precision and care."

"To them, using luck working is no different than using any natural skill. Curse weaving is a parlor trick."

"Using a curse isn't their style." He looks up at the house. "Which doesn't mean they never would. Or that this could not possibly be their trap."

"So . . ."

"So I believe we both have reason to investigate. Reasons that will not allow us to rest until we have answered this question."

"Time to break into the scary house?"

"I'm afraid so."

———

WE START by checking the entrance points. We don't find any traps, but it still seems unwise to throw open the front door and march in. All of the main-floor windows are broken. We select one near the back and clear the glass enough to safely climb through. Once inside, we stand in the kitchen and shine our cell phone flashlights around.

As I squint into the near darkness, Connolly bends to examine the floor.

"Footprints." He lowers his light to show me. "There is no accompanying layer of dust on them, which suggests they're recent."

He snaps a photo.

"Excellent," I say. "Now we have photographic evidence that will help us capture the teenagers who use this as a party hangout."

He frowns at me as he rises. I point to a pile of crushed beer cans in one corner and chip bags on the grimy counter. He continues to frown.

"Kids are using this as a party spot, Connolly."

"That seems"—he looks around—"unsanitary."

I laugh under my breath. "Yep, but not all teens can afford to rent the penthouse suite for a bash. Keep the photo, though. Just because people have used this place to party doesn't mean those are their prints."

I don't say they could be left by whoever set this trap. That would imply there *is* a trap, and now that I'm inside, I'm not so sure. Whenever I try to focus on that curse signal, I can't pick up anything. Then I relax, talking with Connolly, and the sensation comes again, only to evaporate once I notice.

"Do you sense anything now?" Connolly asks, clearly practicing his mind reading.

"I'm not sure. I might have been imagining it."

"Then at least we aren't *intentionally* walking into a trap."

He tries for a smile but can't manage one. It's been a long night for both of us, and it's barely ten o'clock.

I rub my hands over my face and give myself a shake. "Okay, let's get this over with. Quick survey of the rooms—"

Something flickers past the doorway, and I spin.

"Did you see that?" I ask.

"See what?"

"Question answered," I murmur.

I shine my light on the darkened doorway. It leads into the dining room, given the remains of a dinette set inside.

I step toward it. Connolly lays his fingers on my upper arm, but the gesture only urges caution. I keep shining my light as we approach the doorway. Then comes the question of who goes through first. Connolly strides forward, as if there's no question. Yet as he steps in front of me, he has the sense to glance over.

I consider. Yep, I totally want to be first through any door. But this isn't the time to negotiate a bigger slice of the danger pie. I motion that he can go ahead. He adjusts his flashlight beam and approaches. A quick scan, and he steps through . . . and jumps.

I hurry in to find him staring at an empty wall.

"Saw something?" I say.

He nods.

"What?" I ask.

"I don't know. Just movement."

"Yep, that's what I saw earlier. I'd blame rats, but unless they're at least three feet tall and walking on their hind legs . . ."

He nods absently, his attention still on the empty space. Then he eases back.

"It was tall enough to be in my line of sight, which means not a rat, but otherwise . . ." He swings the beam over the space, which is definitely empty, an exterior wall with no doors and a half-broken window.

"Let's get this over with," I say. "I think we're both tired and jumpy. We agree this room is clear?"

He passes his beam over everything, *everything* comprising that broken dinette set. The next room is the front hall. The only object there is the faded photograph of a dilapidated barn. Yep, photographers love rural decay, and apparently people love it in their homes. Not sure why, when they could drive down the road and see the same sight.

I examine the photograph well enough to confirm it's not cursed. Then we move into the living room. When something skitters across the floor, Connolly's arm slams out to hold me back. I bend to see a field mouse huddled under a broken end table.

"Aww," I say. "Isn't it cute?"

"Careful. It could be rabid."

I choke on a laugh. "You are such a city boy, Connolly. Mice don't transmit rabies. Now, if you see a raccoon or a skunk, I'll keep my distance, but I'm fine with mice. Growing up in an old house means spending the winter politely escorting them out the door."

I look around. There's a sofa that's in decent shape, plus two end tables and a chair pulled in from the dinette.

"Party central," I say.

Connolly struggles not to shudder.

"Yep, it isn't the penthouse suite," I say.

"While I would point out I never rented the penthouse—or any hotel room—for a party, I would also need to admit that I never actually hosted such a party. Possibly also"—he coughs—"never attended one."

"Because you were all about the debutante balls."

"I think you're joking, but in the event you are not, no, while we don't have debutante balls, strictly speaking, there are similar events, and they are as tedious as one might imagine. No, my social life was quite full in college. Between trivia night and karaoke night and, my personal favorite, chess night, I was very busy."

He pauses a beat before saying, "That *was* a joke, Kennedy."

"Naturally. You wouldn't be caught dead at karaoke night."

He sighs and shakes his head. "The point is that while my idea of a party may differ from yours, I understand that we can't all rent the penthouse—or even the Motel 8—for our parties, and therefore, I offer no judgment."

"It's the Motel 6 or the Super 8. They're different chains. And, no, before you make any assumptions, I never partied anyplace like this, either. We had bush parties. Or, yes, sometimes at the Motel 6."

As we talk, I circle the room. There are two more old pictures, one a painting and one a photograph, again more pastoral themes. Neither is cursed. That's the end of the main level—kitchen, living room, dining room. Connolly keeps poking around for more, because clearly there must be more. Where's the library? The formal parlor? Even a main-floor bathroom?

When he throws open a door, he gives a small noise of Salvoy . . . until his gaze drops to the stairs descending into darkness.

"Yeah, that's the basement," I say. "And I'm not going down unless absolutely necessary. That is a horror movie waiting to happen." I turn. "There's still the—"

Something runs past the kitchen doorway. I race into the living room as the figure dashes through the other doorway.

"Hey!" I call.

Connolly grabs me before I can keep running.

"Someone's here," I say. "That was definitely human shaped."

He keeps his hand on my arm. I resist the urge to brush him off. He's right—I can't run after a stranger in an empty house.

We proceed with caution to the front door. From there, we can see both the living room and the dining room. Both are empty.

"Circular," I say. "The main level forms a circle. The only way we're catching up is to separate and cut them off."

"Which we are not doing."

I hesitate.

"Kennedy . . ."

"Not doing. Right. Got it."

"Because of the separating part."

I give him a look. "I know, okay? I just—"

His hand clamps my arm, and I spin.

"Hey!" I snap.

I stop as I follow his gaze. He's looking up the stairs . . . and someone's looking down.

CHAPTER NINE

THERE'S a figure at the top of the stairs. A little girl in a dress.

"Holy shit," I whisper.

"Is that . . . ?" he whispers back.

"It's the curse," I say. "That's how they describe her. A little girl in a dress."

"Not a ghost," he says.

"No," I say. "Just an illusion."

I know that, but it doesn't keep the hairs from prickling on the back of my neck. The girl wavers like a ghost, the wall visible through her semi-translucent form. She stares straight into my eyes, and I know that's the illusion at work, but I still need to plant my feet to keep from retreating. Those eyes are empty. Literally empty, nothing but black holes fixed on me.

"She can't hurt us," I say.

Connolly gives a strained chuckle. "That's what I've been telling myself, on auto-repeat, for the last sixty seconds. It doesn't change the fact that the absolute last thing I want to do is what we need to do."

"Go up those stairs."

He grips the banister and lifts one foot. Then he glances back. "Not volunteering to go first this time, are you?"

"Absolutely not."

Another smile, his eyes meeting mine, the warmth of them chasing away the chill from the ghostly girl's gaze.

He starts up the stairs, and she stays there. She seems to be watching me, peeking around Connolly as I climb, but I know that in his mind, she's watching him.

Such a clever little curse. I don't think I fully appreciated that until now. How much work would go into weaving such a thing? I know a few "boo!" curses—standard jinxes where you pick up an object and a sudden apparition or voice makes you drop it fast. This is another level altogether. The difference between building a snowman and chiseling out a marble statue.

"The craftsmanship—"

The girl leaps into the air and rockets toward us.

We both fall back, Connolly staggering against me, only our grips on the railing keeping him from slamming into me and sending us both tumbling down.

I right myself as he catches my arm.

"Got it, thanks," I say. "So, forget that whole thing about her not being able to hurt us."

Even an apparition *can* hurt you if it scares you into falling down the stairs. This hallucination is out for blood, conjuring the vengeful spirit of a dead child.

Not a harmless jump-scare jinx at all.

When Connolly jerks his chin, I follow his gaze to see her at the bottom of the stairs, gazing up, empty-eyed.

"Well," I mutter, "we can see how a simple illusion could kill someone. Or drive them mad. Imagine seeing that beside your bed every night."

"I'd rather not," he says. "But thank you for implanting that suggestion."

"You're welcome." I gaze down at her. "Now that she can't scare us down the stairs, I'm going to try getting a closer look. Better sit down in case she flies at you again."

Most guys would grip the railing tighter and say they're fine. Connolly has the sense to take my advice.

"Careful," he says, while staying where he is and making no move to stop me or interfere or hover over my shoulder. Trusting that it is safe enough and I am smart enough.

Yep, he really is an awesome guy.

If only he didn't come with those parent-shaped pieces of baggage and all the damage that comes from twenty-eight years of lugging them around.

I continue down the stairs, one at a time, my gaze fixed on the illusion. I get close enough to see the girl's dress. There's something about it that seems—

She flies at me, making me stumble back. A clatter behind me as Connolly leaps to his feet, but I'm only a few stairs up, and I just fall onto my ass, facing the front door.

"Did she move?" he asks.

I rise and twist to face him. "She didn't just fly right at you?"

He shakes his head. "She disappeared when I sat down."

"Huh." I draw in a shaky breath. "Okay, so it's definitely a viewer-focused illusion. Also a triggered one. I got exactly the same distance away before she leaped at me. That should make it less scary, right? Knowing there's a trigger, just like a choreographed jump scare?"

"If knowing a scare is fake eliminated the emotional response, we wouldn't have horror movies and haunted houses."

I smile up at him. "True enough."

I take a deep breath and peer up at the top of the steps. The little girl is poised there.

"Yeah, we see your tricks," I say, while pretending my voice is perfectly steady. "We need to search upstairs, and a little illusion scare isn't going to stop us."

Connolly rises. "Ready?"

"Yep, and I'm totally not going to close my eyes and use the railing to guide me up."

He chuckles. "Actually, that sounds like an excellent plan. Safety first."

After two steps up, I decide closing my eyes *does* make sense. It'll keep me from the embarrassment of startling again when she jumps at me.

I grip the railing in one hand and feel my way up the stairs. I should have counted them off, so I won't stumble at the top, but I've gone about ten when Connolly says, "Two more."

"Thank you."

I reach the top and exhale. Then I look around.

"Do you see her?" I say.

"No. We've spoiled her game, I think."

"Mmm, don't count on it. I'd be prepared for jump scares from now on."

We move with care along the hall. I turn toward the first open doorway and brace myself as I step through. The girl doesn't appear. It's a bedroom, with the remains of a bed, including a mattress that someone has laid on the floor, and I do not even want to think about why they did that.

No pictures. No bric-a-brac. Nothing curseworthy. I still circle the room, testing the air, ready for the kid to jump from behind the bed. She doesn't.

Connolly tenses as he steps into the hallway. Then his shoulders relax, telling me there's no sign of her there, either. I follow and see nothing but an empty hall.

At the next door, he goes through first. Another bedroom. Also devoid of both illusions and curses. I'm closer to the door, so I enter the hall first. Still nothing. The next doorway leads to the bathroom. When I catch a flicker of movement, I leap through with an "ah-ha!" only to find myself facing down a tattered curtain as the breeze catches it through a broken window.

I'm turning to tell Connolly when the girl appears right in front of me. I stagger back and hit the toilet. Before I can react, she whips around me, and I'm scrambling out of her way. Steadying hands clasp me, and I nearly jump out of my skin before realizing it's Connolly.

"See?" I say. "Not scared at all. I'm totally over this illusion nonsense."

I glare at the girl, standing right in front of me now. "Did you hear that? I called you nonsense. We have had quite enough of your pranks, missy, and—"

She shoots up into the air, mouth opening in a scream, face contorting, and I stagger back into Connolly. His arms go around me, holding me against him. I wriggle, just a little, embarrassed by my reaction, and he doesn't restrain me, but he does keep a gentle hold, telling me it's okay.

I take a moment to catch my breath. Then I glance back at him, and damn if my heart doesn't pick up speed again. I want to freeze-frame this moment. Steadying arms around me. Warm chest against my back. That strong jaw, those gorgeous green eyes, tight with concern.

Even the smell of him is perfect. Exactly the right fragrance applied with such a light touch that you don't notice it until you're this close, and even then, it barely tickles the senses, a teasing hint of "what *is* that?" I don't know my sandalwood from my rosewood. I only know that I want to bury my face against his chest and drink it in. Which means I'm really kinda glad he's behind me, or I might do exactly that.

I tilt my head to look up at him. "Still mad at you."

"You have every right to be."

I sigh and allow myself to lean my head back against his shoulder. "I hate when you do that."

"Do what?"

"You're supposed to defend yourself. Tell me that you've already apologized and, really, I'm overreacting. That'll piss me off all the more, and I can be properly furious for the proper amount of time. It's much harder to stay mad when you're calm and reasonable about it."

"So I am employing the correct strategy to get back on your good side?"

"Yes, damn you. Now stop it." I pull out of his arms and peer around the room. "Do you see her?"

"No, but as you pointed out, the illusion seems focused on the individual viewer. The fact that I don't see her doesn't mean you won't."

"I wasn't really asking. I'm just changing the subject before I stop being mad at you."

"You are allowed to be temporarily not angry with me for the sake of searching this house, and I will not take it as a sign that you are, in general, no longer angry with me." He puts out his hand. "Deal?"

I shake it. "Deal. Now we have one more room to search before venturing into the dreaded basement." I walk into the hall. "The illusion means the painting is here somewhere. We just need to—"

I stop short. Connolly hurries up behind me.

"You see her?"

I don't answer. I need to catch my breath first. There's no sign of the little girl. What stopped me was a sudden slam of negative curse energy, knocking the wind from my lungs and setting my heart racing.

I take one careful step toward the last room. Then another. The logical part of my brain points out that we've already triggered the curse. It can't do any worse. Yet once again, logic doesn't matter. My heart races so fast I struggle to draw breath. I step through that doorway, and there it is.

The painting.

It hangs on the opposite wall, impossible to miss, the only object in the room. It's the girl from the illusion. She stares out at the viewer with tears streaming down her face. When the painting was an image on a screen, I could roll my eyes at the manipulative melodrama of it. In person, having just seen that girl standing beside me, dread creeps down my spine.

I shake it off and step forward. Connolly catches my arm.

"It's a trap," he says.

He's right, of course. We haven't found the painting by accident. Haven't followed the address to walk into the new owner's home. Haven't even tracked down the spot where the new owner is hiding it. The painting hangs on the wall, waiting for us, and my brain screams that this was a bad idea, such an incredibly stupid idea. We thought we were smart, recognizing a potential trap, but now we're here, in this room, and whoever lured us here has us trapped, where we can't—

Wait.

I shine my light at the wall. There's a message scrawled on the faded wallpaper.

Congratulations, you just passed your first pop quiz!

CHAPTER TEN

LAST MONTH, I discovered the Greek gods are real. Not actual divinities, but immortals with powers who were worshipped as gods. We're descended from those immortals. Connolly can trace his line back to Mars, god of battle luck. And I can trace mine to Mercury, the trickster.

Mercury is gender fluid. Being from a very different time period, she still uses female pronouns and goes by Mercy. I've never met her. I've just gotten messages from her. Tests that I passed, which apparently "win" me a mentoring from the greatest curse weaver of all. I'm not sure "win" is the word, and I certainly never applied for the gig, but I'd be lying if I didn't admit that I've spent the last six weeks eagerly awaiting my first lesson.

I turn on my heel and march out of the room. This time, when the girl appears in my path, I snarl, "Get out of my way," and walk right through her.

I continue down the steps and out the front door. As I inhale deep breaths of evening air, Connolly says, "I hope this isn't a bad time."

I turn, about to answer that question, when a voice answers, "No, not at all. Is something wrong?"

Connolly has his phone out and on speaker. The voice coming

through it is Vanessa Apsley. Better known to history as Venus Aphrodite.

Connolly glances over to see whether I want to explain this situation. I shake my head. I'm too angry to do it properly.

Mercury chose me as her protege. *Me!* It was like getting an invitation to a magical school long past the age where we believe such a thing is possible.

The god of curses herself had seen promise in me. Singled me out. I joke about being special, being the chosen one, but deep down, it'd been a fantasy come true. I couldn't wait for her to reach out and start my training.

Now she has, and I am furious. I expected better. Mercury is the trickster god of the Greco-Roman pantheon. She's a little flighty, a little quirky, and she can drive people around her to distraction. Yes, Vanessa and Marius—Mars—may have suggested I remind them of her, but that seemed mostly flattering. Everything they've told us indicates that her pranks are the kind I like—the fun ones, devoid of cruelty.

This prank may not have been outright cruel, but it is inconsiderate. And, yes, that's a very Connolly word, one that would normally make me roll my eyes. An inconsiderate prank? Aren't they all, at least a bit?

This one is inconsiderate to the point where I'm seriously pissed off. We spent our evening pursuing a painting that I considered dangerously cursed. We broke into an abandoned house, taking the risk that it was a trap. We endured multiple heart-stopping scares because, by that point, I knew the painting was there and couldn't turn around. I went through all that, and worse, I pulled Connolly into it . . . and it was all just a game. A game involving a terrifying illusion that could have sent us falling down those stairs to our deaths.

So no, I don't want to explain the situation to Vanessa. I don't think I could form a coherent narrative. Connolly does—not only coherent but concise, while still making it clear that I am irate, and he agrees with me.

"That doesn't sound like Mercy." The voice coming through the phone now isn't Vanessa's.

"Hello, Marius," Connolly says.

"Vess put me on speaker right after you started. Now, I can be too quick to defend my sister, but . . ."

"Marius is right," Vanessa says. "That doesn't sound like Mercy."

"The message was clearly hers," I say.

"That part does sound like her," Vanessa says slowly.

"Or anyone who knows her," Marius says. "And knows her plans for you, Kennedy."

"Which doesn't mean it absolutely could not be her," Vanessa says. "I can imagine her nudging you to buy a cursed item, pretending it's been sold and sending you on a treasure hunt. Even luring you into an abandoned house. Yes. But it's the nature of the curse that doesn't sound like her."

"The cat tea caddy was one-hundred percent her style," Marius says. "A harmless jinx hiding a puzzle with a greater prize. But a haunted painting? And you say you've heard of this painting before?"

"It's one of a set. An urban legend about an artist feeling compelled to paint them and selling them right away. The paintings are supposed to depict children killed—"

"In a fire?" Vanessa cuts in. "You don't mean the Salvo Costa paintings, do you?"

"Right. It's *Crying Girl*, from the Costa quartet."

Silence.

"Vanessa?" I say. "Marius?"

"We're going to need to get back to you on this," Marius says.

"You're contacting Mercy?"

"We'll try, but that's always tricky. Do you have the painting?"

"It's in the house."

"And you say you saw the little girl? Both of you?"

"Uh, yes. What's going on?"

"Nothing," Vanessa cuts in quickly. "Let us handle this. Can you transport the painting safely?"

"I can."

"Then I would suggest you do that, but only if you can do so safely. Let us look into this and get back to you tomorrow."

We sign off, and I glance at Connolly.

"Something is up with that painting, isn't it?"

"Most definitely." He looks toward the house. "I would suggest we attempt to take it. However, I would also suggest I drive along the back roads until we are certain that curse shield works."

"And you don't have a creepy kid popping up between you and the steering wheel, sending us both crashing into the median and dying horribly?"

"Exactly."

———

Do we agree with Vanessa and Marius that this couldn't be Mercy? I'd like to, but I don't know Mercy, which is a large part of the problem in general. Despite her interest in mentoring me, I haven't heard from her since she first promised that mentoring. While I've tried to be patient, I've started to wonder whether she made the offer on a whim and then skipped off to a new project that caught her eye. Her siblings all consider her the "flighty" one, and that's not a reference to Mercury's winged boots.

I've been called flighty myself, but when it comes to promises and commitments, I'm as grounded as Ani, and I expect the same from others. Being mercurial is no excuse for instability. Though, yes, I'm aware of the double irony there, Mercy being the very source of the word *mercurial* and the fact that the element named after her is known for its instability, in its ever-changing form.

I understand why Vanessa and Marius are defending her. She's Marius's younger sister and Vanessa's younger foster sister. Vanessa and Marius being a couple would be creepy in modern times, but it was different in ancient Greece, and they'd grown up as friends more than siblings.

The point is that Mercy is their little sister. She might test their patience, but they love her, just as I love Hope. If someone told me Hope played a vicious prank, I'd say they were wrong. My sister doesn't have it in her. Does that mean I couldn't be mistaken? Nope. It just means that I can't imagine her doing that.

As much as I want to get this painting safely out of Connolly's car, we need to talk to Ms. Silver again. Was she an unwitting pawn in this game? Or is she part of it?

It feels as if it should be far too late to talk to her. It's not. Okay, technically, it is too late for social visits, but with an hour to go before midnight, it's not exactly the middle of the night.

We pull into the driveway. The house is dark. We didn't call first—we're not about to alert Ms. Silver.

Connolly checks his watch.

"It's 10:58," I say. "Yep, she may have gone to bed and really not appreciate the interruption, but it's not late enough for her to call the cops. And if she does, I'm sure this fancy car can outrun them."

When I start up the drive, he motions for me to wait. He heads to where he can see the left side of the bungalow. Then he crosses the lawn to the right. I think he's checking the side windows for light, but when he walks up to me, he says, "The bedrooms seem to be to the left, if I'm interpreting the window configuration correctly. I'm going to suggest you ring the bell while I watch."

"Ah, to see if a light comes on but she doesn't answer the door. Good idea."

I walk up to the porch and ring. The bell echoes through the house. I glance over at Connolly, who's shading the neighbors' lights from his vision. I edge closer to the door to listen. It stays silent. I back out and look at Connolly. He shakes his head.

I ring the bell again, and this time, I stay where I am, ear to the door. Nothing.

"May I help you?" a querulous voice calls, and I jump, spinning.

An elderly woman stands in the driveway to our right. She has a Great Dane on a lead, the dog nearly as big as her.

"Sorry to disturb you," Connolly says. "We know it's late to call, but we had business with Ms. Silver earlier, and there was an urgent development. We couldn't reach her on the phone, so we stopped by."

"Ms. Silver?"

"The woman who lives here."

"You have the wrong address, son. That's Bert and Mabel's house."

Connolly frowns. "We were here earlier, and we spoke to a woman who identified herself as Ms. Silver. Do the owners have a daughter?"

"Oh, I know who you mean. The plant-sitter."

"Plant-sitter?" I say, coming off the porch.

"They have a friend who stops by to water the plants. I said I'd do it, but they're very particular about their tropicals. Mostly Bert. That man treats them like children. I'm surprised Mabel can drag him away."

"Ms. Silver is their plant-sitter?"

The old woman flutters a hand. "I don't know her name. Never spoken to her. She waves, though. Always smiles and waves, friendly as can be."

"This Ms. Silver," I say, "is she in her early thirties? Dark blond hair?"

The woman laughs. "Goodness, no. She can't be a day under fifty. African-American woman."

"Ah, well, obviously we *have* made a mistake," I say. "Thank you. We appreciate your time, ma'am. Have a good night."

———

As CONNOLLY PULLS from the drive, I groan and thump back against the seat.

"Taylor Silver," I mutter.

"Hmm?"

"The name Taylor. It makes me think of the singer." I glance at him. "Swift Silver. Quicksilver."

"Mercury."

CHAPTER ELEVEN

As we drive into Unstable, we pass a state police car idling at the intersection. I notice because Unstable, while small, has its own police department. We don't want outsiders policing our quirky little town, not when those outsiders might roll their eyes at our paranormal bent and grumble about the inconvenience of managing our tourist trade.

Our taxes pay for a small force, run by Chief Salazar, descended from one of the town's oldest families. If the state police are in town, I presume they're consulting with her on a matter that crosses both jurisdictions. Still, the car catches my eye, so when flashing lights flip on behind us, I know exactly what it is and twist to see the police car on our bumper.

Connolly frowns. "I'm under the speed limit, and there wasn't a stop sign. I do hope this isn't another Breathalyzer test."

I snort a laugh. We'd had an incident where Connolly used luck to avoid a car accident, and the resulting balancing had made him so clumsy the police suspected he was drunk. Then their machine wouldn't work—his bad luck—which only made things worse.

"That's a state police car," I say. "They won't be pulling us over. Just let them pass."

He rolls to the curb a few doors from my shop. It's well past midnight, every window dark, even the pub closed for the night.

I expect the car to continue on. Instead, it stops behind us.

"What the hell?" I mutter.

"It's fine," Connolly says. "Whatever the problem, it'll be nothing more than an inconvenience. It never is, and my luck in that has nothing to do with my powers."

He means that he's a white guy wearing an expensive suit, driving an expensive car. No one's pulling him over thinking he stole the vehicle or has drugs or weapons stashed in the trunk.

Connolly rolls down the window, his license in one hand, the other on the steering wheel.

"Good evening, officer," he says.

A middle-aged man leans down. "Do you know why we pulled you over this evening?"

"No, sir."

"Step out of the vehicle, please. Both of you."

We comply. He doesn't ask us to keep our hands where he can see them. He doesn't rest his hand on his gun. He just steps back and waits for us to get out and then waves us to the sidewalk, where a younger woman, also in uniform, joins us.

"The car is a rental," Connolly says. "The paperwork is in the glove compartment. I presume you'd rather get that out yourself?"

The older officer waves for his partner to do that, and I step out of her way. She retrieves the rental agreement and says, "It's rented to an Aiden Connolly."

Her partner grunts, which I presume means he's confirming that's the name on the license. He's only half paying attention as he circles the car. Then, without saying a word, he goes to the cruiser and climbs in. We wait. A moment later, he's out again.

"I see you have a Lexus registered in your name, Aiden. Seems odd, renting the same vehicle for a drive from Boston."

"My car has been making a knocking noise, and I haven't had time to get it into the shop. I rented this for the trip today."

I try not to grumble in annoyance. The state police have no jurisdiction here, and it's hardly a crime to rent a car when you have one already. Connolly is calm, though, as if this is a perfectly reasonable line of questioning.

The older officer circles the car again. I glance to the younger one for clues, but her face is as expressionless as Connolly's.

"What was the purpose of this trip?" the officer asks.

When Connolly isn't quick to answer, he glances over. "The longer it takes you to respond, the more obvious it'll be that you're making up stories."

"No," Connolly says carefully. "I do not need to discuss my evening with you, and I am trying to determine whether I should request legal representation or simply explain, as I have nothing to hide."

"If you have nothing to hide, you don't require legal representation."

Connolly gives him a humorless smile. "Does that line actually work on anyone, officer? Yes, I know I should insist on speaking to a lawyer, but it's late, and I'm sure there's been some misunderstanding I can easily clear up. I am here visiting my friend, Ms. Bennett"—he nods at me—"who runs the antique shop just over there." Another nod. "We had purchased a painting online for her shop, and we retrieved it tonight."

"The painting's in the trunk?"

"Yes, sir."

The officer leans his hip against the car. "It wouldn't happen to be a painting of a little girl, would it? *Crying Girl* by Salvo Costa? A painting that was reported stolen two weeks ago?"

Connolly's brows shoot up. "That is the painting. I certainly hope it wasn't stolen. We were dealing in good faith with a reputable auction site. If it is stolen property . . ." He glances my way.

"We'll return it, obviously," I say. "Though I'll have to ask for proper documentation to file an insurance claim."

If Mercy stole the painting, I'd give it back. The insurance excuse is a ploy to give me time to uncurse it first. But when I say that, the older officer's eyes glint.

"Insurance. Isn't that your business, Mr. Connolly?"

"It is."

The officer—Platts, I see on his name tag now—waits. Connolly just stands there, as if he, too, awaits more.

"Seems a little suspicious, don't you think, Aiden?"

Not "Mr. Connolly" anymore.

Connolly replies blandly. "I'm not certain how you see that, sir. Yes, my firm insures Ms. Bennett's business. If this is a stolen painting, she will be able to file a claim for the exact amount she paid tonight. That means she won't have lost any money, but she will have wasted an evening retrieving goods she can no longer offer for sale. Insurance or not, she will come out farther behind than before she bought that painting, unfortunately."

"If she paid for the painting. If she can provide all proper documentation of a sale."

Connolly nods. "True, which brings up an important point. I'd actually purchased it on my credit card, for convenience. As it was for her business, she should be able to recoup the loss under her policy, and then I would be repaid, but I will need to check the exact details of that policy. It may turn out that, with the policy I sold her, I cannot recoup my money on the painting, which would be ironic."

"Not ironic," Officer Platts says. "Convenient."

Connolly frowns. "How so?"

Officer Platts pauses, as if he threw that out because it sounded good and now realizes there's no way Connolly could benefit from not being able to recoup his money from his own company. He glances toward his partner for help, but she only shrugs.

"It's suspicious. That's all I'm saying," Platts mutters. He squares his shoulders. "I'm going to need to see that painting, and I'm going to need to see your receipt."

Connolly doesn't even twitch. He only says, smoothly, "Of course, officer. Let me show you the receipt first. May I pull it up on my phone?"

Platts grunts, and Connolly takes out his cell while warning that he's reaching into his pocket, though neither officer seems the least concerned.

Connolly taps his phone a few times and holds out the original receipt. "As you can see, I was the purchaser, and I bought the painting reported stolen."

"And you paid for it?"

"I provided my credit card information, as you can see on the receipt.

As Ms. Silver—the seller—did give us the painting, I can only presume she successfully charged my card."

"You didn't notice? Two grand to eBay, and your credit card company didn't flag that as suspicious? Mine sure would."

There's a pause. Such a long pause that my gut twists, thinking Connolly didn't consider that. But when he answers, his tone is apologetic with just the right hint of discomfiture. "I have what is known as a black card."

The younger officer whistles. "That's a real thing?"

Connolly tugs on his tie, clearing his throat as if embarrassed, though no color rises in his cheeks. "Er, yes. My family has a . . . special relationship with our bank."

"What the hell's a black card?" Platts snaps.

"It means he isn't just rich," his partner says. "He's super rich. Yeah, the bank's not going to call him for spending two grand on a painting." She looks at Connolly. "I gotta ask. Is it an actual black-colored credit card?"

He takes out his wallet, again warning that he's reaching for it. The card he removes is black with a gold edge.

Platts clears his throat and glowers at his partner, but she ignores him and says, "Nice. Still, we are going to need to see that painting."

"Naturally." He glances up and down the street. "If you'd like to examine it in Ms. Bennett's shop, we can do it there. The painting was securely wrapped for transportation, and it will need to be opened. I can carry it to the shop or drive closer, whichever works for you."

"Just drive," the younger officer says. "We'll be right behind you."

Her partner squawks, but she's already heading to the driver's side of the cruiser.

CHAPTER TWELVE

I CLIMB INTO THE CAR. Connolly puts it in gear and rolls forward, barely hitting five miles an hour. That keeps the cops happy, but it also gives us a moment to talk.

"You think Mercy stole it?" I ask. "As part of her test?"

"Possibly."

"She is the patron god of thieves. Could *this* be another part of her test? Dealing with the police? She might have stolen it, but there's no way the police randomly pulled us over when we had it in your trunk. Did she steal it *and* report it?"

"He said it was reported stolen two weeks ago."

"This isn't making any sense."

"I agree. If it's Mercy's idea of a prank, I don't think you want to have anything to do with her, however useful she might be to your career."

"Oh, I've already realized that. This is bullshit, and I'm sorry you've been dragged into it."

"If I was concerned, I'd have already placed a call to my lawyer."

I glance over. "Are you really holding off because you think everything's fine? Or because you're afraid your lawyer will tell your parents you were with me?"

"The police don't have any grounds to charge us."

"You *are* concerned your parents will find out." I study his expression. "Or do you think they're behind this?"

He parks and meets my eyes. "At this moment, I don't know what to think, Kennedy. My concern is that they are about to take this painting, and you'll want to uncurse it first."

I exhale. "Okay. Let's focus on that."

"How long do you need?"

When I hesitate, he says, "That was an unfair question. I'm asking you to rush the reversal of a dangerous hex, which is unsafe." He glances in his rearview mirror. "I can lend you some luck if that would help."

"It would . . . but then you'd need to deal with a balancing while also dealing with an asshole cop who really wants to charge you with something, rich boy."

I try to pass him a smile, but it falters. "No luck, please. If you can keep doing all the talking, I'll unwrap the painting for them and make some excuse about rewrapping it for transportation after they've seen it. That might buy me enough time."

———

I TAKE the painting to a low table that I use to wrap fragile purchases. It also does double duty as a workbench, because I've learned that in a place like Unstable, you don't want to do your repairs in the back. In Boston, customers only wanted to see the final product. In a tourist town, tinkering in the open is seen as artisanship at work, and passersby will slip in to watch me sand or paint.

Hope says I should do my uncursings out in the open, too. I'm sure that'd draw a crowd, but I'm not quite ready for that yet. Tonight, though, I may need to make an exception. There's no way the police are letting me slip this painting into the storage room while they stay up front with Connolly.

"Nice place," Platts says as he struts around. "Antiques, huh? Pretty fancy. You work here, Miss Bennett?"

"It's her shop," Connolly says. "She owns it."

"Huh. Pretty fancy for a young lady like yourself. Must be nice having rich friends who can help you buy all this stuff."

His partner—Grove, according to her name tag—throws me a sympathetic look, but Connolly is the one who stiffens, his face tightening.

"I'm very fortunate," I say. "I have an extremely supportive family and community. And friends, of course. Though one in particular seems to think he can buy an expensive painting and resell it in my shop."

Connolly relaxes. "It was an investment opportunity."

I roll my eyes. "You were never getting someone to pay more than two grand for it, Aiden."

Connolly launches into a mini-lecture on art investment. I'm pretty sure he's just making it up as he goes, but it lets me take my time unwrapping the painting while I'm clearing my mind, opening it to the curse's music.

Curses present differently for each weaver. To me, they are tunes that I must snatch, harmonies I must separate like twisted threads. Why music? I have no idea. I'm hardly what one would call musical. I *like* music, though. I sing in the shower . . . and the car . . . and the kitchen. I love to dance, even if I'm not very good at it. Maybe passion is more important than talent. I love music, so to me, curses present as that.

This one starts singing its deceptively sweet song when Platts barks at my ear, "What's all that for?" and I jump, song shattering.

"What kind of covering is that?" he demands, poking at the curse shield I'm folding away from the painting. He takes a corner. "Why's it so heavy?"

"It's lead lined," I say. "Like an X-ray blanket."

Platts jumps back. His partner stays where she is, across the room, examining a set of teacups.

"Is the painting radioactive?" she asks.

I smile. "I certainly hope not. But we were speaking of urban legends earlier, and this painting has one attached. That's why it's so valuable. Not the painting itself, but the story behind it."

"Cursed, right?" Grove says, as she lifts a little sign from the teacups. "That's the gimmick for your shop. Everything's cursed."

"Formerly cursed. The *formerly* part is important."

"So this is true?" Grove waves at the sign.

"The person who sold them to me swore she heard the funeral march every time she drank from the cups. I didn't find any indication of that, but I still put it on the sign, with the disclaimer that it's what the former owner claimed. Really, they're just gorgeous examples of Salvoian bone china."

"They are very pretty."

"Are you shopping or working?" Platts snaps. "And what's this nonsense about curses?"

"That painting supposedly has one," Grove says. "Didn't you look it up? Owners have said they saw the ghost of that girl. Some went crazy. A couple died. Personally, I don't believe in curses, but yeah, I'd wrap it in lead, too."

Connolly clears his throat. "May I fix either of you a coffee? There are a few pods out here, but Kennedy has a full selection in the back if you'd like to come and choose something."

He ushers them into the storage room while I mouth my thanks. He props open the door so they won't think I'm about to abscond with the painting, but they don't seem too worried. Connolly keeps up a running patter about curses, which Officer Grove seems interested in.

I turn my attention back to the painting. It's half-unwrapped. I don't quite dare expose it entirely. Last thing we need is a ghost popping up in the showroom.

I tune out Connolly and Grove, and allow myself to drift back to the curse. It's right there, whispering in my ear. I'm untangling the tune, hunting for the lyrics. When they come, they aren't in English, and that gives me pause. Is that Italian?

"You're still unwrapping that thing?" Platts's voice startles me from my work.

"I was examining it," I say. "We didn't get a chance earlier. Ms. Silver seemed in a rush, which now makes sense. As I presume you're going to take it, I wanted the chance to have a closer look. It is a legendary cursed object, after all."

He snorts. "It's a creepy painting of a crying kid. Now get that damn blanket off so we can confirm it's the one reported stolen."

"The owner sent a photograph of the signature," Grove says. "I have that here along with a photo of damage to the top left corner. A scorch mark."

"I can see the scorch mark," I say as I tug back the shield. "And the signature should be—"

"Get that damn blanket off," Platts snaps again. "We aren't taking it in that."

"Of course not," Connolly says smoothly. "It's Ms. Bennett's blanket, so she will remove it. I presume you'll want the painting properly wrapped afterward? To protect it for the owner?"

He goes into detail about how they should wrap it and why they might want to do so with such a valuable object. Buying me more time. Before I can focus on the painting again, though, Platts says, "Get that blanket off *now*."

I finish unwrapping it. Grove moves in for a closer look at the identifiers while Platts chugs his coffee. Grove confirms that it's the right painting, and I start wrapping it while Connolly talks, letting me sink back into the curse.

"What the hell!" Platts booms. A crash, and I turn to see him backing away, broken mug on the floor, coffee snaking out, heading right for a rolled-up Persian rug. I lunge to grab the rug out of the way, and Grove says, "Stop right there!"

"I'm just moving that rug before the coffee stains it."

"Stay where you are, please, Ms. Bennett. Ron? What's the matter?"

"Y-you don't see it?"

"See what, Ron?" Her voice is calm and even.

He points in front of him. "Th-the girl."

"Ron, there's no girl— Holy shit!" Grove wheels and nearly drops her phone. Her gaze fixes on a spot in front of her. "What the hell is that?"

"What are you seeing?" Connolly says.

"You know what we're seeing," Platts snaps. "The girl from the painting. You drugged our coffee."

Connolly's voice stays calm. "You made your own coffee, Officer Platts. You selected a pod and inserted it yourself."

"Then you dosed the water." Platts keeps backing away and then stops short and gives his head a sharp shake, muttering, "It's a hallucination. Just a hallucination."

He strides forward. Then he yelps, staggers back and thumps to the floor, hands rising to ward off the ghost.

I glance at Connolly, who shakes his head. He doesn't see it, either.

"Everyone stay calm," I say. "No one has been drugged. This is the curse at work, and I'm a trained professional."

I think I deserve an award for uttering those lines with a straight face. Still, my heart thuds as I realize just how bad this looks, just how much trouble we're going to be in for "drugging" two police officers.

Connolly takes over in his efficient way, as if spotting a curse-born ghost is no different than dealing with a small fire. Remain calm. Don't panic. It won't hurt you. Let the professionals deal with it.

Oh, they aren't buying that. Not even Officer Grove, who'd seemed sympathetic to our plight. Well, she had been . . . up until a ghost flew at her and we tried to claim it was a curse.

I tune them out. It's all I can do. Connolly is reassuring them that whatever they're seeing, it really *is* just a hallucination. Try to ignore it, and don't worry, they can certainly take the coffee machine into evidence for investigating possible tampering.

I'd love to grab my noise-canceling headphones from the storage room. They were a gift from Connolly, the result of a joke bet, and they're the best money can buy, naturally. I use them to focus on curses. I'd also love to get my kit. This seems a simple enough curse that I don't need it, but I'd still like the backup. Can't exactly get any of that now, not when it would mean I could be accused of doing something to the "evidence" of the coffee machine while I'm back there.

I have a few simple uncursing tools here, under the counter, and I can use them if needed. I have to balance the uncursing by casting a curse, but I can do that easily enough with my Magic 8 Ball after the police are gone. I'll be fine. I just need to focus and get this done.

When I focus, I catch the music of the curse quickly enough. It's eager to be heard, like a little girl tripping over herself to be noticed. It's definitely Italian, which makes this difficult. While curses can be in any language—and curse weavers from any nationality—my family is Greek, and most weavers I know are Greek or Italian. I'm most accustomed to curses in Latin or ancient Greek, but there are enough similarities in the languages that I figure out the nature of the curse. It helps that I've seen it triggered.

It's an illusion curse, obviously. Above my pay grade for weaving. As illusions go, though, it's a simple one with a simple trigger. Get within a certain radius of the painting, and you may see the girl herself, flying at you like a tiny Rottweiler.

The curse itself speaks of grief and rage. Does that mean the back-story is true? The painting capturing the vengeance of the girl whose siblings murdered their parents, the girl who went for help, only to be killed by her supposed rescuers? If so, I wouldn't blame her for flying at anyone who came close.

Except the illusion is not the girl herself. Not a ghost. And the part about the artist being possessed is bullshit. This is a curse. The weaver may have drawn on the story—fact or fiction—but it's the work of a real person, and as such, I am able to unweave it.

When I sag against the table, Officer Platts says, "Done?"

I nod, unable to summon the energy to speak.

"Good. Now, you are both under arrest for poisoning two state law enforcement officials . . ."

CHAPTER THIRTEEN

WE ARE NOT ARRESTED. Thankfully. Oh, Connolly goes along with it, preparing to contact his lawyer while advising the officers to call the local police and the crime-scene technicians. Get everyone here and explain to them how Platts freaked out over the hallucination of a little girl's ghost after we mentioned the curse. Also, please be advised that Connolly's lawyer will be contacting pharmacological experts to weigh in on the plausibility of Platts's claim. What exactly does he think Connolly slipped him that would act so quickly? He'd only drunk half his coffee, and Grove barely sipped hers.

Not that Connolly's arguing with officers of the law. Please, take whatever they need for testing, and he almost hopes they find something because otherwise . . . ? Well, otherwise, Platts just hallucinated a ghost on the pure power of suggestion itself. He wouldn't happen to be superstitious, would he?

Connolly wisely focuses on Platts. That lets Grove relax and take a mental step back to evaluate. Maybe she didn't see a ghost after all. Platts said it, and her imagination ran away with her. After all, the painting is right there, with the image of the girl, and the lighting is kind of wonky, and it's really late . . .

I feel a little bad about manipulating Grove. Still, I can argue that she's better off thinking it was just a trick of the mind. If that upsets her partner, maybe she'll get a new one. In the end, she decides she didn't see anything, and the coffee seemed fine, and maybe they don't want to actually arrest us. At least not yet.

Platts sputters, but his reddening face tells me that even without Grove bailing, he's reconsidering his story. Connolly insists they take the coffee machine water and Grove's leftover coffee for analysis, and Platts packages it up, grumbling the whole time.

"We're going to test it," he says.

"I *want* you to test it," Connolly says. "That will clear us in this matter."

"It doesn't clear you in that matter." Platts jabs a finger at the painting. "You took possession of stolen goods."

"Mistakenly," Connolly says. "We used a reputable website, and we will happily provide all required information. If this Ms. Silver was responsible for the theft, I hope she is held accountable. I'm glad the painting is being returned to the rightful owner."

When her partner is out of earshot, Grove says to me, voice lowered. "That was an actual curse, wasn't it?"

I don't answer, just meet her gaze and let her interpret that as she will.

———

THE POLICE ARE GONE. I've locked up the shop, and we leave the car parked out front while Connolly walks me home. We're silent for the first half, as we've been since the police pulled away. Then I say, "Platt isn't dropping this, is he?"

Connolly doesn't answer, and I think that's all I'm getting until he says, "I'm torn between thinking the illusion made the situation worse . . . and thinking it may have made it better. He's not going to pursue that part, which could poison the rest. He may let it drop. We didn't do anything, after all."

"Except not pay for the painting," I say. "And somehow have it in our possession despite there being no Ms. Silver at that address."

"True, but we did speak to the neighbor. She can confirm that we believed a Ms. Silver lived there, and we claimed to have spoken to her. We picked up the painting, drove away, discussed it and then came back for . . . Well, we should figure out why we went back, but otherwise, our story works."

He takes a few more steps. "I will need to contact my lawyer. Just in case."

"Which means your parents will find out." I sigh. "So much for them not knowing you were with me tonight. At least we were on legitimate business." I shove my hands in my pockets. "Of course, if they did this, they already knew where you were."

"Yes."

"The possibility they were behind this?"

"I'm still assessing."

"Can I get a statistical estimate of risk? From the actuarial genius?"

His lips quirk. "This genius requires further data and analysis of said data, but very roughly speaking, I would set the probability that it is fully my parents at 34 percent, the chance it is fully Mercury at 37 percent, the chance it is an unintentional combination at 22 percent and an intentional combination at 1 percent."

"It is way too late to add those numbers up, but I don't think they hit a hundred."

"They do not. That allows a 6 percent probability that neither is involved."

"Right. And unintentional combination means they both did part of it but not working together."

"Yes, and I'd set the *intentional* probability lower than one percent, except that I must allow, within that, for an accidental, intentional combination."

"Uh . . ."

"That they did not realize they were colluding, one or the other party believing they were, in fact, colluding with a third party."

"Okay, now my head really hurts. I shouldn't have asked."

"I have more combinations if you'd like them." He shoots me a quarter smile, and I shake my head.

"In short," he says, "we need to work it out further to properly assess all the possibilities and probabilities, but I believe, right now, we are both far too tired for that."

"Agreed."

———

I DON'T WANT to get up at seven the next morning. I don't want to be to the shop by eight. I want to sleep, perchance to dream . . . as long as those dreams have nothing to do with creepy-kid ghosts and haunted paintings and arranged-marriage contracts and immortals who screw around with mortals for shits and giggles. Yeah, it's probably a good thing I have an eight a.m. showing. It's not as if I'm getting much sleep anyway. My brain ping-pongs from one problem to the next, and when my alarm goes off at seven, it's a relief, even if I'd never admit it.

I'm planning to just grab a cupcake from the counter, but Ani's making breakfast, and since Hope was out late and still in bed, I'm the one who gets the mothering.

"Hope says you were with Aiden last night," she says as I sit down. "You got in late. Everything went well?"

"That depends. Nearly getting arrested for art theft *did* make for an interesting evening."

The fact that Ani doesn't even blink says everything one needs to know about my sister. Also, possibly, about me.

She slides a pancake onto my plate. "Apparently, you have a story to tell."

"I do, indeed."

"Is it going to make me burn the next batch?"

I waggle my hand, giving it fifty-fifty odds.

"Then let me finish, and you can tell me all about it."

I explain over breakfast. As I wrap up, she says, "Everything is fine with Aiden, then? Between you two?"

"Seriously? That's where you started, and after all that, you're still there?"

She takes a bite of pancake and chews before answering. "I liked Aiden. I liked him for you, friend or otherwise."

"Not missing the past tense in that."

"I *don't* like what he did this past weekend. It shed a very different light on his character, and . . ." She sets down her fork. "You were angry. Hurt and angry. Normally, you wouldn't put up with that, but I'm afraid that, in this case, you might."

"You think I'll jump on any excuse he gives."

She meets my gaze. "Did you?"

I look her in the eye. "Yes, he had an excuse. Yes, it was a decent one —family drama, and that's all I can say. But, no, I didn't give him a pass."

"Good." She cuts into her pancake. "I'm sure he's accustomed to that. I don't think he *expects* it—you wouldn't be friends if he was that sort of man—but when you're used to people treating you a certain way . . ."

"Aiden is aware that he isn't as considerate as he should be. We had that conversation. He initiated it."

"Good. Just be careful, K."

"I am being extremely careful. Now, any thoughts on the rest of it?"

"Only that you'll want nothing to do with Mercury if she's behind this. No matter how useful that mentorship might be." She takes another bite of pancake. "It's a similar situation. If Aiden plays you wrong, you need to step away, however much you don't want to. If Mercury has played you wrong?"

"*Run* away, however much I might want her training." I look at Ani. "I will. In both cases. I promise."

A rap sounds at the door. Ani calls a greeting.

"Just in time," Ani says as a tall, broad-shouldered guy walks in.

Jonathan looks at the stovetop where a stack of pancakes stay warm. "I am indeed. Good thing I skipped breakfast."

"Oh, I don't mean breakfast," Ani says. "Kennedy has research questions." She hands him a plate. "But I'll offer breakfast in payment."

"Good deal." Jonathan takes three pancakes. "So what's up?"

Jonathan has been Ani's best friend since they were toddlers, and now that they are no longer toddlers, he should be more than a friend. They are perfect for one another—two uber-responsible, hardworking idealists who cannot get enough of one another's company. Yet since getting to know Connolly, I've stopped teasing them about becoming more than friends. I understand now that this is something that has to happen on its own.

I tell Jonathan about the paintings. He's our local librarian, and while this isn't something he'll find at the library, he's a bit of a research geek, hence the occupation of choice. He knows more about the magical world than we do, even though he's not part of it himself.

As I talk, his fingers tap his phone, accessing his database.

"I can't tell you much about the curses," he says. "Everything I have is on the urban legend, which you've already nailed."

"I know the basics of the legend, but not the actual paintings, beyond the bit in Mom's book of famous curses. Four paintings. *Crying Girl*, which I met last night. *Vengeful Boy*. *Eldest Daughter*. And a fourth that's just vaguely listed as another son."

"That's all I have on the fourth. It's the oldest son, no other details. All four are illusion based. The children—or teens, the last three being older than the crying girl—appear to step from the paintings and scare the viewer."

"Scare them to death?"

"Yes, they're all linked to fatalities. That's really all I can tell you. I'll keep digging, though."

"Thank you."

———

WE LIVE on the same street as my shop. I'm not sure of the exact distance, but I know I can walk there in four-and-a-half minutes and jog in three. Yes, I'm that kind of person, the one who knows exactly how late she can leave.

I'm there at 7:45, early for my appointment. I head in the back door because once tourist season hits, visitors are already up by seven, looking for coffee and quite happy to "pop into" any shop that seems open.

In the storage room, I open my phone to find a message from Connolly. It's a standard check-in that turns into a conversation, just like it would have before this weekend. We don't talk about the painting.

There will be time for that later. We're chatting about our respective breakfasts when a message pops up.

Msg: Congratulations, Kennedy! You've passed your first exam with an A+! For your efforts, you win our special prize. Three to five years in prison for theft over a thousand dollars.

I blink. Then I send it to Connolly with "WTF?" My phone rings.

"How did you receive that?" he says in greeting.

"It's a text message from a string of numbers. I can't tell if it's a foreign phone number or some kind of spoofing address. Is it Mercy's idea of a joke? Tee-hee, wasn't that funny last night when you almost got arrested? If that's her, I don't care how much she could teach me. Not interested."

Another text pops onto my screen.

Msg: Please await further instructions! Failure to comply with all regulations and restrictions will result in possible jail time.

"What the actual hell?" I read the text to Connolly. "If this is really Mercy, and she thinks she's being clever . . ."

I'm struggling for words when a loud rapping has me nearly falling off my chair. I throw open the storage room door to see my eight a.m. appointment knocking on the window . . . with the clock showing 8:01.

I tell Connolly I'll get back to him after my appointment.

"I'll be waiting," he says.

"Thanks."

I sign off and hurry to open the front door.

CHAPTER FOURTEEN

AT MY BOSTON SHOP, I was mostly open by appointment only. It wasn't in the kind of location that saw much foot traffic, and "appointment only" sounded exclusive while allowing me to refinish and uncurse antiques when I didn't need to worry about anyone walking in.

Here, my clientele is ninety-five percent tourists. However, I still offer appointments before and after hours for the monied clientele who expect my full attention and expect to be able to examine a Tiffany lamp without leaning past a sticky-fingered kid in face paint.

Or that's the theory. The reality is that everyone likes to feel special. I presume those appointments will be the final stage of a significant purchase—they've seen a gorgeous Tiffany lamp on my website and just want to have a look before plunking down a thousand dollars. But what I'm getting is people who tell me they're *so* very interested and require a special appointment, and then act like every demanding browser, wanting the owner at their side as they poke about.

This woman falls squarely into that category. She listed three things on the site she wanted to buy, none of them under five hundred dollars. I showed her each, and now she's wandering, getting snippy if I'm not right there when she has a question. Burning questions like "Is this mahogany?" and "Is it Edwardian or Colonial?" about a piece labeled "Solid Oak Salvoian Dresser."

"I open at nine," I say as we reach the hour mark. "I need to unlock the door in a minute or so."

"I'm not done."

"I see that, and I apologize, but there's another customer waiting."

She turns and peers at the window. There's a woman partially obscured by the window graphics but obviously waiting.

The older woman assesses her in a glance and sniffs. "She can wait."

As if hearing her, the woman at the door raps and lifts her watch and then jangles the door. Great. My second imperious customer of the day.

I walk to the door and unlock it. As it opens, I quickly say, "Sorry, I had a private showing that's running a little long. Please look around. I'll be with you in a moment."

I hurry back to the first woman, who fixes me with a sour look.

"So, about the Queen Anne chair," I say. "It is a lovely piece, and reasonably priced. I can show you two online that are more expensive and in worse condition."

"It looked lighter online. That dark wood won't go in my front parlor."

"What about the banquet lamp?"

She wrinkles her nose. "Perhaps. I'll need to think about it. What else do you have?"

Before I can answer, her gaze moves over my shoulder.

"May I help you?" she says.

A voice behind me says, "I believe the question is whether Ms. Bennett can help *you*. You have clearly monopolized her time long enough, with no inclination toward a purchase. In other words, you are wasting her time."

I turn to get my first good look at the newcomer. She's about forty, with an olive-skinned face that looks cut from marble, all perfect angles. Wide-set gray eyes. A little too wide-set, giving her face an owlish look. Those eyes could be dove-soft gray. Instead, they're steel. Gray steel.

She wears a gray pantsuit, and her dark hair is cut short, curls flattened against her scalp as if she glued the unruly locks in place. Everything about this women snaps, "Get out of my way," and I have to bolt my feet to the floor to keep from complying.

The first customer holds fast, but emotions still play over her face. Emotions that I suspect are unfamiliar to a woman of her standing. Intimidation. Fear. Uncertainty.

"Go," the gray-suited woman says. "Now."

"You can't—"

"Can. Did. I need to speak to Ms. Bennett. You may leave."

I clear my throat. "I don't believe we have an appointment, Ms. . . ."

"Athene." Her eyes meet mine. "My name is Athene."

"I don't care what your name is," the older woman huffs. "I had an appointment."

"Which has ended."

Athene strides toward the woman, and while part of me wants to interfere, the rest of me doesn't dare. This is Athene. *The* Athene. No offense to Vanessa, but if I had to pick my favorite god in the Greco-Roman pantheon, it would be Athene. Goddess of war. Goddess of wisdom. Goddess of reason. Also, apparently, goddess of mowing people the hell out of her way.

She herds the woman straight out the door. Then she locks it and flips the Open sign to Closed.

As she's doing that, I text Vanessa.

Me: Athene just walked into my shop. Any advice?

The response is instantaneous.

Vanessa: Stay perfectly still, and she might not see you.

I snort a laugh.

"Something amuses you?" Athene says.

I stuff the phone into my pocket. "Just a joke text." And not much of a joke at all. I do have the distinct urge to stand perfectly still and hope Athene's shark-like focus moves on.

"So Athene, huh?" I say in what is clearly my most professional greeting ever. At least I don't add "cool," like a teen fangirl trying to play it chill. "Pleased to meet you."

"I do not engage in pleasantries. They are meaningless customs that waste everyone's time."

"Even if I really mean that I *am* pleased to meet you?"

She pauses a half second, considering. "If it is a sincere pleasantry, it is marginally less pointless, but only marginally." She steps toward me, the predator closing in on her prey. "You believe you found a Costa painting."

I open my mouth.

"Do not ask who told me. I will only say it was neither Vanessa nor Marius, and I only say that because I know they would be upset if you thought so. They are far too concerned with what others think of them."

"I wasn't going to ask who told you. I was going to say that I don't *believe* I found a Costa painting. I *did* find one. Or, more accurately, I was led to it."

"No, you were led to a fake. I want to know why you lied to Aphrodite and Ares, telling them it was cursed. You knew it was of interest to me, yes? You were trying to get my attention. Now you have it, and you may wish otherwise."

"Wow. You are *intense*. I got that impression from Vanessa and Marius, but one really needs to experience the full force to properly appreciate it."

Her eyes narrow. "If that is meant to be mockery—"

"No, it's meant to be 'step off.' I didn't lie to Vanessa and Marius. I had no idea—still have no idea—what interest you have in the painting. And I sure as hell wasn't trying to get your attention. Kinda busy leading my life, which is complicated enough, thank you very much."

"They said you remind them of Mercury. They are correct."

"Well, right now, I don't take that as a compliment."

"It wasn't one."

"Whatever. Point is that I found the painting. I saw the girl from the curse, as did Aiden Connolly and two very freaked-out police officers. Then I uncursed it before the officers carted it off into evidence."

"Evidence of what?"

"Stolen goods. If you want the painting, talk to the state police. They should have it in lockup. You can confirm it *is* the original. Otherwise, if you—"

"Hello, *hello*," a voice trills, in perfect pitch with the tinkling door chimes. "I do believe I'm late to this party."

"I locked that door," Athene says.

"Not against me."

The woman who walks in looks like Athene, while managing to look as *unlike* Athene as possible. She's roughly the same height, with the same wide-set eyes, hers being blue. Same perfect facial structure, with a sharper chin that gives those wide-set eyes a more catlike appearance. Dark curly hair, just like Athene's, except she's wearing it in tiny pigtails more appropriate for a five-year-old. She's dressed in yellow overalls, a blue newsboy hat and red high-top Chucks. In short, she looks like Athene playing a children's show host, all primary colors and adorable wide grin.

The newcomer bounces over and slaps Athene on the shoulder. "How is my favorite eldest sister?"

Athene frowns. "You mean elder sister. You can only have a single *eldest* sister."

"That's why you're my favorite one."

"Mercury, I presume," I say, and there's a note to my voice that's almost like a growl. She looks over, blinking in surprise.

"That isn't quite the welcome I expected."

"She said she was *pleased* to see me." Athene pulls herself straighter. "She does not seem pleased to see you."

Mercy sighs, leaning against a table for extra drama. "There's been a misunderstanding."

"There always is," Athene murmurs. "One that usually turns out not to be a misunderstanding at all. That is, *we* misunderstand nothing. You misunderstand our tolerance for your nonsense. As for this particular bit of nonsense, I do not appreciate you dragging me into it."

"I didn't drag you into anything, Teeny."

"Do. Not. Call. Me. That."

"The only person being dragged into anything here is me," I say. "That was you last night, yes? Ms. Silver?"

Mercy's eyes glitter. "It was, and I'm delighted that you aren't certain.

That is one of my favorite disguises. If a disguise is close to your own personality, it's easy to maintain but also easy to see through. While distancing yourself from a personality is more challenging, it's always the better choice. There, a succinct first lesson."

She beams, as if expecting a cookie.

"Yeah, no," I say. "I don't want any lessons from you, thanks. Last night's bullshit was quite enough. You can both leave now." I pause. "No, that sounded like a request. Leave. Now. Both of you."

Athene's brows shoot up clear to her hairline. "I beg your pardon?"

I wave around my shop. "This is not public property. It's my shop. I'm going to ask you to take your little tiff outside."

"Little tiff?" Athene says.

Mercy snickers. "Keep going, Kennedy. You're about to give my sister a heart attack." She mimics Athene's crisp tone. "No one speaks to me that way, young lady. Do you have any idea who I am?"

"Out. Both of you." I stalk to the door. "As of now, I'm closed."

"You have really upset her," Athene says to Mercy. "What did you do this time?"

"I honestly don't know," Mercy says, her voice going serious. "You passed the pop quiz, kid. I was testing your curiosity and your determination. Also, your empathy. I'm very fond of empathy."

I snort. "I presume that's a joke."

"Ohh," Athene says. "You really did do something." She lowers herself into an antique chair. "Please, continue. This promises to be quite entertaining."

Mercy throws up her hands. "I'm missing something here."

"Yes," I say. "Empathy. That's what you're missing. The general ability to consider the feelings of others. I like a good prank. Kinda my specialty. But there's fun, and there's cruel, and then there's downright vicious. You didn't just cross that line, Mercury. You pole vaulted it."

Now Athene frowns. "Mercy? There actually *may* have been a misunderstanding. My sister can be the living equivalent of a fart joke, but *cruel* isn't in her vocabulary, much less *vicious*."

"Thank you," Mercy says. "I think."

"Wait a moment," Athene says, rising. "I believe I see the problem.

Ms. Bennett is under the impression you led her to the actual cursed painting. I was in the midst of correcting that mistake when you walked in."

"The original cursed painting?" Mercy shakes her head. "No, Kennedy. I wouldn't do that. The painting is a fake. Did the jinx fail to activate?"

"The jinx where a little girl's ghost comes flying down the stairs at us? Almost makes us fall and break our necks? Oh, yeah, it activated."

Mercy's frown grows. "No, that's the original curse. The real one. You got a fake. When activated, the little girl makes . . . er . . ." She glances at her sister. "Gaseous noises accompanied by a noxious odor."

"I rest my case," Athene says. "Fart jokes."

"Well, then you screwed up," I say, "because we got the real painting."

"That isn't possible," Mercy says.

Athene shakes her head. "I have already informed Ms. Bennett that she is mistaken, though I did not get the chance to explain why. We destroyed all four Costa paintings ourselves. Mercy uncursed them, and I destroyed them."

I lift my hands. "All I know is that I encountered *that* curse on *that* painting. So did Aiden Connolly. If you don't believe us, then check with the state police. Officers Platts and Grove. They both saw it when they came to seize it, and that was a fun explanation."

"Seize it?" Mercy says.

"Someone reported it stolen. Then someone tipped them off that we had it in our trunk. As a prank, apparently."

"That's not a prank," Mercy says. "It's a threat."

"Speaking of threats . . ." I take out my phone and show them the messages.

"I didn't send those," Mercy says. "Yes, I set up the fake painting auction. I made sure you'd see it. Actually, I've tried a few times, but you finally noticed. I played Ms. Silver. I sent you to the abandoned house where you were supposed to find the fake painting. It was a legit test. The introductory lesson in our classes. The painting was fake, and I certainly didn't report it stolen."

"So we hallucinated the police along with the little girl?"

"Someone set you up. The question is why." She frowns. "This is all terribly confusing." She looks at her sister. "Any ideas, O wise one?"

"I will require more information." Athene turns to me. "Tell us everything."

CHAPTER FIFTEEN

ATHENE AND MERCY ARE GONE, and I'm in the storage room, eating icing off a cupcake and wondering about the possibility of getting more. It's that or rummage through the recycling to see whether we left any drops in that wine bottle from yesterday.

I should call Connolly. I've texted, just a simple note to let him know all is well. In other words, I lied. All is far from well, but I'm not ready to discuss what just happened. I need to understand it myself first.

Mercy sent us on the painting hunt. Got it. That makes sense. I'd have grumbled over the wild-goose chase, but if that's all it'd been, I'd have grudgingly admitted we had fun. An unexpected midweek adventure.

Yet Mercy did not do the nasty parts. Not the ghost kid or the police raid. Again, that fits what I know of her. Yet it begs the question, why would someone replace the painting with the real one and call the cops on me?

Is it the real one? Athene and Mercy are convinced they destroyed that. This must be what got Vanessa's attention. I claimed to have encountered a cursed painting she believed destroyed. She dug deeper, and in digging, tipped off Athene, who figured it was a ploy to get her attention.

Someone intercepted Mercy's game and inserted either the original painting or another fake . . . with a duplicate curse. Then they called the cops. Then they sent those texts so I'd think Mercy was behind it.

When the door chimes ring, I practically dive into the showroom, hoping to see Mercy or Athene. Instead, it's a tall, willowy blond with the grace of a runway model and an outfit that suggests she just might be, from her crisp linen dress to her elegant sandals and the delicate gold earring that catches the light as she turns toward me.

"Hello," I say . . . just as I feel a fleck of icing on my lips. I wipe it away quickly. "Please, come in. Feel free to browse on your own, but I'm here for any questions you might have."

"I'm not actually here to shop," she says. "Though it all looks wonderful. You're Kennedy, right? Kennedy Bennett?"

"I am." I manage a smile. "Please don't tell me you're about to serve a summons. Whatever it is, I didn't do it."

She laughs, a tinkling perfection of a laugh. "Full disclosure, I *am* a lawyer. But no, I'm not here on a legal matter." She puts out a hand. "Theodora O'Toole."

The next few moments blur, time stuttering around me. This is Theodora O'Toole. This is the woman whose calls Connolly has been ducking.

Theodora O'Toole. Perfection personified. Elegant and gorgeous enough to be a runway model, but actually a lawyer. Because of course she is.

It's like in seventh grade, when I spent three weeks working on my science-fair project. I'd had a good idea, and I'd worked my ass off, determined to win because that year, the prize was a real telescope and I wanted it so badly. I put my everything into that project, and I was so proud of it . . . and then I saw Molly Miller's project. I'd wanted to run home and cry into my pillow from the sheer humiliation of thinking I could compete against our resident science whiz.

That's how I feel right now. Like the idiot who thought she had a shot at a guy like Aiden Connolly. Sure, he's out of my league, but hey, I don't exactly lack for male attention. I thought I was good enough to enter the competition.

One look at Theodora, and I'm back in seventh grade, seeing my homemade project up against the shining perfection of Molly's, and I am once again wondering what the hell I was thinking.

I manage to put out my hand to shake hers, and I screw that up, too. Is my grip too light? Too hard? Too limp? Too damp? I have no idea, only that I'm sure I screw it up. At this moment, I'm sure I'm screwing everything up.

I release her hand and move behind the shield of my cash desk. "So, Theodora. What can I do for you today?"

"I'm not your enemy."

My head snaps up. "What?"

"With Aiden. I'm not your enemy."

I bite my lip hard, in hopes that'll keep my cheeks from going scarlet. "Uh, okay. *Enemy* in what sense?"

She gives me a knowing look. I meet it with one as blank as I can manage.

"I really don't know what you're talking about," I say.

"I know Aiden spoke to his parents about you this morning. He was with you last night, and they called him on it, and he told them to back off. He also told them that you know about the contract."

That reaction must show because she says, "Aiden didn't tell me. I haven't spoken to him in days. He's not returning my calls. He talked to his parents and . . ."

She sighs, and it is a very elegant sigh, like the softest rush of wind. "Aiden's parents and mine both have immense corporate interests. They are friends. They are also rivals. Now that my parents hope to marry me off to Aiden, there is little that goes on in the Connolly household my parents don't know."

"They planted a spy?"

Her lips twitch. "In our world, there is always a spy or two. My parents told me what happened at the Connolly estate this morning and also told me to get rid of you." She pauses. "Scare you off, I mean. That sounded more sinister than I intended."

"That's why you're here? To 'scare me off.' First, Aiden and I are just friends. Second, he didn't spend the night. *We* spent the evening chasing down an antique. Turned out to be stolen goods, and the police confiscated it."

"That's what I heard, and I'm certain it's the truth because I cannot imagine Aiden coming up with *that* as his excuse. Trying to imagine Aiden Connolly happily spending an evening chasing down antiques and nearly getting arrested for art theft?" She smiles and shakes her head. "Nope. I got nothing."

I bristle. "I can get the police report—"

She lifts her hands. "I don't mean I doubt that's what happened. I mean that if that's the Aiden you know, then yes, maybe you *are* just friends, but his parents have every reason to be worried because he is *not* going through with that marriage contract."

"And you're here to make sure he does?"

She hesitates. "That's . . . complicated. I will say that I am absolutely not here to scare you off. I'm here to introduce myself and to make it clear that I do not consider you a rival for Aiden."

I tense.

She sighs. "I'm doing this all wrong. I mean that whatever you and Aiden have is none of my business. He is a great guy, but he doesn't want me, and I don't want him. I know a way we can both get through this. I just need him to talk to me, and he won't."

The doorbell chimes. In walks a young couple. When we both turn, they hesitate and recheck the Open sign.

"Come in," I say. "Please look around. I'll be with you in a moment."

Before I can return to Theodora, a delivery driver follows the couple in, a large box in her hands.

"Kennedy Bennett?" she says.

"That's me." Before I step up to automatically accept the delivery, I remember the past twenty-four hours. "I'm not expecting anything today. Can you tell me where it's from?"

"It's a personal delivery from"—she checks her tablet—"Aiden Connolly. There's a card taped to the top."

She has me sign for the box. Then she leaves as I eye it.

Theodora laughs softly. "You look as if you expect it to explode."

"After last night, it might. Will you give me a moment? This could be a trick, and if it is, I want to get the driver's info."

I pull off the message taped to the top. It's a standard note card, typed up, as if by the delivery service.

Kennedy,

I promised I would stop apologizing for the weekend, and so this is not an apology. It is a precautionary measure. Purely arising from my concern for your safety.

Aiden

I set down the card and eye the box again. Then I cut the tape and open it.

"Are those Magic 8 Balls?" Theodora says.

I choke back a laugh as I look inside to see an entire crate of the toys.

"It's an in-joke," I say. "Long story."

Her brows rise. "This is definitely not the Aiden I know." She eases back. "I'm glad to see it." She lifts her hands to fend off my protest. "Whether you two are a couple or not, I need him to know I'm not trying to bag myself a husband. Just have him talk to me. Please."

"I will."

"Thank you. I appreciate that." She pulls a card from her chic little purse and sets it on the counter. "In case he's lost my number, but also for you. I know this arranged marriage business must all seem terribly . . . old-fashioned. Outdated." She wrinkles her perfect nose.

"The rich are different," I say, and I say it lightly, as a joke, but a shadow passes behind her eyes, a sadness and an exhaustion.

"It's not just the rich," she says. "It's the magical rich. Never forget the magical part."

"That's right. You're a luck worker."

Her lips quirk. "Even I forget that. Easy to do when I don't ever feel particularly lucky."

She could say that wryly. Ironically. One look at Theodora, and you can spot the life-lottery winning ticket, dangling like a clothing tag she forgot to snip off. But there's none of that in her voice. No "woe is me," either, the whine of a person who has privilege and can't see it. She says it, and then flushes, as if embarrassed, and waves it off.

"Enough of that," she says. "Obviously, I am lucky. Like Aiden. We're just trapped in a family tradition that should have died out centuries ago. The problem is that when something works, you keep doing it. Arranged marriages have worked, financially, and that is all that matters.

I don't want this any more than Aiden does. I just need to talk to him so we can work it out."

"I'll make sure he calls."

"Thank you." She's turning to leave when she spots the open box, reaches in and takes out a Magic 8 Ball. She smiles at it. "I remember when these were a huge fad at my school. Fourth grade, I think? I wanted one so badly, but my nanny thought they were demonic."

"Take that one."

She reaches for her purse.

"On the house," I say. "I apparently have a lot of them."

"Thank you." She opens the small box, takes out the ball and gives it a shake. Then she lifts it to read the message. "Reply hazy. Try again." Her smile turns wry. "Story of my life." She glances at me. "Thank you, Kennedy. We'll work this out. I'll make sure of it."

I nod and watch as she leaves.

CHAPTER SIXTEEN

IT'S BARELY ONE, and I feel as if the sun should start dropping any moment. I've checked my phone a hundred times, hoping to hear from Mercy, while beginning to suspect I won't. The immortals may not be actual gods, but they've been called that for so long they seem to believe their own hype. I've been caught between them before, and this feels very familiar. Even the best of them can be careless with mortals.

Someone used me to get their attention. I've done my part, and now Mercy and Athene have swooped in and set me free. That should be good, but I feel abandoned on the sidelines after getting tackled by the quarterback. Mercy and Athene picked me up, set me off the field and continued on, and I hate it.

Every time the bell rings, I jump. When I'm in the back and hear it, I bolt through, only to see Connolly enter.

"Hey," I say.

He glances over his shoulder, as if hoping that less-than-enthusiastic greeting is for someone else.

"Sorry," I say. "I'm glad to see you. It's just been a very long day."

For both of us, I bet. I'm going to need to speak to him about Theodora. Not yet, though. I just want a few minutes to shelve the personal drama and focus on the more interesting one.

"I was hoping you were Mercy," I say. "Possibly even Athene, but having now met Athene . . . It's true what they say about never meeting your heroes. I expected the kick-ass-cool goddess of wisdom and war, and I got the immortal equivalent of an IRS agent."

When he only blinks, I say, "So did I mention I met Athene? And Mercy?" I walk over to the door, stick up the clock sign and set it for one thirty.

"Come in the back," I say. "I have a story to tell."

———

"THEY BELIEVE THEY DESTROYED THE PAINTINGS?" Connolly says when I finish. "All four paintings?"

"I may need you to confirm what you experienced—ghost girl flying at you and so on. Even Mercy seems to think I might have been imagining it."

His face hardens. "The more I hear about both these two, the less I want to deal with them."

"Gods, right?" I push back on my stool. "Before you got here, I was telling myself I should be happy they've sidelined me. But I feel . . ."

"You feel used," he says. "Perhaps they weren't the ones who used you, but they're all treating you like a messenger service."

"Well, I am descended from Mercury. The original messenger."

I reach for my half-eaten protein bar.

"Please don't tell me that's your lunch," he says.

"Nope, I also had a cupcake, though I mostly just ate the icing."

He plucks the bar from my hand. "Let me find you something better."

———

WE'RE WALKING down Bishop Street. Ellie appears from nowhere to wander along behind us. Apparently, she just happens to be going the same way.

"You know I'm getting food, don't you?" I call back to her. "FYI, it's not frozen custard."

She pretends not to know I'm talking to her. Or not to care. She'll care, though, when I get myself a big salad and she's left staring at a sprig of kale.

We end up choosing a tiny takeout that specializes in crab, clams and crystals. The crab cakes and chowder are amazing. The less said about the crystals, the better.

There's still a line from the lunch crowd, and we join it. Ellie sniffs the air and starts winding around Connolly's legs.

"Wrong person," I say. "He's not giving you anything. You should know that by now."

"I learned my lesson with lacerations," he says.

"Hear that? Once scratched, twice shy. No crab for you." I glance at him and lower my voice. "Though if you do want to win her over, a few nibbles of crab would do the trick. She'll be your bestie for life . . . or at least an hour or two."

"I don't believe in bribes."

"Says the guy who just gave me a carton of Magic 8 Balls."

"That was purely a safety measure, as I said. Not at all because I realize I have behaved poorly and am rather desperate to get back in your good graces." He looks down at Ellie, still winding around his ankles. "You will get no crab from me, Elohssa. I will continue to ignore you, thereby reversing our relationship dynamic. Instead of me reaching out to you and being rebuffed, I shall do that to you until you are so desperate for my notice that you surrender."

"Ah," I say. "You're *that* guy. Word of advice from someone who's been there. It can backfire spectacularly. Tenth grade. His name was Charlie. The cutest ginger in town. Gorgeous green eyes. Bit of a tomcat, but . . ." I shrug. "I was in love. Penny Gray convinced me to do the 'ignoring him' trick. So I did. Pretended I didn't see him no matter how hard he tried to get my attention."

"And . . ."

"Penny totally set me up. Next thing you know, he's following *her* everywhere. She took him home to meet her family, and that's where it all fell apart. He threw her over for her twelve-year-old sister."

Connolly's eyes widen.

"Yep, he also bit her dad. Pissed on the carpet. Coughed up a hairball in the sink. Charlie was bad news."

"Charlie was a cat?"

"Of course. That's what we were talking about, right? Cats?"

We move up in line.

"Anyway, in the end, I realized I'd dodged a bullet," I say. "You can never quite tame an alley cat, not after they've been on the streets a while. If you want to domesticate them, they need . . ." I make a scissor motion. "Snip."

"We're still talking about cats, right?"

The counter clears, and I place my order. Before I can pay, Connolly subtly nudges me aside and orders his. As he does, my phone dings with a text.

Msg: Test two coming up! Are you ready?

I show it to Connolly as his payment processes. Once that's done, we step aside to await our orders.

"May I?" he asks, putting out his hand for my phone.

I pass it over. He types in a reply to the text and shows me.

Msg: Is this Mercury?

I nod, and he hits Send only to get a response that his message can't go through.

"You already tried that, didn't you?" he says. "With the earlier ones?"

"Yep. I tried replying to texts. Tried calling the number. Tried searching on it. They're fake, but yes, I'll keep trying, just in case. I don't want to find out later they actually sent something I could answer and I ignored it."

Our food arrives, and we take it and head out, Ellie at our heels.

My phone buzzes with another text. I sigh as I lift it.

Msg: T-10 minutes. Are you ready? Hope you studied!
Me: I know this isn't Mercury BTW. It's just some asshole trying to sound like her.

Connolly leans over my shoulder as I hit Send.

"Yep," I say. "I know it's going into cyberspace, but it makes me feel better."

When my phone dings, Connolly says, "Ignore it."

I shake my head. "Can't."

I pull it out and check the screen.

Msg: Please show your work when answering the exam questions. How did you arrive at that conclusion?

I hesitate, reading it twice. It's from another number, a string of numerals obviously as fake as the others. Is it a response to my text? Or just more nonsense?

Me: Which conclusion? That you're an asshole?

Msg: No, that is a given. The other please. How do you know I am not Mercury? Are you certain of that response? Please think carefully. Points will be deducted for incorrect answers.

Me: I'm sure enough to risk it. You're not Mercury.

Msg: So she's made contact.

The hair on my neck rises. I show Connolly the string of messages.

"Don't answer," he says. Then he pauses. "I mean, that would be my advice."

"Because I just fell face-first into a trap." I lower the phone. "Damn it."

"I also responded to the message," he says. "And I saw no harm with the one you sent. If anyone is to blame, it's Mercy."

"Athene thought I was trying to get her attention with the painting," I say. "Someone *is* trying to get an immortal's attention. I'm just the messenger, as you said."

My phone has now buzzed twice with messages, and I reluctantly pull it from my pocket.

Msg: Silence must be interpreted as assent. You have made contact.

Msg: Continued silence will be taken as consent. Consent to inflict whatever penalty I deem fit.

I send back a two-word response that has Connolly snorting.

Msg: Well, that was rude. You're upset. You thought this would be all fun and games. It is Mercury, after all. You're her latest bright and shiny project. What could possibly go wrong? I presume you didn't read the fine print before agreeing to mentorship.
Me: I didn't agree to anything.
Msg: Ah, that's why you're testy. The favor of the gods is a double-edged sword.
Me: I don't know who you think I am, but I'm not the messenger you want.
Msg: I won't bore you with a recitation of everything I know about you. Accept that I have studied for this particular test, and I can send a complete dossier upon request. All that is irrelevant . . . unless you force me to make it relevant.
Me: Is that a threat?
Msg: A warning. What matters to me is that you are a mortal conduit to the great Mercury. I have something she wants. Three somethings, in fact.
Me: The remaining paintings.
Msg: Correct.
Me: Not sure she wants them.
Msg: You're probably right. I doubt they match her decor. But she wants them out of the world, as does Athene. Bad memories and all that.

I glance at Connolly, who's reading over my shoulder.

"They're another punishment," I mutter. "Like the Necklace of Harmonia. Seems some curses are a popular way to torture immortals."

I unlock my shop door, and we slip inside.

"I suppose that makes sense," he says. "A curse may only do true harm every few decades, but if you're an immortal, that's a constant reminder that others continue to suffer for your actions."

Another message has blipped in. I ignore it as I flip the sign to Open. I've been closed long enough. I'll need to eat while listening for the bell.

We head into the storage room, and I prop open the door. My phone keeps dinging, reminding me I have unread messages.

I open my sandwich wrapper, spread it on the counter and give Ellie a piece of crab before picking up my phone again.

Msg: I need to speak to Mercury. You have ten minutes to send me her contact information.
Me: I don't have her contact information.
Msg: Tick-tock . . .
Me: I don't have it. She showed up. Then she left. No one has her information. That's why you've come after me. She's impossible to get a hold of.
Msg: And yet you did. You have one hour.

I start tapping in a reply, but I'm so furious I keep hitting the wrong keys. When Connolly arches his brows, I shove the phone across the counter and attack my sandwich.

Connolly takes the phone with another brow arch.

"Feel free," I say.

He sets the phone down sideways so I can see what he's typing and approve it.

Connolly: You're asking me to provide something I don't have. How can I prove a negative?
Msg: Oh, I believe you don't have it. I'm telling you to get it.
Connolly: But without the ability to contact Mercury, how do I obtain her contact information?
Msg: Think of it as a puzzle.
Connolly: A puzzle has a solution. The only solution here is to hope she makes contact in the next hour.
Msg: Then I guess that's what you'll do. Tick-tock.
Connolly: And if I fail?
Msg: You'll get a surprise. And it won't be a nice one.
Connolly: I want to be removed from this equation. I'm not associ-

ated with Mercury. I have not accepted her help in any way. You're speaking to the wrong person.

We both watch the phone as we eat, and the screen stays blank. I want to slap it off the counter. I want to rage and stomp my feet and shout this isn't fair. But whoever is doing it knows it isn't fair, and they don't give a damn. They want Mercy's attention, and they'll use me to get it and punish me when I don't.

CHAPTER SEVENTEEN

"I could try Vanessa," I say. "But there's no way she can get in touch with Mercy that fast."

"Can she get in touch with Athene?"

And there it is. A potential solution to this puzzle.

I let Connolly make that call while I eat. He's known Vanessa longer than I have, and also, I'm suddenly starving. I eat all of my sandwich and half the fries, leaving Ellie glaring as I pick crab bits off the wrapper for her.

Connolly pulls a piece off his half-eaten sandwich and hands it to me. He's on the phone with Marius, or so I presume by the shift of tone that suggests he's talking to his many times great-grandfather. Marius may be the god of war, but he's also very chill, laid back, open and honest in his dealings. Athene is goddess of battle strategy; Marius is the god of battle luck. The head versus the heart. All Marius wants is for Connolly and his brother to be happy and healthy. In short, exactly what their actual parents should want.

When he hangs up, he says, "Did you know they're in Crete?"

"What?"

"Vanessa forgot that part when we spoke last night. They're overseas for the week. Happy to help, and Marius offered to come back and mediate with his sisters, but I said no, not unless the situation gets worse."

"Can they get in touch with Athene?"

"Marius is messaging her now. He apologized for not passing over her contact information directly, but she doesn't like to have that shared, and she can be somewhat forceful in her opinions."

"Understatement of the decade," I mutter.

"I told him you've been threatened with a one-hour response window after which there will be unspecified consequences. I get the impression that Athene may not take that threat as seriously as we'd like, so Marius is giving her thirty minutes to respond or he sends us her contact information."

I laugh softly. "A little battle strategy of his own."

"Precisely."

While Ares might be the god of battle luck, in reality, the lines blur. Marius couldn't have spent millennia in roles of war—general, mercenary, spy, and now head of a company that sells related technology—if he didn't have a head for the art of war.

"So now we wait," I say as I clean up my lunch. "Damn it."

"I know. Let's talk strategy of our own then."

I separate my recycling and waste, each in the appropriate bin, and walk back as Connolly takes out his phone to make notes.

"I've untangled the timeline to get it straight in my head," I say. "First, the paintings are created, which seems to have something to do with punishing Athene."

Connolly's fingers tap, taking notes.

"Then Athene and Mercy destroy them. Or they think they did. Which raises a huge question mark. There's no way Athene destroys a painting if she isn't absolutely certain it's the right . . . Oh."

I'm about to continue when the bell jingles. Two guys looking for a "formerly cursed" object for their apartment. Unlike the sorority girls from yesterday, these two are serious. They're setting up a new place together, and they'd love an antique with a story to tell. Exactly my kind of customers, so I don't mind the interruption. After fifteen minutes of browsing, they pick a platter, and I package it up for them.

"You had a thought before they arrived?" Connolly says after they're gone.

"I did. The power Athene gives her descendants is past perception. The ability to see an object's past. So it'd be impossible to trick her with a fake painting. She *had* to have destroyed the right ones."

"Good point." He taps more into his phone. "That seems to suggest the one you found is a fake with the same curse."

"But not the fake Mercy commissioned for my test. That's where it gets complicated. She gets a fake for my test and puts on a fart-joke jinx. She somehow nudges the listing onto my eBay searches. I see it, and you buy it. But someone swaps it for yet another fake, with the original curse. Whoever did that knew about her test."

He nods. "Which could suggest that the person behind this is the one she commissioned to paint the fake. Whoever it is, they must be close to Mercy. Close enough to know what she was up to with you, which must be a very limited list. That's the only answer."

"Mmm, not exactly," says a voice from the storage room.

The back door opens, and Mercy walks in. She's taken out the pigtails and switched to a braid, as well as changing into jeans and a T-shirt. No longer the kids' TV show host. Just a casually dressed woman of about forty. I hesitate, not completely certain it's the same person.

She sighs. "Yes, it's me. I'm blending. Teeny insists on it. Blend, blend, blend . . ."

"My back door was locked."

Her grin sparks, the other Mercy peeking through. "Was. Wasn't. Is again."

"Where's Athene?"

"I ditched her. I have a three-order maximum with my big sister."

"Three-order maximum?" Connolly says.

"Let me guess," I say. "You let her give you three orders, and then you ditch her."

"Very good." She hops onto the stool. "You must be Aiden."

She puts out a hand. He doesn't take it.

"Mmm," she says. "You're not happy with me, either. Kennedy did tell you I'm not responsible for that curse, right? Or the police?"

"Yes, but you are responsible for her being targeted, solely as leverage over you."

"Kind of like your parents, right? Threatening Kennedy to make you fall in line?"

He stiffens, and before I can assure him I said nothing, Mercy says, "I'm not needling you, nephew. I'm acknowledging that having me do that to Kennedy would be extra annoying. As for how I know about your parents, I *do* take care of my students. Which means I know where all the threats are coming from. I'm going to trust you can resolve that one."

She turns to me. "Marius told me what's going on. You can contact this person?"

I unlock my phone and show her the string of texts. As she reads them, her brows knit.

"I have no idea what this is about," she says. "But I apologize anyway. I've never had something like this happen. Mortal lovers targeted, yes. Mortal friends targeted, yes. But not mortal mentees." She lifts a hand to Connolly. "And because I can tell you're bursting to say it, nephew, yes, if other mortals in my life have been targeted then it makes sense that Kennedy could be. But I only meant that people pester them for a cell phone number."

She taps the phone. "This is next level. For me, at least. I mean, I'm just Mercury. Athene, Paulo and Marius get most of the attention. Hector gets some, Artie, some. Denny and me?" She shrugs. "The advantage to being not taken seriously . . ."

"Is that no one takes you seriously?"

She grins my way. "Exactly. A pain in the ass when you *want* to be taken seriously, but it's ninety-five percent to our advantage." She lifts the phone. "I suspect this is a wrong number. Oh, they think they want me, but they *really* want Athene. Everyone wants Athene."

"And they expect to go through you?"

"I'm easier to talk to, and it's no secret in our corner of the world that Athene and I have been hanging out in New England this past week." She flutters her hand. "Immortal business. Point is, we were together, so they're trying to get to her through me."

She waggles the phone. "Mind if I reply?"

"Go ahead."

Mercy: Okay, you've got Hermes/Mercury/Mercy. What's up?
Msg: That is a poor try, Kennedy. Very poor indeed.

Mercy hits a few keys, switching to a Greek keyboard, and types in a new message.

Msg: I know you also speak ancient Greek, Kennedy.
Mercy: And it seems you do not. Interesting. Allow me to translate.
Mercy: What power is attributed to me that is not mine, and whose is it?

"Oh!" I say. "I know that one. Dream guide. Which is Vanessa's."
She smiles my way. "Nice." Then she taps out a message.

Mercy: Nothing? Seems you're not quite as tuned-in to the immortal world as you pretend to be. Interesting. Here let's try another one. What is the significance of the year 1495?

I glance at Connolly, who only shrugs.

Mercy: Nothing? It's the year those paintings were created.

I whisper, "They were painted in the seventies."
She shakes her head and motions that she'll explain later.

Mercy: The ones you have are fakes.
Msg: Are they? Ask Kennedy about that.
Mercy: Oh, she got the real curse. But not the actual curse. It's a duplicate.
Msg: If you want to test the other paintings, deny my request for a meeting.
Mercy: ???
Msg: Oh, I think you know what I mean. I want a curse.
Mercy: Then find a curse weaver.
Msg: This one requires your very special talent.
Mercy: I have many talents. You'll need to be more specific.

Msg: I want to salt the earth.

Mercy stiffens. I frown and reread the message. So does Connolly, but I can tell he's not understanding it, either.

Mercy: I don't do that.
Msg: But you can.
Mercy: This conversation is over.
Msg: So you accept whatever happens when I find a new home for the next painting?
Mercy: Leave Kennedy alone, and I'll pretend I don't know who this is. I trusted you. You betrayed me, and I'm not sure why, but I'm willing to drop it. Just stop this bullshit and talk to me.

There's no reply.

CHAPTER EIGHTEEN

"You know who's behind this?" I say when it's clear we aren't getting a return message.

"When I first came in, Aiden was saying there's a very small circle of people who could have done this. He's correct. Whoever targeted you knew about my test, and that narrows the list to two people. One person, actually. One mortal anyway. Denny painted the picture."

"Dionysus."

"Right. And there is zero chance he's pulling this crap. Also zero chance he told anyone about it. That leaves the other person, a mortal, someone I . . ." She bites her lip. "Someone I trusted. Well, trusted enough to put the painting up in that abandoned house. It didn't exactly seem like a high-risk endeavor."

She straightens. "It seems I was tricked, which is downright humiliating for a trickster."

"Nah," I say. "It's because you are a trickster that you naturally attract others."

"And in this case, I did know what I was getting. She's a thief."

"You're the patron god of thieves. Which is how you got in my back door now and my front one earlier."

"You really need decent locks. I'll put in good ones later. Least I can do for everything you've gone through here." She looks at Connolly. "Consider the situation resolved. I know who's behind it, and as you could see, as soon as she got me on the line, she stopped targeting Kennedy."

Mercy heads for the door.

"Hold on," I say. "What's this about the paintings being created five hundred years ago?"

"Long story. I'll explain later. Oh, and if Athene shows up, tell her I have everything under control." She glances over her shoulder. "Don't tell her this isn't about her. I'll do that. I want to see her face."

Another wave, and she's out the door and gone.

I turn to Connolly. "What just happened?"

Before he can answer, his phone rings. When he sees who it is, he grimaces.

"Parents?" I say.

"Lawyer. Which is slightly better, but only slightly. I should take this."

I'm about to head into the storage room when the bell jangles, and we motion to switch places. He goes into the back while I handle the customers, a small group of seniors making their way down the street, popping into every shop.

Three of the quartet are baffled by my shop. One doesn't even know what a curse is beyond a "bad word." Two kindly suggest that perhaps I don't want to advertise the formerly cursed part. Then there's the fourth, who thinks it's fascinating and peppers me with questions and leaves the proud owner of a teapot that once bore an ex-hex guaranteeing cold and bitter tea. Her companions are confused—terribly confused—but they assure her it's still a lovely china pot and still worth what she paid, and if this curse thing isn't actually gone, they're sure she could get a refund. I let them know that yes, all my sales come with a curse-free guarantee.

When I head into the backroom, Connolly is staring at the wall. Just staring and frowning, as if a spot suddenly appeared and he's not sure what to do about it.

"Aiden?" I say.

He startles and tucks his phone into his pocket.

"I hope the lawyer news wasn't bad," I say.

"Not bad. Just . . . concerning. Or less concerning? I'm not sure. The good news is that we don't need to worry about being arrested for theft. The state police have no record of the incident."

"What?" I come into the back and shut the door. "You mean Platts and Grove didn't file a report?"

"No, I mean the Massachusetts state police have no record of anything related to last night's incident. No report was filed. No painting was recovered. No painting was ever reported stolen. While they have officers named Platts and Grove, they don't match the descriptions I provided."

"We were set up?" I sink back against the counter. "Okay, now I feel like a complete idiot for not even considering the possibility."

"As do I. However, as my lawyer points out, they were driving a vehicle with state decals and lights. They were in uniform. They acted like police officers. We'd just bought a painting online, and therefore it made sense that it could be stolen goods. The fact that they caught up with us so quickly seemed odd, but we presumed it was a tip-off."

His head snaps up. "You have a camera system for the shop, yes?"

"Uh . . ."

He frowns. "I've seen the cameras. It's the model I suggested, yes? Motion-sensor feed in case of another break-in."

My cheeks heat. "Okay, so, um, I know my insurance policy requires a video camera, and I do plan to get it wired up, but I, uh, it was . . ."

I take a deep breath and plow forward. "I couldn't afford it. Not yet. So I put up the cameras, but I haven't bought the rest of the system yet. I know that could void my insurance if I had a break-in, and it's at the top of my to-do list for when I have extra cash flow, but there've been a lot of expenses, and that one just . . ." I meet his gaze. "I lied about the camera on my insurance application. I don't have footage for last night. I'm sorry."

"No," he says. "I'm sorry. I recommended a very expensive system without ever pausing to consider whether you could afford it."

"I should have admitted it. It was just . . ."

"Awkward." He takes out his phone. "Don't worry about the insurance. I'd never deny you a claim for that. I'm going to make a note to investigate lower-priced options that better suit your needs, while resisting the urge to offer to buy it for you." He glances up. "Unless you'd allow me to—"

"No, Aiden. Please."

Color touches his cheeks. Of all the things that can drive a wedge between people, money tops the list. But to me, that means different money styles. I couldn't be with someone who'd ring up debt and expect me to cover it. I also couldn't be with someone who'd deny me every luxury or splurge. But this is another kind of money issue, when one person has it and the other does not, the gulf so incredibly wide that it seems to taint everything.

I scrape together pennies to pay for big-ticket items that Connolly could cover with a swipe of his black card. For him, overcoming the awkwardness means swiping that card. For me, it means not allowing him to.

"So the police were fake," I say. "While it'd be nice to have their photos, I'm not sure it'd help. We'll know them if we see them again. I don't think we want the actual police investigating."

"That's what I told my lawyer. I was able to be honest with her. She's part of the magical community, so I could tell her it was connected to a cursed painting, and she understands discretion is the preferred course of action. However, it does beg the question of who sent—"

My phone dings with an incoming text. It's a Boston address.

Msg: Painting 2.

"Oh, for God's sake," I say. Then I pause. "Literally in this case. I'm guessing this message is for Mercy. Who did not leave any way of contacting her."

I'm about to ask Connolly for advice when the bell jangles.

"Really?" I say. I push open the door and nearly crash into Athene. She barrels past me and finds herself face-to-face with Connolly.

"You are not my sister," she says.

Connolly only looks at me, as if to say he has no idea how to answer that. Athene reaches to move him aside, but he plants himself, arms crossed.

She sighs. "Marius's boy, I presume. One of the Connollys that he's taken an interest in." Her gaze darts up and down him. "The older one. The responsible one. Adrian?"

"Aiden," I say. "And you missed Mercy, but—"

She turns and strides for the door. I run into her path.

"Hey!" I say. "You're not walking away this time. Yep, I'm a mere mortal and beneath your notice, but I have questions, and I think I deserve answers."

She frowns. "You are not beneath my notice. Who said such a thing?"

"If I'm not, then you'll stop treating me like the corner postbox."

Her frown grows. "I don't understand."

I wave my phone. "I'm the messenger. A way of getting to Mercy and, possibly, you. It's a truly shitty job, one I did not ask for, and I'm going to demand compensation in answers. Mercy thinks she knows who's behind this, and she's gone to confront them. But she must not have caught up with them yet, because they're threatening to release another painting."

"Which one?"

I stare at her for a moment before saying, "*That's* your question?"

"Each painting has a different curse. *Crying Girl* has the most minor of the hexes. Which painting has been released dictates how I should react, based on the statistical harm probability."

I glance at Connolly, who nods. "She means that, with the Crying Girl, there was a very low probability of immediate danger. The painting must be placed. It must activate. It must scare someone poised in a precarious position, such as on a balcony or stairs, where they might fall to their doom. If it was a more dangerous curse than that, it might be best to wait for Mercy to handle it."

I take out my phone.

Me: Which painting?
Msg: The Eldest Daughter.

I show Athene.

"We must go," she says, striding to the door and flipping my sign to Closed. "Follow me."

"Uh . . ." I say.

She turns on her heel. "You want answers?"

"Yes."

"You want to be treated as more than a mere 'postbox'?"

"Yes."

"Then come. I do not require your assistance, but you may join me anyway. You will do as I say. You will not question my orders. I will keep you safe."

"Er . . ."

I glance at Connolly. He grimaces and shrugs. In other words, he doesn't much like her attitude, but it's better than being left on the sidelines again.

"Aiden has a car," I say.

"As do I. We will take mine."

"He's a really good driver. And by 'good,' I mean he'll get us there fast, with minimal regard for traffic laws."

She shakes her head. "I take the driver's seat. Always. Now come."

"Adventure awaits," I say.

Athene wheels again, so sharply I almost bash into her. "It is not an adventure. We are recovering a painting and saving lives, and that is not supposed to be fun."

"Saving lives isn't fun?"

She pauses. "All right, it's a little fun."

She wheels again, and we follow her out the door.

CHAPTER NINETEEN

I DON'T KNOW what I expected Athene to drive, but this fits. A very nondescript, very functional sedan. Connolly tries to take the back seat, but it's small, and I'll fit better, so I beat him to it and tell him he's in charge of navigating. My job is interrogating the goddess of wisdom.

"Mercy says the paintings were from the fifteenth century," I say as soon as she's out of Unstable.

"Yes."

"So they weren't painted in the nineteen seventies?"

"I believe the answer to that is self-evident, Kennedy."

"It's not a question. It's a prompt for you to explain."

"I do not require 'prompts.' If you have a question, ask it."

"Tell me the true history of the paintings."

"Be more specific."

Connolly glances back at me, and I roll my eyes.

"I saw that," she says. "You really are Mercury's child, aren't you?"

"I feel like I'm feeding data into a computer," I say. "You are human, right?"

There's a pause. Such a long pause that I think she's insulted by the jibe.

"That is a question," she says. "Are immortals human? We share the same physiology as humans, yet human also implies mortal. If you'd like me to attempt to answer that question, I can. I've given it great thought. However, if you wish that answer, it will take the remainder of the drive. Perhaps you wish to select another option from the menu?"

She says it deadpan, but she's clearly riffing on my computer comparison, and not at all insulted by it.

"When were the paintings created?" I ask.

"1495."

"By whom?"

"I can supply the name if you'd like, but it would mean nothing to you. As an artist, he was a mediocre talent. This series of paintings is his only lasting achievement."

"Then he's dead. Not immortal."

"Certainly not immortal. Long dead. As I understand it, he died the moment he finished the last painting."

"They were already cursed?"

"No, the woman who commissioned them killed him. He'd served his purpose."

"Damn. Okay. So the bigger question is who commissioned them."

"Also not a name you'd know. Also dead. Not immortal, but of an immortal line. Mine, specifically."

We have to pause there for Connolly to give directions, which is good, because I need a moment to digest that.

"Whoever's behind this said you wanted them gone because of bad memories," I say. "Because they were commissioned by one of your progeny."

"I do not take responsibility for the random acts of my distant descendants. That way lies madness. I only had three children. I am not Aphrodite and Ares with their endless brood. That's no insult to them. They are happy in their domesticity, and their children are a delight to them, as they are a blessing to their children. Three was enough for me. They were fascinating projects, and they turned out exceedingly well, but children are draining. Still, even three offspring still means that I have tens of thousands of descendants. I cannot keep track of them, much less hope to influence them."

"So the connection between you and the paintings is . . ."

"They were created to punish me. While I do not track my descendants, I attempt, when possible, to make myself available to those who wish to understand the power they inherited from me. I don't have favorites, as Ares does with young Connolly here. I don't train students, as Mercury wishes to do with you. But if one of my descendants wishes to seek me out and 'pick my brain,' as they say, I am quite happy to do that."

I wait for her to connect my question to her answer. When she doesn't, I venture, "Did this particular descendant want more?"

"Yes. She was not interested in my wisdom or the gift of my experience. She wanted my favor."

"She thought you really were a god?"

"No, she understood the difference, but I still wield power as a presumed god. I am also a gifted strategist. That is what she wanted. My reputation and my assistance. My favor."

Again, I wait, but apparently, we really are doing this piece by piece.

"Your assistance with . . . ?"

"Are you familiar with the hereditary noble families of Renaissance Italy? The Medicis and so on?"

"Ooh, yes. Nasty stuff there."

"Well, her family was one of those. They were an embarrassment to me. They cheated their way to the top. Cheated everyone who could be cheated and killed those who could not. They were in a dispute with another family, and the matriarch wanted my help in what amounted to a war, not unlike the mafia wars centuries later. I refused. She stalked off in a huff, only to return a month later, begging. Her two sons had been taken captive by this rival family, and she wanted me to help. I agreed . . . if she'd donate fifty percent of her wealth to the poor. She refused."

"And the other family killed her sons?"

"Not intentionally. She hired mercenaries to storm the estate. Even tried to hire Ares."

"He refused?"

"No, Ares set her a condition of his own." Her voice rings with approval, even pride. "He would rescue her sons, as she asked, without harming anyone in the house, and in return, she would not retaliate. Her sons had been taken because she'd killed one of *their* sons, and so the slate would be clear."

"She refused."

"Yes, and so she ended up hiring brutes who botched the job, and her sons ended up dead, along with one of her two daughters."

"And she blamed you?"

"I had refused her pleas, and clearly, I must have interfered with Ares because, otherwise, monster that he is, he'd have happily slaughtered everyone in the house." Her voice drips with disgust. "She knew nothing about us. Knew nothing, and cared to learn nothing. She considered my assistance her birthright, as if I were an ancestral spirit bound to her aid."

"So she commissioned the paintings . . ."

"Commissioned them. Had them cursed. Sent them into the world to punish me. Four paintings. One for each of her children. Their fates were at my feet, as were the fates of anyone killed by their paintings."

Her voice is emotionless, gaze fixed straight ahead. But I don't miss the tightness in her jaw. She feels this. She must, or it wouldn't be a proper punishment. Like Vanessa and the Necklace of Harmonia. Unleash pain on the world in the name of an immortal, and let them suffer for it. Athene suffered, no matter how untouchable she might seem.

"The woman who did this—" Athene continues.

"Can we get a name?"

"No. That is her punishment—to remain nameless, lost to history. She attempted to trick Mercury into cursing the paintings." Another snort. "Because, clearly, the way to recruit a trickster is through trickery. Mercury retaliated as only my little sister can do. She cursed her in return."

"People can't be cursed."

"They can if you're Mercury. It wasn't a malicious curse. She doesn't do that. It was the equivalent of, as you might say, flipping her off. Then Mercury bounded away with nary a backward glance. This woman tracked one of her most gifted progeny, forced her to curse the paintings on threat of death and then killed her afterward. My sister was as invested in ridding the world of these paintings as I was."

"And then . . ."

"We rounded them up. It took centuries, and there were deaths, many deaths. But then we had them all. Mercury uncursed them. I destroyed them, right down to the memory of them."

I open my mouth to ask how that's possible. Then I shut it. There's no "how" to ask here. That must be one of her powers. Her progeny can see the history of an object, the memories it retains. She can destroy even those.

"Okay, so not to be rude but . . ."

"Did I make a mistake? Destroy the wrong paintings? Absolutely not. I could read their history, and I knew they had been made by that artist and cursed by that weaver. I could see that they had been responsible for deaths. We destroyed all four, beyond a doubt."

"I'm still confused about the timeline. I saw that painting. The girl's outfit was modern. There's an artist from the seventies who claims *he* painted them."

Athene sniffs. "He tampered with them. They had been missing for nearly three hundred years. That's why we didn't get to them sooner. An amateur painter found them, 'modernized' the paintings and passed them off as his own, complete with the haunted-children story. We tracked them down after that and destroyed them, but by then, the legend had spread far and wide in the modern world. It lives on, despite the fact that the paintings do not."

"So what did I see? A copy?"

"I can only presume so, and that is where we have the advantage. According to Mercury, the painting you saw has a curse that could be created by any truly skilled weaver. Some of the others . . ." She clears her throat. "There is stronger magic that Mercury can access, though she does not. Historically, some weavers had the knowledge of how to access that magic, but it was heavily guarded, and we believe it is now lost to all but a few weavers."

"Blood curses," I say.

"You've heard of them?"

"Only as ancient history. My grandmother knew of a weaver who did blood curses, but she cut off contact with that person as soon as she found out. We're not exactly innocent good witches—we cast curses—but that goes well beyond an ex-hex."

I pause a moment before continuing, "What you're saying, then, is that you think someone may have duplicated the *Crying Girl* painting, but that no one could do the others. They'd require both extreme skill and a knowledge of blood curses."

"Yes."

This makes sense, and it would mean that, whatever curse is allegedly on the *Eldest Daughter* painting, it won't be the real one. It'll be a watered-down version. Still dangerous, like *Crying Girl*, but not immediately lethal.

The talk of blood curses does nudge another question.

"The person who has the paintings," I say, "the duplicates. They want Mercy to perform a curse. One only she can do. Something about salting the earth."

Athene tenses.

I continue, "I know what the term means. Salt the earth so nothing can grow there. According to legend, the Romans did it to Carthage after sacking the city—"

"They did not."

"Right, because the sheer amount of salt required would be insane for a symbolic gesture. They'd have spent more on salt than they took from the city."

Her eyes meet mine in the mirror. "Impressive."

That'd be more of a compliment if she didn't seem so surprised.

"Wait," I say. "The way you said it . . . You were there?"

"Of course. Who else would the Romans have appealed to, if not Minerva? Which is actually quite annoying. They're on the battlefield, slaughtering animals in my name, and I'm right beside them, dressed as a general."

"As a man? I heard that you refused to use a man's name to translate the Rosetta stone?"

"Because I was forced to assume a male persona for quite long enough. I declared that the modern age had arrived, and I would never again pass myself off as a man in order to be taken seriously." She pauses. "It has been most inconvenient."

"I bet." I glance at Connolly, but he's just listening, deciding wisely not to add to this conversation. "While I have *so* many questions about the Carthaginian Wars, I'll get us back on track. Salting the earth. Is it a curse thing?"

"A generational curse."

I shift as far forward as my seatbelt will allow. "A curse that crosses generations?"

"Yes. Children. Grandchildren. Great-grandchildren."

"Mercy can curse people, right?"

"Yes."

I thud back in my seat and whisper, "Damn."

"Exactly that. It damns the recipient of the curse and all their descendants."

"Salting the earth. Genetically."

"What sort of curse would it be?" Connolly asks.

"Financial is the most common," she says. "Vengeance on a business rival, such as the families I was speaking about. Being able to ensure that not only their rival loses their fortune, but that none of their descendants can do more than cover their basic needs. Then there are the genetic curses. Disease, for one. Cancer. Alzheimer's. Heart disease. Also madness. That was, at one time, very popular."

"When you say *common* or *popular*," I cut in, "you mean Mercy did these?"

"Certainly not," she says sharply. "You know little of my sister if you can imagine such a thing." She pauses. "No, I must amend that. Our father has requested—demanded—such things from Mercury. At one time, he was in a position to force her into it." Another pause. "I should not have said that. I would ask that you never mention it to her." A third, even longer pause. "Please."

"I won't. That's . . . horrible."

"Our father is horrible. I know you have had dealings with Hephaestus, who is indeed our father's son, but truly a son in the sense that he is a weak reflection. Dangerous enough, but there is a petulant child inside Hephaestus. An overlooked and ridiculed child, and the one who overlooked and ridiculed him was his father, for the twisted leg *he* caused. For the rest of us, our mother's love was enough

—we learned to seek her approval and not Zeus's. Hephaestus never could."

She exhales. "That is all more than I meant to say. The question was whether Mercury uses hereditary curses, and the answer is a resounding no—not since she has been out from under our father's thumb."

"I know you didn't mean to tell us that, but it helps. This is going to be particularly difficult for her if it triggers past trauma."

A long pause, and I think she's about to tell me I'm wrong. Then she says, quietly, "Yes. It will."

Athene clears her throat. "As I'm sure you know, there are other immortals with our powers. Some of *them* use hereditary curses. At one time, it was common practice. It no longer is, and while I would love to say that's due to enlightened thinking, it's not. The immortals who did it are gone."

"They're missing?"

She gives what might be a sharp laugh. "I mean they are no longer among us. It is possible to kill an immortal. Very difficult, but possible. It is also possible—with help—to cancel our own immortality, if and when we choose."

"So this person," I say, "who has duplicated at least one of the paintings, wants Mercy to perform a hereditary curse. They've come to her because she's one of the very few who can do it. An immortal who is also a curse weaver."

"Yes. You said she believes it's someone she knows?"

"Someone she trusted, unfortunately. Whoever it is, they had to know about the game she was playing with me. The fake *Crying Girl* painting."

"Whoever painted it?" She pauses. Then she sighs. "No, that would be Dionysus. Those two do love their pranks. He painted it. She cursed it."

"And someone Mercy trusted put it in the abandoned farmhouse where we found it."

"Rosa," she says.

"She didn't give a name. She did say something about it being a thief."

"Then it is certainly Rosa. They have been lovers for a few years."

"Oh. Shit. That's . . . that's going to be rough."

"It was a casual relationship. Mercury never fully trusted her, but she delighted in Rosa's company, and she was exceedingly fond of her. Yes, the betrayal will be difficult. Particularly as I warned Mercury that she was right not to trust the woman."

I expect her to say this with some satisfaction, but there's no Salvoy in her tone, just concern. Mercy might have known better than to trust Rosa, but she still cared about her. Trusted her enough to help with this prank, which would have seemed completely innocuous.

Hey, can you hang this painting in this farmhouse for me? It's a little test for a potential student.

"Is Rosa a curse weaver?" I ask.

"I believe she's a dream shaper. Not one of Aphrodite's, but another line. She used that talent in her occupation. She met Mercury through a mutual friend, and they clicked, as you might say. Or so it seemed, though I was suspicious from the start. Mercury is the patron god of thieves, after all. Just because she couldn't share her curse weaving doesn't mean she couldn't be seduced into sharing some of her skills."

"Or be forced into weaving a blood curse. Rosa wasn't getting far enough with the carrot, so she broke out the stick."

"I'm afraid so."

CHAPTER TWENTY

WE'RE AT THE ADDRESS. It's not the poorest neighborhood Boston has to offer. Not by a long shot. Yet it might be one of the worst in the sense that it has nothing to recommend it. It's surrounded by light industrial, with heavy pollution and no public transit. There are clusters of residential buildings here, all built in the last fifty years, probably taking advantage of one real estate boom or another, when an entrepreneur decided the market was hot enough that newcomers could be tricked into buying a condo in a place like this. It might have worked for a while, but those newcomers would have moved out as soon as they were able, as would every sucker who followed. There is a trio of low-rise condo buildings in this particular area. One is half-demolished, and two bear the signs for future demolishment. Our address is one of the latter.

"Is there an apartment number?" Athene asks.

We both turn to look at her.

She frowns. "They are apartment buildings, are they not?"

"They're empty," I say. "Abandoned buildings in a neighborhood so far from the core that even squatters won't bother. Rosa isn't going to provide a unit number. This is a scavenger hunt."

"I would agree," Connolly says. "The question is: why bother?"

I frown at him and then say, "Right. The address is supposed to lead us to the *Eldest Daughter* painting. Rosa has supposedly unleashed the painting"—I gaze up at the dark-windowed building—"on whom?"

"I would like you two to remain outdoors," Athene says briskly as she marches forward. "In the car, preferably, but please stay a hundred feet from the building. No, two hundred. Yes, stay two hundred feet away."

I jog after her, Connolly beside me. "What does the *Eldest Daughter* painting do?"

"Two hundred feet away at all times—"

I get in her path. "What does it do?"

It's Connolly who answers. "You said the paintings are of that woman's children. Both sons were killed. The youngest child survived. That's the *Crying Girl*, yes? Mourning her siblings. The curses are tied to the children's fates, aren't they?"

Athene's shoulders slump, just a little, before she straightens and says crisply. "Yes."

"You said the other daughter was also murdered," I say.

"I said she perished. By her own hand. I believe her mother led her to believe she would be . . . violated, and so she ended her life. The painting compels others to consider the same. It has led to multiple suicides."

"It only makes them consider it, right? It doesn't actually kill them." I glance at Connolly. "Are you okay going in there?"

"If we stay together, yes."

"Then let's get that painting."

———

WE'VE SPLIT UP—ATHENE going one way while Connolly and I go the other. The curse won't affect her, and if it gets to us, we can call her for help. She impresses that on us multiple times, even providing her cell phone number in case she can't hear our cries.

We thought the threat was that the curse would be inflicted on random people. I'd imagined the painting appearing in a stadium or some crowded place where it would wreak havoc. Now when I think of what it could have done, that is horrifying in a way I struggle to comprehend.

The *Crying Girl* painting could take lives under the right circumstances. Mostly it would do psychological damage from the long-term effects of being subjected to her hauntings, but even then, I'd expect that whoever was being haunted would realize what was happening and get the painting out of their house.

Eldest Daughter is something altogether different, and I can only breathe a huge sigh of relief at finding it in an empty building, where it can't hurt anyone. Well, anyone except us, and that is the point. The address came to me. As Mercy's lover, Rosa would know full well that I don't have Mercy's contact information.

This was never about getting me to put her in touch with Mercy—obviously, she could do that herself. It was a ruse designed to convince Mercy the person contacting her was a stranger. She sent that address after she knew Mercy would be gone. Being eager to impress a god, I'd jump at the chance to help. I'd race to this address and unleash the curse on myself.

Mercy would have been responsible for my death. All because I tried to help her. All because Mercy didn't give in to Rosa's demand.

The building hasn't been abandoned for long. There are still signs of recent habitation—people leaving garbage and furniture in the apartments. It's less than we found at the old farmhouse—that place had the sad air of an estate issue. This is just people moving out of their condos, leaving crap behind because they know no one else is moving in.

The doors have all been left unlocked, which makes searching easy. They'd been nice apartments at one time. Really nice, with huge windows and big rooms and plenty of storage space. Of course, those windows have lovely views of industrial areas, and the appliances haven't been updated in decades, and good Lord, is that shag carpet? Yes, it's been a long time since anyone considered these "upscale" condos.

Even before the building was abandoned, occupancy had only been running at about thirty percent, judging by the number of apartments lacking appliances altogether. After a few apartments, we come up with a system. One person stays at the door while the other whips through. Then we switch at the next one.

We finish the first three floors, checking in with Athene at the end of each. I'm beginning to think we've been led on a wild-goose chase.

"Any twinges?" I ask Connolly.

"No," he says. "I'm not sure what to expect, though."

"Presumably, something like a voice in your ear, calling you worthless, telling you to end it all."

He frowns. "How would that work if I know better?"

I shrug. "Lots of people know better deep down. Doesn't keep them from having doubts, from sometimes feeling worthless."

I open the next door.

"Do you ever feel like that?" he asks before I can slip inside.

I pause. "I compare myself to others more than I should. Whether it's Ani or . . . others." I shrug. "You meet people who are doing so much better, and it can make you feel as if you're not trying hard enough."

"You run your own business."

"So do you, and one of us is doing it a whole lot better."

"Because one of us had every advantage money can buy, Kennedy. If anything, I am in awe of what you've accomplished *without* those advantages."

"I had advantages, Aiden. My dad was a doctor. My mom ran a successful business."

"Yes, but you lost them both. Not every advantage is monetary."

I reach out and squeeze his arm. "Thank you. The answer to the original question is yes, I've doubted myself, but I've never felt worthless, and a voice in my ear telling me that isn't going to send me crashing into the depths of despair. The curse would only work on those who are already teetering on the brink."

"That's . . ."

"Unbelievably cruel? Yes." I ease back on my heels. "I do understand that the woman who commissioned these paintings was in incredible pain. When my dad died . . ." I take a deep breath. "It happened so fast, and I couldn't wrap my head around it for weeks. The shock was too much. I hated the person who hit his car, but she died, too, so there was no one to blame. Then Mom was diagnosed with cancer, and it felt as if Fate would grant us a pass there. We'd just lost Dad. Surely, we wouldn't lose Mom, too. Even by the time we realized the cancer was terminal, we still had plenty of time to say goodbye. But if there'd been someone I could blame for both deaths? Someone I could punish? Hell, yes, I'd have wanted to do that. To punish that person. Specifically that person. The idea of hurting them by tormenting and killing others? I can't even conceive of that level of . . ."

"Evil?"

I balk at the word. I was brought up to be careful with language. As children, we were never "bad"—our behavior was naughty. The woman who was texting while driving and hit my dad wasn't evil—she was selfish and careless and a shitty person, but not evil.

Connolly's right, though. This is evil. It's a breathtaking act of cruelty toward Athene, but it's even worse in its utter disregard for every other person the curses touched.

This women lost three of her children in a day. I cannot imagine her grief. Yet this wasn't lashing out in blind rage. She commissioned a painter . . . and killed him once he'd finished. Then she did the same to the curse weaver. Months would have passed during the process, and at no point did she reconsider her revenge.

Athene is right to refuse to name her. She doesn't deserve it.

Connolly and I search that apartment together, and the next one, too, as if neither wants to be alone after that conversation.

In the following one, I force myself to stay in the doorway while he searches. When we reach the next, he murmurs, "I'll be right here," and I smile over at him and say, "I know." Then I go in.

The apartments all have the same layout. Front hall with a big hall closet. Then the hall turns, with a door to the bedroom on the one side, a kitchen straight ahead and the living area in the corner between the two. I open the bedroom door. It's empty. Long empty, without even a trash bag left on the floor. I back out and—

The *click-clack* of a keyboard stops me. I go still, head turning to follow the sound. It's coming from the living room. I take a step in that direction and see an old sofa. The typing sounds come from across the room where a woman sits at a computer desk. Paper is piled on either side of her computer. As she types, she reaches over, gaze never leaving the screen as she moves a sheet from the pile on her left to the one on her right.

Data entry. I'd done a little of that for a summer job, and I shiver at the memory. Endless typing for rock-bottom wages. The woman is a squatter. Working a job that doesn't pay enough for rent. I'm taking a slow step back when a cat meows. The woman stops typing as a black cat leaps onto her lap.

"Ellie?" I whisper.

The woman swivels in her chair as she reaches for a cat treat. That's when I see her face. My face. Ten years older than I am now, but clearly my face.

I take a slow step backward and smack into a hall table. On it are a series of photographs. Photos of people I know, but otherwise unrecognizable. There's Hope in climbing gear with mountains in the background, Rian's arm slung over her shoulders. Then Ani and Jonathan with two little children, a desert behind them. Other friends, all with partners, some with children. And one, half tucked in the back, of Connolly and Theodora toasting from a yacht.

I want to laugh. Burst out laughing. This is a supposed vision of my future, where everyone else in my life has found love and purpose, and they left me here, in this horrible little apartment, doing a horrible little job. Something went wrong in my life—maybe the shop failed, and I owed so much money I'm still digging out. Whatever happened, it's just me and my cat.

Cue the sad violins . . .

I should laugh, and I don't, because somehow this overwrought, overdramatic scene hits its target, deep in my subconscious.

I'm cursed. Literally cursed. Fall for someone who doesn't love me back, and I could doom him to a terrible fate. It's supposed to protect me —protect my heart—but the problem with curses is that they can backfire spectacularly. Like wishes, Mom always said. How many stories are there of people making wishes only to end up suffering horribly because they didn't think it all the way through? The same applies to curses.

The curse on me was woven by Mercy. She owed Hector a favor, and he demanded payment, and apparently, that's a big deal for immortals. He wanted to punish Vanessa for her affair with Marius. Mercy tweaked the curse to punish false lovers instead of real ones, which meant that the person who should have actually suffered was Hector. Except Hector gave the necklace to Harmonia, intending for it to ruin the marriage of Vanessa's beloved daughter. Since Harmonia's groom truly loved her, the curse had no effect . . . until it was passed on to others and those tragedies *did* hurt Vanessa.

Positive intentions; unexpected negative results.

What if the curse doesn't just punish false lovers? What if it also punishes a lover who wants to give more but can't? In other words, someone like Connolly, busy with his career and his family drama, moving on as soon as a relationship becomes yet another responsibility. A guy like that doesn't deserve to be cursed for honest choices.

I flash back to that cursed mirror. I couldn't see myself in it, and now I think I realize what that meant. I am afraid of disappearing. Of fading from the view of everyone I love and being alone.

My deepest fear is laid out in this room. That everyone I love will move forward, and I'll tumble back. My business will fail, and I'll dig myself into inescapable debt, convinced I just need another loan, another investment, another tweak to save it.

I want to laugh at this pathetic scenario, me with my cat, alone and miserable as I slide toward rock bottom. I know I'm more business-savvy than that, and I'll figure out how to make relationships work despite this curse. But fears aren't always rational, and this one is mine.

Still, there is a world of difference between seeing my worst fear play out and deciding I should end my life to avoid it. I've known people in that mental state, where something like this could push them over the edge, adding to all the other voices that whisper they'd be better off exiting stage left. This is only the painting's first volley, and if I stay near it, the images will get worse, the whispers more insidious.

I knew it was a terrible curse, and now I see just how terrible, how unfathomably cruel.

I march to the doorway. I expect to see the hall empty, me still in that vision, but when I walk out, Connolly is there, where I left him. He's staring blankly.

Lost in his own vision.

I shiver and gently grip his arm. "Aiden?"

He backpedals so fast I stagger away. Then he snaps out of it, blinking at me.

"Kennedy?" Before I can answer, he runs his hands over his face and gives himself a shake.

"I think the painting is close," I say.

He gives a low laugh. "I believe you are correct."

"Are you all right?"

He rolls his shoulders. "Of course."

"Well, that makes one of us. I'm a bit rattled. Just because a vision doesn't trigger suicidal thoughts doesn't mean it isn't really awful."

"Agreed. That was . . . unpleasant."

We stand there a moment. I want to ask what he saw, but if I do, then I have to be willing to share what I saw. I'm sure he's thinking the same. In the end, he says, carefully, "If you want to talk about it . . ."

"Nope. You?"

"I'd rather not."

"Then let's get that painting before it strikes again."

CHAPTER TWENTY-ONE

WE'RE one floor above the apartment where the vision hit. The painting is behind this closed door. I feel it pulsing, an ugly, living thing.

Connolly wrinkles his nose as we pause there. "Do you smell something?"

I inhale. "Garbage and mildew. What do you smell?"

"That, I suppose."

He takes out his phone to try Athene again. We'd called to let her know we were close, but it seems Rosa also installed a cell phone blocker on this floor. Maybe we should have gone to find Athene, but neither of us cared to spend one moment longer than necessary in this building.

"No signal?" I say.

He shakes his head and pockets the phone. Then he puts out his hand, stopping halfway to the doorknob and glancing my way.

I reach for his other hand. "May I?"

"Of course."

He takes my hand and grips it tight, and I do the same to his, grounding us against the curse. Then he turns the knob and opens the door an inch.

"Better to rush in?" he says. "Or take it slow?"

"My gut says grab the painting and run," I say. "Which means we should take it slow."

A smile my way, and he continues pushing open the door until we're staring down a hallway. The smell hits then. It's menthol, strong and medicinal, like the rub my grandfather swore by for chest colds.

"Well," I say. "It's better than rotting garbage."

"Is that the curse?"

I shake my head. "They can emit smells, but I don't see the point of that one. Unless it's meant to evoke the subject—the girl who died. A smell associated with her?"

He steps through the doorway first, which is awkward while holding hands, but he doesn't loosen his grip. He walks through with our joined hands behind him. Then I enter and let the door shut as I move up beside him.

I'm glancing back to check on the door when his grip tightens. I turn to see a young woman at the end of the hall. She's a teenager, maybe eighteen. Now that I know she died during the Renaissance, I can see her outfit better than I could with her younger sister. It's still semi-transparent and could pass for a dress, but it seems to be a nightgown, long and pale, fluttering about her in a nonexistent breeze.

She's staring, her eyes wide with fear. Then she flies straight at me, and I stumble back at the same time as Connolly, our joined hands all that keep me from falling. The apparition smacks into me with a wave of crushing despair that leaves me gasping, panic rocking through me.

The vision downstairs had played on a subconscious but very real and identifiable fear. This is different. It's formless despair and grief, a sudden sense that everything is wrong and nothing will ever be right again.

"Kennedy?"

Connolly's voice cuts through, his free hand on my shoulder, tightening. I force myself out of it, rising to the surface to see his face over mine, pale and drawn, the look in his eyes telling me he'd felt the same thing.

I throw my arms around him. I don't think about it. I just hug him tight, grounding myself with the warmth of him. Then I realize what I'm doing and pull back fast with a mumbled apology.

His arms tighten around me, and I fall against his shoulder, taking deep breaths and feeling his own heart rate slow until we're both back to normal.

"So, 'unpleasant' is the word of the day," I say. "Deeply unpleasant. I definitely preferred the little girl's scares."

"In retrospect, they do seem rather mild." He grips my hand. "Shall we continue?"

"Let me get the shield first. I'm starting to think running in there and throwing it over the painting isn't such a bad idea after all."

I have the shielding blanket in a backpack. Connolly had offered to carry it, but I'd insisted. It's light enough, just a little bulky. I take it out, and he extends a hand.

I pass it over. As soon as he has it, he drops my hand and bolts down the hall.

"Connolly!" I say.

Electricity zings through the air. A light burst of luck, a ward against the vision reappearing. He stumbles as he rounds the corner—a bit of balancing bad luck. Then there's a gasp and a squeak of his loafers that has me sprinting after him.

"Aiden!"

I fly around the corner and bash into him. He drops the shielding blanket, takes me by the shoulders and pushes me back just as I discern another smell beneath the menthol.

I break from Connolly's grasp. When I try to pass him, he blocks me.

"You don't need to—" he says.

I'm already past. Already striding toward the living room. Already knowing what I'll see there.

She sits in a straight-backed chair, upright. There's a moment where I think I'm mistaken, Connolly was mistaken, that the smell led us to the wrong conclusion. The woman in the chair can't be dead. She's sitting upright with her hands gripping the arms. Then I see her face.

Dead.

I back up into Connolly and then twist, and his arms go around me.

"I didn't want you to see that," he says.

"I know," I say. "It's fine."

It's not. Not fine at all. But there's no way in hell I'm retreating and forcing him to deal with this horror on his own. I take a deep breath. Then I head back in, keeping my gaze away from the woman's face.

A flicker to my right. I glance over and see the ghost of the girl from the painting.

"Oh, hell, no," I mutter.

I dive for the discarded shielding blanket before she flies at me. I scoop it up, and then Connolly's there, taking it and running. I see the painting in the corner of the room. The ghostly image appears beside its painted twin. He throws the shielding blanket over the frame, and the image vanishes.

I hurry over and help him wrap the painting. Then we turn back to the woman in the chair. She's in her thirties and has long dark hair with blue streaks, her fingernails painted the same shade of blue.

"Who . . .?" I whisper.

"Rosa," says a voice near the door. We look to see Athene walking into the apartment. "That is Rosa."

There's a bottle of pills on the floor beside the dead woman. Athene walks over and bends to examine it.

"The painting backfired?" I say. "It killed her— No. She was texting me an hour ago, and she's been dead . . ." I swallow as the smell wafts over us. "She's been dead much longer."

"She's bound to the chair," Athene says. "With one hand freed."

It takes me a moment to realize what she means. I stagger back. Connolly catches my hand and squeezes.

Someone bound Rosa to that chair with a bottle of pills, in a room with a painting that would inflict suicidal thoughts.

Athene straightens, clearing her throat, matter-of-fact tone returning. "She has been dead for several days."

"Meaning she didn't send *any* of those texts," I say.

"She also didn't switch out the *Crying Girl* painting," Connolly says.

It takes that a moment to register. It seems as if we went after that painting days ago, but it was just last night. Rosa was already dead.

Pounding footsteps sound in the hall. Athene lunges past us and runs out, leaving us both hurrying after her. We reach the hall to see her blocking Mercy. When her sister goes to pass, Athene grabs her arm.

Mercy tries to throw her off, and Athene yanks her to the wall, pinning her there.

I back up into the doorway, out of sight, my heart pounding. In that moment, I don't see Athene and Mercy. I see Ani and myself five years ago. I'd been at college when our dad died, and Ani had climbed into the car and driven for three hours to give me the news in person, pushing aside her own grief to make sure I wasn't alone when I heard.

I should have broken down in her arms, weak with gratitude as I sobbed for our father. Instead, somehow, my brain insisted it was a mistake. Yes, Ani was mistaken, and she needed to stop this nonsense, stop saying these things, get out of my way and let me straighten this out.

Ani had to physically restrain me, just as Athene is doing to Mercy now. Their voices dimly penetrate the fog of memories, intertwining with the past, me telling Ani she's wrong, Mercy telling Athene the same.

It's a mistake. A misunderstanding. Get out of my way, and let me solve this.

Ani didn't get out of my way. Neither does Athene. Connolly stays behind me, close enough for me to feel the heat of him, and I resist the urge to lean back against him. He's there, and that's enough. Athene is there for Mercy, and that, too, is enough.

It only takes a few minutes for Mercy to surrender. To accept what lies in the next room. She still wants to go in there. Athene won't allow it, and again, eventually, Mercy gives in. She wants to be tough enough to face it, as I did a few minutes ago. But Athene is right—this is not how she should remember her friend and lover.

When I finally move into the hall, Athene is telling Mercy she'll look after arrangements for the body. Mercy only nods dumbly. Then she glances my way.

"We've shielded the painting," I say.

More mute nods. Then she says, "Are you all right?"

"We didn't know her."

"I mean the curse. Did it activate?"

"Yeah. But we're okay. I'm sorry about Rosa."

She takes a deep breath. "She got in over her head. Someone made her an offer. She sold me out, and they double-crossed her."

"Are you sure of that?" Athene says. "When did you last see her?"

"Three days ago." Mercy seems to physically summon energy to continue. "She'd rented a room in Boston to . . . to be near me while I was in the area, and to help with my thing with Kennedy. I dropped off the painting three days ago."

"The fake *Crying Girl* painting," I say. "With the fart jinx."

Her lips twitch, the ghost of a smile. "Yeah, she gave me shit for making her keep it in her hotel room, but I was busy with"—a look at Athene—"our thing."

Mercy continues, "That's why I needed Rosa to plant the painting. I knew it might take a while for you to bite at the eBay listing, Kennedy. In the meantime, I was helping Athene. When you bit, I processed the sale and played Ms. Silver while Rosa planted the painting."

"When did you last speak to her?" I ask.

"The night I dropped off the painting. Otherwise, it was all messaging, and I was busy, so not much of that. I let her know when you'd taken the bait. I didn't want the painting in that house early. Kids had been using it."

"But since Aiden only bought the painting yesterday afternoon, that means Rosa was already dead when you messaged her to put up the painting. *How* did you message her? I thought you didn't have a phone."

She gives me a look. "I'm communication-resistant. I'm not a technophobe. I could message her online."

"Did she reply?"

Mercy shakes her head. "Not until the painting . . ." She frowns, as if thinking. "She sent me a photo of the painting when it was in place and then one of you two at the house. They went to my message service, so I didn't get them until this morning."

"That couldn't have been her," I say. "Yes, she might have been working with her killer, but it's even more likely she was a victim here. Whoever killed her also switched the paintings and—"

"And we'll figure all that out," Athene cuts in. "I need to look after Rosa. Mercy and I will find whoever is behind this and stop them. You two will go home."

"Uh, no," I say. "We're part of this. I am, at least. Whoever *does* have the paintings has made me their messenger."

"I'm resolving that," Mercy says. She takes a cell phone from her pocket. "May I see your phone, Kennedy?"

I pass it over, and she opens both phones and sends the prepaid cell's number to the person messaging me. A moment later, a text dings on the new phone, and she answers it.

"There," she says. "Messenger no more. Athene's right. You two should go home. Leave this to us."

CHAPTER TWENTY-TWO

WE DON'T DROP it there. We're involved, and we want to stay involved. But it's hard to argue when a woman is dead and Mercy is grieving. In light of that, insisting on helping feels more like interfering.

Connolly and I have left them to it and walked three blocks, getting to a better area for calling a ride share.

"I'll take you home," Connolly says.

"In a ride share?"

"No, a car service. That will be more comfortable."

"I'm not arguing comfort, Aiden. I'm saying I don't think we need a hired car just yet. Your car is here, right? In Boston? It's the rental that's back at my place. We can figure out how to get me home later. I'd rather rest first. Take time to clear my head."

"Yes, of course."

He looks up and down the street, as if a sofa might magically appear.

"Your condo is in Boston, right?"

"Er, yes . . ."

Okay, let's be honest. While I wouldn't mind a rest, I'm really angling for a chance to see where he lives. We've been in Boston together many times, but never to his condo, and I've presumed that's just him being careful not to send the wrong message. Now, as he hesitates, I realize there's more to it. He's not going to take me to his condo when he's been telling his parents we're just friends.

"How about a coffee?" I say. "Your caffeine meter must be running low by now. Let's find a quiet place and chill for an hour. Then we'll figure out the best way to get me to Unstable and recover your rental."

"No, no. We should go to my place so you can rest."

"If you're uncomfortable with that, Aiden . . ."

"I am. Very. However . . ." He squares his shoulders. "We need to get this over with."

"No, we don't. If you're concerned about your parents finding out I was at your place—"

"I'm not. The issue is . . ." He shakes his head and takes out his phone. "I'll call that ride share."

———

ONCE AGAIN, I don't drop the matter there. I want him to know, beyond any doubt, that he doesn't need to take me to his place. I give him every opportunity, but he is resolved, which is just hellishly awkward.

Then we arrive at his condo and . . .

"This isn't a condo," I say.

He clears his throat. "Technically, it is an investment property, and it *is* zoned for rental."

"It's a house, Aiden. A house in Boston. Not the suburbs. Not the outskirts. This is a house in the core of Boston."

He clears his throat again but only says, "Yes."

"It's also freaking gorgeous." I walk to the plaque that declares it a historic building.

"It really is too big for one person," Connolly says.

Is that his concern? A show of ostentatious wealth? It's hardly a mansion. While I can't see the whole thing from the sidewalk, it seems smaller than my family home.

"It's what, three bedrooms?" I say.

"Two, actually."

"Then that's perfectly reasonable for a single person," I say. "You said it's an investment property."

"Yes."

"Makes sense. You've invested in real estate, and you're living here while the market climbs. Nothing wrong with that." I motion at the gate. "May I?"

"Of course."

I unlatch it, and we walk in. The gardens are in full bloom. A gardener's work, I presume. While I personally would be delighted to think Connolly had a secret passion for gardening—or any relaxing hobby—I know he'd never find the time to keep up his yard like this.

We climb the steps, and he unlocks the door and then hurries in to disarm the security system. I enter into a small foyer. Lead-glass doors lead to a room on either side and stairs in front of us. Through one glass door, I see an empty space.

"I didn't see the point in decorating a room I don't use," he says.

The other door leads into a study. I look around for a living area. There isn't one. The study attaches to yet another empty space.

"The dining room," he says. "I don't use that, either. It's just this and the upstairs. Well, part of the upstairs. One bedroom. Oh, and the kitchen. I do use the kitchen. That's where I'd eat. Not much point in a dining room table for one."

Is this the problem then? His very empty house? Again, I'd hope for more—some sign he's made himself a comfortable little nest where he can retreat and decompress. As tiny as my Boston place had been, it'd been that for me. Yet Connolly is efficient to his core, and he'd see no point in comfy armchairs or sofas. When would he ever find the time to curl up on one? He has expectations to exceed.

"It's very you," I say.

He glances over. "That is not a compliment."

I smile. "I'd like to see a worn recliner, with a bookmarked novel, but I know that isn't your style. Yours is more . . ."

"Antarctica without the penguins?"

"*Pfft*, no. Who said that? Oh, right. It was me, wasn't it? Fine." I walk into the study. "Your style is a little austere. At least it's a style. And this isn't nearly as subarctic as your office. You have colors here." I point at a painting. "There. I see blue in that . . . What is it anyway?"

"I have no idea. I didn't decorate. Yes, it's not exactly cozy, but I don't spend a lot of time at home. It's a place to sleep, mostly."

He walks to the front window and looks out. "It's a nice house."

"It's a *very* nice house. Seriously. I might tease about the decorating, but the house is *gorgeous*."

"It's not mine." He blurts the words and then rubs a hand over his mouth. "I mean, it is. I own it. Or I will." He squares his shoulders and turns to me. "It belongs to my parents."

"Ah."

"That's why I haven't had you over. At first, I avoided it because I know how it looks. I get letters in the mailbox every month from older couples, professionals, telling me how much they'd love my house for their family. They send pictures of their children, their pets."

"Ooh, emotional blackmail as a sales technique. Classy."

He opens the sheers. "Yes, I resent those letters, but I also feel like a speculator, squatting on prime real estate that some young family would love. I knew how it would look to you. Exactly what you expect. A million-dollar home that I barely use."

He lets the sheer fall and turns to me. "Then it became more than that. I told you I've been trying to save enough to escape that marriage contract. If you found out about the contract and saw this house, you'd wonder why I don't just sell it and pay off the contract."

"Because it isn't yours."

"Yes and no." He paces across the room. "I didn't leave home to live in a place my parents bought for me. I have a little more dignity than that. This was . . . I would call it a graduation gift, but I'm aware of how that sounds when most graduates get a nice watch. When Connolly boys are born, our parents buy us a house. An investment property. They restore it and rent it until we graduate from college and secure a position."

"You get it when you've proven yourselves worthy of homeownership. A responsible adult able to pay the upkeep and utilities."

"Yes, but . . ." He taps his fingers on the desk. "It's also a bribe, of sorts. We grow up being told this will be ours when we have, as you say, proven ourselves. It's also a method of control. And a potential punishment if we don't live up to expectations."

"Rian had a house, didn't he?"

"He did."

"Do I want to ask what happened to it?"

"He was given five years to change course and enroll in college. After that, they . . ." He shoves his hands into his pockets and looks away. "They demolished it."

My mouth opens, but I clamp it shut as my mind boggles at the sheer vindictiveness of that. Rian grew up with the promise of a house, a specific one they'd probably shown him a hundred times. Instead of just reselling it, they destroyed it.

"I am becoming aware of how that may have affected him," Connolly says slowly. "I should have understood before now, but you know Rian. He acted as if he didn't care. And while I admired this house, I didn't grow up dreaming of what it would be like to live here."

I move closer to him. "Rian did."

Connolly is quiet long enough that I think I've guessed wrong. When he speaks, the words come thick. "He used to draw pictures of his house, with his wife and his kids and his dogs. Two dogs. Two kids." A short laugh. "When he was little, there were two wives, too, until I explained that wasn't legal, and he had to look it up. He was very disappointed."

I laugh under my breath. "That does sound like Rian. Not so much the kids and dogs, though."

"That *was* Rian . . . when he was little. He dreamed of things I never did." He shoves his hands into his pockets. "He changed when he got older."

"Did he really?" I ask softly.

His words come even thicker as he turns to look out the window. "No, you're right. I think he just found weapons to protect himself, and those weapons were sarcasm and indifference, and I believed the charade. I believed he didn't care about college. Believed he didn't care about his house. I know better now, but I can't figure out how to tell him that. If I tried, he'd blow me off, make a joke of it."

Connolly inhales sharply. "But we aren't talking about Rian. We're talking about this house. My parents gave it to me when I started my business, and my name is on the deed, but theirs is, too, which is why I can't sell it to repay the debt. Rian used to draw pictures of his family living in his house because that's what it is. A marital home. It's part of the contract. When I marry, I receive full ownership of this house."

He glances at me. "That's why I didn't want to bring you here."

"Because it's the house you're supposed to bring your wife to."

"What?" His brows knit. "No, no. As I said, I never thought of it that way. I didn't bring you because . . . I behave as if I lead a fully independent life. That wasn't an act. I *feel* independent, compared to my brother and my cousins and friends. I am the one who broke away early, and everyone is so proud of me for that, especially my parents." He pushes back the sheers again with one finger and gazes out.

"They want you to feel as if you're free, so you won't notice the invisible chains binding you to them."

"Yes." He stares at the yard. "It's like looking out this window and making the mistake of thinking I'm outside, enjoying the sunshine and fresh air. I'm not free. I am nowhere near free."

He drops the sheers again and turns to face me. "This isn't my house. That's a joke. My business may be mine, but even that's a sham. If I default on the contract, my parents can legally take it from me in payment of my debt, and even that wouldn't cover it. If it would, I'd sell it myself."

"You aren't going to sell your business, Aiden. That's *yours*."

He starts to turn, as if he wants to look out the window again, not to see the view but to break eye contact. He's more comfortable talking while looking out there, and if that's what helps, I'm going to pretend he just wants to look outside. He doesn't, though. He keeps facing me.

"I'll work this out," he says.

"I know you will, and on that note, there's something I need to tell you. I had a visitor today."

CHAPTER TWENTY-THREE

I TELL Connolly about Theodora's visit. I make it clear that she was kind and friendly, but with each word, he seems to age a year.

"I am so sorry," he says. "She didn't mean any harm, but I cannot imagine how awkward that was. I hope she didn't suggest I've said that you and I are anything more than friends."

"She didn't."

"I've been clear, no matter what my parents think."

"I know. Speaking of awkward, there's something else I need to tell you. I'm sure with all her calls, it seems as if she agrees with your parents and is happy to be the, uh, forerunner in this, uh, competition, but she actually isn't."

"She doesn't want to marry me?"

"Er, uh . . ." That's when I see his lips twitch. "You already knew that."

His lips twitch again. "You thought I'd be disappointed?"

"No, just, well . . ."

"Offended, then. I may not want to marry her, but *naturally*, she'll want to marry me. No. I've known Theodora since we were children, and I think she's a fine person, but I have never been interested in her that way."

"I'd understand if you were. Or had been. She's, well, kinda perfect."

His brows knit. "In what way?"

I laugh at that. "Uh, every way, Connolly. She's gorgeous, and she dresses like she's headed to the runway, but instead, she's actually headed to court. Because, of course, she's a lawyer. Smart, beautiful, stylish, rich *and* nice. I can see why she's your parents' top choice."

"Theodora is a lawyer for the same reason I run my own firm. Because our parents could afford the best tutors and best education. She dresses well because—like me—she can afford to indulge in fashion. I agree she is kind, and that is, in my opinion, her most remarkable trait, only because it's so rare in our circles. There are several young women on my parents' list that I hope you never meet."

I nod. "They wouldn't have been nearly as respectful."

"I'm afraid not, which is what makes this all . . ." He exhales and shoves his hands into his pockets. "I will resolve this."

"So if Theodora isn't interested in marrying you, and you know that, why duck her calls? She wants to resolve this, Aiden. She says she has a plan."

"I know."

I throw up my hands. "Then why dodge her? You two can figure this out together."

"Her plan is for us to get married."

I stop, my hands still in the air. "What?"

"She wants us to go through with it. Get married."

I lower my hands. "No, she told me she didn't want to marry you, and you said you know that."

"She doesn't want to, but she thinks we should. A marriage of convenience, she called it."

I pause. "Uh, I've read books about those. It's a one-way ticket to Happily Ever After Land."

His face softens, even if he doesn't smile. "Not in this case. She's thinking of it more as a green-card marriage. We both have contracts we want to escape."

"You *both* have contracts?"

"They're de rigueur in our circle of luck workers. Her plan is that we marry in name only. Live under the same roof with separate bedrooms.

Like roommates. Our contracts don't say we need to *remain* married. She's gone over both in detail. For safety's sake, though, she thinks we should still play the role of newlyweds, publicly, and then after two years, have an amicable divorce. There would be premarital contracts, of course. We'd separate and go on with our lives, contract-free."

"Which sounds very logical, but you don't want it."

"I . . ." He shifts, clearly wanting to look out the window again. "It is logical. An efficient and reasonable solution to our shared problem. I can free myself from the contract and all attached parental expectations by simply sharing a house with someone who'd make an excellent roommate. No one expects a love match, so we wouldn't need to feign romantic attraction. We are agreeing to attempt an alliance that will ultimately fail, and we will go our separate ways."

"But . . ."

"I don't want it," he says. "There are things I wish to change in my life. I'd like to mend fences with Rian. Help him if I can, and if he doesn't want that, then I'll be a properly supportive older brother."

He waves around the room. "I want a proper home where I feel comfortable entertaining friends. If there was one part of this house that truly excited me, it was the pool. I enjoy swimming, and I imagined doing it every morning before work. I haven't even opened it since I moved in. I swim at the gym, when I *get* to the gym."

"You want more," I say.

"More of *everything*, whether it's biscotti with my morning coffee, a pool to swim in before work or an actual week of actual vacation. If I go along with Theodora's plan, I postpone all that to fully inhabit my expected role in the world I want to escape. I know it's only two years, but it feels like twenty, and maybe I'm being selfish and immature, but I want more *choice*. *Now*."

"That isn't selfish or immature, Aiden. You're afraid if you marry Theodora, you'll be sucked back in and forget all that."

"Yes."

His phone rings. He glances down. "Speak of the devil." He shakes his head. "No, that isn't fair. Theodora's not my enemy here."

"She really isn't. You *should* talk to her. Tell her how you feel. Try to come up with an alternate plan."

He stares down at the phone.

"She doesn't deserve you ducking her calls," I say softly.

He nods and answers. As he talks, I wander the office. There's a bookshelf, and I head for it. Before I can start checking out books, I hear him say, "No, not today. I have plans."

He glances at me. "I understand but—"

A pause. "Yes, that makes sense, but even an hour is really more than I can spare right now."

I shake my head and motion that he *can* spare that hour.

"One moment," he says and mutes the phone. "She's inviting me for cocktails and a conversation." He mouths. "I don't want to go."

"But should you?"

He hesitates.

"I can stay here," I say. "We'll go to dinner afterward. You really should talk to her, and it might help ease things if you go over."

Ease them with his parents, I mean. They're sure to hear that he had cocktails with Theodora, and that will reduce the pressure on him. On me, too, but mostly I'm thinking about him.

"You're my guest," he says. "I shouldn't abandon you."

"I'm your friend, not your guest. I'll read while you're gone." I pick up a book. "*The Principle of Financial Reporting for Insurers.* Er, maybe not. Ah, magazines." I take one. "*North American Actuarial Journal.*"

"There are novels on the bottom shelf."

I bend to see a gleaming row of hardcovers. Popular fiction from every genre.

"Eclectic taste," I say. "I like it."

"I . . . haven't read any of them. I bought them last week as a goal for when I have a little time to myself. I'm not sure what sort of fiction I'll like, so I got the top sellers in each category."

I lift one of the mystery books. "I'm on hold for this one at the library. I'll start it now." I thump into his office seat. "I don't suppose I can put my feet on the desk."

He smiles. "You can put your feet wherever you like, Kennedy. I don't relish the idea of leaving you here, though. I'm still concerned about those last two paintings."

"There's an alarm system, and whoever has the paintings won't look for me here." I waggle my phone. "Not a single text since Mercy sent them her number. I seem to be off the hook." I meet his gaze. "Go. Then we'll have dinner together and get your car back."

He unmutes the phone and lifts it to his ear. "All right. What time should I be there?"

CHAPTER TWENTY-FOUR

I HAVE BEEN ALONE in Connolly's house for twenty minutes, and that represents the limit of how long I can pretend this book is more interesting than the chance to snoop through his house. Oh, the book is fine. Great, actually. But I *really* want to look around.

Before leaving, Connolly told me to make myself at home. Help myself to food. Take my book onto the back porch. Even take it upstairs if I'd rather read in bed, given that his office chair was obviously chosen for style over comfort. So I have permission to snoop. It still feels weird, which is why I've been sitting in this gorgeous and ergonomically correct office chair, pretending to read while the crick in my neck whimpers. Finally, I can't take it anymore. I leap up, slap the book down and start to explore.

I check out the kitchen first and snap pictures for Hope. A little aspirational dreamscape that she'll appreciate. The house might predate electricity, but the kitchen is state of the art. I poke around a little, but while I like cooking fine, this isn't my favorite room, and it's clearly not Connolly's, either.

I head for the backyard. He secured the alarm but gave me the code, and I use it before I open the door. I step out onto the back deck and need to snap more photos, this time for Ani, the gardener of our family. To be honest, our backyard is better landscaped, but it's also larger and not dominated by a pool. Still, Connolly's gardener does excellent work with the little bit they have. I hope he gets out here to enjoy it, but the empty back deck tells me that's a vain hope.

I head down to the pool. It's closed, as he said, so I have to use my imagination. It's a little lap pool that makes a perfect oasis of the tiny yard. An eight-foot fence provides privacy, and I can imagine coming out here for a prework dip, enjoying the quiet of the morning.

I envision climbing vines on the fence, ones that bloom bright flowers, turning a dawn swim into a tiny sliver of the tropics. I picture a night swim, those flowers giving off a heady scent, candles burning everywhere, a glass of wine and a book waiting on the deck. No, let's be honest, as much as I'd love relaxing post-swim with wine and a book, what I'm really picturing in that scenario is Connolly. I'm up on the porch with my book, and he's swimming laps, and I look up to see him climbing out of the pool in the moonlight.

Believe me, in that scenario, there is no handy towel in sight, and when Connolly joins me on the deck, he's dripping wet and looking so fine. But I'm picturing more than the erotic scenario. I see past it to the domestic one. What if it wasn't a date, wasn't me staying late while he went for a swim? What if it was just Tuesday? An ordinary evening, both of us enjoying a quiet summer night at home, Connolly going for a swim while I read, and then we'd share a glass of wine before deciding to make an early night of it, me leading him up to the bed we shared?

I want to stick to the first scenario. We're just hanging out together, and he's having a swim, and I'm admiring him, and sparks fly, and we actually follow through on them. An unexpected hookup on the deck. Or maybe a midnight skinny-dip followed by sex beside the pool. Stick with that. Hot and sexy and fun. The other picture tugs at a yearning far more dangerous than lust.

This was supposed to be Connolly's marital home. He may never have seen it that way, but now that idea has taken up residence in my brain. What would it be like—?

None of that. This is the house his parents expect him to share with the woman they choose. Not me. Never me.

Yet it isn't about the house, as lovely as it is. It's the image that sprang up, unbidden. The idea it dragged in its wake.

A shared home. A shared life.

Connolly says he wasn't like Rian. He didn't grow up picturing his future family here. Didn't picture a future family at all. He had goals, and married life wasn't one of them, not because he planned to avoid it but because it was a given for him. He would grow up and marry and have a family. That was settled. Inevitable. The rest were things he'd need to work for, and so he focused his attention there, on ambitions and achievements.

In my own way, I'm the same. There was no arranged marriage in my future, thank God, but it still seemed inevitable. People grew up. They married. They had children. A place like Unstable wasn't as fixed as some small towns on the narrow concept of what constituted a family. It could be two people without kids. A mom and dad with kids. A single mom. A single dad. Two moms. Two dads. Grandparents in place of parents. I'd even had a friend with a mom and two dads, and they didn't bother with the pretense of calling one dad "uncle." That is Unstable. So while I'd been pretty sure my family would be myself, one guy and our kids, I'd known other configurations were possible. Yet the core concept of "family" remained. I would grow up and find a life partner. Not a goal, just an accepted fact.

A few moments ago, I imagined a sexy scene with Connolly, taking our friendship "to the next level." Not friends with benefits, but something close to it. A light, fun, casual relationship. That defines every relationship I've had. Monogamous, yes, because that's my preference. Committed, too, because that's my preference. But monogamous and committed only in the sense that we'd be in an exclusive, long-term relationship, long term being "more than a month and less than a year."

I've never lived with a guy. Never talked marriage with a guy. I don't avoid it. My relationships have just never been that serious. We liked each other, cared about each other and so we stayed together until it was no longer convenient to do so.

Standing on this deck, I'm seeing something else. I'm *wanting* something else, and that's scary as hell when it involves a guy I'm not even dating.

Am I getting in too deep with Connolly? Falling too hard? On the express train to real heartbreak?

Yes. I need to face the truth. I want more. A lot more.

Part of me wants to get the hell out of this house. Text and tell him I have an emergency at the shop and I caught a ride share and hey, let's talk later, "later" being "possibly never."

That's ridiculous, of course. I'd never ghost Connolly like that. I'd never overreact like that. But I feel the urge, and it worries me.

I head back into the house. When I reach to disable the alarm, I see it's already flashing green.

Did I forget to reset it before I went outside? I remember thinking that I'd meant to, but I can't pull up the memory of doing it, so I guess I forgot.

I lock the door and set the alarm.

Consciously, I've accepted that I screwed up and didn't reset the alarm. Subconsciously, I know better, and when a floorboard creaks, I freeze, heart thudding, and I don't for one second think some random thief broke in while I was outside.

I listen, but everything is still and quiet.

Am I wrong? It's an old house, like ours in Unstable. Boards will creak without anyone stepping on them.

I take two steps into the kitchen. Silence. I glance around. There's a butcher's block filled with very expensive, very sharp knives. I slide over and ease one out.

A shadow moves into the doorway, and I swing the knife up.

"Uh-uh," a voice says. "You don't want to do that, Ms. Bennett."

The guy filling the doorway isn't tall, but he's beefy in a way that's at least part muscle. Maybe a few years older than me. Dressed in a suit. He's familiar, and I don't know why until he smiles, a smirk that slams into my memory.

"Travis," I say.

He grins. "You remember me. Good. I do like to make an impression."

I don't know Travis's last name. Or I've forgotten it. Doesn't matter. What does matter is that he's one of the Connolly family goons. Sorry, *security personnel*.

I'd met Travis last month when Marion Connolly sent him and two others to deliver a message to her son. Connolly had canceled brunch, so she'd tracked him electronically and sent three goons to see what he was up to, like any normal mother of a twenty-eight-year-old man.

Two guys stand behind Travis. Probably the same two as last month, but I wouldn't wager on it. My attention had been entirely on Travis because that's where Connolly's had been.

Connolly and Travis grew up together. Travis's mother works for the Connolly family—housekeeper, I think. Travis had been nasty even as a kid, and Connolly had been small and bookish. I suspect there'd been a lot of envy behind Travis's bullying. That might have excused some of it if he'd grown up to realize that he was unfairly taking out his rage on a *product* of the issue rather than the issue itself.

Travis never had that epiphany. He still hates Connolly. Worse, Travis was one of those kids who starts out bigger than everyone else, only to lose steam when he hits adolescence, while Connolly did the opposite.

While Connolly is no longer physically intimidated by Travis, the guy is still bigger than me, and with those two goons backing him up, I pause only a second before lowering the knife.

"What do you want, Travis?" I say.

"It's not what I want. It's what Ms. Connolly wants. You."

"My head on a plate?"

That makes one of the guys sputter what sounds like an honest laugh. I glance over. He's maybe thirty, Latinx, taller than Travis and broad shouldered.

Meanwhile, Travis still seems to be thinking of a comeback. He wants to say something snappy. Vaguely threatening. Preferably insulting and, given our last conversation, definitely suggestive. But it's too much for one comeback, and he's not that clever.

"What does Marion Connolly want with me, Travis?"

"A conversation."

"I'm being summoned to speak to the lady of the manor?" I glance down at my jeans and sneakers. "I don't think I'm dressed for an audience. Let me go home and get changed. Maybe seven? I could do seven."

Travis's mental wheels chug so hard I hear grinding. Then he smirks. "Oh, I bet you could do seven."

I fix him with a level look. He glances at his two sidekicks. Neither of them reacts.

"Do seven," he says. "Seven guys. Probably at once."

The Latinx guy lets out the softest sigh.

I frown. "Seven guys at once? Is there an orifice I'm missing? I mean, two hands plus three possible points of entry. I'm not getting where the other two go. Wait! Do they have really small dicks? Small enough to hold two in each hand? Seems a little awkward, but if you've done it, I'll accept the word of experience."

The other guy—a bulky blond—snickers.

"Let's drop the sex jokes," I say. "They get very old, very fast. Ms. Connolly wants to speak to me. I'm proposing a seven o'clock appointment. Just tell me where she wants to meet, and Aiden and I—"

"Aiden is not invited."

"Ah. It's that kind of talk." I take out my phone to text Connolly. I expect Travis to stop me. When he doesn't, I relax. Yes, they broke into Connolly's house—they obviously know his security code—but this isn't as threatening as it feels. I pop off a text to Connolly.

Me: Your mom wants to talk. I know you'd rather I don't, but Travis is here with two other security guys. Advice?

I hit Send. An exclamation mark immediately pops up warning me that the message can't be sent. My gaze rises to my connection, and a chill trickles down my spine.

"No service?" I say. "In downtown Boston? That's impossible."

"Must be magic," Travis says, his smirk back in place.

"It's a cell blocker," Latinx guy says. "Travis has it. Ms. Connolly insists. General precaution."

"Against anyone calling for help when her goons show up."

The blond guys says, "We're members of her security team, Ms. Bennett. The cell blocking is a security measure."

"Right. Like I said. Security against your target calling for help."

I want to say this is wrong. They'd only laugh at my naiveté.

Duh, obviously, it's wrong. What are you going to do? Call the cops? Even if you got through, our bosses are powerful enough to make this go away.

I want to say that Connolly is going to be furious, and how the hell does his mother think she'll get away with this? More B-movie victim dialogue. Marion Connolly knows exactly what she's doing and how she plans to get away with it. As for Connolly being angry, that's why Travis can't wipe off that smirk. He's loving every moment of this.

Inside, I'm shaking. Inside, I'm also outraged, and I need to stifle both reactions. Don't give Travis the satisfaction.

I resist the urge to address my questions to the Latinx guy. Blondie has drunk the Connolly Kool-Aid. Travis hates Connolly and would happily slap me around if he could. The Latinx guard has shown sparks of actual humanity, but that's like being cornered in an alley by three guys and focusing my pleas on the one who seems the least into it. Just because he isn't attacking me doesn't mean he's my ally.

So I address Travis, as the de facto leader of this goon squad. "How is this supposed to go?"

"It's supposed to go that you come and talk to the boss," he says, slowly, as if to a child.

I motion for more.

Latinx guy answers. "We'll need to confiscate your phone, for security purposes. We'll drive you to Ms. Connolly. She's at the house. You'll talk to her for maybe an hour. Then I'll drive you wherever you need to go. Or Mr. Connolly—Aiden—can pick you up at the house, if you're more comfortable with that." He pauses. "It really is just a talk, Ms. Bennett."

"Then why doesn't she call me herself? Ask me to meet with her?"

Because she doesn't want to give me the chance to tell Connolly. To my surprise, though, he says, "Some kind of painting arrived, and she freaked out. She knew you were in Boston with Aiden, so she sent us to pick you up."

Travis and Blondie's glares tell him to stop talking, but I barely hear him after the word "painting."

"Fine." I hand my phone to him, ignoring Travis reaching for it. "Take me to her."

CHAPTER TWENTY-FIVE

LATINX GUY HAS A NAME: Julian. Which is a relief because it's really awkward even mentally referring to him that way. As for Blondie, he might have a name, but I'm not going to bother using it.

I'm transported in the customary black luxury SUV. Blondie drives, Travis rides shotgun, and I'm in the back with Julian, who might be the best of the trio, but he's still taking me captive, and he doesn't exactly chat me up. It is a silent ride, leaving me to do nothing except fret and worry.

Marion Connolly received a painting today. There's zero chance that's random. Of all the people they could target . . .

I won't say this is the worst. I do not want my sisters or Jonathan subjected to something like *Eldest Daughter*. I could say Marion is the most inconvenient, but that sounds laughably underwhelming. It's true, though. There are a lot of names below Marion on the list of "people I'd least like to see tormented." But she tops another one: the list of people for whom a cursed painting will cause me the most trouble.

I try to question Julian. Has he seen the painting? How did it arrive? Is everyone okay? The last seems to puzzle him. That means the curse hasn't activated. Or so I hope. Still, while his expression conveys confusion, he's not answering my questions. He just keeps telling me that I need to speak to Ms. Connolly.

So I guess I'm speaking to Marion Connolly. Aiden's mother. The cause of all the bullshit in his life. I finally get to confront her. Under the worst possible circumstances.

I'm sorry, Connolly. In advance, I am sorry for anything that is about to happen, anything that is going to fly from my lips, however hard I try to hold my tongue.

I need to keep it together. Focus on the painting. Don't tell this woman what I think of her and her husband and their marriage contract and the hell they've inflicted on their own sons.

For Connolly's sake, I must keep that to myself and let him handle his family situation.

I only hope I can do that.

———

I HAVE NO MORE idea where Connolly's parents live than I knew where *he* lived. I vaguely recall him saying once he had to pop over to his parents' place while we were in Boston, and I figured he meant their house. He didn't, as I realize when the car leaves the city. They must have a place in Boston, a condo or something, but their house is outside, and when the car finally arrives at its destination, I truly understand just how rich the Connollys are.

When we first met, Connolly's surname—combined with the eau d'old money he wears like cologne—had pinged some sense of familiarity. Old Boston family. Old Boston money. It's certainly a common enough Irish name in a town rooted in Irish immigration. Yet I recognized it. When others did, too, I realized he came from more than just a well-off local family. Still, while I can joke about that moneyed cologne and his fashion sense and his luxury cars and his country club life, it still only said "one-percenter" to me. Even finding out he had some kind of exclusive credit card just nudged that up a bit. Huh, he really *does* come from money.

I realize now that while Connolly might seem a walking rich-boy stereotype, he'd actually been downplaying it. The car and the clothes were enough. He wasn't going to flash around his black credit card. He wasn't going to talk about his downtown house. He wasn't the kind of guy who wedged "Harvard MBA" into every conversation. He's been actively trying to cloak that part of his life, and as laughable as his efforts may have seemed, he did manage better than I could have imagined because this house tells me that I'm not dealing with multimillionaires. The Connollys are full-out billionaires.

This house is . . . Well, first, it's not a house. My window might be too tinted to see more than shapes, but we pause at a gate, and then we keep driving, past buildings and vast expanses of lawn. It's not even an estate. It's a freaking compound, and even with the windows up, I catch the distant crash of waves. They own an oceanfront estate less than an hour outside Boston.

As we drive into the compound, though, I'm not straining to see the main house. I'm sure it's magnificent. I don't care. What I'm thinking about is the secured gate we passed through and the high walls that surround the estate. The boundary between the Connolly family universe and the real world. I keep thinking of what Connolly said about being the one who escaped, only to learn otherwise.

Connolly had stepped through that gate. Strode through it into the world, his family at his back. Leaving behind his childhood home. Not taking up residence in one of the guesthouses, not staying in the compound with all the security money could buy. He left this behind for an independent life.

Yet the gate is an illusion. The walls are an illusion. That wall isn't a barrier restricting the Connollys' power to this little corner of the world. They have found every possible way to reach beyond it and tether their son to his family name. A Harvard education . . . with strings attached. An independent life . . . with strings attached. Prime real estate . . . with strings attached.

I can boggle at Connolly for not seeing the strings, but I haven't been putting myself in his place. His parents' control of his life was so absolute that he really *had* felt as if he'd escaped. He'd thrown off the heavy chains of family responsibility and oversight, and so can I blame him for missing the gossamer threads that still bound him to that world?

I blame his parents. They wove those feather-light bonds and let him think he'd escaped, only to reel him in as soon as he started exploring the possibility of more.

As soon as he met me.

No, that oversells my importance in Connolly's life. He'd clearly had the ambition and independence to break out of the most obvious bonds as fast as he could. Meeting me has made him realize he wants more, and to his parents that means I'm responsible. It isn't Connolly opening his mind to the new possibilities reflected in my life; it's me trying to drag him—kicking and screaming—into my mundane middle-class world.

Rather fittingly, as we near the house, it starts to rain. Or maybe it's mist from the ocean. That'd be fitting, too—stake your claim on some of the best property in Massachusetts and end up with nonstop drizzle.

Whatever the cause, the rain streaks the windows enough that I only get a blurred impression of a huge, sprawling house. The SUV pulls into a garage around back. Julian motions for me to wait and then comes around to open my door. I *don't* wait—I try the door myself—but it only opens from the outside.

It's Julian who escorts me into the house. I made the mistake of favoring him earlier, and he's leaped into the role of "good cop." I need to guard myself against that. Remember no one here is going to help me. I can only hope he was telling the truth when he said this was just a meeting.

Julian escorts me through a back door and down several halls, semi-dark with blank walls. Staff quarters. That's the impression I get, though I may have just seen too many old movies.

Julian stops and opens a door, and then we get the sort of corridor I expect, complete with paintings of long-dead Connollys. I don't look at them. I register their existence and the family resemblance and keep going.

"Ms. Connolly is in here," Julian murmurs at last, nodding toward a thick wooden door. "It's Mr. Connolly's office. He's at home, but I don't know whether he'll be joining you."

He opens the door before I can ask any questions. I wouldn't. I just want to get this over with.

"Ms. Bennett," he announces once the door is open.

One look inside that room, and I remember the first time I'd visited

Connolly's office. From his air of old-Boston money, I expected an old-Boston office, complete with massive wood desk, cut-glass scotch decanter and antique globe. Instead, I got Connolly's Nordic, minimalist style. Now I walk into exactly what I'd first imagined, down to the cut-glass bottles and antique globe. The only difference is that it's twice the size of our living room at home. It's half office and half library, the shelves filled with leather-bound editions that I'm sure no one is allowed to actually read.

My gaze goes first to the desk. It's empty. I turn to look into the library and see two wingback chairs. A woman sits in one.

I've seen Marion Connolly on a video screen. Swap gender and hair color, and she's the spitting image of her son, from her pale skin with its scattering of freckles to her green eyes. When I walk in, she doesn't rise until I'm halfway to her, my hand extended. Then she gets up, ignoring the hand, and says in a cool voice with a faint Irish accent, "This is not a social visit, Kennedy."

"Yeah, kinda figured that when your 'security team' kidnapped me."

"Did my men lay a hand on you?"

"They wouldn't let me refuse the invitation, and they confiscated my phone. Call it what you will, Marion. This was a kidnapping."

"You may call me Ms. Connolly."

"No, thanks. You want respect. Show some. Now apparently, you received one of the Costa paintings. I do apologize for that. Sincerely apologize. I've been dragged into something that doesn't actually concern me, and to get the attention of another curse weaver, I'm being targeted with those paintings."

"Is that your story, Kennedy?"

"Um, yes. What do you think? That I sent you a cursed painting? *Here, have a lovely random work of art, as a peace offering. Ha-ha, it's cursed.*"

"Your specialty is jinxes, is it not?" She wrinkles her nose in distaste. "The joker's jinx, I believe they call it? You're a prankster."

"You really *do* think I sent you that painting." I shake my head. "Not my style. Even if it was, you're hardly going to put that kitschy thing anyplace but the trash can."

"Do you even understand what you sent me, Kennedy?"

"I didn't send anything, but if you mean do I know what it is? Yes.

It's one of a quartet of infamous cursed paintings. Supposedly painted by a guy named Salvo Costa, who says they came to him in a dream. He claimed they were inhabited by the ghosts of four children killed in a fire. In truth, the paintings are older than that, and they're cursed."

"So you knew what you were sending. How dangerous it is."

"I didn't send *anything*. As you already know, Aiden bought one of the paintings—*Crying Girl*. It was an investment that went wrong, and now someone is sending the other three out into the world. I presume it came in my name? A gift from me? It's not. Ask your son."

"I know that my son was duped into buying one of these paintings. Duped by you."

I groan. "No, Marion. I was trying to buy it online. Aiden did before I knew what he was up to. You've clearly mistaken me for a gold-digger after your golden boy. I'm not. I'm a friend with no interest in"—I wave around the room—"any of this."

"Yet you let him buy that painting."

"I didn't—" I stop myself. There's no point in arguing. She's going to keep hammering away with her version of events. I just want to get this over and get out of here.

"Show me the painting," I say. "I'll uncurse it if I can or take it if I can't."

"We'll get to the painting. Right now, I want to talk about my son."

"Are we going to have an honest talk? Or one fueled by your delusions?"

Her mouth tightens.

"Look," I say. "You're concerned about Aiden." I'm not convinced of that, but I need to keep this as nonconfrontational as possible. I want to be able to honestly tell Connolly that I didn't make things worse with his mother.

I continue, "Aiden is a great catch. One of the city's premier bachelors. Handsome, brilliant, successful and, yes, rich. Out of my league. I fully acknowledge that, which is why we're just friends. I'm sure you've had us followed. I'm sure you've hacked into our messages. If you had any proof that we're more than friends, you'd show me."

"Aiden isn't the kind of fish one lands so quickly. You're reeling him in. There is no romantic relationship yet, but not for lack of trying on your part."

"You don't know the first thing about me, Marion."

She walks to the shelf and takes down a file folder. Well, I guess I walked into that one.

"You've done a background check," I say. "Great. Show me where it says I've ever chased a guy for his money. Ever let a guy buy me more than dinner."

She opens the folder slowly. I resist the urge to roll my eyes at the drama. There's nothing incriminating in my past. My boyfriends were all like me, middle-class guys scraping by. I have no criminal record. I have an excellent credit rating—my parents taught me to protect that—and my finances may not be in great shape, but they aren't in bad shape, either. I have a little bit in savings. Loans, yes, but I can cover them all, and my shop is turning a profit. For a millennial, I'm swimming along nicely.

She takes her time leafing through the portfolio.

"Tell me about the capital you used to open your new shop, Kennedy."

"An insurance claim. I opened the original shop with my inheritance, and after the break-in, the insurance reimbursed me for losses, which returned my original investment and allowed me to open the new shop. I actually saved a grand a month because of the lower overhead in Unstable. I invest that in an emergency fund."

"An insurance claim . . ." she says. "This insurance claim?"

She passes me a page. I see the header of my old insurer and nod. Then I see the subject line.

Claim Denied.

I frown. "No, this is wrong. They paid out."

"My son paid out. From his own pocket."

"What? No." I skim the page. It's addressed to Connolly, who'd been acting as intermediary. The insurance company denied my claim for "delayed incident reporting." When my shop was broken into, I hadn't been able to report it right away—my sisters had been kidnapped, which was my priority. Connolly had handled that hiccup.

Not according to this.

I shake my head. "They paid."

"Your bank records show a direct deposit. That deposit came from my son's account."

My stomach thuds.

What did you do, Aiden? Tell me this is a mistake.

I straighten and say, my tone as cool as hers, "As far as I know, I received an insurance payout. I have the documentation to support that. If anything else happened, I defy you to find proof that I knew it."

The door opens. For a second, glancing over, I think it's Connolly, and my heart leaps. The man who walks in has his bearing, his stride, his height and build and red-gold hair. That's where the resemblance ends. The man glances over with a face that reminds me of Rian's, aged thirty years and skewed.

Liam Connolly.

I don't know much about Connolly's father. Most of what Connolly says is either about his mother alone or his parents together. That could give the impression of a man who stands in his wife's shadow, but the little I did hear suggested it was more a case of Liam Connolly letting his wife handle the domestic side of the household so he didn't need to bother with it. Connolly's occasional comments had squashed any hope that he had a supportive and loving father. More like a largely absentee one, happy to heap responsibility on his wife, expecting her to run the home and her share of the business.

When Liam enters, he gives me a once-over, and there's just enough objectification in it for me to tense. He's not judging my clothing or my manners or my upbringing. He's checking my appearance, as if that will surely explain his son's interest. A flicker of disappointment tells me it doesn't.

He nods to me and continues on to his desk. Marion Connolly waits, clearly expecting he's grabbing something before joining us. But he sits down and pops open a laptop and sets to work.

This is a domestic matter. None of his concern, though we're welcome to use his office because he's an understanding guy.

Yeah, maybe I'm misinterpreting the situation, but I can't help but kinda hate Liam Connolly even more than I do his wife.

A look passes over Marion's face. That moment where she expects him to join her—to help her—and then has to reorient herself when he doesn't . . . again.

She clears her throat and reaches into her folder to pass me another paper.

"Please explain this, Kennedy."

It's a letter from Connolly. Written on his company stationery and signed with a flourish. Sent to the family lawyer, it directs them to begin a monthly ten-thousand-dollar withdrawal from the "active" portion of his trust fund, to be sent to an account in the name of Kennedy Bennett.

I read it, and I laugh.

"You find something amusing?" Marion says.

"I'd joke that I'd love to know where the money's going, 'cause I'm not seeing it. But really, I'm laughing that you think I'd believe such an obviously fake letter."

Her expression doesn't change, and I peer at her. "You *did* write that, right? Please tell me your investigator didn't dig it up and you actually believe that Aiden would be stupid enough to ask his *family* lawyer to wire me monthly payments from his *family* trust fund."

"My son can be naive in matters of financial security."

I snort. "You mean he can be naive when it comes to believing he has any financial privacy. Trusting when you tell him that his trust fund is his to do with as he likes. He knows better, and he would never do something this blatant."

"So you're accusing me of writing that?"

"Maybe someone else did and planted it. I have no idea. I can guarantee, though, that I'm not getting ten grand a month from Aiden, and no paper trail will prove otherwise. The only thing he buys me is food—dinner and whatnot—and I pay for his as often as I can." I pause. "Oh, wait. He did give me a gift earlier today. A flat of Magic 8 Balls, which probably set him back a couple hundred bucks."

"Magic 8 Balls?"

"It was a joke."

"My son does not make jokes, Ms. Bennett."

I shrug. "Apparently, he does now. I don't know anything about that insurance claim." My gut twists thinking about it, but I plow forward. "And I don't know anything about payments from his trust fund. What I do know is that you've been the victim of a nasty prank aimed at me, through the Costa painting, and I apologize."

"Nasty prank? Is that what you call it?"

"Not really. It's vicious and cruel, and I hope no one was hurt."

"Someone was hurt. One of my staff."

My gut twists again. "I *am* sorry. I can absolutely guarantee, though, that no matter how it came into your possession, I had nothing to do with it."

"Are you certain about that?"

I pause again. "No, I misspoke. Like I said, it's about me. Sending it to you was about making things uncomfortable for me. I meant that I didn't deliver it. I don't know which painting it is or what it does. I've never seen it. I will, however, handle it."

Marion walks to a shelf and picks up an iPad. She comes back to me and hits the screen. It's security camera footage showing a figure in a hoodie at the delivery door. The figure leans the painting against the side service gate and hits a bell. Then they walk away.

I pause and enlarge the picture. The movements and size suggest a woman, though the hoodie and shapeless sweatpants make it hard to say that for certain. She's about my size, and while her hood is pulled up, a long strand of dark hair escapes.

"It's someone who looks vaguely like me," I say. "Dressed in over-sized sweats. Keeps her face averted from the cameras but lets that one matching strand of hair slip out." I tap the time. "When this was delivered, I was with Aiden, in Boston, with a third party, tracking down another painting."

"What *third party*?"

"I'm not at liberty to say. The important part is that I was with Aiden. He'll vouch for me." I meet her gaze. "I presume that will be enough. He is your son, after all."

"Enough of this, Marion," says a voice behind me.

I'd forgotten Liam was there. I turn to see him rising from his desk.

"Either the girl is telling the truth or she's not going to," he says. "She's right about one thing, though. We can speak to Aiden. He wouldn't lie to cover for her when that painting injured one of the staff."

"Are they all right?" I say.

He waves aside my concern. "Just a scratch. More of a shock than anything. She's been given the rest of the week off." He walks from behind the desk. "Let's get this over with. The painting is downstairs. You can take it or uncurse it or whatever you need to do. I just want it gone."

"I am sorry—"

"Yes, you've said that. I don't really care whether you're sorry or not, Ms. Bennett. I just want you to take your cursed painting and leave."

I glance at Marion. Her jaw sets, and in that moment, she looks like her son when he doesn't want to do something but knows he should. After a moment, she gives a curt nod.

"Fine," she says. "We're done here."

"Then I'll escort Ms. Bennett to the painting, and Julian can drive her back to Aiden's."

I hate to leave this unresolved, but the woman wants a reason to hate me, and this gives her one. I'm exactly what she expected. A gold-digging curse weaver who lacks the intelligence to threaten her more subtly than this.

I glance at Marion one last time and then follow Liam from the room.

CHAPTER TWENTY-SIX

LIAM CONNOLLY HAS CORRECTLY DEDUCED that I'm no threat to his sphere of interest: the business empire. That doesn't make him an ally, by any means, but it does mean that this may be where Connolly can focus his own efforts. Use his father's disinterest in me to sweep his mother's target from my back.

Yes, I hate the idea of suggesting Connolly pit his parents against each other, but they've been doing it to their sons for years, so I feel only the most perfunctory stab of remorse at such a Machiavellian plan.

Liam said the painting was in the basement. True, but it's not in the same building as the house. Also, it's raining, which makes this a very inconvenient trip across the property. We enter another building. A guesthouse? I don't know. Like I said, it's raining, and also we go through the back door.

"Smart getting it out of the main house," I say as we descend steep stairs. They're my first words since we left Marion, and Liam only says, "Yes."

"I probably can't uncurse it on-site," I say. "I'll need to transport it, and for that I require a shielding blanket."

"Which would be . . . ?" he asks as he opens a door.

"Like an X-ray blanket. Lead lined."

He takes out his phone and taps a message to someone. "If we don't have such a thing on the premises, I will have one brought immediately. By the time you've finished examining the piece, it should be here."

Yes, there's a definite advantage to this guy wanting me out of his house pronto.

"As soon as it arrives, I'll take the painting," I say. "Even if I think I could uncurse it without my kit."

He leads me down a hall, and I let my thoughts drift. I'm relieved I didn't call Marion out on Connolly's marriage contract. I wasn't completely nonconfrontational, but I was as close as I could manage without letting her walk all over me, and Connolly would never expect that. I can legitimately tell him the entirety of the conversation without smoothing over my behavior.

The entirety of the conversation . . . That insurance letter . . .

Connolly, please tell me you didn't slip me the payout after my claim was denied.

If he did, while his heart would have been in the right place, I can't accept the money, and if I don't accept the money, I don't have a shop, which means I've lost my inheritance and—

I struggle for breath and force myself to focus on the positive: I met Marion Connolly and did nothing to make things worse for Connolly or myself. Except I also couldn't do anything to make them better or—

Hey, let's focus on the painting! A cursed painting behind door number two! It hurt a staff member, but not seriously. This would be one of the boys. *Vengeful Boy* or the unnamed older brother. It would help if I knew what either curse did beyond making the subject seem to step out of the painting.

I also need to speak to my sisters. I'd be freaking out a lot more about that if they didn't know about the *Crying Girl* painting incident last night. If whoever's behind this sends them the fourth painting, they'll know what to do about it. So will Jonathan. Still, I want to speak to them.

With all these thoughts zipping through my head, it takes a while for me to realize where I am. In the basement of an empty building. Alone with Connolly's father. Walking down a creepy subterranean corridor.

I slow, and I'm about to say something when he opens a door. I hesitate, but it's a little late for me to decide I'm uncomfortable with this. I should have asked for a guard escort. Or agreed to have Marion accompany us. Also, it's not as if Liam led me into the basement for no reason. It's a cursed painting. They put it here to keep it as far away as possible.

Liam disappears into the room. I approach the open doorway with care. My purse is back at Connolly's house. My phone is with the security team. It's just me, alone and defenseless.

I move into the doorway and see an empty room. "Where's the painting?"

Liam points at a closed door.

When I arch my brows, he sighs. "It's a cursed painting. I'm not walking into the room with it, Ms. Bennett. That would be your job."

Logical, but I still take a step back. "You know what, I don't see much point in me checking out the painting. Just get me a blanket, and I'll take it out."

He shrugs and taps his phone as he joins me in the hall. Then he grabs me by the shoulder and shoves me into the room. I wheel, fists rising. Something hits me. Not a blow but a smack of existential dread, sending me reeling back, gasping, my heart hammering.

My feet tangle, and I land flat on my ass, pain jolting up my tailbone. When I try to scramble up, my feet twist, and I fall, my knees cracking against the concrete.

"Bad luck," I whisper.

"I suppose, being around Aiden, you are far more accustomed to boosts of good. My son may see himself as tough and ruthless, but there's a little too much of his mother in him. A moral compass that keeps him from achieving his full potential. Like his mother, he prefers to use good luck, and only in small doses. Too much good aimed at himself —or bad aimed at his rivals—is cheating. His mother's influence again."

I stay where I am, knowing if I rise, I'll only fall again. "There's no painting, is there?"

"Of course there is. Marion wouldn't have brought you here otherwise. It's past that door, which is where you'll be, too, if you prefer not to help me resolve this issue with my son."

Liam takes out his phone. "I have your banking information, Ms. Bennett. I propose wiring you five hundred thousand dollars to tell my son you don't wish to see him again."

"I'm *not* seeing your son. Not like that."

"I know." He sighs. "Again, a touch too much of his mother's honor. He likes you, which means he won't do the convenient thing and get it out of his system with a week in Paris. But he *does* like you, which is *very* inconvenient." He lifts his phone. "Half a million dollars."

"I'm not a gold-digger."

"If you were, you'd be a very poor one, indeed. 'Gold-digger' is my wife's theory because she needs to cast you as the villain. Fair play and all that. I don't actually give a damn what you are, Ms. Bennett. I only care about what you are not: a suitable wife for my heir."

My *heir*. Not *my son*.

He continues, "I have a dynasty to protect. My father passed it on to me, and his father to him. I will pass it on to Aiden. I'd like to see him develop more cutthroat instincts, and I believe he will."

"With the right wife."

He considers and then shakes his head. "No, the wife herself doesn't matter. What matters is that he can tick off that particular checkbox and focus on his ambitions. A wife to provide sons, run his household and help his business interests."

"A wife who can do it all. Just what every woman wants."

"Some women do. Just look at Marion. Yes, Connollys expect a lot from their wives, but there's one thing we don't expect: romantic sentimentality. That's what I wish to protect Aiden from. Falling for some girl who'll distract him from his work. Who'll have him gallivanting into the countryside chasing antique washbasins."

A roll of his blue eyes. "Aiden is already distracted, and he isn't even sleeping with you yet. Do you know what he did last week? Set up a college scholarship for his cleaning lady's son. And reached out to some group inquiring about internships for low-income students."

Both these come as news to me. Of course, they would. He'd do it quietly. Because it's the right thing to do. Not to impress me. Which impresses me all the more. He's trying to be a better man . . . and it's the last thing his father wants.

"Take the money, Ms. Bennett."

"Or else?"

He sighs. "I'm not going to threaten you. I am strongly suggesting that you take the money and allow Aiden to continue in the life he's always wanted. If you care about him, you'll want that, too."

"He's twenty-eight years old. I think he can decide what he wants."

"No, actually, he can't. He isn't his brother. He hasn't been in the world, meeting girls like you. He has done what we've asked of him, and if there's a downside, it is that he's led a sheltered life. You are a bright and shiny novelty. Nothing more. I just need him to realize that before he veers too far from the plan."

"Maybe you should let him veer from the plan. Remap it. You want him to marry a luck worker? Give him a couple more years. He's still young. Let him see the wider world first."

"An Amish rumspringa?"

"Why not? It works for them. Let Aiden see what's out there and come back."

He shakes his head as if I'm a very amusing child. "Take the money, Ms. Bennett. Otherwise, there will come a day when you will look back on this moment and wish you'd made another choice. That isn't a threat. I won't 'make you regret it' or anything so banal. You will regret it because you will see that I offered an opportunity to secure your future. You don't have one with my son. You realize that, I hope."

"I'm not trying to snag a wealthy husband. We've already established that."

"Remove money from the equation. I have the feeling that's an obstacle, and you'd prefer him without it and all it represents. You can't have that—I think you realize that. There is no separating him from that part of his life. But what you want is *him*. The man beneath the millions. Very sweet and romantic and also very naive. He will have his fling. He will move on, as he always does."

"Then why worry about it?"

"Because this isn't his usual fling, with someone of his own class to decorate his arm at a charity dinner and have a little fun with afterward. I have no doubt of the same end result, but in the meantime, he is distracted in a way he never is, and it couldn't come at a worse possible time."

"Because of the marriage contract. You want to see him paired off with Theodora O'Toole."

"Theodora would be an excellent choice."

"What if Aiden isn't *her* choice? What if *she* doesn't want this?"

His lips twitch. "Has she told you that? Clever girl, our Theodora. But you're drawing this out, and I have things to do." He lifts the phone. "May I wire you the money?"

"No."

"You *will* regret it one day. You'll look back and realize you traded financial security for a fleeting affair that ended in heartbreak."

"I don't care."

"All right then." He circles wide around me, as if to be sure I don't think he's coming at me. He opens the door and waves inside. The light is on. Across the room is a painting. It's a teenager holding a saxophone.

Vengeful Boy? He looks calm and thoughtful.

"Your painting," Liam says with a wave.

I walk closer for a better look. Then I say, "What did it do?"

He shrugs. "Marion knows. I didn't bother with the details."

He moves aside to let me through. I step into the doorway and stop. Then I back up. "I'd like the shielding—"

He shoves me. One hand between my shoulder-blades, shoving me into the room. I stagger, the bad luck still in effect. When I spin, he slams the door shut.

"Hey!" I pound on it.

"I wouldn't bother with that," he calls from the other side. "No one will hear you. I'm going to give you some time to reconsider my offer."

His voice grows softer as he walks through the adjoining room. The other door shuts behind him, and I am alone with the cursed painting.

CHAPTER TWENTY-SEVEN

I EYE the painting from across the room. Then I glance at the door.

The obvious answer is to forget the damn painting and check the door. Except I'm in the room with the painting, and I have no idea what it can do.

I sidestep toward the door, my gaze on the painting. I turn the doorknob. It doesn't budge. Did I expect it to be unlocked? Honestly, that strikes me as exactly the sort of thing Liam Connolly would do.

Lock Ms. Bennett in the basement? Of course not. The door was open. She wanted time with the painting to try uncursing it. She could have left whenever she wished.

It's locked. I heave on it, even knowing the chance of me being able to break it is lower than the chance it was left unlocked. Still, this is just a basement room. Not a prison cell. Not a subterranean dungeon. It could be a flimsy door I can eventually break. It is not. It's solid wood with a brass handle, and the hinges are on the other side, so I can't remove those.

I shout for help. Yes, he said not to bother, but also, yes, that's another thing I'd expect from him—warn me it won't work while there's actually someone right upstairs who could hear me. So I shout, but no one comes.

I manage all that without activating the painting. Maybe I'm out of range. Two options then. Stay right here until Liam returns or uncurse the painting.

I'm trying very hard not to freak out at being locked in the basement. When Liam Connolly returns, I'll tell him yes, I'll take his damn money. He'll wire it. Probably make me sign something promising to never see his son again. I'll walk away and figure out how to handle the situation from there, which ultimately involves returning the cash and reneging on the deal.

Liam wants to lock me into a contract, as he did to his son. The difference is that Connolly spent the money—on tuition and college life—before realizing the full nature of his obligation. If I don't touch the money, I can repay the cash and get out of the contract.

The only question will be how I handle it with Connolly. If I tell him what his father did, it'll drive a wedge between them. I'm all for Connolly getting some distance from his supervillain parents, but he needs to do that for himself, on his terms.

What if I *don't* mention the deal and he finds out? This isn't exactly the sort of thing I can brush off, pretend I didn't think he needed to know his dad offered me a half-million dollars and kidnapped me when I refused.

What if I *do* tell him, and it doesn't trigger any kind of explosion? If Connolly just sighs and says he's very sorry?

I can't worry about that. Get out first and then decide what to do.

As for the painting, I'm torn. I feel cowardly sitting outside of its activation range, but is there any point in getting closer and taking that risk?

Ani would tell me to sit my ass on this floor and wait. Jonathan would agree. Connolly, I think, would hesitate, feeling the pull of curiosity, but would ultimately do the practical thing and wait.

I should wait.

I *will* wait.

Maybe if I just got a little closer . . .

Nope. Not after the *Eldest Daughter* encounter. I might want to uncurse that painting; I do not want hours of being tormented by my deepest fears.

And yet, even with the *Daughter*, I only had to get out of her way to stop the visions. I know where the boundary is. Maybe I could just . . .

Stop that.

I look at the painting. From here, the boy seems like a teen from the seventies. Saxophone in hand. Longish hair. Solemn dark eyes. Black turtleneck sweater. A face that fifteen-year-old me would have found swooningly cute.

From what I know, though, this is not the original painting. It's actually a teen from the Renaissance era. I squint, trying to see it. Imagine not a turtleneck but a high collared shirt. Not a saxophone but a trumpet or other period-appropriate instrument.

What happened to you?

This boy's mother might have been monstrous, but that doesn't mean he was. His little sister grieved for him. These children didn't deserve their fate. Athene isn't to blame for it, though. Their mother is. She made choices that led to the deaths of her children, including this boy.

I itch to see the painting up close. We know these are copies. Is there something that would help me date it? Tell whether copies were made in the seventies, when the originals were altered? Created later, after the originals were destroyed? Or created recently, to launch this assault against Mercy?

We've lost the *Crying Girl* painting. Mercy has taken *Eldest Daughter* and cut us out of the loop. I'd like the chance to examine this one.

Get closer. Activate it. Decide then whether it's mild enough—like *Crying Girl*—that I can barrel through and endure the curse while I undo it. I might not have my Magic 8 Ball here, but I'm quite happy to relocate the curse onto the damn doorknob if I need to.

I start forward, braced for visions of any kind. Are my thoughts drifting anyplace unpleasant? Is reality shifting in any way? Do I catch the shimmer of a ghostly vision before me? No, no and no.

I make it all the way to the painting. Then I stand there and wait. Still nothing.

Okay then.

The painting is propped on the floor. I kneel to get a better look. Up close, I can see the brushstrokes. I can also make out minute scratches in the paint. That would seem to suggest it's not brand-new, but I keep investigating. Touch the paint. Scrape lightly. My nail doesn't seem to do anything.

I run my hands over the frame. This is where my expertise kicks in. I know a few things about checking for fake-antique artwork. I know even more about furniture like frames. This one looks antique, but it's cheap. Old, rather than valuable. Maybe 1940s.

I touch the paint again. The antique-shop owner in me wants to be careful, but even without the curse, I wouldn't resell this painting. Too many bad memories for Athene, whether it's the original or not. I want it destroyed. So a little damage to answer my questions is reasonable.

I can hear the curse whispering, and I momentarily open myself to it, but that whisper is too soft, and I can't catch it. I block the sound and focus on the painting.

I'm running my index finger over the saxophone when pain slices through my finger. I yank back. Blood wells up on a small paper cut. I squint at the painting, but I see nothing there that would have cut it.

Then I remember what Marion said, that one of her staff had been injured by the painting. I stare down at my finger. Okay. Well, as curses go, this would be a mild one. Nasty but mild.

I clean off my finger and continue examining the painting. There's a spot on the boy's neck that seems lighter. A ragged edge where the top of his turtleneck alternates between black and dark gray. I rub my nail along the lighter part. The paint cracks. I peel off a pinky-nail sized piece to see lighter paint below—paint that matches the background color. It leaves a divot at the top of the boy's turtleneck. I find the edge of the removed piece and carefully scrape.

When my fingernail scrapes through to the canvas, I try the other angle and manage to peel off another small piece. I keep working at it, sometimes going too deep and sometimes managing to separate the two layers of paint. It takes a good ten minutes to clear just over an inch, but when I do, I see an older layer, one that shows the boy wearing a shirt with a high lace collar. The lace is scalloped, and when someone repainted it as a turtleneck, they evened out the neckline.

I ease back on my heels, still crouched. So this seems to be a duplicate of the original, rather than a later copy. A second portrait of a Renaissance teenager turned into a "modern" one in the seventies.

I reach for the curse again, clearing my mind until I catch the whisper of Latin. Yet, I can't quite catch the words or the music.

My gaze drops to the saxophone. Pretty sure that's not a period-appropriate instrument. Yep, when I get closer, I can see the flaws in the overpainting, just like with the collar. The artist in the seventies—or whenever it was "touched up"—used an object of a similar size and shape from the original. A long and slender object that the boy's fingers rest atop.

The perspective of the painting means that the bottom of the saxophone is missing—there's just part of the curved bell coming up from the base, and the more I look at it, the more the proportions seem wrong.

I run my finger up the keys of the sax—

Ouch!

I yank my hand back to see a second paper cut. Really? I glower at the painting. All right, so it seems that I cut myself if I touch the saxophone. The rest is fine.

I bend to squint at the sax. Whatever is under it is significantly thinner. Also, the color of the sax is unusual, more metal-gray than bronze.

Metal gray. Sharp. Thinner than a sax. Sharp.

Oh! I know what it is. He's holding—

The boy leaps from the painting. All I see at first is a blur of motion that has me tumbling back onto my ass. Then he's right in front of me. A teenage boy wielding a sword.

He slashes. Pain slams down my arm, and hot blood rushes up.

What the hell?

I scramble backward, crablike, but he keeps coming, his face cold and determined.

Vengeful Boy.

This is what I saw in his face. Not fury. Icy resolve.

He swings again. This time I manage to dodge, only the tip piercing my leg, pain still making me gasp. He lunges at me, and I scramble to my feet and run to the door.

It was safe there.

It is no longer safe there.

I have my back to the door, and he's right there. Before I can run, he swings the sword, and it hits me in the neck, and in that moment, I think I am dead. I feel the blade go in. Feel it cut right through me and see it swing out the other side.

I don't die. It takes a second to realize that. The absolute horror of that moment steals both breath and thought, and when I realize I'm still alive, there's a second, even more horrifying moment of thinking I've been decapitated and I'm still conscious.

Then I see him lift the sword again, and I snap out of it and run. I run all the way to the other side of the room and plaster myself against the wall as I shout for help. The boy runs at me, sword raised, and I scream that I'm not his enemy; I didn't hurt him or his family. I know it doesn't matter. This isn't a ghost. It's a curse-triggered hallucination. I don't care. I'm terrified and alone, and there is blood dripping from my arm and hip and neck, and this boy is so angry, rightfully angry.

He's rushing at me, and I'm backed into the corner, as far as I can get from his painting. He's running at me, his face that impenetrable mask of cold, and I'm bracing for the blow, telling myself it will hurt but nothing more. He pulls back the sword . . . and disappears.

I don't move. I barely breathe. I brace myself for him to return. Nothing.

I take two steps forward, and he lunges from his painting again. I force myself to close my eyes. If I can't see him, does that break the spell?

The blade rams into my chest. I feel the pain of it and the cold of the metal, and I stagger back, gasping. He yanks the sword from my heart and lifts it to swing again, and I turn and run for the corner. When I'm there, I twist and see him lunge at me, only to vanish a couple of feet away.

I am outside the range of the curse. I thought I was when I stood in the doorway. I wasn't. I just hadn't activated it.

I slide to the floor and breathe. It's a while before I stop shaking. I touch my wounds. They're all shallow cuts, barely scrapes. They sting like paper cuts, and blood wells along each, but I'm okay. As long as I stay right here, I'm okay.

I force myself to look across the room at the painting. I should have tried harder to access the curse. If I had, I'd have been warned. I might even have been able to uncurse it. I was able to unweave the one on the little girl's portrait without my tool kit. This one is similar, with the added effect of the sword. Like Marion said, terrifying but not deadly—

not unless your heart stops in terror, as mine almost did. Worse than the little girl, but not as bad as her older sister.

The saxophone hides what would have been a sword in the original painting. Did I trigger it when I touched the sax? No. I did that earlier, and nothing happened. I don't think there is a trigger per se. It just randomly activates on someone in range.

I take a deep breath and lift one foot to start forward, but I can't bring myself to follow through. I know it's just an illusion. Well, yes, there are also the cuts, which hurt, but they're not fatal, right?

None of that matters. *Vengeful Boy* is as terrifying as *Eldest Daughter*. I keep flashing back to seeing that sword coming at my neck, feeling it cutting into my neck, thinking it had actually—

My breath quickens until I'm gasping for air. I look at the painting, and I want to march over there and uncurse it. I want to be strong enough to do that. Honestly, though, maybe I'm making excuses, but I'm not sure toughing this out would be strength as much as pride and stubbornness. I'm safe here, in this corner, and Liam will come down soon. I'll take his damn money to get out. I just have to wait a bit.

CHAPTER TWENTY-EIGHT

FOUR HOURS.

I have been in this corner for four hours. My legs ache, and I'm hungry, and it's after ten at night, and I haven't seen Liam. Haven't heard anyone. Twice I tried venturing from my corner, only to be driven back by the boy with his sword. Once I gritted my teeth and ran to the painting, quickly realizing just how foolish that was. It takes time to hear a curse, much less unweave it, and that work requires my full focus. I'd barely caught the first strands of the curse's music before I ran back to my corner, bleeding from three fresh cuts.

I'd crept to the door again and tried getting it open. I couldn't. I already knew that. I just didn't know what else to try. I'm trapped in a box with that door and a painting. I'd battered at the door until the curse triggered anew and the boy stabbed me in the back.

Are my sisters wondering what happened to me? I missed dinner, but they knew I was with Connolly, and I'd said not to expect me. If I don't show up, they'll think I'm spending the night with him, which neither will question, being too pleased that we finally moved past friendship.

What about Connolly himself? There's no way he went home, found an empty house, shrugged and settled in to binge-watch TV for the evening. His father will know this, which means he'll have taken steps to ensure Connolly doesn't wonder where I am.

The Connollys have my phone. It's locked, but I'm sure Liam Connolly has people who can hack it enough to send a text to Connolly.

Took a ride share home. Sorry! There's a lot going on, and I need a little quiet time. Talk tomorrow!

Connolly would get that message and think I'd been uncomfortable in his "marital home" and needed time alone to work it through. He'd grant me that time. Pop off a quick text saying he understood, and when he didn't get a reply, he wouldn't question it. He'd give me my space.

No one knows I'm missing. No one will know until tomorrow, and even then, is it possible for Liam to delay the inevitable? Use my phone to tell Connolly I need more time. To tell my sisters I'm taking a day off with Connolly and can they put up a note in the shop, thanks! Eventually, they'll all realize something is wrong, but Liam could buy himself a good twenty-four hours before anyone knows I'm missing.

Twenty-four hours. Curled up in a corner. Hungry, thirsty and scared. Cut and bleeding.

I keep telling myself Marion and Liam Connolly aren't monsters. They can't be if they raised sons like Connolly and Rian.

I remember how Liam lamented the traits Connolly inherited from his mother. A sense of fairness. More, too. I hesitate to say softness because there is none of that in Marion Connolly. But have I misjudged the situation, just a little?

Liam said Marion needs a reason to hate me. A reason to keep Connolly away from me, too? Connolly wants to be with me, at least as a friend, and so she casts me in the role of gold-digger to justify her interference. But is that enough? She's not a stupid woman. There's a limit to how hard she can sell herself that story in the absence of proof.

If Connolly really did pay for my insurance claim, that would seem to be proof. Still, it's a little wobbly, especially if he did it under the radar, making me think my insurance paid out. That letter to the lawyer, though, would cinch it. That would be just the evidence she needed to convict me.

The letter is fake. I know that. Someone gave it to Marion, and it annihilated any doubt that I was after her son's money and could therefore be swept aside, by force if necessary.

Liam wrote that letter. I'm sure of it. Oh, he'd sigh at the need for such subterfuge, but he'd still do it. Write the letter. Have the investigator find it and deliver it to Marion. There, see? Kennedy Bennett is evil, and you must stop her, Marion, before she destroys your son.

I'm not evil. Neither, I think, is Marion Connolly. Oh, I do not want to cross her, in any way, but I don't think she's the gorgon she's been painted as. That'd be Liam Connolly. The bastard who sics his wife on me as if she's the family guard dog while he lounges at his desk, and then, once she's run out of steam, he locks me in the basement with a cursed painting.

I don't care if you're not a gold-digger, Kennedy Bennett. I just don't want you with my son.

No, it isn't about his son. He doesn't want me throwing a wrench in the gears of his so-called dynasty.

I'm fuming over that, letting the heat of my anger burn through my fear, when there's a soft click across the room. I leap to my feet as the door opens.

"I'll take your damn—" I begin. Then I stop as Julian walks into the room.

"If Mr. Connolly sent you—"

Before I can finish, the boy bursts from his painting and charges, sword raised. Julian flinches, only to steel himself, as if knowing it's an illusion.

The boy swings his sword, the blade slicing through Julian's side. The guard hisses, eyes widening in shock. He staggers back. I run to him, and yet, while that altruistic impulse blazes, it does not fail to notice—a heartbeat later—that Julian has staggered backward through the open door.

Julian is on the floor, eyes wide as he clutches his bleeding side. I vault over him and race down the hall.

"No!" he shouts. "Wait!"

I stop and turn back to see what he wants. Ha! No. I keep going, picking up speed as I bear down. Behind me, he scrambles to his feet, shoes squeaking on the concrete floor. Then the thump of his running feet. I reach the door and twist the knob. I'm throwing it open when he grabs me.

I kick and punch as he tells me I don't want to do that, don't want to go out there; he's here to rescue me.

Oh, well, in that case . . .

I fight harder. I see the blood on his shirt, from that paper-thin cut, and I slam my fist into it. He yowls and doubles over, releasing my arm, but when I race up the stairs, he catches my foot, and I almost fall flat on my face.

"Just listen to me," he says. "Do you want to get out of here or not?"

"What the hell does it look like I'm doing?" I say as I kick.

"Escaping into a heavily guarded estate surrounded by a ten-foot fence with security cameras. A mile from the nearest neighbor. In a thunderstorm."

As if on cue, thunder crashes.

"You aren't getting away without help, Kennedy. My help."

I want to fight. Tell him to go to hell. I don't trust him. He brought me here. Into this.

Yet I see the truth in his words. I saw the high gates and guards and the rainstorm.

"You can't escape without my help," he says again.

"You. The guy who brought me here knowing what they had planned."

"No, the guy who brought you here knowing what Ms. Connolly had planned. To confront you with proof you were taking advantage of her son and sent her a cursed painting."

"I never—"

He lifts his hands. "I didn't say I believed it. I had no opinion either way. Yes, I had to force you to come with us, which sucks, but I wasn't lying when I said it was just supposed to be a talk. I trusted her. None of us knew what he had planned."

His gaze rakes over me. "Shit, you're *really* hurt. I knew he was a bastard, but this is next level. Ms. Connolly had nothing to do with it. I can promise that."

"Can you?"

"I can, because right now, she's in the house, telling Aiden she has no idea where you are, that yes, you came for a talk, but Davey drove you back to Aiden's house hours ago."

"Aiden is here?"

He snorts, relaxing a little. "That got your attention, huh? Yes, he's been here for a couple of hours, arguing with his mom, who genuinely has no clue what he's talking about. And his dad has gone golfing."

"Golf—golfing?" I sputter.

"Well, I figure he's at the country club bar. Or with one of his mistresses. He has a few."

He says that casually, as if it's to be expected, and I guess it is for a guy with Liam Connolly's wealth and moral compass, but I feel a stab of sympathy I'm sure Marion wouldn't appreciate.

I keep thinking I couldn't hate Liam more, but here he strikes a new low, leaving his wife to face their son—who's furious about something she knows nothing about—while he saunters off for an evening with a girlfriend.

"Nice boss," I mutter. "You have excellent taste in employers."

"Oh, Liam Connolly isn't my employer. I work for . . . another party. And after this, I'm sure I'll be reassigned, which is a relief. This is a nest of vipers. Well, one viper, one pit bull and their two messed-up kids."

He shakes his head. "You can't pick your family, huh? Anyway, I'm here to help you, not because I'm a great guy, but because someone else might never talk to me again if they found out I stood by after what Liam did to you. That person's opinion matters more to me than any job. I'd just rather not get shot running out after you."

"There are armed guards?" I'm sure I sound naive, but I hadn't seen anyone with a gun so far.

Julian hesitates, as if considering how to answer. "Not that I know of, though I'm tempted to tell you otherwise if it'll make you listen. Point is that I don't trust that Travis *doesn't* have a gun, and I know he'd happily use it on either of us. He's not a fan of mine, either."

I look up the stairs. "You need to get me into the house. I'll tell Aiden I'm fine, and—"

"Oh, no. Save the confrontation for another day, okay? I know you all have magical powers, and I'm not ready to get caught in the crossfire."

"We don't have that kind of—"

He lifts his hands. "Don't care. You and I are slipping through the rain to the main house. We're going in the side door, but only to cut across to the garage. Aiden's car is there. I have his keys. He left it running in front of the house when he stormed in. You're getting into his back seat, and then I'm going to find a way to let him know you're safe, and he'll come out, and you two can drive off into the sunset. You can handle the rest however you like . . . after I'm gone, please."

I want to argue, but again, it's really just impulse. I'm angry and still scared, and this is one of the people who made these hours of hell possible. Yet Julian's right, too. Who should I confront? Marion? I'm not entirely convinced she knew nothing about it, but I suspect Julian is right. Do I tell her what her husband did—tell Connolly what his father did—when I'm still freaked out and furious, and the true target of my rage is off screwing his mistress?

"All right," I say. "I still don't trust you, though. One false move, and I'm running straight to Aiden. He's the only one I trust."

"Good call," he says. "Now, let's go."

CHAPTER TWENTY-NINE

JULIAN IS right about the storm. It's not a gentle summer shower, but a full raging storm with howling wind and pounding rain and flashing lightning. It's as if Zeus himself has unleashed his fury on this house. Except the actual Zeus is apparently the kind of dick who'd think Liam Connolly is a fine fellow and probably join him for a fun evening of "golfing" and screwing around.

Julian had brought an umbrella, which lasted until he reached the door before surrendering to the storm. We have to make a run for it. I eyeball the distance. Maybe fifty feet. I'll get soaked, but honestly, that'll probably be the least crappy thing to happen to me tonight.

The one advantage to the storm is that no one is watching. I'm not even sure anyone *could* see us, between the driving rain and the pitch-black night, lit only by flashes of lightning.

Julian warned me not to flee on my own. Warned me that I wouldn't make it.

I'm not so sure of that now.

Which means I'm not so sure about him. About his motives.

But Connolly is in the house, where we're running. That's my safety zone. Make it to him, and I'm home free.

Except Julian is the one who told me Connolly is there . . . and that he conveniently moved Connolly's car into the garage around back.

The side door is ahead. A darkened doorway leading to a darkened part of the house.

I glance to the side. I should make a run for it. No one's out here. No one's watching. Follow the driveway to the fence and climb. I can climb it. I know I can.

I'll wait until Julian is opening the door. He thinks he's tricked me, and I'm complying. I just need him distracted—

"No!" A voice booms from inside. "You listen to *me*!"

Connolly. I know that voice, even if I've never heard him raise it.

I hesitate only a moment before I follow Julian in.

Julian motions me to silence as he shuts the door. I listen for voices, but they've gone quiet. Or gone back to normal tones, their voices lost in this huge house.

"This way," Julian whispers.

I have to force myself to follow. I need to allow him to lead me until I can figure out where exactly Connolly is. Then I can decide my next move.

We're moving along a dark hallway when Marion's voice rings clear. "I need you to calm down, Aiden. I don't know how many times I can tell you she isn't here."

"And I'm telling you I know she is. Did you really think I gave you my actual security code? I'm not that stupid. I gave you a visitor code, and you're the only one who has it. I check my logs daily. I know when you've sent someone into my house. As soon as I found Kennedy gone, I checked. You used your code."

"Yes, I've already admitted that. I invited her here for a talk. Which we had, and then she left. You've spoken to Davey. He says he dropped her off at your house."

"I wouldn't trust Davey to tell me the sky is blue. You did not 'invite' Kennedy. You took her. Her phone turned off minutes after my alarm did."

"Seems I'm not the only one keeping tabs on her."

"I had a tech contact check it after Kennedy disappeared from my house and wasn't reading my messages. She would understand that."

I have no problem with what he did, but I also no longer feel the compulsion to march in there and tell Marion so. Hearing Connolly has calmed my fears. I shouldn't interfere. Just let Julian take me to Connolly's car. Wait there. It'll be safe.

Marion continues to insist she has no idea where I am and that, yes, perhaps Travis got a little overzealous and confiscated my phone, but I have that back now. Just ask Davey.

"Is Davey the blond guy?" I ask.

Julian only rolls his eyes, which I guess means yes. I presume that Liam had Davey take the fall here for two reasons. One, he didn't trust Julian—rightly, it seems. Two, if he had Travis lie about returning me, Connolly would be even more suspicious, given the history between them.

Marion and Connolly are somewhere to my left. We pass near enough to the room that I can hear them even when Connolly lowers his voice. Then we keep going. Julian's gesturing to a door ahead when there's a tremendous boom, the entire house shaking with it. Someone screams, and an alarm shrieks, drowning out the screams.

Julian grabs my arm.

"Hey!" I say, yanking away.

His grip only tightens. The alarm stops, voices rushing in to fill the void, people shouting.

"Why the devil isn't the generator turning on?" Marion says.

"Come on," Julian whispers.

"Did you do this?" I whisper, tugging against his grip.

"No, but I'm sure as hell taking advantage of it."

He pulls at me. I pull back. The power's out, and the generators aren't coming on, and something is wrong. I didn't imagine those screams.

"I'll check the utility room," Connolly says from the other room. "Go see who was screaming. I think it came from the staff quarters."

When Julian tries to drag me, I dig in my heels.

"They're separated," I say. "Let me talk to Aiden."

"I'll do that."

"No, I can—"

He yanks my arm.

"Hey!" I say.

He starts to drag me, and when he throws open a door, it's pitch-black inside, and all I can think of is Liam opening that door downstairs, forcing me through into that terrible empty room with the painting.

"No!" I say. "Let me go!"

"Kennedy?" Connolly's voice echoes through the halls.

"Just get in here, and I'll—" Julian starts.

I yank harder. "Let me go!" I kick at him, and he swears but doesn't release his grip.

Running footsteps, and a figure rounds the corner we just passed. Connolly sees me and stops short. Then he sees Julian and charges.

"Wait!" Julian says, backing up fast. "It's not what you think. I rescued her. I'm on your side, buddy."

"On my side?" Connolly says between his teeth. "Do you think I don't realize you're the O'Toole family spy?"

"Fine, yes, but—"

"Let her go."

Julian blinks down at my arm, as if he forgot he was holding it. He drops it fast and backs up, hands rising.

"I rescued her." He waves at the door. "I was putting her in your car."

Connolly doesn't seem to hear him. He holds both my arms gingerly as he looks down at me.

"Are you—?" He sees my cut arms and sucks in a breath. "What did they do?"

"I'm fine," I say. "I just want to go. Please. Let's get out of here."

Connolly's gaze rises to Julian's. "If you did this to her—"

"He didn't," I say. "He got me out of where I was being held. Maybe he was rescuing me. Maybe he was taking me to the O'Tooles."

"What?" Julian says. "No."

"Don't know. Don't care. I just want to leave. Please, Aiden."

Connolly glowers at Julian one last time and then bustles me into the garage.

———

As Julian said, Connolly's car is in the garage. So maybe he was telling the truth about the rest, but I only care that my ordeal has ended, and I'm with Connolly. His parents won't harm me while he's here.

He doesn't say a word as we get into the car. Just starts it up and drives to the door . . . only to realize the automatic opener doesn't work during a blackout. He murmurs, "Just a moment," and it's a testament to how unsettled I am that I nearly scamper out after him, just to stay close. He heaves open the door. Then he's back, and it's a silent drive to the gate, where he needs to do the same thing.

It's still storming, a driving rain that has him soaking wet when he climbs back in. I reach into the back seat where there's a folded blanket from our last picnic. I hand it to him, and he wipes off his face as the car rolls through the gates.

"I'm sorry," he says. "I know that sounds like a ridiculously weak thing to say. My parents kidnapped you."

"You mother kidnapped me. Your dad's the one who held me captive."

The words barely leave my lips before I'm wincing. "That came out wrong. I mean, I, uh . . ."

"You wanted to find a gentler way to break it to me? Let me know that my father is an absolute bastard who set my mother up while he went off to the country club? Probably seeing a girlfriend while he's at it?"

"Uh . . ."

A soft, bitter chuckle. "Yes, Kennedy, I know what my father is. The problem is always that I can never quite tell how much my mother knows. It's too easy a trap to fall into. If I know one of my parents is . . ."

"A supervillain?"

The chuckle lightens. "Don't say that to his face. He'd take it as a compliment. Well, no, he'd grimace and sigh and say you're misunderstanding, but at heart, he'd be pleased. Yes, if I know one parent is villainous, I cannot help but raise up the other one, even when they are hardly a superhero. It's easy to see our father as the root of all evil, and our mother as a saint, which she is not and does not pretend to be."

He glances over. "You believe my mother didn't know he was holding you captive?"

"Ninety-nine percent sure, especially after hearing your conversation with her. She honestly thinks Davey took me home."

His hands tighten on the wheel. "And what really happened?"

I don't answer.

"Kennedy?"

"Can we talk about this later? Please? I'm fine, and I just want to forget it for a while."

He relaxes his grip. "Of course. I'm sorry. I'm just . . ." He glances over. "I know you're *not* fine, but are you okay? I see cuts. Do you need to go to a hospital? Or see a doctor? I know someone I could take you to, even at this hour."

"They're paper cuts. From another Costa painting. I will tell you everything later, but for now, yes, I'm not 'fine,' but I am okay. I'll be even more okay when we're far from here."

"All right. If you need anything . . ."

"If you could find me a burger, I would totally take that."

"I will. Then I presume you'd like to go home?"

"If that's okay."

"It's absolutely okay."

We reach the end of a quiet road. The lights of Boston shine to one side, but he turns the other way to bypass the city. When we see the neon glow of a fast-food place, he says, "Is that one okay?"

"Right now, any one is okay."

He turns into the drive-thru. I place my order, and he doubles it. When it comes, he passes the bag my way. I start to hand him his burger, but he shakes his head.

"It's all yours. I don't feel much like eating."

"I felt the same way a few hours ago. Now I think I could eat both burgers from the sheer adrenaline rush of relief." I pause as he tenses. "I'm kidding. It wasn't that bad."

He looks over. "You're *not* kidding. It *was* that bad. You don't need to minimize it for me, Kennedy. I already do that too much when it's me or Rian in my father's crosshairs. At least, I know I won't do that with you." He grips the wheel. "Which I should have thought when it was my younger brother bearing the brunt of it."

"Growing up in a dysfunctional family means you can't see the dysfunction. It feels like normalcy. You trust your parents to do the right thing."

He slants me a glance. "Because you know all about family dysfunction."

I lick ketchup off my fingers. "I have a college friend who took a bottle of pills. I found her in time. She's been in therapy for years and is just beginning to realize that she's not as worthless as her parents said she was."

He flinches. "That was presumptuous of me."

I shrug. "My family is awesome. That makes it easy to think I don't know anything about non-awesome ones. The truth is that I don't—not from personal experience. I'm just saying that, from where I stand, the mistakes you made with Rian were understandable. Also, you aren't your brother's keeper, and he doesn't want you to be. From what I've heard, you did a lot to protect him. Still do."

"Maybe, but I do so with a jumbo-sized side order of exasperation. I need to stop that."

"Nah, just downsize to kiddie-sized. Rian still needs a little big-brother exasperation."

I hand him a fry, and he takes it.

"So to totally change the subject, how did cocktails with Theodora go?"

He tenses again and then rolls it off. "Unfortunately, that doesn't change the subject as much as you hoped. I think she set me up. Set *us* up. Before I went over, I said I was with you, and I couldn't stay long because you'd be waiting back at my house."

"Damn."

"Yes. I agreed to join her for cocktails, and while I was gone, you were kidnapped from my house. Either my mother asked Theodora to lure me out or Theodora let my mother know you were alone at my house. I'd said you were with me in hopes she would extend the invitation to include you. The fact she didn't makes me all the more certain she set us up."

I want to protest. To say I'm sure it's a coincidence. Yeah, defend Theodora based on a fifteen-minute acquaintance, during which she swore she was on Aiden's side and not my enemy.

I remember what Liam said.

Has she told you that? Clever girl, our Theodora.

"I didn't expect this of her," he says. "Which just goes to prove that I am a terrible judge of character."

"I liked her, too. This doesn't mean she's evil. Just more ambitious than we've given her credit for. If she did set us up, it was with your mother, whose plan seemed to be just talking to me."

I take a bite of my burger and then hold out another fry. He accepts it and nibbles the end, after which it disappears, as if dropped into the door pocket.

The windshield wipers fill the silence. The rain seems to be letting up, and the wipers slow. Connolly turns onto an even quieter back road.

"I need to ask you something," I say. "And I need an honest answer."

"Of course."

"It's about my insurance claim."

There's a beat pause, and my heart clenches, but when I look over, he's only frowning at the change of subject.

"What would you like to know?" he says.

"Did the insurance company reject it?"

Another pause, one that now has my heart speeding up.

"Aiden?"

He sighs. "Yes, they rejected the initial claim. I didn't mention it because you were worried enough already, and I could handle it."

"How did you handle it?"

"I strode into their office and insisted—demanded—that they accept your claim." His lips twitch as he glances over. "That sounds so much more impressive than the truth. I accessed policy documents from their firm and discovered they were rejecting you based on a misapplication of a clause that didn't appear in other policies. Which meant that they were wrong to deny your claim, but also that they'd taken advantage of a young business owner, a fact they would not want publicized when they promote themselves as an entrepreneur-friendly firm. The first part meant they had to pay you, and the second part encouraged them to do so expediently."

"Your mother has a copy of the original rejection. She thinks you paid my claim."

"Certainly not." The GPS warns him to turn ahead, and he eases off the gas. "If I couldn't resolve it, I would have positioned myself as a potential investor in your business, but that proved unnecessary." He glances over. "Did you think I'd snuck the money into your account?"

"No, but she claimed she had proof it came from your bank."

"It didn't. I'll double-check the records, but I suspect she misunderstood the investigator or outright lied to see your reaction."

"Makes sense." I fold away my empty bag. "However, I am waiting for my ten grand a month sugar-daddy payment."

"Then I fear you will be waiting a long time, as I should hope I'm not old enough to qualify for the role." He turns the corner. "Dare I ask what that's about?"

"Your mom has a letter, signed by you, directing your lawyers to wire me ten grand a month from your trust fund."

His shoulders slump. "So either she forged it herself, or my father did, and she believes it despite the fact that, were I to do such a thing, I would certainly be more discreet. Also, it's not *my* trust fund until I marry, and anything I take from it is a loan, which is added to my debt."

"You should make sure no one is funneling ten grand a month off your trust fund."

"And by *no one*, you mean my father. Yes, I'm sure he is. Partly because my mother would have checked to be sure the withdrawals were occurring, and partly because it's ten thousand a month he can keep off the family books. Probably to pay *his* girlfriends. I'll make a call in the morning—"

The car jolts with a cough I know well. Connolly snaps up, looking in his rearview mirror as if expecting we've been hit. The car jerks again.

"Tell me you aren't out of gas," I say.

"Impossible. I never let it drop below half—" Another heave, and he steers it to the shoulder of the road. Then he taps the gas gauge, as if it isn't digital.

"Out of gas?" I say.

"Not according to this." He turns off the car. When he restarts it, the gauge plummets and warning lights flash, complete with beeps.

"Seems you should have taken her to the shop after all," I say. "She's glitching."

"I suspect this particular problem began an hour ago."

"You think someone sabotaged your car at the house?" I pause. "Wow. I still managed to sound shocked at that."

He only grumbles, turns off the car and then restarts it, as if that will help.

"It's not a computer, Aiden. We're definitely out of gas. I know the symptoms, having coasted home on fumes so I wouldn't need to fill the family car."

Connolly reaches for his phone. Then he taps his pocket.

"You left your phone behind?"

"No. That isn't possible." He keeps tapping. "I didn't take it out . . ."

When he trails off, I say, "You *did* take it out, right? Probably to show your mom something? And then between the blackout and finding me, you forgot it. Well, this is retro. Stranded on a deserted road without any cell phones. At least you have your wallet."

"Hmm."

I peer out the side window. "The rain has stopped, and we can't be far from a gas station. Did you see any back the way we came?"

He shakes his head. "I should have stayed on the highway."

"I like the back roads myself. Just not when someone drains our gas tank." I open the door. "We aren't in the middle of the Mojave Desert. It can't be more than a mile to the next gas station."

"If it's open."

"It's not even midnight." I climb from the car. "Let's go have ourselves an adventure."

CHAPTER THIRTY

WHEN CONNOLLY PICKS BACK ROADS, he *really* picks back roads. I'm not even sure where we are. I keep reaching for my phone to check, but yep, without phones, we only have the car GPS, which we left when we abandoned the car itself. We really should have checked it for service stations. I don't say that now. It'll only make us kick ourselves harder for our understandable distraction.

With the rain gone, it's a nice evening for a walk, and we make the best of it, tramping along the dark road, lit only by the flashlight that Connolly remembered to grab from the glove compartment. Forest frames the road, and the storm left a hazy heat that shimmers around us. A hauntingly beautiful night . . . right up until the sky opens and rain slams down again.

"Run back to the car?" Connolly shouts to be heard over the thunder.

"I think I see lights ahead," I yell back. "And it's at least a mile to the car. I say we make a run for it."

We run until our empty road joins with a busier one, and there, right around the corner, is a travel center, complete with diner, roadside motel and gas bar.

We race to the gas bar, only to find it dark, with a Closed sign on the adjoining diner. I sluice rain off my face as I peer around. Then I point at the motel. A light shines in the window.

We race to the door. Connolly yanks it open and ushers me inside. The smell of mildew makes me wrinkle my nose. A bull of a man sits behind the counter, his feet up as he watches a sitcom on a tablet. Something in his profile strikes me as familiar, but when he turns, I don't recognize him. He's wearing a tank top that shows off massively muscled arms, and there's an air of dissolution about him.

"We need gas," I say. "We ran out down the highway."

"Gas bar's closed."

Connolly pulls out his wallet. "I'll pay triple."

"You can only buy gas at the diner," the man says.

"Is there anyone there?" I ask.

"Nope. Gas bar's closed. Diner's closed. Only thing open is this motel."

The man's gaze slides down my soaked shirt. Connolly sidesteps in front of me, and the man chuckles under his breath.

"Looks to me like you might want to get that girl a room," the man says. "She could use some warming up."

"May I borrow your phone?" Connolly says. "I'd like to call a tow truck."

"Be cheaper to just stay. You're not getting anyone out here at this hour."

"May I try?"

The man shrugs and waves at an old-fashioned dial-phone. Connolly picks it up and then hesitates, as if trying to figure out how to use it. He takes a card from his wallet and dials in a number. He waits. Waits some more. Glances at me, frowning.

"I'm not getting an answer," he says.

"Yep, no one's coming out at this hour, son."

"It's a twenty-four-hour service. I'm not even getting their voicemail."

The man puts out a broad hand. Connolly gives him the receiver. The man lifts it to his ear and then chuckles.

"You kids never used a landline?" he says. "There's no dial tone. And before you ask, no, I don't have a cell. Not all of us can afford one. Judging by that shirt of yours, though, son, I think you can afford to treat the lady to a good night's sleep." His eyes sparkle. "Or a good night's something."

I glance out the window, where the rain pours down. There are a half-dozen cars in the parking lot. We could see if someone has a cell phone, but it's almost midnight, and I don't want to disturb people's rest for a non-emergency.

"Let's just get a room," I say. "We can buy gas in the morning."

"A fine idea," the man says. "Diner opens at seven, same as the gas bar. Now, we're a little busy tonight, but I believe I can offer you the honeymoon suite."

I shake my head. "Two beds, please."

"Well, now, that's a shame." He looks at Connolly. "You want me to tell the little lady I don't have anything with two beds? I can do that for you."

"No," Connolly says. "I would like you to rent us a room with two beds, for which I will pay you the same price as the honeymoon suite, so there is no need to upsell."

"I was trying to help you out. Kids these days." The man pulls over a book and runs a thick finger down a row. "I *am* charging you the honey-moon suite rate, though. Since you offered."

"That's fine."

"It'll be one fifty."

Connolly pulls out sodden bills, which the guy takes without asking for ID. Connolly signs something, and the guy passes him a key with a plastic room tag on it. Connolly stares at it.

"Your room key, kid," the man says. "You've never seen one that isn't electronic?"

I take the key. "I have. Thank you. Have a good night, sir."

"Better than yours," he says. "But don't say I didn't try to improve it."

———

I UNLOCK OUR ROOM, push open the door and flick on the light as we hurry out of the rain. Inside is a king-sized bed and a jacuzzi.

"The honeymoon suite," I say with a sigh. "Figures."

Connolly takes the key. "You wait here. I'll get us a proper room."

I catch the back of his wet shirt. "Don't bother. It's a massive bed, and we're adults. Plus, that jacuzzi tub looks kinda awesome right now, and I doubt it's a standard feature. Ooh, is that complimentary champagne?" I pluck the key from his hand. "We're staying."

"I'm not sure I dare drink champagne that comes free with a hundred-and-fifty-dollar suite."

"All the more for me." I look up at him. "I'm joking. If this really bothers you . . ."

"No, you're right. It's a very big bed. And you've earned that hot tub and champagne."

"Excellent. Then it's decided." I yank off my shoes, letting water ooze into the carpet. "We may also owe a cleaning bill."

"Fine by me."

I head to the jacuzzi. While this didn't look like the most promising motel, it's perfectly nice inside. Clean and tidy, and when I turn on the jacuzzi taps, blessedly hot water pours out.

"I suppose I should . . ." Connolly looks around the room. "I could take a shower while you have your bath."

"If you want a shower, go for it," I say. "If you're trying to give me privacy, I have a bra and panties and bubble bath. You can rest on the bed or join me in the tub, where I will be enjoying . . ." I lift the sparkling wine from the ice bucket.

"I believe you aren't supposed to drink in a hot tub," he says.

"It's a jacuzzi. Totally different thing. And if you point out that both contain hot water and therefore both come with the same warning, I will remind you that you do not need to share my tub or my bubbly, though you are welcome to both."

He looks from the filling tub to me. "Are you certain you wouldn't mind?"

"We are about to have a conversation that will go so much better with a hot bath and booze." I walk to the closet, open it and pull out two thick robes. "Get out of that wet clothing and into this.

When you come back, I will be in the tub, demurely hidden by bubbles."

He accepts the robe and heads into the bathroom.

———

I TURN my head when Connolly disrobes to climb into the tub. I don't even sneak a peek, because that would be wrong, and really, I was kinda hoping he'd say, "You don't need to look away—I'm wearing my boxers" so I could ogle guilt-free. Sadly, he does not. Still, since it's not exactly a hot tub, it isn't as if we're submerged to our necks. I'm up to my armpits, which has him turning away sharply.

"It's a bra, Connolly," I say. "Not even a sexy bra. Basic black bra."

"Yes, of course." He clears his throat and, with great care, returns his gaze to let it rest on my face. I do not let my gaze rest on his face. I check out his shoulders, his upper chest, his biceps, all very nice. Then I hand him a glass of wine.

"You don't need to drink it," I say. "Just let me pretend I'm not drinking alone."

He takes a sip, as if at a wine tasting. Then another.

"Interesting," he says. "It doesn't taste *bad*. Just different."

"Well, as someone who has had a lot of cheap bubbly and little actual champagne, I place this firmly in the cheap bubbly category. But yes, it's not necessarily bad. Just lacking the palate of actual champagne, I say as if I know what that means."

His lips twitch. "I'm not much of a wine connoisseur myself. I have developed a few standbys, some of which I order with friends and some I order with people I wish to impress. Personally, I'd prefer a nice cocktail, but in my circles, that means a martini or a Manhattan, neither of which is quite to *my* palate."

"Meaning not sweet."

His smile grows. "Exactly. Were you to check my fridge at home, you would find a half-dozen bottled coolers, all pretty shades of pink and electric blue."

"Then I should have checked your fridge and stolen one to enjoy on the back deck, which is gorgeous, by the way."

"Thank you." He sips the wine. "And that eases us into the subject we must discuss. How you got from my back deck to wherever my father put you."

"It's a bit of a long story."

He meets my gaze. "How much you want to tell me is obviously up to you, but I'd like the whole thing."

I nod and begin.

CHAPTER THIRTY-ONE

I'VE FINISHED. I told him everything. Well, almost everything. I don't tell him that his father tripped and shoved me, and when I explained about the painting, I downplayed it. Not as bad as *Eldest Daughter*. Just paper cuts, which I can't even feel now. The last part is true, mostly because of the sparkling wine and the hot water and the unbelievable relief of just being here, safe with Connolly.

I don't mention any of the terrifying moments, especially that one where the sword went through my neck. I'll deal with that on my own because, if I'm being honest, I think anyone else—even Connolly or my sisters—would struggle to truly understand the horror of it. It's a thing one needs to experience, and in trying to make someone understand, I'd experience it again. I know it was horrifying. I know I'm safe now and was never truly in danger, so I'll take that as comfort.

Connolly doesn't let me rush through the painting part. He makes sure I'm okay, and I can honestly say I am, at least in this moment. That is enough. So I move on and finish the story.

When I'm done, Connolly sits quietly for a moment. Then he says, "How desperate do I sound if I'm relieved my mother doesn't seem to have been involved in your captivity?"

"It sounds as if you're a normal guy dealing with abnormal family problems."

"Abnormal." A snorted laugh bubbles up, and he takes another sip. "That is one way of putting it."

"Your mother honestly believes I'm a gold-digger and you need her protection."

"Because my father fed her the evidence to support her delusion."

"I never said—"

"You don't need to. I will straighten this out with my mother, though I'm not sure how much that helps." He gazes into his bubbly. "I'm not sure how much any of it helps."

"I'm sorry about your father."

A snorted laugh. "Do they have Hallmark cards for that? Condolences on having a raging dick for a dad?"

"Given how many crappy parents exist, they should. I'm sorry you have to deal with that, and I'm glad I see nothing of him in you."

He takes a gulp of his bubbly. "That was what I saw. With the *Eldest Daughter* painting. Me, as my father. I had children, and I was treating them the way he treated us. I was treating y—" He stops with a quick cough. "I was treating my wife the way he treats her. That is what I fear most. What if he was like me when he was young? What if he turned into that? What if I will?"

"You won't," I say firmly, meeting his gaze. "Trust me, he was never like you, and you will never be like him."

Connolly slams down the rest of the glass and gives his head a sharp shake. "Enough of that. So apparently, Kennedy Bennett, according to my father, you are a bad, bad influence."

"Next thing you know, you'll be granting people paid sick leave."

He wags a finger. "My employees already have full health benefits, including paid sick leave . . . partly because from an actuarial standpoint, it makes sense to encourage sick employees to stay home rather than infect others. And, yes, also, it's the right thing to do and I'm not a complete monster. It's just . . ."

He lifts one shoulder in a shrug. "Meeting you made me take a closer look at my choices. I can focus too hard on the end goal and blinker myself to the rest. It's not as if I had a sudden epiphany that I come from privilege and should share. I always *tried* to be a good and equitable employer. My employees know they can come to me for anything."

"Like keys to a bathroom that isn't locked?"

He lifts his brows.

I grin. "When I snuck into your office to uncurse that mirror, I talked to one of your staff. He'd been there for two years and was too intimidated by you to ask for a key to the staff washroom . . . which isn't even locked."

He stares at me. Then he snorts a laugh that turns into a full-on fit of laughter, edging dangerously close to giggles.

"You're drunk, Connolly."

He shakes his head. "Just tipsy. The thought that anyone actually finds me intimidating . . ."

He chokes on a laugh, sinking deeper into the bubbles.

"Drunk," I say.

"Tipsy." He lifts his empty glass. "Were I drunk, I would tell you exactly how I feel about you, Kennedy Bennett. I'd make my confession in all its embarrassing glory."

My heart thuds, and I force my tone light. "You kinda just did, Connolly."

"No, I said I *would*, and I said it would be embarrassing."

His eyes glitter, and he reaches for the bottle. My heart trips so fast I can barely breathe.

He waggles the bottle, in case I don't understand that he's asking for permission to tell me how he feels. To take another swig of bubbly, a little liquid courage, yes, but mostly it's that question.

Do you want to know, Kennedy? Am I taking this conversation somewhere you don't want it to go? If so, just make a joke and snatch the bottle from me, and we'll step back onto safe ground.

Do I want to know? Oh, hell, yes.

Do I want to take this conversation there? Absolutely.

Yet *want* and *dare* are two very different things.

Am I ready for this? That's the big question. Not whether I want it at some point, which is an enthusiastic yes. Am I ready *now*?

Earlier today, I'd have been uncertain. A few days ago, after he ghosted me, I'd have said hell, no. But I look at him now, watching me, and I do not want to lose this chance. I do not want to lose him. To risk him taking any subtle rejection as a permanent "not interested."

I can't urge him to confess his feelings just to avoid missing my chance. I need to be ready to hear whatever he has to say.

Listen to him. Talk to him. Admit that I want more from this relationship.

Am I ready for that?

I take the bottle away, and his smile freezes as he tries to find another expression, one that doesn't showcase his disappointment. I tip the bottle over his glass, stopping when it's halfway full.

"There," I say. "Then I'm cutting you off. Tell me what you really think of me, Connolly."

He takes a sip of the wine. "I think . . ."

He freezes. Then another quick sip, and he blurts. "I think you're awesome."

A laugh bursts out of him and shakes his head. "Did I really just say that? Apparently, cheap bubbly resurrects my twelve-year-old self."

"Hey, I'll take *awesome*."

"Good. But I have more." Another sip, and he meets my eyes. "You joked once about being special. How you've always wanted to be special. Well, you are. You're incredible, Kennedy. You're smart and funny and fun, and you don't put up with my bullshit. When I hired you, it was purely business. When you walked away from my offer, I was secretly impressed, but mostly just annoyed because it was terribly inconvenient. Then you pulled a gun on me."

"*Fake* gun."

"A real one would have spun this in an entirely different direction, and if you were that person, we wouldn't be sitting here now. The fake gun. The exploding pen. Calling me out on being an asshole when I was most certainly being an asshole. That's when I started coming up with excuses to get to know you better. Help rescue your sister. Take you to meet Vanessa. Oh, yes, we *could* go our separate ways, but that would be most unwise. We really should stick together. Because I wanted to stick together."

Another sip of wine. "I kept finding more excuses. You needed help with the insurance claim. Help with opening your new shop. Then I didn't need reasons. We were becoming friends, and I could just say I wanted to see you. Hang out together. So very normal . . . and not normal for me at all. I was leaving work on time to see you that evening. Extending my lunch hour to bring you a picnic. Taking a weekend off to go antiquing. That's when I got cold feet."

"Ah."

"In my defense, I was also worried about what my parents might do, with good reason as you see. I wanted to remove that target from your back, and stepping away seemed the most expedient way to do so. But yes, it was also ego."

"Ego?"

"I am accustomed to . . ." He seems to search for wording. "To setting the parameters for relationships."

"You mean you're usually the pursued, not the pursuer."

"I was going to say that, but it made me sound even more egotistical. I tell myself I am just very, very busy, which I am, but apparently, if I want to be with someone, I can make the time. That was new ground, and it was uncomfortable. You know me. I don't take chances. Ever."

I remember Rian saying that shortly after we met. He'd said I had to make the first move because his brother never would.

Connolly continues, "I don't take chances because chances are risk, and what is at risk here is my pride. I've realized I want to spend time with you. As much time as possible. I wake up in the morning, and I'm looking for your texts. I bought that new watch so I don't miss one. In short, I was acting like a boy with a crush, and because I'm not accustomed to that, it started to feel dangerous, even obsessive. So I backed off, and I hurt you, which is the opposite of what I intended."

"You weren't remotely obsessive, Aiden. You were a guy who seemed to enjoy my company as much as I enjoyed his."

"I'm sorry for backing off."

I nod. I won't say, "It's okay," because it wasn't, but his apology is accepted.

He goes quiet after that. The silence stretches as I wait for him to drop something into it. No, I'm waiting for him to drop something very specific into it.

I want to get to know you even better, Kennedy.

I want this to be something more.

I like you. Do you like me?

When he doesn't say that, I realize he already has, in his way. He has stepped as far from his safe corner as he dares, and now it's my turn.

I need to meet him halfway, and that should be so easy. I just need to follow his example. Tell him what I really think about him. Reciprocate.

And I freeze. Me. Impulsive Kennedy Bennett. The girl who walks up to a guy in a bar and says, "You're cute" and asks him to dance. The girl who has no problem being the first to say, "I like you."

This is different. This isn't telling Connolly I think he's cute or that I want to go on a date with him. I could say that. It's all he needs, more than he expects probably. But I don't just like him. I'm falling for him so hard it terrifies me.

Connolly says he has always been the pursued. I may have pursued, and yet we aren't all that different. I set the parameters, too. Keep your (emotional) distance. Let's have fun. Enjoy each other's company. Revel in our time together. That time will be relatively short because this isn't going anywhere. An express train to Funsville. That's the end of the line. Friendship. Companionship. Sex. Mutual respect and affection and nothing more.

This is more.

Say something, damn it.

He made the first move. I need to meet him halfway. Hell, meet him a quarter of the way. He already did the heavy lifting of going first, so there's nothing to risk.

Start by reaching for my champagne flute. At least do that much, and he'll know I'm about to follow his lead.

I get as far as lifting my hand from the water before I freeze.

"Your cuts," he says, pushing from the tub.

"W-what?"

"Your cuts. You need something for them." He's out of the tub and drying off. "The front desk should have bandages."

I protest, but it comes out as a wordless noise. He doesn't hear. He's already in his robe, and then he's out the door.

Connolly is gone. He's decided I have nothing to say, and he has literally retreated as fast as he can.

Tears sting. I rub the back of my hand over my eyes, only to get bubbles in them, which makes them sting for real.

Am I really going to mess this up? Lose this chance?

I can make a dozen excuses. We've both had a bit to drink. It's been a long and difficult day. What if we say something we'll regret? What if we say something we don't mean?

Will I say something I don't mean? Only if I say nothing at all. The wine and the difficult day aren't going to make either of us confess something we don't feel.

The door opens, and I'm still in the tub, staring at the bubbles swirling around me.

"Aiden," I say, looking up. "I—"

"Out," he says, his voice ringing with false cheer. "Let's get those cuts fixed up. I have bandages." He lifts a dusty plastic case. Then he turns his back to me. "There. I'm not looking. Your robe is right there."

I envelope myself in the robe as I rise. "Aiden, I—"

"On the bed." He pauses and gives an awkward laugh. "That does not sound good. On the bed, because it's the only place to sit. Get comfortable, and let me take a look at those cuts."

I sit propped up in the bed and put out my arm. He examines the thin cut as if it were a gaping wound. Focusing on that so I don't see his disappointment. Also, letting me know that it's okay if I don't feel the same way. He hasn't stormed off to nurse his wounded pride. He hasn't said to hell with me. He's here, taking care of me, whether I want to move this relationship forward or not.

"I think . . ." I begin. Then I blurt. "I think you're totally hot."

He sputters a slightly drunk laugh. "Okay . . ."

He looks over, sobering. "You don't need to find something nice to say, Kennedy. You don't have to feel the same way. I'm not going anywhere, unless you'd rather I did. Given the choice between friendship and losing you in my life, there's no choice to be made."

My eyes prickle again, and I nod. "I wasn't done. Not sure why I led with that. Well, it might have something to do with the fact you're in bed with me, wearing a robe and looking after my injuries. Totally hot."

Another sputtered laugh. "Fair enough, though I'll point out I'm still on the edge of the bed."

"I'm cursed," I blurt.

He meets my gaze. "I don't care."

"You have to, Aiden. It's important."

"Is it?" He shifts, moving up onto the bed as he applies a bandage to my neck cut. "I believe it's only important if I have any intention of playing you false. That's the curse. It punishes false lovers. If anything, my problem has always been the opposite. I'm too honest, especially when saying things women don't want to hear, like being clear that a fling is never going to be more, that I'm not interested in more."

He finishes affixing the bandage and shifts to look me in the eye. "I am not afraid of your curse because I would never do you wrong. I don't make false promises. I don't tell pretty lies, even when they'd get me something I want."

"I think I'm falling for you, Aiden." I blurt the words before I lose my nerve.

Then I stop, steel myself, and say, "No, I *know* I'm falling for you, and it scares the hell out of me. You're complicated. Your life is complicated. I don't do complicated. I pick easygoing, uncomplicated guys with the bare minimum of baggage. That's not you, and part of me wants to run in the other direction, and the other part says this is *why* I don't date complicated guys. Because I *like* your complications. I like the fact I can never quite figure you out, and you're always surprising me, and you're never what I expect. I'm not so keen on the *family* drama, but that's part of the package, and I'm okay with it."

I stop and take a deep breath. "Oh, boy," I murmur. "That was a lot."

He holds out a bandage. "Do you want another one of these?"

I snort a laugh. "Not really."

He moves closer, his face coming to mine. "How about one of these?"

"Yes, please," I whisper, and he leans in to kiss me.

I fall into the kiss. It's light and gentle, careful and considerate. His arms go around me, pulling me to him, and then one hand moves to the side of my face.

"Anything else you'd like?" he says as he pulls back from the kiss.

"What's on offer?"

His gaze meets mine. "Everything."

"Well, in that case, I'd like what's in the top drawer of that nightstand."

His brows knit. He smoothes them, as if trying to hide his disappointment.

I point at the nightstand.

He pulls open the nightstand drawer. Then he gives a soft laugh as he pulls out a package of condoms.

"It is the honeymoon suite," I say. "Fully stocked, apparently. And we wouldn't want them to go to waste."

"We would not," he says, setting the box on the nightstand as he slides into bed with me.

CHAPTER THIRTY-TWO

WE AREN'T SLEEPING. Just lying in bed, quiet and breathing, legs entwined. Connolly has his eyes shut, and I'm running my fingers over his chest, bending to inhale the smell of him, still there, faintly lingering, even after a shower and bath.

"I can stop if you want to sleep," I say.

"Absolutely not." He opens one eye halfway. "Everything's all right?"

I smile. "Everything's definitely all right. I'm just taking advantage of an opportunity." I run my finger down his biceps. "Have I mentioned you're hot?"

He smiles. "Once or twice."

"Should I stop *that*?"

"Certainly not."

"That's the first thing I thought about you, Aiden Connolly, when you walked into my shop." I trace my fingertips down his forearm. "Damn it, why do all the hot ones have to be such assholes?"

He chokes on a laugh. "I will take that as a compliment."

"The hot part or the asshole part?"

"Both, of course." He half opens the other eye. "For the record, I will provide equal attraction-related compliments in due course, along with equally intent physical explorations. However, to say them now would make them seem obligatory. As for any reciprocal explorations, to attempt those now would not be in my best interests. I'm going to exercise my asshole right to be selfish, lie here and enjoy."

I ease my fingers down his stomach and stoke the inside of his thigh. "You do that."

He inhales sharply as my fingers move. A low groan, and he reaches for me. I take his hand and push it back onto the bed.

"Uh-uh," I say. "You're lying there and enjoying it, remember?"

"I can manage both. Enjoy and reciprocate."

"Nope, you claimed 'lie there and enjoy,' so that's what you're doing, whether you like it or not."

He sputters a laugh. "I rather think that would defeat the purpose."

"Whatever. It's the rules."

His eyes dance. "Is it?"

"It is."

"Are you sure?"

I shift my hand, and he groans. "Absolutely sure."

"Well, if you insist, then I suppose I have no choice but to—" He grabs me around the waist and flips me onto my back.

"Hey!" I say as I laugh. "What are you doing?"

"Following the rules," he says as he kneels between my legs. "With a necessary amendment."

"Uh . . ."

"One of us has had a much rougher evening than the other. That rough evening is, regrettably, the fault of the other. That other is a selfish asshole with a tendency to think of himself first, and so you must indulge him."

"That makes no sense, Connolly."

"Of course it does. I feel terrible about what happened earlier. I want to make amends. Therefore, you must indulge me." He crouches over me, grinning down. "Now, lie there and enjoy it, whether you like it or not."

I do like it. I like it very much.

IT'S ALMOST DAWN, and we're still wide awake, lying there again, catching our breath. Into the silence, I say, "The answer is obvious. Blackmail."

He glances over at me. "If that's a game, I'm in, but I need at least ten minutes of recovery time."

"Oh, I think I need more than ten minutes. Which is why I'm changing the subject. You need to blackmail your parents. At least your dad. I'm still undecided regarding your mother."

"Aren't we all? Dare I ask what you mean by blackmail?"

I lift onto one arm. "You know their secrets. Use them to get out of the contract."

"That is . . ."

"Too much?" I sigh. "I know."

"No, I was going to say it's an excellent idea."

"I was joking," I say. "Mostly."

"Perhaps, but now you've planted the seed. I'll need to see what I can do with it. The biggest problem is that, if I successfully blackmail them, it will impress my father, which I'd rather not do."

"I think the more important thing is getting out of that contract."

"That is the *most* important thing."

When he reaches for me, I catch his hand and twine his fingers in mine. "I need you to do that for you, Aiden. Not for me. Not because of me. It must be one hundred percent because you want out of the contract, whether I'm in your life or not. Otherwise, that's a very bad way to start."

"Agreed." He slants a look my way. "So is this a thing?"

"A *thing*? Why Aiden Connolly, are you asking me to have a thing with you?"

His cheeks color.

"Have I mentioned how hot you are when you blush? And when I say that, you blush even more. So hot."

He makes a rude gesture.

"Did you just swear at me, Aiden Connolly? First, you ask me to have a thing with you. Then you start cursing me out."

"I was ensuring we are on the same page. Avoiding any misunderstanding."

"Are you asking me to go steady with you, Aiden?"

He sighs. "You aren't going to make this easy, are you?"

"Fine. Are you offering an informal contract to enter into a monogamous committed relationship with you?"

Another sigh. Deeper.

"If you are, I accept," I say. "For five thousand a month."

"I thought it was ten?"

"Nah. You're really good in bed, so that gets you a fifty percent discount." I consider. "Unless you're willing to replicate the experience at least twice a week, with an equivalent level of expertise. Then your discount rises to 99.5 percent."

"You want ten dollars a month?"

"You must be a math whiz or something. I want a cupcake a week. That's my price. Take it or leave it."

He leans over to kiss my shoulder. "I believe I'll take it."

"Woo-hoo. I have myself a sugar daddy who'll pay in actual sugar." I waggle my brows. "Both the literal and figurative varieties."

He sighs and thumps back onto the bed. I prop up on my elbow beside him, hand on his chest.

"We need to talk about the paintings," I say.

He winces. "I'd rather talk about my family, and that's saying something."

"I know." I trace my fingers over his pecs. "We don't have to talk about it now. We don't need to talk about either the paintings or your parents now."

"Except we do," he says. "Because both are threatening you. Let me take care of my parents." He meets my gaze. "They are not going to hurt you again. I'll do whatever it takes to make sure of that."

"I'm more concerned about them hurting you, and I don't want you to do whatever it takes if it endangers your business. That's my line in the sand, Connolly. If your business is at risk, talk to me before you make any decisions."

"I will. As for the paintings, we'll call Athene and Mercy as soon as we have a phone. No more of them running off and leaving you to face the consequences."

"Agreed, but I think the best way to resolve this *isn't* to rely on the immortals. It's to solve this mystery ourselves."

"Find out who's behind it?"

"Yes, and I have a theory about that. Well, not about who's behind it but about how to find that out. I inspected the painting, and it's old. I can't say for sure it's contemporary with the originals. It'd need a lab analysis for that. But it *is* Renaissance-style art painted over to match the seventies redo."

"Either it's the original, or it's a very old copy. It wasn't painted and cursed just for this. Whatever *this* is."

"There's the rub. What is *this*?" I sit up and cross my legs. "Someone is tormenting Athene to convince Mercy to weave a blood hex. A generational curse. The more I think about it, the more I don't buy that."

When he doesn't answer, I add. "That doesn't mean I think Athene and Mercy are lying. They believe the story. I don't."

"I agree. It all seems very haphazard."

"Throwing paint—well, paintings—at the wall to see what sticks. Whoever's behind this is all over the place. Interfering with Mercy's 'lesson' for me. Sending fake cops after us. Threatening me by text. Then sending us running to an empty building where we discover Rosa's body. And while that's happening, they send yet another painting to your parents. Half of it is aimed at Mercy, and half at me, apparently to threaten Mercy by using me but . . ." I throw up my hands. "It's a mess."

"Chaos," Connolly murmurs. "It's not a plan. It's planned chaos."

"Intended to have even the goddess of wisdom and strategy running around like a chicken with her head cut off."

Connolly sits upright. "If it's about getting Mercy to weave a curse, it shouldn't even involve Athene. Yet it clearly does."

"Right. So the chaos targets Mercy, and the paintings pull in Athene, who wants them gone and also wants to protect her little sister. Convenient that Athene and Mercy just happened to be together when all this started."

"Because they were working on something. That's what Athene said. They were busy doing something together, and now they're not."

"They're distracted," I say.

"We've arrived at the same conclusion independently. Well, I did after you nudged me, but I'd already concluded that the plot seemed suspiciously random. We mostly arrived at the same conclusion independently, which strengthens its statistical validity as a theory."

"Have I mentioned how hot you are when you talk stats?" I lean over and kiss him. "So we accept that as a valid theory?"

He smiles. "That I'm hot when I talk statistics?"

"Nah, that's established fact. We now think whoever is behind this scheme doesn't want a generational hex. They picked something so extreme that Mercy would never agree. Which implies they know Mercy has been forced to do those curses in the past. An impossible demand means she'll stay distracted rather than agreeing and getting back to what she was doing before. Do we have any idea what she *was* doing before? With Athene?"

"I hoped you might."

I settle in beside him. "It's almost six. The gas bar opens at seven. We'll get gas and fetch the car, call Mercy and tell her they're being misled."

"Whatever it is, it's local."

"Hmm?" I glance over at him.

"The issue they're resolving is local. Boston, New York, somewhere in New England. I had been thinking earlier that Athene must have been in the region already, considering how promptly she showed up in your shop. We know Mercy was nearby but busy, which is why she had Rosa set up the painting."

I think about it. "In other words, I wasn't chosen because I'm Mercy's super-special protégé. I was nearby, and Mercy was testing me while she was in the area."

"I still think you're special."

I kiss him. "And I appreciate it. In fact, I appreciate it so much that I'm going to get the coffee maker going for you."

I rise from bed. "I presume you weren't planning to get an hour's sleep before the gas bar opens."

"I was not." He rolls from bed. "Let me handle the coffee maker. You rest."

"I am far too wired to rest. I saw vending machines in the lobby. I'll grab us candy bars for breakfast." I stop. "Or I would, if I had any cash."

He opens his wallet and hands me a five.

I take it and say, "Just so you know, this isn't a down payment for this month. You still owe me four cupcakes."

"I'd like to know where in Boston I can get four decent cupcakes for ten dollars."

"Fine. You can go as high as twenty, as long as they're good. Or you just get me two, as long as I get repayment in other forms."

I waggle my brows. He laughs and shakes his head as I gather my robe and head for the door.

CHAPTER THIRTY-THREE

YEP, I'm walking out of a motel room wearing nothing but a robe. Connolly did it last night, so I reason it's fair game at a place like this. Also, it's six in the morning, and the robe is long enough that no one knows what I do—or do not—have on under it.

The biggest problem with my current attire is the lack of proper footwear. I get two steps before I'm dancing on one foot and looking down to find myself barefoot on a crumbling sidewalk. Huh. It hadn't seemed that bad last night. Right, because it was pouring rain, and I was really a lot more concerned with what the *room* looked like.

I continue picking my way along. It's wonderfully quiet. Of course, that makes me wonder how loud we were last night and how thin the walls are and whether we disturbed our neighbors. But hey, it's a roadside motel. I'm sure people expect that. Also, the parking lot had only been dotted with cars, so we probably didn't even *have* neighbors.

It's silent now as I make my way along, catching only the singing of birds and the *flap-flap* of something blowing in the breeze.

I reach the office, grab the doorknob, yank . . . and nothing happens. I give it a twist and yank harder. The door flies open, sending me stumbling back.

Damn. Hopefully, I didn't break the door. I prop it open and step in, blinking against the darkness. It stinks, too. Last night, I'd noticed the smell of mildew under an air freshener; now it's just mildew.

There's no one at the desk. I turn toward the vending machine, just inside the door.

The machine is empty.

I frown. I think hard, but I don't remember whether I did more than notice there was a vending machine last night.

A squeak sounds behind me, and I turn just as a rat races across the floor. I jump, stumbling back. That's when I see the front desk, now that my eyes have adjusted to the dark. It's . . . crooked? No, not crooked. The entire top is bashed in, as if someone took a sledgehammer to it.

What the hell happened in here?

As I look around, I notice debris on the floor. The rat nest in the corner. The cobwebs hanging from every surface.

I race back outside, the door slapping shut behind me. Then I stand outside the office and catch my breath. When I squint against the morning sun, I'm looking at an empty parking lot.

There were cars and trucks here last night.

That *flap-flap* sounds again. I follow it to a sign. A big weather-beaten sign anchored by one post where there'd once been two.

I pick my way to the sign.

For Sale.

A faded For Sale sign that has weathered at least one winter. My gaze sweeps the motel and diner and gas bar. They're all closed. *Permanently* closed, with yellow tape around the gas pumps and broken windows in the diner.

I'm dreaming.

I fell asleep beside Connolly, and I'm dreaming.

No, I fell asleep in that basement room, and I've been dreaming ever since.

That's the easiest—and worst—explanation, yet I know it's not the answer because there's been nothing unreal before this moment.

As wild as last night was, it's all grounded in reality. I can tell myself I must be dreaming if I think Connolly actually confessed his feelings for me—and then turned out to be such a passionate and considerate lover —but that's bullshit. Dig past all my insecurities, and I'd already known he was interested in me as more than a friend. His lovemaking wasn't unexpected, either.

Maybe only this part is a dream? Or dream shaping? Vanessa's progeny have the ability to shape dreamscapes. Yet something else nudges at me, another idea, not yet ready to be voiced.

I touch the sign and feel the dirty cardboard. I hear it flapping in the wind. I take one last look around, and then I run back to the motel room, letting stones dig into my bare feet.

I throw open the door. The room is empty, and my stomach drops into free fall. Then I see the light under the almost-closed bathroom door. It opens, and Connolly comes out.

"Coffee's on," he says. "I poured you a cup . . ." He frowns at me, poised in the doorway, one hand on either side of the frame. "Kennedy?"

"Does this room look normal to you?" I say.

His frown grows.

"Any sign that it's an illusion?" I say.

The furrow between his brows deepens, but he says, "No. That's definitely coffee I just drank. Or I certainly hope so."

"Come outside," I say.

He doesn't question; he just follows me onto the sidewalk. His feet touch down, and he readjusts as he steps on crumbling concrete.

"Was it like that last night?" I say. "The sidewalk?"

"Crumbling? I didn't notice it when we arrived. I did when I went to get the bandages. I felt it, at least, and then I saw it was in poor . . ."

He trails off as he looks around. "There were cars."

"Yes."

As he walks, he shades his eyes against the rising sun. "Is that tape around the pumps?"

"Yes."

I stay where I am while Connolly walks to the pumps and then back to the motel, circling past the front office before returning to me.

"We are awake, yes? This isn't another dream shaping?"

"We're awake."

"Everything's closed. Has been closed for months. What we saw last night was an illusion." He glances at our room and shudders. "Tell me I didn't just drink year-old coffee."

"Not sure you'd notice at this hour, but no. We did not imagine having hot water and power to run the jacuzzi or—thankfully—clean linens. I thought last night that our room was remarkably clean for this type of place. That's because it was staged. Everything outside was an illusion, though you could still feel the crumbling sidewalk when you walked on it barefoot. Someone made up the room and turned on the power for us."

"The man at the front desk? Was he an illusion, too?"

I shake my head. "I don't think you can interact with illusions."

Connolly continues standing there, staring out at the empty lot. "I know a couple of illusion spinners. They can't do anything on this scale. Maybe if they worked together?"

He runs a hand through his hair. "I can't even wrap my head around this one, Kennedy. So we ran out of gas and randomly ended up here, where an illusion spinner was waiting with a restored honeymoon suite for us?"

"I haven't worked it all out, either. It's big magic. Huge magic. The likes of which I can't quite comprehend."

I shiver against the morning chill and rub my arms, and he comes over to put his arms around me. I twist to lean into him, his hands locking around my waist, the warmth of him against my back.

"I do have an idea, though," I say.

"Go on."

"The immortals have stronger powers than we do, right? Plus extra powers we lack."

"Yes."

"And illusion weavers are descended from . . ."

He sucks in a breath.

"Should I keep going?" I say. "Or am I overthinking it?"

"Keep going."

"That painting last night bothered me. It was so . . ."

"Traumatic."

I start to deny it. Traumatic, no, no. Nothing like that. Instead, I lift one shoulder and say, "Vastly unpleasant. But beyond that, it's one hell of a curse. I've seen more dangerous ones, but I'm not sure I've ever encountered one that elaborate. *Crying Girl*'s illusion is relatively simple.

I'd like to think I could replicate it, though I wouldn't want to. With *Eldest Daughter*, the illusion is also simple, but the visions of our so-called futures require serious curse weaving. My grandmother might have been able to do it. So *Eldest Daughter* is within the realm of possibility. *Vengeful Boy* is a whole other level. A pursuing illusion that can inflict physical damage goes beyond curse weaving."

"It would require illusory magic."

"Serious illusory magic, combined with serious curse weaving. Last night, when we got here, I thought the clerk looked familiar. Then he turned, and I lost that impression."

"Hector," Connolly murmurs. "He vaguely resembled Hector. I thought it was just because he was a large man."

"So I put all that together, and I remember who forced Mercy to do blood curses. Who would know, better than anyone, that it would be traumatic to even bring that up. Which is what this person wants. Mercy distracted. Athene distracted along with her."

"Pretending to want a blood curse would trigger Mercy's trauma. Get her so focused on avoiding it that she doesn't look closely enough to see flaws in the supposed plan. Doesn't realize she's being intentionally misled."

I nod. "I'm hesitating with the theory because, just last night with the storm, I was thinking it was as if the god of thunder conjured it up. I don't want to be leaping to a conclusion because of a passing thought."

"You're not."

"So the guy at the front desk last night? The one who set all this up? The one Athene and Mercy were trying to stop from doing something before they were derailed by the paintings?"

"Zeus."

King of the gods himself.

CHAPTER THIRTY-FOUR

WE HAVE WORKED out a potential theory. We have even worked out who seems to be behind it. Yes, there are some signs it wasn't Zeus—like the texts where he seemed to not know ancient Greek—but those would be red herrings to throw us off the trail. It was him. We're almost certain of that. All that remains is to tell Athene and Mercy so they can get back on track and stop their father from whatever the hell he's up to now.

That would be much more easily done if we weren't in the middle of nowhere, without cell phones or a car. We check the motel office. The phone is actually dead, which makes far more sense given the state of the building. I'm shocked he got the power going.

We check the pumps. Definitely no gas coming out, even if we could find something to carry it in, and presuming Connolly's car is still there and functional, which I doubt.

Once more, we are pawns in this game. Zeus's game. Strand us in the middle of nowhere to not only remove us from the board but also get Mercy and Athene looking for us. He'll make sure they realize we're missing. Just another wrench thrown in the works.

Is it ridiculously elaborate for what it accomplished? Yep, but from what I saw last night, Zeus is having a blast shuffling us around his game board. Oh, sure, the goal is to distract Athene and Mercy, but he's not going to turn down a bit of fun while he's at it.

We need to get to a phone. Connolly has his wallet with his credit card, cash and ID. That will get us what we need. Call Athene and Mercy, and then we can figure out how the hell to get home.

We set out in the direction we'd been heading rather than turning back toward the car. There has to be a house or a real gas station nearby. We're barely outside Boston.

Or that's what we thought.

Whatever kind of illusion magic Zeus spun, it's serious stuff, because we are not where we thought we were after all.

The road we've been walking down is closed. Permanently closed. I don't even want to know what makes a state shut down a road. Radiation leak? I'm joking . . . I hope.

What I know is that there are no cars on it and no houses, either. Just trees hemming in a dirt road. Unless that's an illusion, too, and we're actually walking down a regional highway with cars honking and swerving to avoid us. At this point, I don't trust anything I see.

We talk as we walk. What do we know about Zeus? Well, his greatest achievement may be that he makes Liam Connolly look like a minor-league villain, the sort who'd die in the movie's opening sequence.

For me, Zeus has always been the sterling example of my least favorite literary trope—the middle-aged guy who gets away with everything because he's powerful and charming. The eternal man-boy who's never been expected to grow up or take on an ounce of real responsibility, and certainly not to give a damn about anyone else. The world—especially the women in it— exist to amuse and serve him.

I once went to a lecture where the speaker talked about Zeus's affairs, using Leda as an example, and I got up and walked out. That wasn't seduction. It was rape.

The mythological Zeus used his charm and his power of illusion to trick, coerce and force women to have sex with him. From what I've heard, that goes for the real Zeus, too.

In myth, Hera is the evil one, the jealous harpy who punishes the women Zeus seduces and assaults. As I've heard from Vanessa and Marius, the real Hera was very different. She raised Zeus's offspring by other women. She helped the women he wronged. She was a mother figure in every way, goddess of hearth and home.

I think her children would have rather she stuck a knife between her monstrous husband's ribs, but every abused woman deals with the situation in her own way. Also, Zeus is immortal, so that knife-thing probably wouldn't have done any good.

Hera's children loved her. I use the past tense there because she's been gone for decades now. Her children loved her and did their best not to judge her, and so I won't, either. The one who deserves all the judging is Zeus.

We walk about two miles before we reach an intersection and find a gas station that is definitely not an illusion. Connolly gives the teenage attendant a hundred bucks to borrow his cell for five minutes.

Connolly doesn't call Mercy. We can't without my phone, which has her number. He must call someone else. Then we wait. We stake out a place on the opposite corner where there's a little pull-off, complete with picnic tables. Connolly bought candy bars—and two fresh coffees—at the gas station. We're eating those and talking while Connolly discreetly checks his watch, monitoring the time but acting as if he's not the least bit worried that the person he called won't show up.

Nearly an hour passes. Enough time for my own gut to begin twisting in worry. We can get another ride home easily enough. That call was more. So much more. It was Connolly—a guy who doesn't take risks —taking a huge one. Giving an ultimatum that relies on something he's not sure he can rely on. His mother's love.

When the car appears, he's on his feet. I'm sitting on the table edge, and I stay where I am as he walks toward the oncoming vehicle, his entire body rigid until he can tell there's only his mother in the car. Even then, he only relaxes a little.

Marion gets out. She doesn't slam the door, but she closes it with a decisive click. She strides to Connolly and wordlessly slaps both cell phones into his hand. Then her gaze fixes on me.

"I suppose this was your idea?" she calls over.

"Because I'm not capable of demanding something on my own?" Connolly says. "No one pulls my puppet strings, Mother, and it's an insult to imply it. Kennedy isn't your enemy."

"She—"

"I did not pay her insurance claim. It was initially denied but later approved, as they will confirm. Nor am I funneling money to her from my trust fund. You can follow that paper trail yourself. Or you can refuse to dig deeper in either instance because your delusion is a convenient one." He pauses for a beat. "Convenient for both you and my father. Do with that what you will."

"If you're implying your father—"

"Do with that what you will," he repeats, enunciating each word. "I think you knew it would always come down to this. Choosing your husband or your sons. I have little doubt you'll continue making the choice you've always made."

"I have never—"

"You know what choices you've made. It's up to you to decide how far down that road you plan to travel. I only know that I'm not taking another step down it with you. The marriage contract has nothing to do with me or what's best for me. It's about control. You took advantage of my youth, and you let Dad steer me into making poor choices that only pushed me deeper into your debt."

At this, she flinches. The rest, no, but when he accuses her of being unfair, that hits home.

"The contract wasn't my idea," she says, her voice low. "You know that."

"Yet you stood by and let it happen. I'm not marrying Theodora, Mom. No matter how much you want me to."

She frowns. "Theodora has *never* been my choice."

"So you didn't have her call me yesterday for drinks . . . leading me away so you could kidnap Kennedy?"

"Certainly not. I—" She stops. Pauses, as if thinking it through. Then she says, crisply, "If it was a setup, I was unaware of it."

"Dad then."

"All I know is that Theodora is his choice. I'd hardly try to match you up with a girl who is sleeping with the hired help."

"Sleeping with . . . ?" Connolly says, frowning.

"Julian, right?" I say as I walk over. "You all knew he was the O'Toole's spy. You didn't kick him out because it's better to know who the spy is and keep him from overhearing anything critical. When he 'rescued' me, he said he was doing it for someone else, someone who means a lot to him. Theodora."

Marion rolls her eyes. "Yes, I'm sure the boy is quite enamored. Just as I'm sure Theodora is doing nothing more than enjoying the adoration of an attractive young man."

"Wait," I say. "So if Julian is hooking up with Theodora, he's smitten and she's just having fun. But if I were with Aiden, I'd be a gold-digger and he'd be my hapless victim?"

Her lips tighten, but she doesn't rise to the bait. She knows I'm right. As Liam said, Marion Connolly has woven the version of this story that suits her needs.

"May I have my phone, please, Aiden? I need to let my sisters know I'm okay. And you two need to talk without an outsider jumping in."

He passes over my phone.

I turn to walk away. Then I sigh and turn back. "Nope, can't do it. I'm physically incapable of walking away without saying my piece. I'll just keep it short."

I look at Marion. "I think your son is awesome. That's why I'm hanging out with him, in spite of all his family complications. I defy you to find a shred of evidence that suggests I'm after his money. If that's not the problem, then . . ." I meet her gaze. "Your husband may be a world-class asshole, but at least he's honest enough to admit he wants me gone because I'm not good enough for his son."

"It isn't about me," Connolly murmurs. "It's about protecting his dynasty."

I hadn't said that earlier, but I'm sure Connolly has heard the sentiment often enough.

I only shrug. "If it's not about you, then it should be."

I meet Marion's eyes again. "I hope that your real concern is Aiden. Not some family dynasty or any bullshit like that. If you don't think I'm good enough for Aiden, say so. I'd hope to prove otherwise, but at least then we know where we stand. I only know where I *don't* want to stand. Between you and him. I'd give anything to have my mom here, telling me a guy isn't good enough for me."

I exhale. "Okay, that's enough. You two talk. I have sisters to assure I'm alive and well."

I don't look at Marion. I don't dare check her expression. Instead, I pass a wan smile to Connolly and continue across the park to make my call.

————

I TELL Ani what happened last night. Well, kind of. She already knew I'd been heading to Boston chasing a painting with Connolly. I wouldn't have left Unstable without telling her. I'd also let her know we were fine afterward and staying in the city for a bit. Now I tell her I was caught in a storm with Connolly, and we ran out of gas and, in our distraction, left our phones in the car as we went for help. We ended up at a motel, where we spent the night, and she can read whatever she wants into that. Of course, she "reads in" the truth, and she is delighted enough that she forgives me for dropping off the face of the earth.

When I finish that call, I glance over to see Marion and Connolly still talking, so I phone Mercy. It rings through to a generic voicemail. I go to leave a message, but it cuts me off after a few words.

I call again and spit a quick and unintentionally cryptic message. "It's Kennedy. Plan is distraction. Met your daddy dearest. Call ASAP."

As I hang up, Connolly is walking back to me. Marion waits beside the car.

"No luck messaging the god of messages," I say. "I had to leave one. A very, very short one."

He shakes his head. "My mother is offering us a lift to my car. We could summon a driver instead, but . . ." He looks along the very quiet road. "Of course, it's up to you."

"That motel room is looking pretty good right now. It was clean. Running water and electricity."

He smiles. "I think a day of rest is an excellent idea. However, I should hope I could do slightly better than that motel. The Four Seasons, perhaps? Or the Mandarin?"

"Ooh, how about the Liberty?"

His brows rise. "The former jail?"

"Turned luxury hotel."

He laughs softly. "All right, the Liberty it is. Their best room. We'll hide out there until Mercy calls . . . and then we'll give her the information she requires while we spend the day in bed ordering room service."

I sigh dreamily. "I knew there was a reason I wanted a rich boyfriend. I get to sleep in a jail and pay handsomely for the privilege."

I glance at his mother. "Speaking of which, at some point, we're going to need to tell her things have changed between us. While I'm not exactly in a rush to do that, I don't want to give her additional ammunition against me."

He squares his shoulders. "Let me do that now."

"You don't have to. I promise no public displays of affection."

"Well, in that case, I absolutely want to do it now." He passes me a half smile. "I'd rather get it over with. Also, the fact that we got together after last night can be laid directly at their doorstep."

"Their attempts to keep us apart actually brought us together. Romantic *and* ironic. I like it."

Before he goes, I catch his arm and whisper, "You might want to cast a bit of luck for this one."

He smiles. "I think I will."

CHAPTER THIRTY-FIVE

CONNOLLY TELLS his mother about us, and I expect an explosion aimed my way. Or, possibly, *his* way for being "foolish" enough to fall for my gold-digging ways. Neither happens. I stay back, but I can't help following the drama, which is very undramatic. She listens as he explains. Then she moves farther away, and they speak intensely for a few minutes.

When they return, Connolly is calm, and Marion is . . . Again, I'm not sure. She isn't angry. She certainly isn't happy. She's just quiet. Very quiet.

I could imagine danger in that calm, but I don't sense a storm. I look at her, and I see Connolly when he withdraws into his thoughts, working things through. Maybe that's just wishful thinking. Whatever was said, Connolly is confident enough to suggest we take Marion up on her offer of a lift. I insist on the back seat while also insisting he sit up front with his mother. I'm trying to reiterate my message there. I'm not getting between them—not unless she forces me into that position.

"I think you should stay away from the house for now," Marion says as she backs onto the road. "Away from your father."

"Agreed," Connolly says.

She stops at the Closed Road sign and peers past it. Connolly directs her to take another route.

"I would also suggest, strongly, that you resist any urge to publicize your"—she clears her throat—"change of relationship. It will be easier for me to sort out the contract without that complication."

"And how do you intend to sort it out?" Connolly asks.

For a moment, she says nothing. She'd hoped he wouldn't ask for details, that he'd just trust her. He doesn't, and she can't expect him to.

"You do not need to worry about the debt coming due on your birthday," she says. "That isn't to say I will erase the debt—"

"I wouldn't ask for that."

I want to say it should damn well be erased. It was student debt incurred by a responsible and hardworking young man whose parents could afford to send twenty sons to Harvard—or, better yet, two sons and eighteen scholarship kids. They made it worse by taking advantage of his youth and naiveté, encouraging him to rack up debt with fancy apartments and lavish student living when—if he'd understood it was going onto his bill—he could have opted for a nice campus residence.

I see unfairness here, but it isn't my place to point it out. Even if he were given the option, Connolly would repay the money. He needs to cut every invisible bond.

"I would like two years," he says. "I can manage that. I would also like the obligation to marry removed. Should I somehow fail to repay the debt, I would be subject to normal penalties. And I will move out of the house by the end of the week."

"That's your house, Aiden."

"Not unless I can find a way to pay for it, which I doubt. You may take it back. Though I would suggest you sell it rather than drive a wrecking ball through it."

Her full-bodied flinch is almost a convulsion. Then she lowers her voice and says, "I had no idea he planned that. I would have stopped him."

"Then you should have said something. Even after the damage was done." Connolly glances over. "And I don't mean the damage to the house."

She's saved from a reply by her phone ringing. She glances irritably at the screen and then jabs the Answer button.

"Yes, Lauren?" Marion says, her voice sharp.

"Where is my granddaughter?" The words come not as a question but as a demand.

"I have no idea. I'm a little busy this morning. I—"

"She's with you, isn't she? You or that son of yours."

Marion's face tightens, and her words snap, cold as icicles. "I am currently with 'that son of mine.' Neither of us is with Theodora."

"My apologies for eavesdropping," Connolly says. "But we're in the car, and you're on speakerphone. I did see Theodora last night around five, but when I left, she was going out for dinner with friends. Is something wrong?"

"Don't you pull that with me, boy," Lauren says. "I know what you're all up to. You and your parents and my daughter and that husband of hers. You are going to drag Theo into this marriage kicking and screaming. I'd say you'll do it over my dead body, but I suspect that would present only a minor obstacle."

"We are not with Theodora," Connolly says, his voice calm. "I don't want to marry your granddaughter any more than she wants to marry me, and my mother has agreed . . ." He slants a question his mother's way. Marion nods. "She has agreed to drop this arranged marriage foolishness entirely. I am not getting married anytime soon, and when I do, it will be to the person of my choice, who will not be your granddaughter."

"If you're looking for Theodora," Marion says. "I'd suggest you call your former pool boy."

"What?"

"Julian Navarro," Marion says. "Worked for you, I believe. The pool boy. Cliché, but true."

"I have no idea what you're talking about. I haven't seen Julian in years."

"Because he went to work for your son-in-law. First on his security detail and then on mine, as a spy planted by your daughter and her husband. A spy who is also sleeping with your granddaughter."

I expect the older woman to sputter. Instead, she snorts and says, "Good for her. I always liked Julian. However, whether your gossip is true or not, that doesn't explain my granddaughter's disappearance. I have spies of my own, and I know my daughter and son-in-law were well aware of Theodora's reluctance, and they were scheming to overcome her objections, by force if necessary."

"Force her into marriage?" Marion sounds horrified, as if that wasn't what she'd been doing to Connolly. She doesn't see it that way. Not a shotgun wedding. Just strong encouragement to follow family tradition.

"Don't sound so shocked, Marion. I know what you luck workers are like. I have it on good authority that Theodora was at her parents' home last night, and there was a loud argument about marriage. Then my daughter and her husband left, and my contact presumed Theodora was staying over, sleeping in her old quarters. This morning, my daughter hadn't returned . . . and there was no sign of Theodora."

"Perhaps, but if they are forcing a marriage on her, it's not to Aiden."

"Because he's there, in the car with you, apparently opposed to this union."

"Very opposed," Connolly says.

"In that case, Aiden, perhaps you ought to consider why you are in a car alone with your mother. Where she might be taking you. My granddaughter seems not to be the only one in danger here."

"Oh, for God's sake," Marion says, her Irish accent thickening. "I am not driving my son to a forced wedding. How would one even manage such a thing in this world? They'd get an annulment by morning. Aiden's car broke down, and I picked them up—at his request—and now I'm driving them to his car."

"Them?"

"Yes, Aiden and his girlfriend."

So much for keeping *that* a secret.

Marion continues, "I'm sorry, Lauren, but I can guarantee you that we are not arranging a wedding for Theodora and Aiden. It was your daughter and son-in-law who pushed the match. We were letting Aiden make his choice, and his choice is that he doesn't want to follow our traditions. At least not for now."

"Not ever," Connolly murmurs.

Lauren cackles. "Oh, she's not going to take that one so easily, boy. But you keep at it. Don't let them trap you into—"

Marion clears her throat loudly. "The point, Lauren, is that we have no idea where Theodora is. Now, if you'll excuse me, I need to ask Aiden why his car was abandoned along a closed road."

She disconnects the phone as the car rolls to a stop. "Your car is down there?"

"Evidently," Connolly says, checking his phone.

"A road that is closed at both ends, with your vehicle in the middle. How did you fail to see the signs?"

"Possibly illusion magic," I say. "Also possibly we were both really tired, and I was too busy stuffing a burger in my face."

"And rain," Connolly says. "Don't forget the rain."

Marion sighs and steers her car around the sign.

CHAPTER THIRTY-SIX

WE FIND Connolly's car not far past that sign. It's in perfect working order, including having a full tank of gas.

"You hallucinated the empty tank?" Marion says.

"No, whoever is toying with us refilled it," Connolly says.

"A very considerate adversary?"

"He probably thought it was funny," I say. "Got a laugh out of picturing us here, scratching our heads and saying 'I know it was empty last night.'"

"What exactly have you two gotten mixed up in?"

I take it as a sign of progress that she doesn't instead demand to know what I've dragged her poor *son* into.

"It's related to my gray-market contacts," Connolly says. "Contacts that are extremely beneficial, but yes, it does mean navigating a treacherous landscape."

"Well, as long as you're careful," Marion says.

I have to bite my cheek at that. Marion has no idea we're involved with immortals—or that such things exist. She knows only that even before Connolly met me, he'd been getting into the so-called "gray market" of magic workers. It *is* dangerous, yet her warning sounds like she's telling Connolly to be careful swimming in the deep end.

"I'll follow you back to the highway," Marion says. "To be sure the car is in proper working order. Then you may continue on with your day."

"And you'll remove whatever tracking device you have on my car?"

Her brows shoot up. "You've just admitted you are involved with potentially dangerous people, Aiden. You cannot expect me to surrender my only way of finding you. What if you go missing along with Theodora? Knowing where you are is a safety precaution."

"One you misuse."

She flutters a hand. "I promise that I will only check it in circumstances where I have legitimate reason to believe you are in danger or I have not heard from you in more than six daylight hours."

Connolly hesitates, searching the promise for loopholes.

I clear my throat.

They both look at me.

"Is the tracker really on his car?" I say. "Because if it was, then you would have gone after him last night, especially if he seemed to be stuck on a back road for hours. Yet you seemed surprised to discover where we left the car."

"Because I hadn't checked since Aiden left."

"Since Aiden stormed from your house midargument? Took off during a blackout and left his phone behind?"

She says nothing.

"The tracker is in his phone," I say.

Connolly shakes his head. "I have my phone checked monthly for both hardware and software tracking. It's in my car. She only ever finds me when I'm driving."

I turn to Marion. "It *is* in the phone, right? You just let him think it's in the car by not admitting you know where he is unless he's in it."

We lock gazes. I arch my brows.

Marion throws up a hand. "Yes, in the interests of full disclosure—to prove that I am attempting to be more honest, Aiden, it is software embedded in your phone."

"What?" Connolly says.

I turn to him. "Ask her to remove it. Then grant her access to your regular phone tracking."

Like normal parents do when they have a valid concern about their kid's safety.

They sort that out while I wander out of earshot. Do I jump when I hear the engine start? Whirl around, fearing I'll see the car roaring off, Connolly kidnapped and dragged to the marriage altar? I know it's ridiculous, but if last night taught me anything, it's to never underestimate the Connollys.

Marion is not absconding with her son. She's starting her car while he walks over to me. I relax and get into his car.

Connolly pauses and says, "I suppose we should presume Zeus put a tracker in the vehicle while he was filling it?"

"I doubt he came here with a gas can himself. He'll have minions, like the other immortals, and probably twice as many. He only shows up when it amuses him. But, yes, definitely presume we're being tracked by him in some way."

We climb into the car. When he pulls from the shoulder, I say, "Should we be concerned about Theodora?"

He glances over as he turns the car around.

"I don't want to be," I say. "I want to head to a hotel and spend the day in bed. But I can't quite figure out what role to cast her in. She seemed nice when she came to the shop. Nice and also . . . sad? Melancholy?"

I shrug. "It struck a nerve, so maybe I'm being too sympathetic. You did agree she was nice, though. And yes, we suspect she had an ulterior motive for inviting you to cocktails when I was conveniently left alone in your house. Still . . ."

I sigh and thump back against the headrest. "Tell me I can ignore it. Theodora is fine. Off to brunch with her parents, and her grandmother is panicking for no reason, and either way, it's no concern of ours."

I look over. "Tell me it's no concern of ours."

"It's not."

"And yet . . ."

He sighs as we reach the highway. "I have three voice messages from Julian. I haven't listened to them. I presumed he wanted compensation for helping you."

"But after that call, you think it's about Theodora."

He sighs again.

"We should call him back."

Connolly taps the console screen to bring up his call log. He's about to tap the button to return Julian's calls when my phone rings.

"Where are you?" a voice says when I answer.

"Uh, who is this?"

"Athene, of course. Where are you?" The briefest pause. "I hear road noise. You're in a car? With Aiden? Put me on speaker."

"Yes, ma'am."

I hit the Speaker button and say, "You are now live with Aiden and Kennedy."

"What's going on?" she says. "You left a frustratingly vague message on my sister's voicemail. We really need more details than that, Kennedy."

"Mercy has her voicemail set to a five-second window," I say. "I couldn't leave more. Is she there?"

"Yes, and I'm sure you'd rather speak to her, but I have confiscated her phone."

"I'm here," Mercy's voice comes in. "You're on speaker, kid. What's up? I couldn't quite make out the message. Someone's father is a distraction?"

"No, your—" I stop. "Aiden and I have a theory about who's behind this. We think it doesn't have anything to do with a blood curse. Well, it kind of does, but only because the person responsible knows how much that would upset Mercy."

There's silence on the other end. Then Athene murmurs, as if to her sister, "I told them what this person is demanding." Then to us, sharper, "Continue."

"We think this is all a distraction aimed at you two. The paintings aren't modern copies. They seem to be contemporary with the originals, and then also overpainted."

"Yes, we are aware of that. I have analyzed *Eldest Daughter*. May I presume you've seen another?"

"*Vengeful Boy*. It was sent to Aiden's parents, supposedly courtesy of me. I believe there were two sets of paintings. The woman who commissioned them *really* wanted her revenge. If you got hold of one set, another still exists. Anyway, that's not the point because the paintings aren't the point. They're a smokescreen. Someone has targeted me with the paintings, forcing you two to run around trying to save my ass—and the asses of everyone who comes into contact with them."

When I pause, Athene says again, "Continue."

"I wasn't targeted because I'm Mercy's new mentee. I was targeted because I'm a convenient mortal whose well-being Mercy might care about. Convenient because I'm in the area. You two were here, in this region, handling another problem. Yes?"

"Yes."

"Let me guess. That problem involves your father. Zeus."

Silence. Then Mercy starts swearing. Athene cuts her off with, "I see where you're going with this, Kennedy. You believe Zeus is distracting us via these paintings."

"Yep, and we know it's Zeus because we met him last night. Big guy. Looks like Hector, but a helluva lot more charming?"

"You met Zeus himself?"

"Well, that's our guess. We ran out of gas—very unexpectedly. We ended up at a motel where the night clerk tricked us into taking the honeymoon suite—nudge-nudge, wink-wink. We woke this morning to discover the entire motel has been closed for months. Same with the road . . . which is also way off our route. I can't even quite conceive of that level of illusion magic, so maybe we were hallucinating—"

"No," she says crisply. "That would be him."

"Definitely him," Mercy says. "Ridiculously over-the-top, and coming from me, that's something."

"He was amusing himself," I say. "Having fun with us before getting back to whatever business you two were trying to interrupt."

"Yes," Athene says dryly. "There is no matter so urgent that it cannot be set aside for a bit of amusement, particularly at the expense of hapless mortals."

"Well, these two hapless mortals will leave you to it. We have another problem to deal with. The case of the disappearing debutante."

Mercy chuckles. "Dare I ask?"

"Aiden's arranged-marriage partner has vanished, along with her parents, and her grandmother thinks she's being forced to the altar . . . only not with Aiden, apparently."

Silence. Then Mercy says, "What?"

Connolly cuts in. "By arranged-marriage partner, Kennedy only means that the young woman was the primary prospect on my parents' candidate list, and I was on her parents' list. There was no marriage forthcoming."

"That isn't—" Athene clips off the rest. "Would this young woman be Eleanor O'Brien?"

"Nope," I say.

"She's Eleanor's cousin," Connolly says. "Theodora O'Toole."

"What's going on?" I say.

A beat of silence. Then Athene says, "We may know who Theodora is about to marry."

"Uh . . ." I say.

"Zeus," Mercy says. "They're marrying her to Zeus."

CHAPTER THIRTY-SEVEN

I SPEND the next sixty seconds deciding I very clearly am still asleep, and I'll wake to discover I'm in that motel room with Connolly, and the motel is most certainly not closed down. We never met Zeus. We just ran out of gas and ended up at a regular roadside motel.

My first reaction to that? A pang of sharp disappointment, not for what happened in the motel but for what happened twenty minutes ago, those moments when Marion Connolly seemed to understand what she'd done to her sons and want to make amends. The rest can be a dream, but I desperately want that to be true.

Why do I think I'm dreaming? Because there is no way the paintings problem can be connected to Theodora and the arranged-marriage world of the luck workers.

It can't, can it?

Turns out, it can, and that's fifty percent coincidence and fifty percent a collision of magical worlds.

Zeus is in the market for a wife. Hera died decades ago, and I suspect he cut loose and had himself a blast after that, his only reining influence gone. But there's a reason he hadn't left Hera millennia ago. He needed her. Oh, he'd rather have had looser reins, but she'd also kept him from getting himself into anything he couldn't get out of again.

Hera was balance and restraint. She was his goddess of hearth and home. Who would keep the home fires burning for him? Who would keep his finances in order? His home in order? Give him a place to lay his head when he wanted a bit of peace? That is, according to Athene and Mercy, what Zeus had with Hera and what he wanted again. Which meant he needed a wife.

Zeus had been in the area wife-shopping, and his daughters had been trying to figure out who he was targeting so they could run interference before some mortal girl made a horrible mistake.

If an immortal wants an arranged marriage, where better to look than the luck workers of Boston, New York and Philly? That's where the Irish branches of Marius's offspring ended up, and they practice arranged marriage.

Except that isn't quite what Zeus wanted. Or it's not the direction Athene and Mercy were looking. He wanted a reminder of his Hera, a descendant of *her* line. That's where the O'Tooles came in. Eleanor is Theodora's cousin on her maternal side, which is descended from Hera. When Athene and Mercy started closing in on Zeus, he fed them false clues pointing at Eleanor. The truth is that the ideal mate was descended from Hera *and* from luck workers.

Oh, and there's one more thing Zeus needs. A little extra that Theodora won't even realize she possesses: semi-immortality. Yep, the young woman I'd envied in my shop really does have it all—money, beauty, brains, *two* types of magical powers and a genetic aberration that means she's going to live one hell of a long time.

That's the theory anyway. Mercy and Athene know Zeus wants a semi-immortal wife. They know he'll be able to recognize semi-immortals, using a power the others don't possess. And since Theodora is a descendant of Hera—and cousin to their initial suspect—they're certain she's Zeus's new bride-to-be. Her parents had used Connolly as a bait and switch.

Oh, we'd love it if you married Aiden Connolly. What? You don't want to? Hmm, well here's a second option . . .

They let everyone—even Theodora—think Connolly was the one. Theodora expected that, and so she wouldn't be surprised by a flurry of preparations. She also wouldn't be overly alarmed if they tried to force her hand. Connolly was a decent guy—he'd never force her into marriage, whatever her parents might want.

Only Connolly isn't the bridegroom. And the guy who is? Well, he's never taken no for an answer, not from a woman, and he's sure as hell not going to start now.

———

WE NEED TO FIND THEODORA. The first step is to contact Julian and see what he knows. That would be much easier to do if he'd answer his damn phone. He called Connolly several times. He also left messages, which Connolly hasn't retrieved until now.

It starts off innocuously enough. Julian's making sure I'm okay and letting Connolly know he had nothing to do with my kidnapping. Oh, and could Connolly please call him ASAP?

When Connolly didn't answer that one, the next became more urgent, Julian shedding his "just need to chat" camouflage. Then comes the final message.

"Damn it, Connolly. You aren't getting back to me, so fine. It's about Theodora. She's missing. Her dad had heart palpitations—allegedly—and her mother was freaking out, so Theodora went home at just before midnight. I know she got there. Then she vanished. She's not answering her cell, and my friend finder shows it's still at their condo in Boston."

A pause then. "As for why Theo has me on Find My Friends, well, I hope I don't need to spell it out. I went by her parents' condo. It's empty. Theo's gone, and with all this marriage bullshit, I'm really hoping it has nothing to do with you."

Connolly calls and texts Julian, but there's no response. We drive back to Boston, where we meet up with Mercy and Athene, and we still haven't heard from Julian. The next time we call, it goes straight to voicemail, as if his phone's dead.

"Do we have any idea where her parents would take her?" I ask Connolly.

We've switched into Athene's car. We're in the back while she drives and Mercy rides shotgun. Mercy has, once again, changed outfits. Today, she's gender neutral, no makeup, hair partly pulled into a Samurai-style tiny ponytail, with an untucked Oxford shirt, rolled up chinos and sandals.

"They have a Boston condo according to that message," I say. "What else?"

Connolly doesn't reply.

"*Is* there anything else?" I press.

"Yes, and that's the problem. I'm not even sure where to begin. Between investments and businesses, they own at least a dozen properties in Boston. They have an estate, but it's closer to New York, where they have several more properties."

"I believe I can narrow that down." Athene pulls over and takes out her phone.

"Please tell me you have a tracking device on your dad," I say.

Her lips tighten. "I would prefer you did not refer to him as my father. That implies a relationship he never held in any more than a biological sense."

"Just call him Zeus, please," Mercy says, twisting to face us with a small smile.

"As for tracking him," Athene says, "he is far too savvy for ordinary methods, and to be bluntly honest, I do not wish to expend the effort finding better ones when it might mean I feel obligated to actually keep an eye on him. This is a special case. Our mother would want us to warn whoever he intends to marry. We expected that he would have wooed his new bride with charm and promises, and we'd need to set her straight. Instead, it seems he's skipping the formalities."

"Which makes this a rescue mission," Mercy says.

"Yes, and while I do not know precisely where he is, I have managed to track his general whereabouts." She lifts her phone. "A marina."

"The yacht," Connolly says as Athene pulls from the curb. "Yes. They own a yacht."

"They're taking her into international waters," I say. "Is that a thing? Can they force a marriage easier on the high seas?"

"I have no idea," Athene says. "But if there's any loophole for Theodora to get out of this wedding, Zeus will have closed it. To the marina it is."

———

ON THE WAY, I remember to ask Athene and Mercy about the remaining painting.

"You don't need to worry about that," Athene says briskly. "We are resolving this."

"Right . . ." I say. "And you told me I didn't need to worry about anything after the first painting. And after the second. I'm worried."

"Agreed," Connolly says.

"Yeah," Mercy says from the front seat, twisting to face us and her sister. "They need to know, Teeny."

"We are not allowing them anywhere near—"

"Athene?" Mercy says. "If you want to put on your earbuds, listen to your white noise app, you do that. You don't need to hear this, but they do."

"I am driving. I cannot put in earbuds. And I do not need to block this conversation." She glances at us in the rearview mirror. "The eldest son was a devil. His mother's demon spawn."

"She means that figuratively," Mercy says.

"Obviously," Athene snaps. "There is no such thing as demons."

"Have you met our paternal DNA contributor? Also, technically speaking, we might all be what humans call demons. We actually *are*, as the so-called Greek gods. With the rise of monotheistic religion, most so-called pagan gods were recast as demons."

"Stop that," Athene says. "I'm driving."

Mercy grins at us. "What Athene means is that she doesn't want me tossing philosophical questions into her brain while she's focused on something else. She gets very easily distracted."

"I do not."

"Take the Christian devil himself. Is he not a fallen angel? That means—"

"Stop."

"If you're trying to derail *us*," I say, "that won't work, either. I want to know about the damn painting."

"Sorry," Mercy says. "Yeah, in the case of the older son, the apple did not fall far from the monstrous-Momma tree. You recall the beginnings of the drama. Momma insisted Athene get her sons back and rain down hellfire on her rivals. Athene refused. When Marius also refused, she hired mercenaries. They rescue the two sons, but in trying to wreak vengeance, the older one is killed. The younger one escapes, with his enemies hot on his heels. He dies fighting them."

"And his sister—terrified by their mother's stories of what will happen to her—commits suicide."

"Yes. What's missing from that version is the *reason* the other family pursued the younger son. Remember, this wasn't the ancient world or even the medieval one. We're in Italy, during the Renaissance. One family might kidnap—or even kill—the members of a rival family, but they're not chasing them down the street with swords. Not unless they have a really good reason."

"The older son gave them that reason," I murmur.

"From what I understand, the younger son just wanted to get the hell out of there. The mercenaries came, and they were under orders to kill as many members of the rival family as possible, but younger son wanted none of it. He fled. His older brother did not. Nor did he march downstairs and confront the sons of that rival family, who were all in the courtyard wagering on a cockfight. He went to the nursery."

"Oh!" I say.

"Yeah, I won't go into details. There were children, and young wives. All unarmed. When the men of the family heard the commotion and discovered what the oldest son had done, they killed him and then went after *his* family in retribution."

"Okay." I take a moment to process that. "So what does the painting's curse do?"

Athene and Mercy exchange a look.

"We don't know," Mercy says. "That was the one we targeted first. We knew it was the worst. In the decades before we caught up with it, it had two owners. Two people had been murdered. A third was dead by her own hand. The fourth was in a mental hospital."

"Two couples," Athene says. "In each case, one of the partners murdered the other. One of the killers took her life, and the other went mad. We do not know exactly what they saw—only that it compelled them to murder their spouse."

"It's the worst of the paintings," Mercy says, her voice low. "From the worst of the siblings."

"But you don't need to worry about that," Athene says briskly. "We are resolving this now, before Zeus can find a use for that particular painting."

CHAPTER THIRTY-EIGHT

BY THE TIME WE ARRIVE, there's no sign of the yacht. Connolly speaks to someone. Don't ask me who—harbormaster, marina master, whatever. Athene accompanies Connolly, which will help get whatever information Connolly needs, but I'm also sure she just goes along because she's not about to rely on his account afterward. She wants answers firsthand.

They return twenty minutes later.

"The yacht left nearly an hour ago," Connolly says.

"Is that odd?" I say. "They kidnapped her last night. Why wait until now to sneak her out to sea?"

"It seems they aren't *sneaking* her anywhere," Connolly says. "Theodora arrived with her parents and several others. She wore a bridal gown and was beaming and chattering away with her bridegroom."

"Who is definitely Zeus," Athene says. "I interrogated the woman we spoke to, and her description left no doubt."

"Did it also leave no doubt that Theodora was going along willingly?" I ask.

"We spoke to three people," Connolly says. "All saw the wedding party, and all said Theodora seemed fine, but they also were watching from a distance. Her father cleared the area before bringing her from the car. One person said she seemed to have had a few glasses of celebratory champagne already."

"Drugged," I say. "They're making sure witnesses see her, apparently under no duress. So what do we do now?"

"Follow that yacht," Connolly says.

I grin. "I love it when you say that."

———————

WE'RE TAKING Connolly's speedboat. His family's, actually, though Rian uses it most, not surprisingly. Seems the Connolly family docks here, too —with their yacht, this speedboat and a sailboat.

When Mercy sees the speedboat, she whistles and nudges me. "That's a cigarette boat."

"Huh."

"You have no idea what that is, do you?" She socks me in the arm and calls to Connolly, as he's getting into the captain's seat. "Good luck impressing this one. You could take her out in a fishing boat, and she wouldn't know the difference."

"Which is exactly how I like it," he calls back. "Now, if everyone can take their seats . . ."

The boat slices through the water like a rocket, and before long, I'm up in the front, where I can get the full effect.

"I feel like I'm in a James Bond movie," I call to be heard over the noise.

He only smiles at me. Connolly took it slow coming out of the marina, but once we hit open water, he showed us just how speedy this speedboat is, and we're flying along, in hot pursuit of a luxury yacht.

It isn't long before we spot them on the radar. That's the beauty of a very expensive boat—it has all the technological bells and whistles. Connolly can determine which is the right ship and set a course straight for it.

When the yacht comes into view, I try not to gasp.

A cruise was on Mom's bucket list after the cancer diagnosis. We all went on a Caribbean one and decided there was a good reason we'd never been on a cruise before. Not our thing, really, though we did have fun and made plans for an expedition to the Antarctic, the trip of a life-time. We never took that trip. Mom's cancer advanced enough that she canceled the voyage while she could still get a refund, being Mom and not me, who would have held onto the tickets and prayed for a miracle.

The point is that I've been on a cruise, and that's what this yacht reminds me of—a small and exclusive cruise ship. The idea that it's intended for a single family boggles my mind.

Once we've spotted the yacht, we have a problem. It's not a house we can sneak into. Hell, I don't even see *how* to sneak in when the deck towers a story above our little boat.

Connolly throttles the engine. "There's a docking area around the other side for bringing smaller craft along."

"Like when you hitch an ATV on the back of your motorhome?" I say.

"Er, yes, something like that."

Mercy stifles a laugh. Connolly explains that we could dock there to access the yacht. The problem is that he's as close as he dares get without raising suspicions.

"Do you have scuba gear?" I ask. "We could slip up underwater."

"I presume that is a joke," he says, "but no, while Rian and I do have scuba gear, it is not on this boat."

"Shame, because while I *was* joking, I'd give it a shot. Total James Bond moment." I look at him. "How long can you hold your breath?"

"Fifteen miles off the coast in the North Atlantic? About as long as it would take me to die of hypothermia. I believe our only real option is to openly approach and hope they haven't loaded the cannonballs."

"*That's* a joke, right?"

"Of course. Cannons are notoriously inaccurate. They'd equip their security force with long-range sniper rifles."

"Also a joke?"

Before he can answer, Athene cuts in, "While you two are having far too much fun, I can suggest another option." She points up at the sun, high overhead.

"Uh . . ." I say.

Athene sighs. "If we navigate in the correct direction, the sun will obscure the boat. I inherited some illusion magic. I can ensure anyone looking over the side is uncertain whether or not they see us or a mere reflection of the sun."

"All right," I say. "Let's give it a try."

———

WE HAVE SUCCESSFULLY SNUCK up on the yacht and are now at the back where a wide door leads to the interior. That door is at least six feet above us and also closed—a giant hatch that, according to Connolly, can electronically open into a ramp for the toys within. Which is very cool— I'm fond of a good WaveRunner myself—but I'm not sure how we're supposed to get inside.

"Safety features," Connolly says. "There is a ladder leading up to the hatch." He points, though all I see is a blinding wall of white. "Also, there's a manual override, accessible from the exterior, in case of emergencies."

"What about pirates who happen to know where to *find* the emergency override switch?"

"It will set off an alert if used."

"Then how do we sneak on?"

"I will remain in the boat. When they come to investigate, I'll say I came to stop the wedding to my intended bride."

"What? Wait. No."

"I don't actually want to marry Theodora, Kennedy."

I roll my eyes. "That is *not* my problem with the plan, Connolly. You're throwing yourself at their mercy as a distraction. And then what? We rescue Theodora and leave you to take the fall? Possibly a literal fall, off the gangplank."

"There isn't a gangplank. They'll just toss me overboard." He lifts his hands. "I'm joking. I will go in there, full of righteous fury at being robbed of my intended, and then I will storm off in a huff when I realize she doesn't want me. By the time I leave, you'll have Theodora."

"No one who knows you is going to buy that for a second."

He straightens. "Are you implying I wouldn't come to *your* rescue, were you kidnapped for a forced wedding?"

I pat his arm. "I mean the righteous fury and indignant huff. They'll know you're acting."

"Again," Athene cuts in. "You two are adorable. However, Kennedy is correct that, while Aiden's plan is noble, it won't work. I will take that particular role in this scenario, minus the fury and the huff. Also minus the betrayed bridegroom. You will sneak on, and I will distract them, having tracked my father and come to stop the wedding. He will believe that, and it won't bother him overmuch, as I have been 'sticking my nose into his business' since I was a child. He'll resolve the family squabble with me while you rescue Theodora."

"Great," Mercy says. "Then we've got ourselves a plan. Can we get on with it? Before someone hears us chattering out here?"

"Let the rescue effort commence," Athene says. Then she pauses. "First, though, let me give you some advice. Potential strategies, depending on what you discover inside."

Mercy groans but waves for her sister to go on, and Athene does.

CHAPTER THIRTY-NINE

WE'RE ON THE YACHT. That took a combination of powers: Athene's illusions, Connolly's luck and Mercy's sneak skills. Yep, curse weaving is pretty much useless in spy craft. I don't even have my damn 8-Ball, having left it in my purse back at Connolly's place.

Connolly's power is much more useful in a situation like this. He doesn't use good luck. That would cause a rebalance, which he cannot afford here. Instead, when a crew member gets close, he pulls the same trick his father did on me—throwing a little bad luck the guy's way, which also charges up Connolly's good luck. Sigh. I really need to work on my superhero skills.

We leave Athene behind to face Zeus's wrath. Or his amusement, apparently, because as he comes down to meet her, it's obvious he isn't even vexed. Just amused.

Mercy leaves us the moment we're certain Zeus is distracted and no one thinks there are other stowaways. Her job is to double-up on her sister's role—standing by to provide distraction, in case Connolly and I are spotted. We need to get to Theodora. If she's with others, then Mercy will take on her secondary disruption task and lure away whoever is with the bride-to-be.

And where would we expect to find a bride-to-be on her wedding day? In her room, getting ready. Or in her room, being held captive until the ceremony.

Connolly leads me to a stairwell and then up. "Her room is the third down," he says. Then he pauses. "Which I know from when we were children."

"I wasn't going to make any assumptions, Connolly," I say. "And if there was another explanation, I'd only care if you found your way to that room tonight."

He shakes his head. "Theodora and I never . . . Well, there may have been a kiss. But we were twelve." He stops. "I didn't need to disclose that, did I?"

I lean over and kiss him lightly. "You did not. However, now that you did, I think it's adorable. Third room, right? And we should presume there might be people in other ones?"

He nods. We'd heard the sound of merrymaking earlier, and Connolly had said it was coming from the front deck, where he could make out the voices of Theodora's parents. We hadn't heard Theodora herself, and we're hoping that means she really is in her room.

We creep toward her door, listening at each one we pass. They're all quiet, and when we strain, we can still hear the party going on upstairs. Apparently, no one is the least concerned about Athene being on board. Zeus will handle it.

At Theodora's door, we listen for an extra moment. Then I tap one fingernail against the door, and we wait, Connolly poised with a shove of bad luck if a guard answers. When the door finally cracks open, it's Theodora. She doesn't open it the rest of the way, just stands there, face against the crack, eyes widening as she sees me.

"Kenn—"

I motion madly for silence as Connolly moves where she can see him and whispers, "If you're not alone, make an excuse to come out."

She throws open the door and waves us inside. When the lock spins in her fingers, she hisses in frustration, as if she's forgotten they disabled it.

"What are you two doing here?" she whispers.

"We're your shotgun-wedding rescue team," I say. "We know what's going on."

"How much do *you* know?" Connolly whispers.

"That my parents have sold me to Zeus, who is apparently an actual person."

"Okay," I say. "That's pretty much the story. We have a boat outside. We can get you out of here."

She empties her expression. "I appreciate that, but I'm fine."

"You're . . . ?"

"Fine," she says firmly. "I'm going to marry the king of the gods, and apparently I'm a god myself."

Her voice hitches with barely suppressed hysterical laughter. She swallows it back. "Sorry, let me rephrase. He's an immortal. The most powerful immortal of all. I'm merely semi-immortal—a demigod, if you will. Seems like a match made in heaven. Or Mount Olympus, at least."

"Theo," Connolly says, his voice steady. "What have they given you? Something to eat? Drink?"

"No, Aiden, I'm not drugged." She meets his eyes. "Pupils normal, yes? I might feel as if I've stepped into *The Twilight Zone,* but it's a good shock. I am about to win the ultimate status marriage. The epitome of feminine ambition."

She shakes her head. "Sorry, yes, I might not have been dosed, but I am a little giddy. Light-headed, I think. I haven't eaten since last night. I can't take the chance they *will* drug me."

She straightens. "I'm doing this because I want to. No drugs required. No shotguns, either. Now I really do appreciate what you two are doing —and I owe you for taking the risk—but you need to go before someone comes to get me."

"No drugs or shotguns required," I say. "Just a boyfriend, held captive until you go through with the wedding."

"Boyfriend?" She gives a light laugh.

"Julian Navarro."

Her face spasms, and when she speaks again, her voice is a half-octave higher. "I don't know what you've been told, Kennedy, but I'm going through with this because I want to. I've made this choice."

She meets my gaze. "I'll be fine. I can handle it."

I want to grab Theodora and shake her. I know Julian is being held captive, his life threatened. She didn't even bother to finish denying it.

Why not admit the truth and let us help her get out of this? She's a smart woman—brilliant, I bet. Ambitious, driven and confident. So why the hell go along with this?

Because it's how she was raised. Just like Connolly. When I met him, he'd seemed enviably independent. Running his own business—a thousand times more successful than my own—and acting like a responsible adult, not a twentysomething trying out for the role.

Connolly knew exactly what he wanted from life, and he moved toward his goals with the breathtaking confidence that he could achieve them. Meanwhile, I wasn't even sure what the hell I wanted from life. I constantly shift my goalposts to match my skills and abilities.

Yet Connolly and Theodora are lions in a zoo, feeling like masters of their domain, blind to the walls that keep them in. They were raised in that cage. They don't know any better. They accepted that a spouse would be chosen for them, and when they were old enough to realize they didn't want that, they didn't rebel—they just calmly tried to find loopholes.

Theodora has never considered going to her parents and telling them where they can shove their arranged marriage. She knows the consequences, and here is my own weak spot—unable to truly believe any parents would force their children into such a thing. Theodora knows better, as does Connolly. So they devise their own solutions.

Connolly will renegotiate his debt. Theodora's original plan had been to marry Connolly with the shared understanding they would separate in a couple of years. That didn't work out, and now the stakes have been raised.

Her lover is being held as surety that she'll marry the immortal Zeus. So what does she do about it? Scream and stomp her feet and refuse? Flee and hope she can save Julian? Nope. She'll go through with the marriage and figure out a solution later.

Yes, it's her choice, but she's still making it under duress, and I argue with her. So does Connolly. Zeus isn't some senior-citizen billionaire she can marry and divorce. Once she's in, she's in. At least let us bring Athene to talk to her. To explain what being married to Zeus means and help us devise a solution.

"Athene?" Theodora gives a high laugh. "Of course. If there's a Zeus, there's an Athene." Her eyes glisten. "I used Athena as my online name all through high school. She was my favorite goddess."

"Same," I say. "The reality is . . . Well, she's a little more intimidating than I'd like. Not exactly warm and cuddly. But I'm sure the same has been said of many successful women."

Her lips twitch. "True enough."

"May I bring her? Or bring you to her? Just for a talk. I swear we won't try to take you—"

The door swings open. Zeus walks in, two burly men flanking his rear. Connolly sidesteps fast, getting in front of me.

Zeus looks between Connolly and me. "Poor Theodora. Your former intended has thrown you over for good. I thought he was just dallying with the hired help—you two have that in common—but he jumps to protect his fair curse weaver, leaving you to look after yourself."

"Which I can do just fine," she says, lifting her chin.

"I'm sure you can, love. But soon you won't have to. If there's any sting from young Connolly's defection, it will fade quickly. You've traded up. Vastly."

"I know. And yes, they came to help me escape, but the fact I'm still in this room means I refused the offer. They'll leave now."

"Yes, they will." Zeus waves for his guards to take us. "Escort Ms. Bennett to the storage room. My future in-laws will take care of Mr. Connolly."

"Whoa!" Theodora says, rocking forward. "There's no need for that. Just take them back to their boat. My parents don't need to know." She looks at Zeus. "Please. Let's not ruin our special day."

"You are very pretty when you plead, Theodora. I'll have to remember that."

"Take them to Athene. Please."

His brows rise. "Are you certain? My men here just threw my daughter overboard. She'll be fine—she is immortal, after all. These two are not."

"Just escort them to their boat. They'll leave."

"Enough." His voice hardens, that jocular air evaporating. "I said no. I do not like to repeat myself. It's a lesson you should learn quickly."

Theodora ignores the threat. As they argue, Connolly flexes his fingers, preparing to launch his luck. I clutch his other arm and whisper, "Five," and then begin to count down by tapping on his arm. I ready a curse. I can't do much without preparation, but I can cast a little jinx.

Before I hit the end of the countdown, the guards lunge. Connolly throws himself to meet them, and I start my cast . . . only to see Connolly stumble, his fist striking air. No, his fist strikes an illusion as the real guard grabs him and a third grabs me, appearing from nowhere.

Theodora leaps in, but two more men appear from the hall, and before I can blink, I'm being dragged out, one beefy hand over my mouth. I kick and struggle to no avail. I catch a stifled grunt, Connolly landing a blow, but then we're in the hall, and I'm being dragged in one direction, Connolly in another. Zeus leads my guard, who hauls me down two flights of stairs. Then Zeus raises a hand.

"Mercy?" he says. "I know you're there. I can smell you, child."

No answer.

"You don't think I was prepared for you?" Zeus says. "Your sister didn't come alone. I was surprised to find the two mortals with her, but I knew you would be."

Still nothing. Zeus sighs and motions for us to continue. He rounds the bottom of the stairwell and moves into the hallway. Then he stops, looks and listens before continuing on. He gets five steps before Mercy drops from a hatch in the ceiling, landing in between us.

"Hello, my darling baby girl," Zeus says.

"Don't call me that," Mercy growls, every trace of the happy-go-lucky trickster gone. "You murdered someone I cared about."

"Did I?" He frowns. "Are you sure?"

My captor starts leading me backward. I try to make a noise to warn Mercy, who's facing off with Zeus, her back to me. My captor only tightens his hand over my mouth and lifts me off the floor as he retreats.

"Don't you even pretend—" Mercy says.

"Oh, I'm not pretending. Are you sure your dear Rosa is dead? Did you actually see her body? Or did Athene shield you from the sight of your lover's decomposing corpse? I didn't murder your girlfriend, child. What would be the point? She's much more valuable to me alive, so I can tell you to back the hell off, or I *will* kill her."

At that moment, either Mercy hears something or she realizes she's being distracted. She wheels to check on me, and Zeus lunges at her. That's all I see. A final moment of action before my captor carries me around the corner. I fight harder, but I might as well be struggling against a gorilla. He carries me halfway down a hall, throws open a door and tosses me inside.

"Enjoy," he says. "Oh, and don't bother screaming. It's soundproof."

He slams the door. I expect to fall into darkness, but there's a light on. I turn slowly and look around. An empty storage room. I stop, my gaze falling on the far wall.

A painting.

I lift my gaze to the face of the oldest son, sneering down at me.

CHAPTER FORTY

As I STARE at the painting, I remember the others—the angry grief of the younger daughter, the haunted fear of the older daughter, the grim resolve of the other son. All had accurately portrayed the effect of the illusion. Accurately portrayed the subject of the portrait, too, I presume. The youngest, grief-stricken and furious, lashing out at anyone who came near. Her older sister, terrified of the fate her mother described. The younger son, determined to avenge his brother and sister. This is the oldest, and had I not known his fate, I'd have thought he looked like a typical young nobleman. Or a typical guy of Connolly's social circles. His chin held high, his gaze oozes hauteur as he smirks down at the peasants and tries to decide whether any of the girls are pretty enough to bed. A harmless playboy, easily dismissed.

I know better. And knowing better, I see more in those eyes, the same way I had with the younger daughter and son, their seemingly placid expressions masking their cold rage.

I remember what Mercy told me about this "boy." About what he'd done. About the fates of those who triggered his curse. Mostly, I think of what he did in the nursery, the horror of it overpowering everything else. Knowing that story, the lift to his chin and the smug smirk on his face take on a whole other meaning. Not a renaissance frat boy, but a socio-pathic monster.

He massacred the children and wives of his enemy. Not because those children and wives did anything to him. No, he killed them to avenge himself on his captors.

The worst of it is that he probably wasn't an actual sociopath at all. How many women and children in history have shared that fate? Murdered to hurt a man, their lives nothing more than daggers to the heart of the true target. Classical literature is full of it. Just look at Medea, murdering her own children to hurt her faithless husband. That is what truly enrages me, looking on this painting. I see a monster, and I know he is just one of thousands who decided a woman's or child's only worth was as a tool to wreak vengeance against another.

I look at this painting. At a young man in riding pants, one foot on a chair, posed to show off his eighteen-year-old physique to full measure.

It takes a moment for me to realize what is wrong with the picture. It hasn't been retouched. I'm looking at a full-blown Italian Renaissance portrait, right down to the frilled cuff peeking from under his riding jacket sleeve, and the hand below, bedecked with rings and gripping a silver-handled riding crop.

Even Salvo Costa hadn't wanted to touch this one.

I stay where I am. I learned my lesson with *Vengeful Boy*. I don't need or want a better view. If I'm going to be trapped with it, I am staying right here in this—

The room goes dark. I back up fast, hitting the wall and plastering myself there. I reach for my phone. Yet when I touch my back pocket, I feel stiff fabric. I pat my hip and reach down and then experimentally move my legs.

I'm wearing a dress.

No, I *think* I'm wearing one. I'm caught in a powerful illusion. Remember that. The light did not turn out. I am not wearing a dress. My cell phone is in my back pocket. Focus on pushing past the illusion—

Someone whistles. It's the first notes of a tune I don't recognize. I wheel toward the noise. It comes again, and I back up.

Stop that. No one's there.

Am I sure?

Another three notes. Then the slow roll of a footfall. I take a step sideways and bash into another wall.

"Little birdie wants to flee," a male voice whispers. "Little birdie trapped with me."

The same three notes follow. Not a tune, but birdsong.

I squeeze my eyes shut. I am not hearing a birdcall. I am not hearing a man's voice. I am not hearing a footstep. I am alone in this room.

Am I sure of that?

The other illusions didn't have sound. Only image. That made sense.

What about the one at the motel? Zeus's illusion?

I struggle to think even as the whistle comes again, raising the hairs on my neck. Did I hear anything at the motel that wasn't real? Voices in other rooms? Cars in the parking lot?

I don't think so. Visual only, even that giving way to other senses, like when I'd smelled mildew in the front office or Connolly felt broken concrete underfoot.

"Little birdie," the voice croons. "Can you flee, little birdie?"

It's not an illusion. That's the cruel irony of it. Yes, I'm imagining that I'm wearing a dress. I might even imagine that the lights went off. That's the illusion part, and then a *real* person has slipped into the room to torment me.

Well, if he's real, I can fight.

I back against the wall, shivering and hoping—if the lights are really on—I look suitably terrified.

"Little birdie cannot fly. Little birdie's going to die."

The man lunges, shoes squeaking. I charge. I hit him in the stomach, and he gives an *oomph* as he sails backward. A very real, very human *oomph*.

I smile as I bounce back on my toes, fists raised. My tormentor is real. One of Zeus's minions sent to play the part of the eldest son, combined with an illusion that makes me think I'm one of the monster's victims, fleeing from the nursery.

"Little birdie pecks and claws," the man says. "Little birdie—"

He hits me midsentence. I'd been poised, waiting for the rest, as he expected. I didn't hear him move, and his fist slams into my jaw. I flail blindly, but I'm falling back. A foot snags mine out from under me, and I go down hard. Before I can react, he's on me, hands around my neck.

I flash back to another fake attack. A dream shaper making me think Connolly attacked me.

Not real. Not real.

Except it is. This isn't Connolly. It's not a vision, either. There is a man on my chest with his hands around my throat, and I did not expect that. I thought it was one of Zeus's games. Tormenting me. Frightening me. It is not. This is real.

I gasp and claw at my attacker, who doesn't seem to notice. His hands keep tightening. I lose consciousness for a split second, and that fuels my rage and resolve. I pull my knee up into his kidney. He gasps, and his hands loosen on my throat. The lights flicker, and then come on, and I can see him.

It's not the monstrous boy in the painting. It's the same guard who'd brought me here. Ordered to stick close until I triggered the curse and he could play his role.

His role. Not to frighten me. Not to threaten me. To put his hands around my neck and squeeze until I passed out.

To kill me.

I slam my fist into his throat. He falls back, holding it. The lights flicker again. I leap on him before I lose sight of my target.

Another flicker, and the room goes dark, but I have him. He's below me. My hands find his neck. I dig in my thumbs before he can throw me off. I get my hands around his neck.

"How do you like it?" I whisper.

He struggles, bucking and writhing. I wait for the inevitable blow. A punch. A kick. He's a burly guard. I might have startled him, but he will fight.

He doesn't fight. He only struggles beneath me as my hands tighten. White-hot rage sears through me. I'm in the abandoned house, stumbling back from the little girl's ghost. I'm in the empty condo, seeing my worst fears play out in loneliness and failure. I'm in that basement, ducking and flinching from a sword, feeling it cut through my neck.

Now this. Now Zeus sends someone to kill me.

Kill me.

The rage licks hotter. Underneath it, though, a little voice whispers, cool and rational.

Something is wrong.

You're overreacting.

My rage wants to incinerate that voice. Overreacting? This guy tried to *strangle* me. If I let him go, he'll finish the job.

Overreacting? How many times have I heard that? How many times have I admitted that someone frightens me, a situation concerns me, and been told I'm making too big a deal of it. Being dramatic. Such a drama queen.

Except this time, I *am* overreacting. This isn't me. I wouldn't kill someone unless I absolutely had to, and my attacker isn't fighting.

Why isn't he fighting?

Something is very wrong.

I jerk back, yanking my hands from his neck. Then I breathe. Deep inhales.

"Talk to me," I say.

He only writhes and wriggles.

I rub my eyes. I blink hard. It's still pitch black.

Is this the illusion? Or are the lights really out?

The illusion. The curse.

We asked Mercy and Athene what it was. They didn't know what happened, only the outcome.

The murderous outcome. Two owners who murdered their spouses. One killed herself afterward. The other was committed for a mental breakdown.

A mental breakdown that caused the murder?

No, a breakdown when they realized what they had done.

"Oh!" I gasp, falling back.

My attacker doesn't leap up. He just keeps struggling.

Not talking. Only struggling.

I crawl around and feel my way up his side. I reach his arm. It's pinned behind his back. *Tied* behind his back. I feel upward until I find his face. There's tape over his mouth. Something breaks then, some kind of spell, and I hear him making muffled sounds against the gag.

"I'm going to pull this off," I say. "I don't know if you can hear me."

I start to pull, and he jerks his head, ripping the rest away. Then he gulps air.

"Aiden?" I say, tentatively. I know it's him. I could tell when I moved my hands up his arm and over his face. That note in my voice isn't fear that I'm wrong. It's horror for what I did.

"It's okay," he croaks.

"No, it's not," I say, my voice cracking as tears spring to my eyes. "Oh, God, I am so sorry. I thought—I thought—"

"I know," he says, and I feel him rocking against the ground. "I'd give you a hug, but my arms are tied."

I quickly find the rope and start untying it, explaining the whole time how I'd seen the guard attacking me, strangling me, and then the curse did something, enraging me, making me think I had to kill him or be killed.

The moment his hands are free, he pulls me against him. "I know. I *knew*. That wasn't you. You would never do that. I understood."

His words hit me, and I'm slammed again back to Vanessa's house, the night a dream shaper made me think Connolly attacked me. I remember Connolly's horror, even as I'd said I understood it wasn't really him. The horror of realizing what "he'd" done to me, of knowing that image was now implanted in my brain.

"I'm so—"

His hands find my shoulders, squeezing. "No more apologies. This is something Zeus did to us. It wasn't you." He pulls me against him. "You figured it out in time."

"What if I hadn't?" My heart hammers. "What if I—? That sick *bastard*."

"Agreed. This wasn't a game. Vanessa has said he's so much worse than Hector. I didn't believe that. I do now. My father did the same thing, locking you in a room. Seems they have a lot in common." He pauses as I untie his feet. "Seeing that—the commonalities—I get a better idea of what my mother endures. I can look at what Hera put up with for the sake of her children, and while her children wish she'd made another choice . . ."

He trails off, and I hug him, understanding his meaning, and the new light it shines on his mother. We're still hugging when a voice whispers, "Little birdie . . ." and I freeze.

"Kennedy?"

"You didn't hear that?"

"No. Is it the curse?"

"I think so. Either that or we're not alone in here." I pause. "It is dark, right?"

He chuckles. "It is."

"Okay, well, in case you trigger the curse, I think it's supposed to be the eldest son stalking one of the wives, maybe even attacking her. In her illusion-fueled rage, she fights back."

"Killing her supposed attacker, who turns out to be her own husband." He sucks in breath. "That is an abominable curse."

"It is, and while I think it probably only strikes women, be aware of what it does."

"I am. Our next step, then, is getting out of here."

"Yeah, there's a door. It's locked."

"It is if you don't have the key."

Silence.

Then he says, "That would be so much more impressive if you could see me holding up the actual key card."

I feel around until I find the edges of hard plastic. "Ooh, very impressive. How'd you get that?"

"Two guards carried me down. I snagged it from one of their pockets as he was putting me on the floor. Took a bit of luck. Now we just need to figure out how to use it from this side of the door."

CHAPTER FORTY-ONE

THE KEY WORKS on both sides of the door, probably to keep anyone from getting locked in the storage room. After we escape, I pause two seconds to hug Connolly—now that I can see him—and then we make our way along the hall.

We get twenty feet before footsteps sound. We duck into a room using the key card. The footsteps pass. They're light steps, not at all what I'd expect from the burly guards. On a hunch, I peek once the steps pass by, and I see Mercy's back.

"Mercy!" I stage-whisper.

She turns. In one hand, she holds a key card. Seeing me, she sighs and waves the card.

"So much for my daring rescue," she mutters. She catches a glimpse of Connolly behind me and exhales. "Good, you're both fine. Now we need to get you off this boat."

"The last painting is down the hall," Connolly says. "We'll want to take it if you can't uncurse it quickly."

She glances down the corridor and then slowly turns to me. "That's where he put you. Where he put both of you. What happened?"

She says the last two words slowly, as if she can already guess.

"I figured it out in time," I say. "Right now, that's all that matters, but it is a horrible curse." I glance at Connolly. "Diabolical."

"That *bastard*," she hisses.

"What about Rosa?" I ask carefully. "Was he telling the truth?"

"I don't know. He has video of her with today's newspaper. Proof of life. Or proof of recent life. She isn't on the ship, and if she *is* still okay, it's because he wants leverage over me."

She waves a hand. "My problem. I'll deal with it. Get the painting. Get off the boat."

"And Theodora?"

Her face falls. "She's determined to go through with the wedding."

"Because your lover isn't the only one he's threatening."

"Okay, well, I'll figure that out. For now, we need to get you both to safety. Head that way while I get the painting."

"We'll go with you," I say.

She starts to argue, and then shakes her head and waves us onward.

We reach the room. Connolly opens the lock, and Mercy pushes the door, and we step into the darkness. I'm reaching for my phone when there's a click. Light fills the room, and there stands Zeus and his two guards.

"Came back for the painting?" Zeus says. "I thought you might."

We turn, and he says, "Don't bother fleeing. While I presumed you'd want the painting, I covered all the bases."

The door opens, two more guards walking in.

Zeus continues, "There are also a few of my men holding your sister captive. She climbed back on the ship, naturally. So tenacious, our Athene. Never knows when to quit. Kind of like your mortal friends here."

He meets Mercy's glare. "Oh, don't give me that look, little one. I wasn't going to let Ms. Bennett kill her darling beau. I'd have stepped in once he lost consciousness." He smirks. "Probably."

Zeus turns to the guards. "Escort them upstairs. They seem determined to crash my wedding, so we might as well let them."

———

We're on the main deck, in a large open area where a marriage officiant waits. Theodora's parents refuse to look our way. They're seated at the front, along with a few guests. Chairs are pulled in for us. We take our seats—Connolly, Mercy, Athene and I.

We've barely sat when the doors fly open and Theodora strides in, wedding gown hiked up in one hand.

"I appreciate your impatience, my dear," Zeus says, "but that wasn't your cue." He motions, and the sound of organ music fills the air.

"Not yet," Theodora says, and the music stops.

Zeus's mouth tightens. "If you've had a change of heart—"

"I haven't. I just want to know what you did to Kennedy and Aiden. And don't tell me nothing. There are bruises around their necks. I could see them from the balcony."

Zeus sighs. "They are fine."

"They're fine now, but you did something." She lifts a hand. "You don't need to tell me what. The point is that it made me think of something. I want a boon. A wedding gift."

His lips twitch. "Oh, that is coming. Tonight, my dear."

She starts to roll her eyes but stops herself and straightens. "I want your promise that you won't hurt me. Not me or my family or my friends, including Aiden and Kennedy."

"All right. I will never physically harm any of those people."

"Not physically and not financially."

His brows shoot up. "Financially?"

"You will do nothing that could financially harm them, which would include attacks on their businesses, their homes, or their reputations."

"You really are a lawyer, aren't you?"

"I am, and this is my prenup. No physical or financial harm shall come to my family or friends. Nor any physical or financial harm to any of their loved ones."

"*Their* loved ones?" His brows climb higher. "That seems a bit excessive."

"No, because you'll note that I specified physical and financial harm to those I care about. I did not include emotional harm because that is difficult to quantify. Instead, I include harming *their* loved ones, which would be the primary method of inflicting emotional pain."

His lips curve into a smile. "Well played, and now, understanding the purpose, I will agree."

"Blood oath," Mercy says.

"Yes," Athene says. "You must demand a blood oath, Theodora. It is a form of a curse, and my sister can weave it on your behalf. Zeus must swear to your conditions, bonded with blood, enforceable by a curse that, if he breaks his oath, he suffers whatever he has inflicted two-fold."

"She doesn't need—" Zeus begins.

"That sounds fair," Theodora says.

Zeus stomps to the dining table—laid out for the wedding feast—and snatches up a knife. Everyone flinches, even his own guards. He slices across his palm and strides to Mercy.

"Do it," he growls. "Quickly."

She weaves the curse. It's nothing like I've ever heard before, but the form makes sense. It has a trigger, and it has consequences. It's also elaborate enough that it'd take me days to cast it . . . and she does it in less than a minute.

Zeus strides back to the table, grabs a linen napkin and clutches it in his fist, staunching the blood. Then he marches to the officiant and snarls, "Get this done."

I squirm in my seat. I cast an anxious glance at Athene, but she's staring straight ahead. Mercy meets my look with a small, sad smile.

So that's it, then? Theodora has made her choice and protected herself as best she can, and there's nothing—

"One last thing," Athene says, her voice ringing out over the officiant's words.

Zeus wheels on her. "No." He jabs a thick finger at her. "Your mother indulged you, Athene, but I will not. There is no 'one last thing.' You got your blood oath. Now be silent, or I will silence you myself."

"Will you? You never have before."

He takes a step toward her.

Mercy clears her throat. "Athene is right. There is one more thing."

"Don't you start—"

"Theodora," Athene says. "Do you wish to be semi-immortal?"

Theodora blinks. "I-I am, aren't I?" She looks to her parents, who haven't said a word, and then to Zeus, who's glaring daggers at his daughters.

"Yes." Zeus spits the word. "Otherwise, we'd hardly be here. I'm not about to marry a mortal girl."

I glance at Athene at the same time Connolly does.

"True," Athene murmurs. "You'd hardly marry a mortal. So, I ask again, Theodora. Do you *wish* to be semi-immortal?"

"No!" Zeus's bellow shakes the entire room, champagne flutes chattering. "Don't you *dare*."

He advances on his daughters. Mercy flinches but comes back firm.

Athene stands her ground. "Theodora? You may surrender your semi-immortality."

"Wh-what?" her mother sputters. "Certainly not. You've been given a gift, Theo."

"No, you've been given a curse," I say. "One that landed you right in a monster's path."

"You keep out of this," Zeus snarls.

"Uh-uh," I say. "Careful now. You just swore a blood oath not to hurt me."

Mercy straightens then. "Theodora? Athene is right. I can rescind your immortality. Curse you to be mortal. It requires your permission, which doesn't make it very effective as a curse but . . ." She shrugs. "It's a technicality."

"My daughter is lying," Zeus says. "She doesn't need your permission. It's a true curse, one she inflicted on her own mother."

Mercy flinches again, but Athene lays a hand on her shoulder.

"No," Athene says. "Mercury is right. She can only rescind the immortality of the willing. Our mother was willing. She asked for it."

"She did not!" Zeus thunders, and champagne flutes topple, shattering on the deck. "She would *never* have done that."

"She did," Mercy says, her soft tone almost apologetic. "She was tired. She wanted to go. We told you that. She told you that. You just wouldn't listen."

"You are a lying little trickster. Always have been. It doesn't matter anyway. I gave the oath in return for Theodora's hand in marriage. If she doesn't go through with her end, I don't have to go through with mine."

"Uh, no," Mercy says. "That wasn't part of the deal."

"What?"

"You didn't stipulate a condition," Theodora says. "You just made the promise."

I see the look on Zeus's face. Connolly does, too, and we both start to run toward Theodora before he strikes her. Instead, he wheels and lashes out at her father. He hits Mr. O'Toole in the side of the head, and the man stumbles back . . . as an invisible force smacks Zeus back so hard he stumbles and falls, blood trickling from his ear.

Zeus throws his hands up, and the sky splits open with a thunderous crack. The bright sun vanishes, swallowed by night-black clouds. There's one eerie moment where the thunder dies, and the clouds seem to just hover there. Then the clouds burst, and the rain pours, wind howling.

A tablecloth goes flying, everything on it sailing through the air. I grab Connolly just as a glass salad bowl whips past his head. He yanks me down onto the deck. We start to slide as the boat—this huge yacht—lurches. Connolly grabs my hand and drags me toward the side, where we latch onto a railing.

I squint to look around. Everyone's running for cover. Someone screams. It's one of the guards, hanging off the side.

"Theodora!" I shout to Connolly.

"She's fine. The curse protects her."

"Not from Zeus kidnapping her. That's what he's doing. Distracting us while he gets Theodora out of Mercy's way before she can take her immortality."

There's a moment when Connolly hesitates. I know what he's thinking. The same thing I am. What does it matter to us? Theodora is a family friend of his and nothing to me, and if Zeus can't hurt her, then leave her to her fate. She'd said she'd go through with it. Let her.

Connolly pauses only a moment before his jaw sets. I nod, and he grabs my hand, wrapping his tight around it. The ship no longer lurches dangerously, but it's rocking with the force of the gale, and the deck is wet with rain, that rain driving down.

Connolly keeps hold of the railing as we pick our way toward the bow, squinting to see what's going on. Athene is shouting orders. Mercy is helping Theodora's father. And Zeus stands there, smirking, arms crossed over his chest.

He just stands there. Unmoving.

And there's no sign of Theodora.

CHAPTER FORTY-TWO

"Illusion," I hiss in Connolly's ear as I motion at Zeus. "He's an illusion. No one's realized it yet."

He looks over.

"He took Theodora," I say. "Where would he go?"

"To the deck we came in. There are boats there."

Still gripping my arm, he starts out, presumably in the direction that will take us to the middle deck. The yacht lurches again, and my foot slips, but Connolly catches me just as a plate flies past. We keep moving.

"Kennedy!" Athene shouts. "Aiden! Stay here! It's not safe—"

"Illusion!" I shout back, waving at Zeus. I'm about to say he's taken Theodora, but she realizes it and runs toward us with Mercy following.

As we move, the storm eases. That's not a good thing. It means Zeus is close to achieving his goal and no longer cares about stalling us.

We pick up the pace. When we reach the steps, Connolly slips on water, but he rights himself before I can grab him. The stairs have a nonslip coating, essential for a boat. We still hold tight to the railing as we descend.

We reach the "toy storage" space just as Zeus is climbing into a small speedboat. Theodora is already in it, slumped unconscious over the seat. Mercy runs, vaults and lands in the boat before her father sees her. He spins on her, roars and charges . . . and Mercy and Theodora both disappear.

Zeus turns on Athene. He snarls at her, furious at his own magic being used against him, but it's only a moment before he's on the deck, marching toward a spot, as if he can see Theodora and Mercy.

I weave a curse as fast as I can. A little jinx that—along with the inch of water on the deck—has him doing a pratfall. It's barely a stumble, but it's enough to infuriate him, and he wheels my way.

"You can't touch her," Athene says calmly. "If you want someone to fight, fight me."

He turns back to Mercy and Theodora. He stops. They're gone, and apparently, that's more than the illusion magic.

Zeus stalks along the side of the boat. "How did I raise such silly daughters? What does this girl mean to you?"

"Nothing," Athene says behind him. "It's our mother who mattered, and the knowledge that she would want us to stop you from enslaving another wife."

"Enslaving?" he snorts. "I left for months on end, and she remained happily at home. No one bound her there."

"*You* bound her. With threats. Against us. Your own children."

Zeus slows and turns with a sneer. "Is that what she told you? She lied."

"She told me nothing. I heard you threaten her. When she tried to leave, you lamed Hephaestus."

"I never—"

"I heard it!" Athene's voice fills the room, echoing off the walls as she advances on him. "I heard it from your own lips. Mother tried to tell me I'd misunderstood. She didn't want us to know the sacrifice she made for us. Always for us."

"She made her choice. And so did this girl."

"Is that what you tell yourself? You choose a woman, and you threaten to harm her loved ones, and when she agrees to be with you, you say it was her choice?" Athene sneers at Zeus. "You are a child. A selfish, petty tyrant of a child."

"I am still your father and—"

He stops and turns back to the other side of the room, as if he heard something.

"Mercy!" he says. "You don't want to do this. Remember that I still have your girlfriend."

He takes out his phone and hits a button. A clip plays. I can't quite hear it, but I'm sure it's Rosa—or it's supposed to be. Zeus drops the phone back into his pocket.

"If you steal my bride's immortality, I'll kill your girlfriend. Remember that."

I glance at Connolly and mouth something. We walk toward Zeus. When he turns, we stop a few feet away. He only shakes his head and turns back toward where his daughter presumably hides with Theodora.

Another look at Connolly. He nods, and I ease forward. An electric charge fills the air. It takes Zeus a moment to recognize it. When he does, he spins, and his elbow catches me in the shoulder. I stagger into him and then fall back.

"Really?" he says, glaring from me to Connolly. "I might hurt myself if I harm you two children, but if you annoy me enough, I'll take that chance."

I scamper back, out of his reach, but not before I raise the phone Connolly's luck burst helped me pick from Zeus's pocket. I lift it to catch his face, and the phone unlocks. He swipes at me, but Connolly's between us, taking the blow. Connolly staggers, and Zeus falls, thudding to the deck.

Zeus leaps up, snarling, only to find himself facing off with Athene.

"I have his phone!" I call to Mercy. "It's unlocked."

"You think that'll help you find her girlfriend?" Zeus says.

"Uh, it already did," I say, flipping through the messages. "You texted the location to one of your guards earlier, telling them to move Rosa there." I raise my voice. "I know where she is, Mercy."

I call out the address, and Zeus lunges at me, but Athene blocks him.

"What does it matter?" Zeus says, throwing up his hands. "If you take this girl from me, I'll only find another one."

"And we'll be there to stop you," Mercy says, rising from behind a WaveRunner, Theodora standing with her. "You keep trying, and we'll keep stopping you. If you want to marry so badly, find someone who wants to marry you back. A woman who genuinely jumps at the chance to marry the almighty Zeus. Should be easy enough. But where's the fun in that, right?"

Zeus stalks over to where they stand. He stops in front of them and looks at Theodora.

"You can feel it," Mercy says. "She's lost her immortality. Which means you don't want her anymore."

His hand flashes out, a sidelong smack for Mercy, almost casual. She ducks it, and he snorts and keeps walking.

"Don't think you got away with this," he calls back, without turning. "I'll have my revenge."

"We have no doubt of that," Athene calls after him.

"Or no doubt you'll try," Mercy murmurs. "Which will keep you out of trouble for a little while."

Athene turns to her sister, giving her an affectionate smile, and Mercy hugs her, and they stay there, holding each other as their father walks away.

———

ROSA IS ALIVE. Zeus makes no effort to stop Mercy from getting to her. As Athene says, he won't embarrass himself further. He's gone to lick his wounds, and then he'll bounce back as if nothing happened, as if he decided he didn't really want to get married after all. Not yet, at least. Maybe someday. To the right woman. Yep, he's just going to sit on that for a bit.

Theodora frees Julian, who was being held by her parents as "insurance" against her backing out of the marriage. After nearly being thrown in the ocean by their son-in-law-to-be, they've decided they'd like Theodora to find herself a new groom. Is Aiden Connolly still available?

Yes, so it seems poor Connolly wasn't the O'Tooles' first choice. Oh, I'm sure he had been, until the almighty Zeus threw his hat in the ring. Then with Athene and Mercy dogging Zeus's heels, Zeus had to cook up a diversion. The O'Tooles' former groom-of-choice is sneaking around with Mercy's new protege? That gives him an idea.

As we suspected, there'd been two sets of the paintings. The woman who commissioned them knew Athene would eventually chase down and destroy the one set. Then, if Athene heard stories of them after that, she'd dismiss them as mere rumors. After all, she'd destroyed them herself.

It seems that Zeus knew there were duplicates, and he knew who had them. When he needed a distraction for Mercy and Athene—and he knew Mercy had Dionysus paint *Crying Girl* for my test—the answer became obvious. Get that duplicate set and use them to keep Athene and Mercy busy while he sealed the deal for Theodora's hand in marriage.

Was it all just a bit too over-the-top? Unnecessarily complicated and elaborate? Absolutely, because Zeus wasn't just distracting his daughters while buying a bride. He was having fun. Unleashing deadly paintings on mortals? Kidnapping his daughter's girlfriend? Using a corpse to make his daughter think her girlfriend was dead? So much fun. Or it is if you're a narcissistic monster, the kind of parent who torments his own children and then insists he was just kidding around.

Mercy has three of the four paintings. We aren't too worried about the first one—I uncursed it, and wherever it is, it's harmless. She'll destroy the others. Afterward, she'll spend some quality time with Rosa, and then she'll get in touch, and my training will begin. At least one good thing came of this whole mess—I've proven my worth, and there will be no more tests, just lessons and mentorship.

Connolly and I are back in Unstable. Temporarily. The hotel is booked for tonight, and he's promised a five-course meal in bed. I'm not quite sure what constitutes a five-course meal—multiple desserts, I'm hoping —but I'm not going to argue.

First, though, I want to explain everything to my sisters in person. I also need to check on my shop. I'd closed early for a "personal emergency" yesterday, and Hope hadn't been able to open until this afternoon, having work of her own in the morning. I feel terrible having the shop closed that long. Connolly understands that I need to touch base—with my sisters and my shop—before I can truly relax, and if that involves a round-trip to Unstable, so be it. I kinda love him for that.

I kinda love him for a lot of things, and I'm pretty sure there's no "kinda" about it. I'll put a pin in that. My curse means we'll never rush things, and that's good. We have time to do this right, and I'm going to do that.

It's Thursday night, and the shop closes at seven, earlier than it will on the weekend. We walk in at 6:45. As much as I wanted to go home, I left the yacht soaking wet and wearing yesterday's clothes. Connolly's place was on the way, so we stopped in and set my clothes on a quick wash cycle. We may also have found other things to do while we were waiting, because even a "quick wash cycle" takes a while, and Connolly is nothing if not efficient in his use of time.

I've brought a special delivery for Hope—her favorite Boston sushi. Yes, Boston is not exactly known for its sushi, but compared to what you can get in Unstable, it's phenomenal.

I'm walking in when I see the mirror. It's uncursed now, but for a split second, I freeze, terrified of not seeing my reflection. Earlier, I thought that meant I was afraid of fading from the lives of others. Now I realize it's that, but more, too. I struggle to see myself clearly. I'm constantly comparing myself to others—Ani, Hope, Connolly, Theodora —and feeling small and invisible. Feeling "not enough." That was my biggest flaw, reflected back at me. Feeling invisible compared to others. I need to work on that, and I will.

I push that aside and continue in before Connolly notices my pause. Then I stop again and stare . . . as a half-dozen pairs of eyes stare back at me. Seven, if you count the black cat poised, gargoyle-like, among the dolls.

"Uh, Hope . . ." I say.

She's at the counter with a customer and waves that she'll be with me in a moment. Connolly walks over to the prominent display of dolls.

"Seems someone took advantage of your absence," he says.

"I was away twenty-four hours. Where the hell did she get all these so quickly?"

"Language," Hope trills as she walks over and moves a doll into an empty place. "You were gone twenty-*nine* hours. A few are from my collection. The remainder I've been keeping in storage, waiting for the right moment."

"The moment when I was out of the shop and fighting for my life against the king of the gods?"

"Oh, please." She rolls her eyes. "You weren't fighting for your life the entire time. You were shacking up in a cozy little roadside motel with this one."

"We didn't sleep together," I say, just to see that knowing grin fall from her face. Also, there *was* no actual sleeping involved.

"What?" she says.

"Is it just me?" Connolly says. "Or are those dolls really creepy?"

"That's the point," Hope says proudly.

"Are they supposed to look like they're watching me?"

"Yep. Isn't it cool?"

Connolly shakes his head. I give Ellie a pat and then hand Hope her sushi bag.

"So you two aren't . . . ?" she says.

"Together?" I say. "Of course we are."

She exhales. "Good. I thought—"

"We're together right now. We've been together all day. Most of yesterday, too."

"Except for the part where my father kidnapped you," Connolly says.

"Right. But then you rescued me."

"That's very romantic," Hope says. "So, then you two . . . ?"

"Actually, I believe Julian rescued you," Connolly says. "Was that romantic?"

"Not a bit."

Hope clears her throat loudly. "Are you or aren't you?"

"Aren't," I say. "We aren't staying long. Sorry."

I start to walk past Connolly. He grabs me around the waist, and I lean in and kiss him.

"Yes!" Hope says, yanking out her phone.

I quickstep away from Connolly.

"Hey!" Hope says. "I need photo evidence for Rian."

"Photo evidence of what?" I say, and then kiss Connolly again, too fast for her to snap a photo.

I crook a finger, and Connolly follows me to the storage room door. We zip inside, and I shut it before Hope can catch up. Then I lean against the door, hands around his neck.

"You're together!" Hope calls through the door. "I know you are."

"Yep," I call back. "We're together in the storage room. Maybe we're making out. Maybe we're finding proper antiques to replace those godawful dolls."

"Don't you dare!"

"Don't I dare make out with Aiden?" I pull him to me. "Too late!"

He laughs against my lips, and then he kisses me, and I decide maybe, just maybe, I have never been luckier in my life.